Son of Dust

Books in the Loyola Classics Series

Amy Welborn, general editor

Catholics by Brian Moore

Cosmas or the Love of God by Pierre de Calan

Dear James by Jon Hassler

The Devil's Advocate by Morris L. West

Do Black Patent Leather Shoes Really Reflect Up?
by John R. Powers

The Edge of Sadness by Edwin O'Connor

Five for Sorrow, Ten for Joy by Rumer Godden

Helena by Evelyn Waugh

In This House of Brede by Rumer Godden

The Keys of the Kingdom by A. J. Cronin

The Last Catholic in America by John R. Powers

Mr. Blue by Myles Connolly

North of Hope by Jon Hassler

Saint Francis by Nikos Kazantzakis

The Silver Chalice by Thomas Costain

Things As They Are by Paul Horgan

The Unoriginal Sinner and the Ice-Cream God
by John R. Powers

Vipers' Tangle by François Mauriac

Son of Dust

H. F. M. PRESCOTT

Introduction by Mike Aquilina

LOYOLA CLASSICS

CHICAGO

LOYOLAPRESS.

3441 N. ASHLAND AVENUE
CHICAGO, ILLINOIS 60657
(800) 621-1008
WWW.LOYOLAPRESS.ORG

Originally published in 1956 by the MacMillan Company, New York.

The author is indebted to Mrs. Bridges, Mrs. Daryush, and the Oxford University Press; to Mrs. Ayscough, and to Messrs. Constable & Co., Ltd., for permission to quote extracts from copyright poems and translations by Robert Bridges, Arthur Waley, Mrs. Ayscough and Miss Lowell, and Miss Helen Waddell. Houghton Mifflin Company kindly granted permission to quote from *Fir Flower Tablets* by Florence Ayscough and Amy Lowell.

Cover credit: Corbis

Series art direction: Adam Moroschan
Series design: Adam Moroschan and Erin VanWerden
Cover design: Judine O'Shea
Interior design: Erin VanWerden

Library of Congress Cataloging-in-Publication Data

Prescott, H. F. M. (Hilda Frances Margaret), 1896–1972.
  Son of dust / H. F. M. Prescott.
      p. cm.
  ISBN-13: 978-0-8294-2352-5   ISBN-10: 0-8294-2352-4
  1. Normandy (France)—History—To 1515—Fiction. I. Title.
  PR6031 .R38S66 2007
  823'.912—dc22

                                                              2006030599

Printed in the United States of America
06 07 08 09 10 11 Versa 10 9 8 7 6 5 4 3 2 1

Introduction

Mike Aquilina

It has been several decades since Yale University Press last published a romance novel. But then, it has been several decades since H. F. M. Prescott produced her academically acclaimed— yet spellbinding and best-selling—volumes of historical fiction. She has had no successor.

Most of her novels, like this one, *Son of Dust,* are indeed romances. They're against-all-odds love stories, with nail-biting and page-turning plots, ample feats of derring-do, caddish treachery, heroic fidelity, and a constant and powerful undertow of sexual desire.

Three things, however, set Prescott's novels apart from the bodice rippers arrayed in the drugstore: (1) their historical precision, (2) their spiritual and philosophical depth, and (3) their literary artistry. She did not write costume pageants or steamy melodramas. She produced imaginative histories. Yet she wrote them with such simplicity and sensuality that the consumers of popular fiction kept her works on the charts.

Hilda Frances Margaret Prescott was born in Cheshire, England, in 1896, the daughter of an Anglican clergyman. She studied at Oxford and Manchester and held master's degrees from both. She taught briefly at the high school and college levels before turning full-time to writing in 1923. Her first three novels are set in medieval France, the third being *Son of Dust,* published in 1932.

Her novels often revolve around questions of religious, political, and romantic allegiance—and these categories are inseparably intertwined, making for high drama. Characters measure their duty to God against fidelity to a difficult lover or a demanding duke. For Prescott, erotic desire drives much of human history, whether personal or international. Yet it is a providential force; God made the world that way.

In religion, Prescott's sympathies were decidedly Anglo-Catholic, and these set her apart from other historians. Mainstream English authors, both academic historians and historical novelists, tended to read Protestantism back into pre-Reformation events. Their heroes were proto-Protestants, their villains venal "papists." The Mass was shown to be idolatrous; "Romish" doctrines, customs, and traditions, such as relics and monks, shown to be superstitious. The church, starting with the pope, was held to oppress its people and keep them in ignorance. With the Middle Ages read this way, the anti-Roman revolt of the Reformation was seen not only as inevitable and necessary, but also as a grand victory for human freedom and enlightenment against popish tyranny and ignorance.

But Prescott would have none of that. She respected medieval civilization and recognized its profound sacral foundations. As an Anglo-Catholic, she believed that the Church of England had lost something at the Reformation, however "necessary" that event was. Her characters are Catholic believers who go to Mass, pray for the dead, venerate the saints, and don't begrudge any bit of it. Roman Catholic critics and readers felt at home in her pages, as they will today. And so will many of today's leading academic historians. Prescott anticipated, by fifty years, the historical reconsiderations of the late twentieth century, especially the work of J. J. Scarisbrick, Eamon Duffy, Christopher Haigh, and others. Since Prescott died in 1972, she did not live to see this movement's triumph at the close of the twentieth century.

Son of Dust draws from the chronicles of noble families in Norman France in the eleventh century. The action takes place in the years just before the Norman invasion of England and the Battle of Hastings (1066). Indeed, William the Conqueror (Guillelm of Normandy) plays an important role in the drama. The novel's plot, however, concerns quite another battle, one that is certainly not confined to any period in history: the ever-present conflict between spirit and flesh (see chapter 5 of St. Paul's letter to the Galatians). Traditional Christian doctrine holds that the sexual drive is powerful and good, but it is not simply benign. Original sin has left us with a San Andreas–sized fault line running through our sexuality. In no other area of life are we so prone to self-deception. Yet, like nothing else in life, erotic desire holds out the promise of love, happiness, companionship, and fulfillment. Eros, says Pope Benedict XVI, is "that love between man and woman which is neither planned nor willed, but somehow imposes itself upon human beings."

Prescott's characters represent a variety of approaches to the problem. Robert of Saint Ceneri and his wife, Aelis, enjoy a satisfying, natural happiness in their love. Raol Malacorona aspires to be pure spirit and reject the flesh as something beastly. Geroy is content to indulge the beastly, committing adultery and casual rape over the course of the story. Fulcun longs for pure love yet lives by all the wrongheaded clichés of courtly romance—that true love should be spontaneous, forbidden, perilous, desperate, and adventuresome. As he and Alde consummate their sinful love, they cover over the true nature of their deed with sweet euphemisms and rationalizations.

But God is not fooled. Prescott's universe turns on the principle of sacramental realism. There is nothing merely symbolic about her portrayal of the mysteries of faith. The cleric Herfast is "dirty, ignorant, drunken, but a priest," and dire consequences follow upon his decree of excommunication. At Holy Communion, a priest "laid God . . . upon Mauger's tongue." The sacraments are more real than anything in creation, and any breach of their discipline, any impiety, can bring on horrific consequences, in both the natural and supernatural orders. The marital bond is no less real than the character of holy orders, no less sacramental than the presence of Jesus in the Eucharist— and the marriage bond is just as intolerant of compromise.

Thus, Fulcun and Alde's illicit union, though gilded in their own fevered imaginations, is a mortal sin. Committed in a state of nature, it evokes Eden and creation's primal couple, Adam and Eve. And within the novel their adultery functions as a sort of original sin—bringing death, devastation, and disenfranchisement to the entire Geroy clan and its lands.

Sin leads to further sin, and to a darkened intellect that cannot choose well or wisely. Conflicting loyalties and a warped sense of duty almost always follow in the wake of adultery. It takes the entire novel for Fulcun and Alde to extricate themselves (by God's persistent grace) from their tangled bonds.

The artistic miracle is that they do, and rather believably. They ascend from eros to a higher love, a diviner love—agape—climbing a difficult path of renunciation, purification, and healing. It is not spoiling the ending to say that over the course of the story, they grow in self-knowledge, discipline, repentance—and they achieve a full, and dramatically surprising, redemption.

H. F. M. Prescott's novels are great acts of restoration—not only for her characters, but for her readers, too. The chronicles of medieval Europe, especially England, were for many centuries distorted by partisanship. History is always written by the victors, and in England the Protestant regime prevailed. From the sixteenth through the nineteenth centuries, historians committed to a cause, both religious and patriotic, perpetually ground the old axes of the English Reformation. And literary artists were no less to blame. Alfred Tennyson removed the sacramental character from the Holy Grail legends and recast them as Broad Church Anglican quests for the world's most prized antique—but nothing more.

As academic history grew more agnostic, it actually gained a greater degree of objectivity. It rose above the controversies swirling about the Reformation—or at least it stood apart from them. Hilda Prescott, as an Anglo-Catholic, also stood above the fray, though she kept her profoundly Christian convictions and sensibilities.

In spite of the work of Eamon Duffy and the art of Hilda Prescott, pop culture is still dominated by what some scholars call "the Monty Python school of history"—that is, the certain knowledge that the Middle Ages were irredeemably bad times, because ordinary people bathed little, read less, lived in serfdom, and sometimes died of plague. In *Son of Dust,* we see that those times—though surely flawed—were about as civilized as our own. If the medievals lived with social injustices, sexual depravities, and ignorance, well—we should read the newspapers—so do we.

You need not be a habitual reader of romances to get caught up in this powerful love story. You need only be human. Nor need you be a scholar of history to become rapt in scenes from many centuries ago. But by the book's end, you might be able to pass a history exam, in spite of yourself. Learning should always be so enjoyable, and so good for the soul.

Mike Aquilina is coauthor of The Grail Code: Quest for the Real Presence *and author of many other books on Christian history, doctrine, and devotion. He is vice president of the St. Paul Center for Biblical Theology and has been cohost of five popular television series.*

Son of Dust

Truth bids me say 'tis time you cease to trust
    Your soul to any son of dust.
'Tis time you listen to a braver love,
    Which from above
    Calls you up higher.

Crashaw

So let us love, dear love, lyke as we ought:
Love is the lesson which the Lord us taught.

Spenser

Genealogical Table of

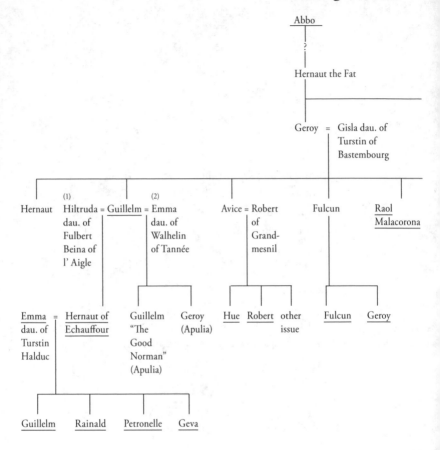

Abbo
?
Hernaut the Fat

Geroy = Gisla dau. of Turstin of Bastembourg

Hernaut

(1) Hiltruda dau. of Fulbert Beina of l' Aigle = Guillelm = (2) Emma dau. of Walhelin of Tannée

Avice = Robert of Grandmesnil

Fulcun

Raol Malacorona

Emma dau. of Turstin Halduc = Hernaut of Echauffour

Guillelm "The Good Norman" (Apulia)

Geroy (Apulia)

Hue   Robert   other issue

Fulcun   Geroy

Guillelm   Rainald   Petronelle   Geva

Note on the Genealogical Table

I have taken liberties with some members of the Geroy family. Thus Fulcun, son of Geroy, is called in the story Fulcun of Montgaudri. Actually he was known as Fulcun of Montreuil; Montgaudri was not among the Geroy lands. Also, Geroy, brother of the younger

the Geroy Family

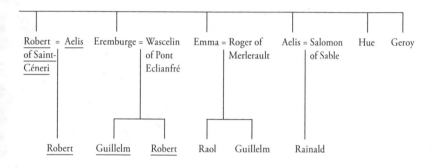

Gui Bollein = Hodierna

Robert = Aelis	Eremburge = Wascelin	Emma = Roger of	Aelis = Salomon	Hue	Geroy
of Saint-	of Pont	Merlerault	of Sable		
Céneri	Eclianfré				

| Robert | Guillelm | Robert | Raol | Guillelm | Rainald |

Fulcun, survived to be an annoyance to the monks of Saint-Évroult when Hernaut Geroy was in exile.

The names underscored belong to those persons who take part in the story; the names not underscored may therefore be forgotten.

Foreword

Hernaut the Fat, Hernaut the Breton as they called him in Mayenne, was the first of that house to come out of Brittany. He prospered, and before he died he was lord of lands that lay close along the Norman border. His son was Geroy, a short, sturdy, resolute man, so cheerful and quiet in his ways as to seem peaceable. He was not, though; he loved trouble, and he found it both pleasant and profitable to play a game between Mayenne and Normandy. Guillelm of Belesme was doing just the same, and he and Geroy grew fast friends. It was with Guillelm that Geroy went to one of Duke Richart of Normandy's Christmas courts.

Richart the Fearless knew a good fighter when he saw him, and he always wanted to make friends in Mayenne, so, as they rode back one day in the snow after hunting wolves in the woods near Fécamp, he says to Geroy, "Heugo of Echauffour will give you his daughter if you like. She'll have Echauffour and Montreuil when he dies, for she's the only one he has." He looked at Geroy, and then said, "And he won't live long." Geroy said he'd take the girl.

But he did not. He saw her once, and that was when they were betrothed, and he thought, "Poor stock! I wouldn't breed from a mare that looked so ramshackle!" He did not see her again because she died two months after, and a week after she died Heugo her father died too.

Geroy swore when he heard it. He thought they might have waited a while till he had married her. But he cheered up when Duke Richart said he should not miss his lands for that. And so on the day after Easter Day the duke put into Geroy's hands a gray-green ash stave and then a chunk of moist sod that had one daisy just opening in it. The stave was for Montreuil and the sod for Echauffour.

So there was Geroy with the Mayenne lands—Courcerault and Montaigu, Gandelain and la Pooté and the rest, and with Montreuil and Echauffour that held of Normandy. He was a great man now; he married one of Turstin of Bastembourg's girls; he saw her pass through a slant of sunshine in Turstin's hall at Bastembourg, and he wanted her, and did not rest till he had all her tall, splendid, fresh strength for his own. That was how the Norse height and the Norse red-gold hair came into the family, for of all the sons that Gisla bore him (and she bore him seven, as well as four daughters), only Robert was a low man like his father, and he had flaming hair when he was a lad, all curls.

The first child they had was born the year that folk feared would be the last of the world, the year 1000. They called him Hernaut. Next it was another boy, Guillelm; then a girl, Avice; then, one after another, three lads, Fulcun, Raol, and Robert. After those came three girls, Eremburge, Emma, and Aelis, and then another boy, Hue, and last of all Geroy, that they called Red Geroy.

But though the house had prospered, it had not much luck. Geroy died before his time, and within ten years of his death Gisla was dead too, and of all their sons only three lived—Guillelm, Raol, and Robert. The girls were all alive, and married, and Fulcun, who was dead, had left two sons, Fulcun and Geroy, bastards by a Breton wench that Fulcun had brought back from Caharel—the hold looking over the Breton sands toward St. Michael in Peril, from which Hernaut the Fat, the first Geroy's father, had come. Fulcun brought her to Montgaudri, willing enough, for anyone could see that she loved the ground he went on, but she ran away from him before three years were at an end, and before he had quite tired of her. He was very angry when she went; he always swore that she went with a Norman horse coper. But he was wrong. She had gone back to Brittany on foot and glad of the pain that put something between her and the sin of love that had so hurt her and must therefore be so black.

She came to the house of nuns at Dol and sat on the side of the road by the gate with her long black hair trailing over her hands as they lay in her lap. She did not ask to go in, but when they brought her in she did not refuse. Only she turned her head to watch them shut the door behind her, because she knew that it was shutting her away from Fulcun. She lived there for six years and then died; she did not even know that Fulcun was dead already. Of the two little lads she did not think; it was enough to have to keep Fulcun out of her mind. As for loving—she must try to love God and his Christ, who were kind; Fulcun had not been kind.

After his eldest brother's death Guillelm Geroy was head of the house. He was the wisest of them all; not so ready for a quarrel as his father, but as good a fighter when he was in it. His one unwisdom was to trust other men to be as honest as he was. He was a broad, tall man with a brown, plain face; he stooped a little when he walked and had a way of standing leaning against the wall with his arms folded and his chin on his chest. He married Fulbert Beina's girl from l'Aigle, but she died in bearing him Hernaut, so he married again and had two sons more, but as soon as they were grown those two went into Italy where the Normans were swarming; but Hernaut stayed in Normandy.

The first Geroy had been friends with Guillelm of Belesme, but that Guillelm was dead now, and his three eldest sons died soon after; one of them, men said, was strangled by a devil in his sleep for his wickedness, but he was not worse than his brother Guillelm Talvas, who lived.

This Guillelm Talvas and Guillelm Geroy had never been friends; as time went on they had more than one score against each other. Once they were accorded and gave each other the kiss of peace, and after that Guillelm Geroy ceased to think about Talvas; he was a coward, a liar, and a trichard, and he had murdered his wife pretty surely, but it was the devil's business, not Guillelm Geroy's.

Talvas did not cease to think about Guillelm Geroy; he could not forget him; and he thought that someday he would so deal with Guillelm Geroy that Guillelm Geroy would never be able to forget him either.

So, when Talvas made a great feast for his second wedding, he bade to it, among all his neighbors and the friends of Belesme, Guillelm Geroy, but none of the other Geroys.

Guillelm Geroy was at Saint-Céneri when he got the message, and Raol Geroy was with him. It was Raol who read out the writing, for he was as learned as any clerk, and that was why he was called always Malacorona, as it were "spoiled priest," because there was nothing else clerkly about him, that anyone could see, but his learning. Raol said neither good nor bad that night about Talvas's wedding feast, but next morning he says to Guillelm in his ear, "Do not go to Alençon."

Says Guillelm, "What, have you been asking your devils what will be?"

Raol told him not to mind whom he had asked, only take the counsel. Everyone knew that Raol could look through time into tomorrow and that he had secrets of healing; and when they were angry with him they would say it was devils who told him what would come.

Guillelm would not listen. He said he was not afraid of Guillelm Talvas. He went, on a shining June day, with twelve knights only; he would not have Raol with him, but he took for his esquire that time young Fulcun, Fulcun of Montgaudri's son by the Breton girl, a lad of fifteen.

It was three days later that one of the house wenches came screaming to Raol as he sat in the tower. As he went down he did not rightly know what was her news, but he knew soon enough. At the gate there was a little crowd, and when Raol pushed into the midst of it he found Guillelm Geroy leaning heavily over young Fulcun of Montgaudri, who had him round the waist; Guillelm Geroy with his face all bloody, and bloody pits for eyes. That was Talvas's work.

They brought him up to the tower, and there Raol saw to him. He bathed the raw sockets and laid ointment on. Guillelm lay as stiff and still as a log while he did it, but Fulcun, holding the water in a wooden bowl, shook so much that the water lapped over, and Raol swore at him.

It took a week to send round to all the Geroy kin and bring them to Saint-Céneri. Robert Geroy and Hernaut, Guillelm's own son, were the last to come in, for they had been to Courville, near Chartres, where there were Geroy cousins. They rode in one noon, and all rode out the next, a hundred men, and thirty of them knights.

Young Fulcun of Montgaudri went with them, this time as Robert Geroy's esquire. It was Robert who had brought up the two lads that dead Fulcun had left. They came, after burning two villages, in sight of Alençon through the last trees of the wood. Robert turned in his saddle because he heard a strange small sound behind him. Young Fulcun was grinding his teeth. He said, suddenly, as though he were very glad to speak, "It was here. I came out of the wood, riding back from hunting with the first of Talvas's people. I saw . . . him . . . coming along the grass at the edge of the road, feeling with his feet, and his hands out, groping . . . and the sun shining. Talvas laughed."

Robert swore. Fulcun cried out, "Oh, sir, kill Talvas!"

They could not do that because Guillelm Talvas of Belesme shut the gates of Alençon and would for no burning nor wasting of his lands open them and come out. The Geroys, when they had done all the harm they could, must needs go home. It was on the way back that Robert said to Raol Geroy that Fulcun would make a good fighter. "He's slow," says Raol. "Hernaut is far the better."

"Hernaut is almost a man grown," says Robert. "And when Fulcun's angry . . . They call him 'the heron,' you know."

Raol said that that was because he was such a long lad.

"Well," said Robert, "he hits like a heron too when he's angry, straight and hard."

"He's a bastard," says Raol. Robert said that so was the duke, and they left it at that.

Blind men have little place in the world; Guillelm Geroy, after three black years, went from it into the abbey at Bec, and from there came to Saint-Évroult, when Avice Geroy's two sons, Robert and Hue of Grandmesnil, built the abbey in the woods near Echauffour, and they and Raol and Robert Geroy gave to the monks plow lands and mills and wood and water. But though he was with his own kin there—Robert of Grandmesnil was prior—Guillelm Geroy could not stay. Once, he went on pilgrimage to Jerusalem, and then at last, when there was talk of sending some of the monks to beg for gifts for the new stone cloister from the Normans who were gone to Apulia, blind Guillelm Geroy made the abbot send him. That was the spring of 1053.

Robert, now Robert of Saint-Céneri, and Raol Geroy said him farewell at the crossroads below Echauffour. They watched him out of sight, tall and stooping, and heard the clack of his staff on the stony road die away to nothing. He had gone with two young monks to lead him, but he was in the dark. Robert Geroy sat on his horse in the sunny road and did not care that the tears were running down his face. He began to curse Talvas and all the Belesme.

Raol, thin and dark-faced more than any other of the Geroys, turned on him suddenly and bade him be silent. "It's the will of God," he cried in a strange hard voice.

Robert of Saint-Céneri stared at him. He was too simple to understand what was in Raol's mind. He only said, "You're mad."

Raol stared back almost as wild as if Robert spoke the truth.

"Would I not lose my eyes to save my soul?" he said, and swung his horse about, and left Robert to follow his reckless gallop.

Before even they heard the news that Guillelm was dead in Gaeta, Raol had gone away one evening from Saint-Céneri without a word. He went to Marmoutier, the abbey that looks over the wide shallows and gold sand shelves of the Loire, and there his crown was rightly shaved at last.

So Robert of Saint-Céneri was the only one of Geroy's sons left in the world. He kept Saint-Céneri and the Mayenne lands; Fulcun son of Fulcun, a grown man now, held Montgaudri from Mayenne too, though the Normans always said that Montgaudri should hold of Normandy. His younger brother,

Geroy, the other son of the Breton girl, lived at Montgaudri with him; Geroy had a wife Alianor, Baudri of Boquenci's second girl, and she had borne him one child, a boy, Baudri.

Hernaut, Guillelm Geroy's eldest son, held the Norman lands of the house, Montreuil and Echauffour. He had married Emma, Turstin Halduc's daughter, and had two sons already and was like to have more. The Geroys were a great house still. Robert Geroy had even married the duke's cousin Aelis— though she brought little dowry with her he trusted that she would bring him friendship with Normandy.

But sometimes Robert, whose fiery hair was graying to gold, would forget his cheerful carelessness and sit biting on his fingers and frowning under his big fair eyebrows at nothing. Then Aelis, who was fond of him, would cry out at him to stop scowling, and he would look up and laugh.

But he wished that he had by him even one of his own brothers. They had used to ride out seven, and a man is strong in his kin.

Chapter 1

The expense of spirit in a waste of shame
Is lust . . .

Shakespeare, *Sonnets*

I

Fulcun stood at one of the windows of the tower at Montgaudri; it was the window that looked out over the castle yard where the hens were picking, and where the washing hung from the line between the two old thorn bushes, for it was Monday. Beyond the castle yard was the little town, mud-and-wattle houses, yellowish-colored and thatched with every shade between the fresh brown-gold of last year's work and the dead gray of twenty years back, huddled anyhow among orchards and patches of ground where the peas and beans grew in fresh rows. Beyond the houses and the orchards and around it all ran the wooden pale of the township.

Behind him in the room, Dame Alianor, Geroy's wife, who had just finished setting up the warp of a new length of linen, settled herself on the bench and began to work the loom with a quick, sharp clack. Dame Alianor was a thin, frail, bitter woman, hardy and reckless in her heart but weak in body. She was the daughter of that untamed old quarreler Baudri of Boquenci; she had run away from Boquenci with Geroy one night in spring close on ten years ago. Before that, when they used to meet secretly in the dim flour store of the mill at Boquenci, where the air was dusty and full of the deep measured beat of the rushing water and the turning wheel, she had worshipped Geroy. Now she did not.

Down below in the yard one of the men was driving in a fresh stake behind the castle pale; Fulcun had found yesterday that some of the old wood was rotted. It was not bad enough to shift yet, but he had told Osmunt the steward it must be strengthened. The pale was made of stout oak and beech trunks cut in half lengthwise and rammed deep into the earth with the rounded side out and the flat within to the yard.

Fulcun watched the man swinging up the heavy mallet and bringing it down on the wood—the sound came to him just a fraction of time after he saw the mallet fall. But though he watched the man intently he was not thinking of the work; only the regular shock of the blows seemed to mark the time of the pulses that beat in his brain and through him, till he felt he was himself the smitten vibrating wood.

Fulcun stood a moment longer, but he was not now watching the man at the pale. His eyes had been caught by someone crossing the strip of green between Osmunt's orchard and the alehouse. It was Custance; she had a bag slung at her back and a stout long stick in her hand; she must be going along Montgaudri hill to Johan, her father, who had the sheep in the valley end.

It was Custance, who was in his mind day long and night long. This morning he had known when he got up that today he would come upon her—somehow. He often did know at the beginning of a day that he would certainly find her before evening. And standing at the window just now he had known something more, though he had not cared to think about it too much—he had known that today was the day, come at last, almost against his will, when he *must* find her. He could not let her keep him off any longer with her fierceness and her silence and with the straight stare of her cold yet stormy eyes. After all, she was only his serf's girl; her father Johan wore Fulcun's iron collar about his neck.

And yet for ten minutes and more he stood there still, his fingers gripping the sill of the window as if someone might tear him from it. Custance had gone out of sight and now appeared again on the open hillside beyond the town. He could see her clear; she was half a mile away by this time, walking steadily.

He turned sharply from the window and went across the room and down the stairs into the hall and out to the door of the tower. Dame Alianor had started at his suddenness, and the servants in the hall stared as he went past them; he did not look back. He took the outer stairs two at a time with his sword held up in his hand.

In four minutes he was riding out of the gate of the castle; in six he was beyond the pale of the town and out on the open, warm hillside. The hill was empty, but he knew his way. He remembered now that he must not hurry while he was in sight of the tower. He settled down in his saddle and rode soberly, but his fingers were sweating on the bridle.

It was high summer, and the sun so great in his afternoon strength that the cloudless sky was drained of all color but a faint, languid blue. It was very hot on the hillside, but now and again a little wayward wind brought with it a puff of clean coolness and then died, and the warm air closed again. There was no sound but for the grasshoppers, and no movement but the swallows' long, delicate, gliding lapse, as they skimmed the slope below the level of his feet.

He pulled up and looked back. Montgaudri had sunk behind a lift of the hill. He turned and for one second sat still in his saddle staring at nothing, feeling nothing but the thundering shake of his heart in his chest. Then he was riding with the wind going by his ears, and the soft thunder of the hooves to listen to instead of the other that had made him almost afraid.

He saw Custance before him; he passed her at a gallop as though he did not see her, and then, a quarter of a mile beyond (he could not tell why he went so far), he pulled up and sat on his horse, waiting for her to come up.

As she came he watched her bare brown feet on the warm grass; her black hair gleamed in the sun like a crow's wing, her eyes were on the ground. He knew well enough that she had seen him, but he guessed that she would not look up till she saw the shadow of his horse; he was not sorry for that, for he could look at her the better when he had not to meet her eyes. He wanted to look at her mouth, red and stubborn with a sulky droop, and at her brown neck, and at a tear in her old yellowish-white woolen gown that let him see her knee as she moved.

She looked up, and he jerked his head back, and next minute he was out of the saddle and by her. She stood still and looked no higher than his throat that was on a level with her eyes. He stretched out his hand and laid it on her shoulder and clutched it hard. She did not wince, but she lifted her eyes and said, "What do you want?" She did not call him "master" or "lord," and she looked at him without a change of the dark color in her face.

He said, dropping his eyes from hers to the little hollow at the base of her throat, "Where are you going?" though he had meant to say something quite different.

She told him. "To my father. He's with the sheep away there," and she nodded beyond him over the hill. "I've bread for him." She had a goatskin bag slung across her back.

Fulcun, staring down at her, shifted his hand from her shoulder to her arm and moved closer. He had hold now of both her arms, but she stood still.

"What do you want?" she said, and her voice was more angry than afraid.

She could feel Fulcun shaking. He told her, "You." He snatched at the stick, tore it from her hand, and threw it away, then he dragged her against him.

She fought herself off with a sudden surprising fierce strength, and as they stood for a second she cried at him, "Like as your father had your mother!"

Fulcun's chin went up as if she had struck him. He was not glad to be a bastard, though many men those days thought little of it.

He said through his teeth, "I do not care," and put out his strength again, and held her, struggling, for a moment glad to know that he must be hurting her. But he thought she would never stop fighting to get free.

She was tiring. He tightened his arms and heard her give a sharp breathless cry. He bent to get at her mouth, but she wrenched her face away. She had no strength for more than that; yet he could see how even now the muscles of her throat were all straining against him.

For a long second he was quite still, only holding her desperately close with all his strength and staring down into her face. Her eyes came up to his, glaring, wild with the terror and frantic impotent hate of an animal taken in a snare.

He knew that he could have her body now if he chose. He knew suddenly, and with a great rush of blind pain, that it was no use, since she hated him like this.

He cried out, "Custance, won't you let me . . . let me? . . . Can't you see I love you, Custance!" And then lifting his head, "Oh! I can't force you . . . Let me!"

She did not answer, only she struggled faintly against him. He held her a second longer because it was so hard to let her go, and then he loosed his arms about her—it was no use to keep her. She pulled away from him as far as she could.

He said again, "Can't you understand? I love you. I only want—" He stopped because he did not know himself what it was he only wanted. It was a great deal. It was more than the thing his body wanted. "I love you," he said.

But she had never learned what love was. She grew fierce as she felt herself safe, and she did not know at all what it was that had kept her safe.

"No," says she. "I want none of that," and suddenly broke away from him and ran. As she went by his horse she clouted it on the shoulder, and when the animal bolted he heard her shrill laugh.

Left standing there, Fulcun had to choose between catching her or catching the horse. He went for the horse, but it was a young wild stallion and it had been scared, so it got away.

By that time it was too late to catch her. She was gone, and she had made a fool of him. There was little forbearance in his mind when he gave up chasing the horse. He came back, hot and angry, and sat down on the grass. He would wait. She must come back this way, and she should not leave him laughing again. As he sat there he tugged up handfuls of the wiry, fine grass and flung them from him.

But as he waited, his anger died. What took its place was first a great soreness. He lay full length and buried his face in the grass and longed for kindness from her—just that, kindness and gentleness. And then, because he was young enough still not to believe in any final denial, he began to hope. He rolled over and lay at ease on his side, seeing the world very great because his eyes were on a level with the smallest creatures—he could see no more than a multitude of grass blades close by, and beyond, the great green shoulder of the hill, and beyond that again, a steep of sky.

He thought, "But I'll teach her to love me. They say a woman always loves a man afterward. And I'll be as gentle as I can." He let his mind slip into sweet imaginings, part of pure passion, part of something that should be afterward. She would open her eyes from the languor of past delight and he would be waiting for them. He would look down into her solemn, wide, unsmiling eyes and find that she was glad of him, as he was of her. And they would walk home together in the dusk, very close; but while he was thinking of the touch of her along his side, something in him, deep down in his unknown mind, was craving for a contact that was not of the body, but something closer yet.

He lay there long, dreaming with his eyes open, and a sound—a small, distant, regular beat—came to his ears for a long time before it reached his mind. But he heard it at last, and raised his head, and then sat upright. Cortilly church bell was ringing for Vespers.

He listened to it for a minute, frowning. Herfast was ringing it, that rascal old priest with gray bristles all over his face and a dirty, half-grown tonsure on his head. Herfast spent most of his time digging in the croft round his cottage. When he had to go to church (and he did not trouble the church much, but today must be some feast) he would spit on the ground and wipe his hands on his gown and go with no more care than that. He was an ignorant old fool too. He knew no more than a few prayers, and no one could hear them, he gabbled so fast; so they might be right or wrong. And besides, for as long as Fulcun could remember, he had kept a wife, if you liked to call her so, a gray-haired woman now, with watery eyes, but she had been plump and almost comely once.

It was only old Herfast ringing the bell in the dusty, dim tower of the church. Fulcun tried to keep his mind on that. Why should he care though Herfast rang all night? The faint, cracked voice of the bell meant nothing to him. He clapped his hands over his ears to shut it out. He shut out the sound, but he shut himself in with his thought.

Here he was on the hill, in the warm-breathing world, where the sun would soon go down and color everything with evening, and he was waiting here for Custance for his body's fierce delight. And there, in the wattle church in the valley, where it would be twilight now, God sat. It was God who spoke in the hoarse discordant voice of the bell. God forbade him.

Fulcun jumped up and began to tramp about, hasty and aimless, through the low-growing, trim whin bushes and back along the smooth sheep tracks. God forbade him his delight because it was sin. God forbade it, and Custance must soon be here. But why need he listen? He stood still once in his roaming and lifted his head. The sun had gone down behind the high slopes of Perseigne forest that rose opposite the bare flank of Montgaudri hill, but above, the sky was full yet of colored light, and very high up there were some small fine clouds, warm with the sun, and softly cruddled like the wool of a sheep's fell.

Fulcun thought, "God is up there too!" and because the sky was full of gentleness, and peace, and the remote but tender beauty of the evening, his thoughts ran suddenly aside. If God was . . . like that at all . . . would he not allow it because of the tenderness there was in love?

He stood there staring up, and then he muttered, in case God should not understand, "I love her—it's not all lust."

The bell rang on and then stopped. He turned, listening to the silence, and it was a rebuke. He had wanted an answer, but now he knew that no answer would have made any difference. Presumably God had known it too.

He flung himself down on the grass, his face hot, and his heart too, with a dogged, uneasy rebellion. The light in the sky was changing and fading to something more chill and pure. Soon Custance would be here.

He sat up with a shock of all the blood in his body. Someone was coming along the hill top.

But it was not Custance. It was a man. He saw that it was Geroy.

Geroy came near. Fulcun fixed his eyes on the iron shoe of his scabbard that lay beside his leg on the grass. He only looked up when Geroy stood over against him, looking down.

"It is hot," says Geroy. He looked hot.

"Where is your horse?" asked Fulcun, because he must say something, and then he wished he had said anything else, for where, at that rate, was his own?

"It went from me." Geroy looked back the way he had come. "I got down to—to see to one of the sheep and the brute bolted. It will be at Montgaudri by now very like." He did not want to stay and talk, but as he moved on he thought he must say something.

"What are you doing here?" he says over his shoulder.

"Nothing," says Fulcun, and then, because he did not want Geroy to ask more, he nodded toward him. "What have you been doing to your hand?"

Geroy snatched it up and looked at it and put it behind him.

He said, "A dog bit it," and moved on. He wanted to get away from Fulcun. Not that he cared what Fulcun might say.

He went off with a swing of his shoulders, whistling, and then, when he was a little bit away from Fulcun, smiling to himself.

Fulcun did not watch him go. He was only glad that he had gone so easily and without question. For the sun was down, and Custance must come very soon. He had thought she would have been here before this.

Then he saw her coming and stood up. She came very slowly. He felt the blood going up to his face and his hand was so hard on his sword hilt that it shook. He had a thought then. He slipped his cloak from his shoulder ring and laid it down on the grass. There would be dew soon. He put the silver ring into his pouch. He was surprised as he did it that he could think of such small things.

He took two strides toward her and then stopped. Custance had stopped too.

She stood there with her hands at her mouth and her knuckles crushed against her teeth. He knew that she was biting her own fingers. He saw that; he saw her rent gown that showed the curve of one breast; he saw a green grass stain all down her side from shoulder to knee; he saw a bright red bruise on her cheek; and he knew that she shook so that she could hardly stand.

He said "Custance!"

She turned her head aside as if she wanted to find a place to run to, but she did not run.

"Custance, what has happened?" he asked her, but he knew, and she would not tell him.

"Who?" he said after a minute, and went a step toward her. He meant no harm—he had forgotten that he had ever meant it, but she went back with a strangled cry. When he stood still again she dropped her hands from her mouth and suddenly huddled the gown together across her breast.

"Lord Geroy," she told him, and her eyes came up to his and he saw loathing in them, ugly and agonized. She loathed him, with Geroy, because he was a man.

When she had gone on, stumbling stiffly along the road, her hands again at her mouth, Fulcun stood there very still for a long time. He moved at last, but only to sit down, his knees drawn up, his head down on them, and one wrist clenched in the other hand. Twilight came and the dark, but he dared not move because of the thoughts that went round and again round in his head.

This afternoon she had gone away from him. He had not taken her by his strength as he might. She had gone away. And while he had sat here waiting, Geroy— He gripped his wrist tighter and heard himself give a strange grunt of pain. But in the blackness of his mind there was not only pain; there was shame and loathing too. Geroy had done what Fulcun had waited to do. Fulcun knew now the vile face of it—this was the work of the flesh.

Sitting there as the dusk turned to dark, and as the stars came out and wheeled slowly over the dim crowns of the hills, he hated himself, and Geroy; he hated the whole of humankind. He knew now, he thought once with a kind of drunken clarity, how God must hate the vile and shameful flesh.

He got up at last, his hair dank with dew, and dew beads all over the iron of his scabbard. A nightjar screamed as it hunted somewhere over toward Belesme. As he went he heard a fox barking down in the valley, but they were small sounds in a great loneliness. He came, without any satisfaction, in sight of the lights in Montgaudri tower. He was not glad to leave the empty hills; there at least he was only one man moving in a great space of clean air, but in Montgaudri there were men like a herd of cattle, men doing the shameful work of the flesh even now in the dark. And Geroy was there—Geroy. He hated Geroy—a vile hate it was.

And Custance was there too, in that little cottage near the gate. He wanted her still—and that was vile. His thoughts, sharpened by weariness, would not be controlled. He could not keep the crowding imaginations from his mind, and yet he sickened at them.

II

Fulcun came from the dark stairway of the tower at Montgaudri into a dim and smoky light. The hall was hot that May night, though the fire was out, for they had barred the shutters, and up in the rafters the smoke hung yet like a cloud. It was so late that down here, round about the hearth, the house serfs already lay sprawling or huddled, and as Fulcun stood, the heavy air was full of a faint mutter of sound; snores, long-drawn sleepy sighs, the sharp rustle of straw when someone flung over to be more at ease.

Fulcun looked down at them, and beyond to the other end of the hall where the light burned—two torches stuck in brackets, whose flames, sucked aside now by the draft of the opening door, swayed, wreathed in drifting smoke.

At the high table with his back to the torches Geroy sat. He was drinking. Fulcun saw the light burn and blur on the silver rim of the horn as he lifted it. There were two other men with him—no, three, if you were to count the fellow who lay sprawling with his face on the table, Walchelin the Freeman by his bald head. On Geroy's left Osmunt the steward sat, big and black-bearded. On his left was a small man, gray-haired.

Geroy drank and lowered the horn and leaned over the table peering into the shadows.

"Who is that come in?" says he.

Fulcun did not answer. The gray-haired man was Herfast the priest from Cortilly. He must have come up to Montgaudri as soon as he had said Vespers.

Fulcun went up the hall, stepping over the sleeping serfs. He saw that the three at the table were all very drunk, Osmunt the least of them. Besides, Fulcun thought, Osmunt had done him no wrong, but to look at Geroy stabbed him with a fresh torment of hot jealousy, loathing, desire, and shame. And Herfast—Herfast had rung that bell this evening that Fulcun had listened to on the hill, and here he was, a drunken swine of a priest who kept a woman. Fulcun felt that he and they were all deep sunk in mire—they were all men.

He stood a moment looking at them across the table as if they were strangers. Geroy's face was flushed and his eyes very bright. He had both his hands now spread on the table, palms down, to keep himself steady. He had laid the horn on the table and the wine dribbled from the lip and spread in a dark shining pool. He stared at Fulcun standing there in his gray gown, long and lean, with his thin face hard and shut, and lines about his mouth.

Says he, with a loud laugh, "What mischief have you been at this summer night, Fulcun Heron?"

Fulcun's eyes dropped to Geroy's left hand. There was that fresh red gash on the back of it—shaped like a crescent moon—the mark of teeth.

Geroy felt his look and snatched his hand off the table. But Fulcun did not ask again how he came by the mark. He knew.

He said to Herfast, "Welcome, priest," and nodded to Osmunt. To Geroy he said, "Who is serving you? I'm hungry."

Geroy told him. "Baudri. He's gone for more wine."

Fulcun went round the end of the table and sat down by Osmunt, but not close to him. Osmunt turned and said, "If this weather holds we'll be shearing sheep in a week."

Fulcun says, "Aye," and thought of Custance going to Johan, who was with the sheep. When Baudri came in with an earthen jar of wine, he told him to fetch bread and meat and another horn. The lad brought them and Fulcun began to eat and found that he was indeed very hungry. He did not pay any attention to the others, nor they to him, except that Osmunt turned to him now and again at first. But he soon stopped even that; everyone was used to Fulcun's fits of silence.

Geroy was telling stories, all of the same kind, and when he and the others had done laughing he would lay his arm over young Baudri's shoulder and explain to him the point of the tale. When Baudri laughed Geroy was pleased. "You're young but you'll learn," he says. He was very fond of Baudri, who was a well-made little lad with bright blue eyes and a sweet singing voice.

Fulcun finished eating and leaned down and reached for a handful of rushes to wipe his knife on. When he had done that he shut it and put it back in its sheath at his belt. As soon as Baudri had given him some more wine he would go off and leave them.

Geroy and the others were merrier now. Osmunt was talking very loud of a girl at Cortilly. Herfast said she was a rare one. Fulcun thought to himself with sour unwilling amusement that Osmunt had better not talk so loud because Richereda slept in the great chamber next door, and she was known to have a tongue and little respect for her husband's size.

Then Geroy cried, cutting across the end of Osmunt's tale:

"But hark ye—hark ye—I'll tell you—"

He began to tell them that the Cortilly girl was a slut to Johan Shepherd's Custance. "And today, look you," Geroy lapsed into giggles but pulled himself up. "Today—" he went on.

Fulcun listened because he could not move. When he did move he sent his chair back with a crash that rang through the hall.

Geroy and Osmunt and Herfast turned, staring, their faces blank with surprise. Down in the hall folk sat up from their straw and stared too.

Fulcun did not know what was in his mind and in his face till he felt Osmunt catch his wrists and found that the steward was standing between him and Geroy. But he knew then that he had wanted only to take Geroy's throat in his bare hands and choke the words there.

Geroy was standing now. He tried to push Osmunt away so as to see Fulcun. Fulcun stood quite still and Osmunt let his wrists go, but he did not move aside, and then Geroy's legs betrayed him and he sat down abruptly.

"Curse you, Fulcun," he says very loud and angry. "What flea's bitten you?"

Fulcun remembered suddenly that Geroy could not know—could not guess. He muttered, because he could not think of anything to say:

"It's your foul mouth. I—" Then he caught sight of little Baudri's face, flushed and scared. "Can't you keep it shut in front of the lad?"

Geroy, who had honestly forgotten Baudri, and almost forgotten Fulcun, growled something that no one heard.

Fulcun wanted nothing now but to be away from them. He turned to Baudri. "Pick up that chair." He waited, and then, "Now—away to bed with you." He drove the boy before him to the door.

As he went through after him and turned to latch it, Fulcun heard Geroy cry out something with a great shout of laughter. The words came to him and stuck in his mind, though just then they had no meaning for him because he could think of nothing but Geroy's tale. Geroy had told it well. Fulcun could see it happen in his mind.

Out on the tower under the clear stars, Fulcun was for a moment eased. Then his thoughts caught him up again, and for an hour he tramped, over and back across the narrow space as fast as he could go, and his iron scabbard-shoe rapped on the pale every time he swung about. He could not go fast enough to outpace his thoughts.

It was all aimless torment, until at last a new thought came. For a minute he stood still, now for the first time hearing Geroy's words that had been in his ears since he shut the door of the hall.

"Ho!" Geroy had cried. "There'll be another of us with a shaved crown soon."

Fulcun went on with his tramping, six steps and turn, six steps and turn, but he went slower and almost stopped sometimes and then on again.

Was that the way of it? Was it the only way to escape from the hot and shameful torment of human flesh? If he went to Saint-Évroult and they shaved his crown and gave him a gray gown and a rope instead of a sword belt, would that set him free? He tried to reason it out and could not.

Then suddenly he went over to one corner of the tower and knelt down and pushed his head and his clasped hands against the hard, still wood. He did not pray, but somehow his thoughts cleared.

This must be the way. A sudden thought of Custance in his arms this very afternoon stabbed and frightened him. If he were a monk, shut up in a square, guarded cloister, he would be safe; he could separate himself from his own flesh, and from more than the flesh, because he had wanted more. In his sick mind he now assembled, under one shamed condemnation, one terrified loathing, both lust and love.

He sat back on his heels and stared dully, in a great weariness, at the sky. The stars were very bright; those over the horizon trembled like white flames. It must be nearly dawn.

It was a week after that night, one wet noonday just before dinner, that Fulcun went out after Geroy into the yard. Geroy was hurrying because of the straight pelting rain, but Fulcun caught him up in the stable.

"Geroy," says Fulcun, "I am going to Saint-Céneri tomorrow."

"Oh, aye," says Geroy, and that was all. They were not good friends these days. Fulcun blamed himself but could not speak friendly to Geroy. Certainly he could not tell him what he intended.

Next morning, a fine, fair morning with a galloping wind and white cloud, Fulcun mounted in the yard at Montgaudri. He rode armed, and as he settled himself in the saddle and took his spear from Osmunt and felt the fringes of the white and blue banner that hung from below the spearhead slide across his hand, he thought, "I shall not ride out like this again!" The thought was strange and painful.

Osmunt's lad, Neel the Archer, came with him, and a couple more Montgaudri men, freeholders from the valley. When they were all mounted Fulcun stooped and kissed Geroy and waved his hand to Dame Alianor and little Baudri up on the outer steps of the tower. Then the horse moved on from a pressure of his knee.

Just as they came to the gate they met four or five of the women of the township coming in with their buckets swinging on the yokes to draw water from the castle well; it was the only well in Montgaudri. Custance was among them. Fulcun saw her, and then he saw nothing else.

He rode out of the gate looking neither to right nor left. He forgot that this was the last time he would ride armed out of Montgaudri. He did not look back.

Custance, as she hurried to draw up her second bucket before the other women should go away and leave her, thought unwillingly of Fulcun, with a heavy, angry ache that she did not understand. Geroy had wronged her; but Fulcun—he had betrayed her. So she felt and did not in the least know why. She caught the bucket from the hook and had it swinging from the yoke again. As she turned to go, someone said:

"Well, wench! Not even good morning?"

It was Geroy. She raised her eyes for one second.

"No," she said, with no breath to say more. She hurried by him clumsily so that some of the water slopped out of the buckets and splashed on the dry, trodden ground. She must catch up the other women, but they were almost out of sight.

He went after her.

Chapter 2

Thou lovest all the things that are, and abhorrest
nothing which thou hast made: for never wouldest
thou have made any thing, if thou hadst hated it.

And how could any thing have endured, if it had
not been thy will? or been preserved, if not called by
thee?

But thou sparest all: for they are thine, O Lord,
thou lover of souls.

Wisdom of Solomon 11:24–26

I

The castle of Saint-Céneri stands high up above the quick-
running Sarthe on a rocky bluff around which the river makes
so sharp a turn that the town and castle are set almost on an
island. The castle is at the extreme tip of this tongue of land and
looks down directly on the clear shallows and deep flashes of the
river, dark with long weed, and on the smooth worn heads of the
big boulders that are bare in summer but waterworn by the full
winter floods. Across the river the opposite bank is rocky too,
but not so high nor so steep. There is a strip of good grazing land
on top of it, and little paths trodden by the cattle lead down
from that to the pebbly drinking places. Beyond the narrow
meadow there are woods, and more woods, piling up to meet

the sky. Saint-Céneri is a quiet and sheltered place, very pleasant in summer; and summer or winter every room of the castle is full of the fresh sound of running water.

The sheep-dipping pool is not immediately below the town, but a mile or so away down the river, at a place where the water makes a sudden elbow round a jutting point of smooth blue rocks. The water is thigh-deep just under those rocks, and there, for as long as folk have lived at Saint-Céneri—and that is as long as there had been men with flocks in Maine—there, on the shore just above the blue rocks there has been a sheep pen and, enclosing that pool of slower deep water from the shallow hurrying stream that swings round the rocks and away, a paling of stout stakes driven into the bed of the river, making Saint-Céneri's sheep-dipping pool. Everywhere else along the river, beyond a narrow meadow, the woods rise steeply, but just by the sheep pen and the pool there is a wider space, and an open, sunny, grassy slope running down from the high valley side to the river.

On the morning of the sheep shearing—that is the morning of the 3rd of June—young Robert, Robert Geroy's son, was up as early as the sun. Robert Geroy himself came down not much later. Robert Geroy was over fifty now, short, but broader in the shoulders than many bigger men, his face square and fresh-colored, with a boy's look when he smiled, and when he did not, the mouth of a man who knows that men are born to trouble. He smiled now as he watched the youngster striding to and fro bare-legged, in his old green gown, with his chin on his chest, scowling at the ground. Little Robert frowned heavily, muttering something, and pointed at the corner where the wood stack was; then he put his hand to his side and tugged at an invisible but doubtless very weighty sword.

Robert watching him thought, "What the devil is he doing? Who is it walks so?" and then knew that it was Fulcun of Montgaudri who would walk up and down like that, scowling and smiling.

Robert stood still, his eyes smiling, and the ends of his big mouth. He was thinking half of little Robert and half of Fulcun as he used to be—though he was never stocky and fair like this boy, but long, thin, and dark, with fits of silence that Robert had thought were sullen, and tried to cuff him out of, till he found it no use; untidy, uncertain; now lazy, now more eager and quick than any; unaccountably fierce, unexpectedly indifferent. Robert had not understood him then, and did not understand him much better now that he was a grown man, but he loved him. Geroy, whom he had brought up along with Fulcun, he understood, he thought, well enough. "Soft—a coward," Robert called him to Aelis; but she said that he was a handsome lad and pleasant. Robert had answered, "Pleasant? His dogs don't like him." Neither did Robert.

Young Robert looked up, saw his father, forgot altogether what it was he was playing at, and ran to him.

Says he, "Sir, the sun's up above the pale. Look! Can't we be going to the sheep pool?"

"No. It's too early yet," says Robert shortly, just as he would speak to one of the men, so that young Robert's chest swelled with pride. When his father turned off toward the carpenter's shed young Robert fell in beside him. "You mustn't wash sheep," says Robert, "till the sun is up enough to dry them out of hand."

Young Robert, close alongside as a dog, asked, "Why?"

"Because they take cold." Robert of Saint-Céneri liked to teach young Robert. He liked to think of the lad a grown man, with Saint-Céneri, and la Roche d'Ige, and Gandelain, and Hauterive in his hands; with the sheep to see to and the harvest, the knights to lead and the serfs to rule; keeping safe the lands and woods, the cattle and the corn. Young Robert had been born after he and Aelis had been married ten years. Robert wished the boy were older. Still, he was a strong lad and no fool; he'd grow and learn fast.

Says young Robert suddenly, skipping in his walk, "Sir, why ought sheep to be sheared the Eve of Barnaby?"

Robert didn't know himself. "It's the day to shear sheep, if the weather is fair," says he, and that was enough for young Robert. They went together into the carpenter's shop and together bent over a plank laid along the great balk of fissured, hacked wood that had been a fir tree in the woods when Rou came up the Loire in his long dragon ships; and now, littered deep with sawdust, was Hardre the carpenter's bench and had been his father's bench before him.

Robert ran his finger down the grain of the clean wood that lay there. At the end of the plank young Robert, not knowing why it was done, faithfully and unobtrusively copied him. The grainings in the wood, he thought, were like the small fishes that swam in the pools of the Sarthe, with rippling light rings shivering round them and making visible the transparent water.

Says Robert, "That's good oak."

Young Robert touched it again with his stubby fingers and then dived them into the soft sawdust. "Sir," says he, "what is it for?"

"A new great chest. The old chest is so warped it's not safe for keeping charters and treasures in." Robert stooped again over the wood and smoothed his hand along it, palm open. "That's been seasoned more than a dozen years. Longer than you've been alive. It's from Short Close Wood. The best oaks are there," he says, and went out again with young Robert following.

As they crossed the yard young Robert said, "Sir, what is 'warped'?"

Robert told him, and then, "Go and fetch me bread and a horn of wine from the kitchen."

Robert ate and drank, sitting on the end of the high table in the new hall he had built—it was of oak and thatched, with patterns on the thatch and a weathercock at one peaked end; it was much bigger and pleasanter than the old hall up in the tower, but it seemed dark after the sunshiny morning outside. When Robert had had enough, and young Robert had finished what he left, Robert says, "Now! Time to go."

As they went out Dame Aelis was standing on the tower steps. She was scolding a man who had brought in two hens for the rent of his croft. She said there was no flesh on them. She waved her hand to Robert and young Robert but did not take any more notice of them.

Robert got upon his horse that Ansgot the steward had ready, young Robert took hold of his stirrup, and Ansgot mounted on a mule. Then they started.

❧

They had not been gone for half an hour when Fulcun of Montgaudri came to the town gate. The porter there told him that Robert had gone down to the sheep shearing.

"Oh," says Fulcun, and sat still in the saddle for a minute. Then he said, "I'll go after him." He wanted to find Robert and tell him at once that he was going to Marmoutier, where Raol Geroy was, to be a monk like him.

He got down out of the saddle and said to Neel the Archer, "Unarm me." So Neel unarmed him there in the road, and laid the mail coat over his own saddle and gave the spear and helm to the porter to hold, and opened the saddlebag and took out Fulcun's gray gown, and put it on him. Then Fulcun mounted again, left them there, and rode off.

He crossed the ford and went up through the steep paths among the hazel bushes and out on to the town meadow and on along the river bank. The sun was shining above, and everything was still and hushed in the early morning shadow and dew-drenched, sweet-smelling coolness; only before him the air was full of the low, desolate crying of the sheep and the shriller answer of the lambs.

He came to the opening of the valley and the sunshine was here—he could see it, above the darkness of the highest trees, flung down into the deep hollow, a palpable great slant of light. He was in it now and felt the warmth on his cheek as he passed from the line of shadow.

He came that same minute in sight of the sheep pen and the noise of all the commotion there burst out at him; the shouts of the men, the loud crying of the beasts, the great splash and fresh shouting as each wether was flung from the pen to the washers in the pool.

Robert of Saint-Céneri was standing above the pen with his feet apart and his fists on his hips, watching. Ansgot the steward was by him talking. Robert listened and nodded without looking at the man.

Farther off Fulcun saw young Robert. The children were all at the shallows of the stream beyond the sheep pool, with bunches of whins and thorny bushes tied on poles, waiting for the odd scraps of wool to come bobbing along on the rippled glinting of the water. When any came they caught it on the thorns and raced with it up the bank, and stuffed it into a goatskin poke that Herold the shepherd had hung for them on a thorn bush.

Fulcun for one second watched it all as if he had no part in it; then someone shouted and pointed. Robert turned, stared, lifted his hand, and came toward him. As Fulcun swung out of the saddle he was thinking, "I am going to Marmoutier. I must go to Marmoutier."

He went forward quickly and kissed Robert's hand. Robert kissed his cheek and told him he was very welcome. "And I hope you'll stay," says he. "There's a couple of hawks you can train for me."

Fulcun looked away. Now that he had found Robert he did not want to say, "I am going to Marmoutier." He was very glad when young Robert came galloping up with shrill cheers. He thought Robert could not have noticed that he had not answered. But Robert, whose habit and inheritance it was to command men, had noticed. He said to himself, "The Heron has something on his mind."

He pulled off young Robert, who was swarming up one of Fulcun's legs, and sent him back to his wool gathering. Then says he, "Tether your horse and sit down. I'll be here soon. I'll steal you some of the sheep-washers' drink."

He went off grinning like a lad.

Fulcun sat down. He had tied his bridle and stirrup together and the horse moved slowly away, grazing. It was the young black stallion, and the sun shone with a lovely moving gleam along its shoulder and quarter, and the red harness was red as fresh blood. Fulcun saw it as if he had never seen it before. He stared at it, scowling. That small piece of the beauty of the world, like the dew and waiting stillness of the valley, and like the pleasant warmth of the sun on his face—he could not tell if he loved or loathed it. He thought miserably and dumbly that he must loathe it because he loved it.

Robert came up. He had in his hand a beech-wood cup of the sheep-washers' drink that the wenches had just brought— ale and boiled milk, and crumbled bread, and spice.

"That's for your welcome," says he, and gave it to Fulcun and dropped down on the grass beside him.

Fulcun drank it slowly, saying nothing, because there was nothing to say except one thing.

Robert gave a sudden big laugh. "You know," says he, "your serf is a born fool. Here we came, not a minute before nine, and I said we'd begin." He turned to Fulcun with a twist of his big mouth and a grin. "D'you think they would? Herold said the sun must shine on all the gorse clump up there," he jerked his head back. "I said that gorse clumps grew, but Herold called his son and old Goisbert; they all said we must wait! I'll have that gorse clump rooted up," says Robert, cheerfully truculent; only he was not thinking much of the gorse clump; he was wondering if Fulcun would out with it now.

But for a long time Fulcun said nothing, and Robert said nothing either. Robert thought to himself, "I can't talk forever while he thinks whether to tell it out or no."

Then Fulcun said suddenly, "Sir—I must be a monk."

So that was it. Robert turned and looked at him. He was not smiling now.

"And why?" says he, and looked away from Fulcun's face because it was so darkly unhappy.

It took Fulcun a long time to think what to say. Then— "Because of my foul sins."

"Oh! Which!" Robert asked.

"You're laughing at me," Fulcun cried.

Robert shook his head so soberly that Fulcun knew, even when he smiled, that it was in kindness.

"Which?" says Robert again, and knew that Fulcun had turned to face him. He met Fulcun's eyes.

"Of the flesh," Fulcun answered, with a steady somber look.

Robert said, "I told you last year you should marry."

"That's no use," Fulcun cried sharply, "It's all foul—it's all—" He stopped short and for a minute stared straight at Robert's eyes, as rigid as a man struck through the body, who stands still a long instant staring before he falls. Robert had not time to think over that strange thing that he had left half-said before Fulcun broke out with a rush of words telling him of the last months—of Custance—Custance—Custance.

It was a difficult tale to follow. Now it was how he had watched her dancing round Montgaudri Stone with other girls, and all her black hair flying out—or had come on her bent under the faggots she had been gathering in the woods; now it was how she had gray eyes and dark brows, mostly frowning—and her lips were red—and— Then that was bitten off unfinished because he must not remember or think of it. And now he would tell Robert that old Johan beat her. "I came on him once," Fulcun says, "beating her with a ragged stick. Her—her neck was bleeding. And she didn't cry out." He looked at Robert as though there were no one there, and said in a very small voice, "And she is . . . a good wench. She'd . . . have none of me, never . . . never . . . and . . . but—" He stopped a long minute, and then he put his head down between his fists and told Robert of that evening on the hilltop.

Robert listened, his eyes on his own green leather boots, and when Fulcun stopped he sat for a long time silent, biting at his fingers and frowning, with his great bushy fair brows drawn together. It was like Fulcun to talk of a serf girl like this. "I couldn't take her," Fulcun had cried. "It was no use—was it?"

But anyway, since Geroy had had her, it was too late to say, "Go home and have her up to Montgaudri tower. You'll be weary of her soon."

In the end Robert went back to what he had said before.

"My lad, it's what I told you. You should marry. Get a wife and get sons on her. You'll have forgotten this wench in a month."

Fulcun said quietly, after a silence, "No. I must go to Marmoutier. The flesh—it's all foul. It's all sin. I know now."

"Oh!" says Robert, and then, cheerfully but not lightly, "I don't know it. Is it sin for me?" and he looked along the river to where young Robert stood thigh-deep in the bright water. Fulcun looked too and could see no light in his mind. He shook his head and muttered, "No . . . I don't know," and they sat silent.

Robert was trying to understand. He was not used to thinking about what he felt and did, but now he must, so that he could answer Fulcun; only he wished that either he had been a wiser man, or Fulcun—not so mad.

He set himself to think of what he felt about Aelis, and it became clear to him, as he thought, that he was very fond of her. But he could not bring himself to be ashamed of anything in that. Looking back and remembering her dumb and trembling obedience when he first brought her with him to Saint-Céneri, and remembering that night soon after, when, shuddering and half-sobbing, she had held his head down on her breast while she whispered to him that it was bliss for her too—remembering these things and more, he admitted that there might be something there to be ashamed of—though for his part he was not ashamed—not he.

But for the other things there were in love—no. He had never thought of it before, but now he was very glad to know that there was much more love between him and his wild girl than he had ever guessed. He was glad because he was sure, now he thought about it at all, that such love was good.

He turned to Fulcun.

"Listen to me," says he in his big, confident, masterful voice, "I'll tell you. It is different if you marry. This wench—well—" He let a wave of the hand pass for all that Fulcun wanted of her. "But a man's wife is more than that. Of course"—he frowned at Fulcun to keep him quiet—"of course there's that as well. But there's more." He was frowning now at his own square brown fist on his knee; he found these things very difficult to put in words. "There is," he said slowly, "a great . . . a great kindness . . . and care." He shut his mouth hard. Then, "Very great," he said.

Fulcun was silent a minute, then he gave a kind of impatient groan.

"For you!" he says, stumbling over the words. "Your—your heart is clean."

"Rats!" cried Robert angrily. "I'm a man like you."

"Mine's not." Fulcun finished.

Robert snorted. "Don't talk nonsense!" but Fulcun was staring past him, intent on something else.

He said, after a minute, "I know now that this is what I've feared—always."

"What—to be a monk. Was that why you would not marry?"

"No . . . I don't know," says Fulcun vaguely, and went back to his own thought. "Robert," he said, "I always feared that he'd never suffer me to love any human creature. Now—" He stopped and sat there by Robert, not daring to look at him, nor say more, only waiting for him to answer and say that was all a mistake.

But Robert did not answer. He had shot his bolt and now sat silent. He picked up a dry twig out of the grass and stared hard at it; then he snapped it sharply in his fingers and, lifting his hand, threw the slight, light thing from him with all his strength.

"Well," says he, "if you must be a monk—you must." He was thinking, "There aren't many Geroys left to stand together—but he doesn't care for that."

Fulcun said stubbornly, answering Robert's voice, "My uncle Guillelm was a monk—Raol is now."

Robert turned to him with a heavy look.

"Aye—so—" he said, and Fulcun understood.

He cried out, "Robert—sir—"

Robert cut him short. "No! No! You must not care for any human soul," and scrambled up, and stamped his foot on the ground, and stood for a minute biting on his fingers.

Then he looked down at Fulcun with a queer shamed look, and yet half laughing.

"I wish I could take a rope's end to you these days," he says.

Fulcun laughed too, but for both of them it was sorry laughter.

II

It was evening when Fulcun rode beside Robert, back along the valley toward Saint-Céneri. Young Robert was up behind Fulcun, and Fulcun carried young Robert's stick with the dripping whin bush like a spear. He was merry with the boy, but Robert Geroy rode in silence. Behind them came the sheep washers and the rest of the men, except the shepherds, who, with the sheep and the ranging dogs, brought up the rear.

When they came to the riverbank the sheep were driven into the town meadow that had hurdles set about it to keep them in.

Young Robert says to Fulcun, "Did you know you must drive sheep into hold after May Day to keep them from the corn?"

He was very proud of himself when Fulcun said that he was glad to learn it. Robert turned and grinned at Fulcun.

The horses went down slowly and idly into the cool water of the ford, dark now with the shadow of the high banks, yet lucid. Fulcun's beast snatched at its bridle, and when he let it, put down its mouth to the water. He sat there in his saddle a moment while it drank, in the midst of the river that hastened by with a smooth, fresh mutter. Behind were the dark woods, and over them the golden sky; before him rose the cliff and castle—the rocks pale as dry bone in the shadow, and above warmed almost to rose where they faced the sun. He would have looked longer—Saint-Céneri was as much—even more—his home than Montgaudri—but young Robert clamored to race his father home.

Fulcun pulled the horse's head up and rode after Robert. They caught him up and passed him among the hazel bushes, but they heard him coming after them calling to his horse. When they broke out on to the meadow he was riding abreast of them, and young Robert yelled with delight as the horses gathered themselves together and plunged on across the open hill.

Before them stood the gate of Saint-Céneri. There were serfs coming in with axes and billhooks over their shoulders, and a woman in a red hood was driving a donkey in at the gate. Nearer to them, striding forward along the road, went a very tall, thin man in a monk's gown. He walked fast, swinging a long staff. It was young Robert who shouted, "It's Sire Raol!" but before he shouted both Fulcun and Robert had reined in.

As the horses strained and slowed they looked each other in the eyes, but they said nothing. Fulcun was thinking, "This is the will of God," and he was afraid. Robert thought, "He'll go with Raol."

They rode on in silence till Robert cried to the striding monk, "Ho! Raol, welcome!" and swung off his horse.

They went into the town together, but when Robert was for going to the castle Raol stopped.

"I can't sleep with you up there," says he.

"Why not?"

"I am forbidden. I should have gone on straight to Séez, where my business is for the house."

Robert says rudely, "Then why did you come here?" He was angry with all monks tonight.

Raol Malacorona turned round in the road.

"I'll go again."

Robert swore, "Death of God!" Then, "I'm sorry, Raol."

They went on; the two brothers knew each other; there was old affection between them, though they had never agreed well together.

"But," says Robert, "where will you lie tonight?

"At your priest's."

"Will you? He keeps a woman." Robert did not stop quite short of teasing.

Raol told him he should be ashamed to have a priest like that in Saint-Céneri.

"He's not the only one in Normandy. Besides—it's not my business. It's Bishop Ivo's in Séez."

"Well," says Raol tartly, "I don't suppose he takes her to church. I'll stay there tonight."

They parted at the gate of the little church, by the black yew. Fulcun thought he had never seen Robert so ill-tempered.

His temper did not mend, either. When they came into the castle, Robert, before ever he got off his horse, began to shout for the wenches to get a couple of cloaks, and meat, bread, and wine, and for a man to fetch a truss of hay from the barn, and then to carry down all to the church for Lord Raol. He was very impatient, hurrying them.

Fulcun went into the stable. When he came out, Hodierna, Ansgot's wife, had the food and wine in a rush basket, and a lantern, and one of the men was coming from the barn with a truss of hay on a pitchfork.

Fulcun went over to Robert; he was standing with his arm through his bridle, frowning at nothing.

"Sir," says Fulcun, "I'll take them to Lord Raol," and took the basket out of Hodierna's hand.

Robert looked at him. "Oh! And a truss of hay over your shoulder?" he jeered.

"The man can bring that." Fulcun was not angry. He knew that Robert knew why he went to Raol Malacorona tonight.

"Well," says Robert, "I must thank you, must I?" He flung the bridle to young Robert, who stood listening, and went off across the yard to the tower. Fulcun watched him. For all that it was not his fault, he was ashamed, and for all that Robert had gone in anger, Fulcun felt that human kindness went with him.

He came, in the last light of the evening, to the little church and went in. It was almost dark inside. Raol Geroy got up from the trodden earth floor in front of the altar.

Fulcun told the man where to put the hay; he tossed the cloaks down on it and set the basket by them. After that he and the servant went down on their knees, and Raol blessed them, but when they had got up and the servant had trudged out with a sort of scared side glance at the place where God lived, Fulcun lingered.

Raol says, "What do you want," and stood waiting, but for a moment Fulcun did not answer. In the dim dusk of the church he could not see Raol's face under the cowl, only he caught a pale gleam where Raol's eyes must be. He had never had much love for Raol, nor Raol for him, and he had to try not to see in his mind what was far clearer than the man before him in the twilight—the Raol Geroy that had been at Saint-Céneri when

Fulcun was a boy—that big-boned, hawk-nosed man with the narrow, glancing eyes; impatient, hard-tempered, given to long, controlled fits of anger that made the lads fear him far more and love him far less than Robert with his brief rages; Raol Geroy that had made most people half afraid because of his learning, and his silences, and his sudden wild brilliant talking. Fulcun must not remember that this man was Raol Geroy; it was Brother Raol, the monk.

Fulcun cried out suddenly, "Why did you go to Marmoutier?"

Before Fulcun spoke, Raol, seeing his rigid stillness, had guessed what was coming. He said, "I went to escape from my own sins. I was afraid."

"Afraid?" cried Fulcun. So he understood—even though he was Raol Geroy! "To be a monk?"

Raol told him harshly, "No. To be in torment to eternity."

That struck Fulcun silent a moment. It was true that a man might well fear to be so, but there was no room in his mind for that fear just now. He stared into the dusty shadows beyond Raol. The church smelled damp and unused; there was a little blur of grayish light showing in one place through the worn thatch. With his eyes on that Fulcun understood that there were two things that he feared; himself, and the flight from himself. He went back to those.

"Sir," he said, "have you . . . have you . . . when you were in the world did you know the love of a woman?"

Raol Malacorona moved sharply and hit his chest with his clenched fist.

"When I was first in the world," he said, "I lived in that sin as the swine in mire."

Fulcun muttered, "I can see that God would have us leave the work of the flesh—"

"It is putrid rottenness."

Fulcun bowed his head. That was true. He had learned it.

"But," he said, and again peered at Raol's dimly gleaming eyes, "but will he have us love no human thing—nothing—nothing?"

They were almost the same words that he had used to Robert that morning; but then he had told Robert the thing was so; now, to Raol, he cried out for denial of it, because he could not hope that Raol would deny.

Raol turned from him to the altar for a long minute. As if in a vision in the dark he saw Fulcun's soul struggling to free itself from heavy, strong chains that were the flesh. There was a blaze of fire too in the vision, and Fulcun's soul tried desperately to wrench itself away from the snatching flames. Raol turned back; he drew himself to his full height, as tall a man as Fulcun but as thin as a winter tree. He put out his hand and laid it on Fulcun's wrist.

"Fulcun Geroy," he said, "choose as you will—every man chooses for himself. But I tell you—I dread—I dread to care for any mortal thing. I fled away to Marmoutier to be alone—only alone can a man find God. Do you think that God will share—" His voice rose high and harsh as it used to do when he was angry—"Do you think God will share a soul's love with any other thing? He will not. Be sure that he will punish." He stopped and Fulcun heard him grind his teeth. "Tonight I came here because my folk are here . . . and Robert . . . he laughed at me for it. So I was served." He took his hand from Fulcun's wrist and turned half away. After a minute he said, "Will you weigh human love against God's pardon? Will it ease you to be loved by any human flesh when you lie together in the flames of hell? For God is jealous . . . angry and jealous."

Fulcun stood dumb. He could not think; he was lost in the dark. He knew only that it was not the anger of God that he had feared; it was the love, insatiable as fire, unappeasable as hate, relentless as the tide of the sea; the love that demanded from his quailing soul no less than all its love in return. But just now he did not even fear that. Something had, not answered, but blotted out fear.

Outside a man passed by whistling; then there was silence, and still neither of them moved nor spoke. But Raol was thinking, "He'll be down on his knees in a minute." He knew how men broke all of a sudden. He waited; it was a moment when time stood.

At last Fulcun moved, slowly and uncertainly. He shifted his feet and looked vaguely round about the shadowy place.

"No—" he said, very low, as if he spoke to himself. "But I can't understand—" He broke off again. He stood a minute more, then sighed, and turned slowly away. The gray twilight came in as he opened the door; it narrowed and was cut off. The latch clicked. Raol was left alone.

⚜

Going back through the town with the little houses and the orchard trees sharp black against the colorless sky, Fulcun ceased even trying to understand. Just now it seemed unnecessary. Instead he gave himself over to the dumb but potent persuasion that had touched and mastered his mind as he had stood facing Raol in the dark church.

In that moment he had known that Raol was wrong, and his own fear as idle as a child's fear in the dark. But why? The answer, only it was no answer, was—Robert Geroy's cheerful face and his blue eyes, looking hard, half smiling, wholly kindly, into Fulcun's, this morning.

Raol was wrong—that knowledge flowed into Fulcun's mind and spread. Then a greater tide followed it, lifted him, and carried him out of the reach of thought or argument into a dim certainty of safety. It was kindness itself that had him; it was too close all about him for him to need to lift his eyes and call it God. He gave himself over to the flood, and it bore him up.

He was at the door of the hall. He lifted the latch and opened it. The blaze of light, warm-colored, and the warm air, burst on him like a sudden flowering of summer. In the instant that he stood there, blinking in the glare, he forgot everything that was not familiar and easy.

He went up the hall toward the high table, and as soon as his eyes could see he saw that Robert was watching him come. Aelis was there too—Fulcun had forgotten that he had not greeted her, and now he did not notice her offended sharp stare.

Guion was there too, Yvo Geroy of Courville's lad, and his younger brother Berenger, that Yvo had sent to Robert to bring up. They stood together behind Robert, but Fulcun did not greet them, nor did he greet the men of Saint-Céneri he knew—Hardre the Black, and Ranof Badger, and Neel of the Crooked Nose, and the rest.

He sat down opposite Robert and said to him:

"Sir, I'll stay awhile at Saint-Céneri with your leave."

"Good," says Robert, and that was all.

Chapter 3

Par la grace infinie, Dieu les mist au monde ensemble.

Rousier des Dames

I

Next morning Raol Geroy went on his way to Séez. Robert, Fulcun, and Guion of Courville—all of his kin at Saint-Céneri but little Robert—went with him as far as the river, and there they three knelt, and he blessed them and said farewell. They watched him go across the little wooden footbridge. He passed under a young ash tree and they saw the light leaf shadows chase quickly down his back; then they lost sight of him among the trees of the wood.

The other Geroys mounted their horses when he was out of sight and rode back to Saint-Céneri. Robert was silent and frowning, but Fulcun felt as if today the world was somehow new, and all of it important. He stared at a bank that was bright with a tangle of bright wild roses and thought he had never seen them so deep a color before. If then his blood reminded him of Custance, and if it hurt afresh to lack her in the midst of all the bounty of summer, he set his teeth and fought with himself—neither his body nor his mind should want her, since his will was set against it.

That was how it went for him at Saint-Céneri in the weeks that followed. He must fight, and the fighting hurt, and sometimes, lying awake while young Guion and Neel and Ranof slept, he would despair of peace. But between the nights there were busy days and every evening Custance was farther off. All told, Fulcun was not unhappy.

It was Robert of Saint-Céneri who was, for him, strangely uncheerful. Fulcun, selfish in his own preoccupation, did not notice it at first. Then, one evening as they were sitting on their cloaks upon the platform at the top of the wooden steps that led up to the door of the tower, Fulcun did see it. It was a fair evening after a showery day and the air was sweet. Fulcun looked up at the tower, wood in its two upper stories, and now streaked black like an old tree with the rain that had fallen. Up on top, against the sky that was still blue at the zenith, he could see the head and shoulders of Guion Geroy leaning over the pale; everyone else had gone up there.

Fulcun turned to Robert, to say something about the last litter of puppies. But he did not say it, for Robert was staring out over the yard at the pale golden west, with his big mouth set and his eyebrows frowning. Fulcun watched him, and in a minute Robert turned and looked at him, lowering, and then began to talk.

"There's trouble coming," says he, "in Maine. Count Hue—he's a sickly fellow—he's thirty—no, not that—twenty-eight maybe, and bald as an egg already. And if he dies—he nearly died last year—the boy Herbert is five." He began to drum on the hollow planks with his fingers. "That'd be a nice morsel for the Bastard in Normandy, or Geffroi Martel in Anjou. They'll both try to gobble it."

He was silent a minute, scowling at the dying light, and then:

"I rode to Mayenne at Easter. It was Geffroi of Mayenne set me thinking. He had a guest there, Gautier of Pontoise—his wife is the child Herbert's aunt, old Count Herbert's daughter. Geffroi was all for me swearing to Gautier to be his man and make him count of Maine, if Count Hue dies while the child is a child. I didn't—but—"

He stood up, as if he had finished, but then he said, "I asked Raol when he was here; he's the wisest of us since Guillelm died, but he would say nothing, only that the kingdoms of this world were dead ashes." After a minute he looked down at Fulcun with a rueful smile. "I doubt I'm not clever enough for this," he says.

A day or two after that, Fulcun rode out with Robert to hawk along the Sarthe where the woods opened beyond Gandelain. Guion was riding behind with the dogs, leashed. He was a dark-haired handsome lad, and he knew it; he had an idea of his own dignity and was apt to sulk. He was sulking now because he had tried to cast his hawk in the woods and had lost it, and Robert had laughed at him.

Robert stared into the suffused but dazzling light of the gray summer sky with his eyes puckered up against the glare. He pulled up, so did Fulcun, and instead of the jingle of the hawk's bells and the noise of the horses they heard nothing but the open silence of the still day.

"Sir," says Fulcun suddenly, "why not ride to Guillelm of Normandy this summer and see how he will deal with you?"

Robert did not take his eyes from a heron that flew with a long slow sweep of great curved wings a mile or so down the river.

"What for?" he asked.

"Why," says Fulcun—he had thought it out and he was eager—"then in the autumn you can go to Martel in Anjou, and then, when you have talked to all three of them you can choose between Guillelm the Bastard and Martel and Gautier of Pontoise."

"He's coming this way," cried Robert, and whipped off the hawk's hood and slipped the jess and tossed the hawk up with the falconer's yell.

For the next hour or two Fulcun forgot even to wonder whether Robert was thinking about what he had said. They took a heron and two bittern and a curlew and then they stopped to eat the bread and bacon and eggs that they had with them. They lay at their length on the bank of the river that ran here smooth and wide and deep, and the dogs sat watching them with eyes yearning for scraps. Guion had come out of his sulks and was merry now; he said he was sure he would find his hawk in the wood as they went home.

"Oh yes," says Fulcun, and stopped because he shivered. "It'll be there still, I expect," he finished.

Robert lifted his head from his arm and laughed.

"A goose treading your grave, Fulcun?"

"Or another man lying by his love," says Guion.

Fulcun was frowning. Then he lifted his head and looked across the river and watched a brown dragonfly darting and gleaming above the reeds there. He gave a little laugh suddenly.

"He's welcome," he said.

Robert of Saint-Céneri thought, "That sounds like truth," and he was right.

On the way home, when they had left Guion behind, whistling in the wood for his hawk, Robert said suddenly to Fulcun:

"We—I mean I might ride to Guillelm's court. There would be no harm done. They used to say that Gandelain and your Montgaudri should hold of Normandy, though they never did. That was why I've never been to Guillelm. But they've forgotten it now."

"I'll come," says Fulcun.

Robert looked at him. "I'm glad," he said.

Fulcun turned and grinned at him. "And will you get me a good marriage there?"

Robert says, "I promise you." Then he laughed. "Ho! Fulcun, we'll go. And Geroys prosper when they go into Normandy."

The day before they left, a hot and sultry day with distant thunder, Dame Aelis came down from the tower and called to one of the men to know where Lord Robert was. Aelis was flushed to her hair, her hands were dirty, and there was dust on the skirts of her blue gown. She had been busy all day over the bales they were to carry with them roped across the saddles of the pack animals; there were sheets to take, and coverlets, and Robert's faldstool—the little one with the red and blue painted stars on it—and cups and knives and wooden bowls for the table, and cooking pots, and one wooden chest with spices in it, and another one that held her gilded lamp shaped like a man riding a dragon's back, and Robert's gold-and-ivory collar and precious things like that. And then there were clothes to pack up—all their finest clothes—her gown with the English embroidery, and the silk mantle that Guillelm Geroy had brought back from Jerusalem for Robert the first time he went on pilgrimage, before Talvas caught and blinded him. It was of white silk with a shimmer of gold in it, because there were threads of gold woven through the weft, strong shining threads made with a core of silk wrapped round with thin cowhide strips that had the pure gold leaf stuck to them with gelatin. There was a pattern on the mantle too—a pair of animals in blood color and scarlet red that faced each other with their stiff claws up. Dame Aelis was proud of Robert's mantle and she had folded it carefully with lambs' wool in between the folds to keep the gold safe; she did not grudge her trouble that hot day, but all the same, when she came down through the old hall in the tower on her way to the kitchen to see if they had remembered to pack the new spit, she was tired and ready to be angry.

Robert was in the old hall at the window that looked north into the town. Fulcun was there too, and Guion Geroy and one or two knights. It was cool here because the shutters were closed, and the men were sitting about on their cloaks and on cushions, with a big wooden dish of cherries in the midst. She thought, "Little they have to do—the lads will pack their arms and that's all!" She knew that Robert called her but she pretended not to hear.

"Aelis, here!" he cried again. She went over to them and stood with her hands clasped tight in front of her.

"You called me, sir," she said.

"Aelis," says Robert, "go and get out that gear in the old black chest. Raol's gear that he left here when he went to Marmoutier. I want it for Fulcun. He can't go to court in that!" and he pointed.

Aelis looked at Fulcun. She was not glad to do this for him.

She said, "Why didn't he bring his stuff from Montgaudri? If that old gray gown he's got on is good enough for us—"

Robert stopped her by getting up to his feet and putting his hand on her shoulder. "Go and do as I say," says he, and gave her a push hard enough to let her know he meant it.

When she came back, hotter and angrier still, she had a heap of clothes bundled in her arms and trailing to her feet. They were of all colors, some bright, some faded, but most of them rich and fine, for Raol Geroy had always gone gay.

She tumbled them down on the floor and pushed them with her foot before she went away across the room. But at the stairway, safe from any brief anger of Robert's, she turned.

"I hope," says she, in a thin, unfriendly voice, "that they'll bring Fulcun luck—*he* didn't have much!" and she jerked her head toward wherever Raol might be now. Then she went.

Robert muttered something about women's tongues. He was put out. He thought it was an unchancy thing to say.

No one spoke for a second, but Fulcun stretched out his hand to the pile of clothes, and then stopped.

From very far off came a long, lazy mutter of thunder that paused and dwindled, broke with a single short concussion and ceased.

"I knew there was thunder in the north," says Ranof. "We'll ride into it tomorrow unless it clears."

Fulcun pulled out from the heap a white wool gown, and a scarlet, and a blue cloak, as blue as borage.

He said to Robert, "Sir, by your leave I'll take these."

Robert nodded. "Is it enough?

Fulcun said it was.

They rode next day, twelve knights not counting Robert and Fulcun, and Aelis with two other women; Guion Geroy went to carry Robert's shield and Robert bade his younger brother Berenger serve Fulcun, for Fulcun had sent back the Montgaudri men a month ago. There were a few freeholders with bows, and many servants to drive the baggage animals; altogether a great crowd. They all rode out of the gate of Saint-Céneri at six o'clock in the morning and along the bank of the river toward Préz-en-Pail. The men did not ride armed; their mail shirts and helms were in the bales on the packhorses' backs, and their shields too, in goatskin covers. They carried only hunting spears; on their fists Robert and some others had each a hawk; and loping along beside the horses, discreet and solemn, came half a dozen big deerhounds with their smooth, unhurrying pace.

They went by Carrouges, avoiding Alençon because it was Belesme land, though the only Belesme left now except old

Bishop Ivo of Séez was a woman, Mabille, Talvas's daughter, Rogier of Montgommeri's wife. But they counted it Belesme land for all that Rogier held it, and besides, neither Robert nor Fulcun wanted to ride up to the gate out of which Guillelm Geroy had come, groping in the sunshine, with the cur dogs barking after him, and Talvas's men jeering and shouting them on.

They spent one night in the field near Carrouges, sleeping in the tents they carried. The thunder stood all about them but did not break. There was wind and harsh, spitting showers, but it was pleasant enough weather for riding when the sun came out, sudden and hot in the high blue sky that seemed higher and greater because of the bulky clouds that floated there.

At Écouché they heard a wild tale told by a peddler who had come from Évreux that Martel had gone by from Anjou with two hundred knights on his way to take the king at Paris. But they heard too for certain that Duke Guillelm was at Falaise; so they had not far to go to find him.

They had not so far as they thought. It was in the oak woods about Trun that they heard horns blowing, and Robert bade leash up the dogs lest they should get away and join the hunt. Then they rode on listening to the horns, and to the silence that fell suddenly.

"They've killed," says Robert.

Aelis said, "Yes. Perhaps it is my cousin hunting."

It was. Half a mile on they came on the hunt in the midst of a long green ride. Three foresters were flaying a buck, and the dogs sat about, slavering and waiting for their share of the entrails. A dozen or so of knights stood by leaning on their spears—one of them had the knife in his hand that had cut the deer's throat when it went down.

Robert of Saint-Céneri got off his horse and went toward them. Fulcun followed him.

The man with the knife turned. He had a smudge of blood on his cheek and his hands were red. His brown shock of hair was rough and there were leaves and twigs in it from the low branches he had ridden through. He was a big man, almost as tall as Fulcun and far more solid. He watched Robert hard as he came up; he was frowning, and it darkened his eyes so that they looked almost black.

Says he, as Robert Geroy slung off his cloak for courtesy and let it drop on the grass and stood in front of him:

"You're Robert Geroy of Saint-Céneri?"

"Aye, Duke Guillelm."

"Have you come to do me homage for Gandelain and Montgaudri?"

"I have not," says Robert. "I hold all I hold of Mayenne, as Fulcun my nephew holds Montgaudri."

Guillelm looked at him, frowning darker, but Robert was cheerful.

"They are both Norman land," Guillelm told him sharply.

"I don't know it."

Guillelm said, "Your father served my father well." His voice meant more than the words.

Robert looked at him with a jerk of his lips.

"Your father was a good lord to mine," says he. "He gave him land in Normandy. My nephew Hernaut has it."

Guillelm stared at him a minute, very black; then he laughed suddenly.

"Well, I'll be your good lord too—if you deserve it." He kissed Robert on the cheek. "We'll talk about Montgaudri and Gandelain afterward."

Then Robert said, "My wife, your cousin, sir, is here." He went away from Guillelm and lifted her down from the saddle and brought her to the duke.

She would have kissed Guillelm's hand, but he said "No, she should not, because it was all bloody," and he kissed her. Then Fulcun came. The duke held out his hand and Fulcun kissed it. It smelt of blood like a butcher's.

After that they got into the saddle again. Guillelm said he would not hunt more today, so they all rode to Falaise together, the duke going between Dame Aelis and Robert Geroy. Fulcun, following, watched Guillelm. He was very broad in the shoulders—any fighting man could see that he was a fighter. His build was a little loose and slovenly, but Fulcun thought only so as to make for quickness. He had a very sober, reserved look, and a way of frowning that darkened his eyes, but when he smiled you saw that they were a fair fresh blue. Fulcun did not know it, but that was the only thing in which he was like his mother, the tanner's lass that Robert of Normandy had made the mother of a bastard.

As Fulcun rode behind he heard Robert Geroy's big, sudden laugh; and Guillelm was laughing too. Fulcun said to himself that things looked well.

Within the pale of Falaise they parted, for Guillelm said there was no room for them all to lie up at the castle. But he said they must eat there whenever they pleased, and tonight for certain. Then he left one of his people to take them to a tanner's wife who would lodge them, and so rode off with his fist on his thigh.

"Tanner's wife?" says Robert behind his hand in a great whisper. "Duke Guillelm's own folk!"

Aelis cried angrily, "Hush!" Though the duke was out of hearing his man was not. But Robert only laughed.

II

At supper in the great hall of Falaise Robert Geroy sat that night at the duke's left hand, and Guillelm would have young Guion Geroy of Courville and Berenger to serve them; little Robert, in a fine new gown, very solemn and a little nervous, stood with the duke's own two sons—the fat, cheerful Robert Short-legs and Red Guillelm—and carried the wine about the table. Dame Aelis had gone up into the tower, where Duchess Mahalt and her women ate at the times of the great courts.

Fulcun sat at one of the lower tables; by ill luck he got separated from the Saint-Céneri knights and found himself sitting among strangers. On one side of him was a fat, gray-bearded knight who attended only to his food; he did not speak except to the servants as they went about with the wine and the spits of meat.

On the other side of him sat one almost as silent; a heavy, dark-haired man who kept his head down most of the time; when he raised it to look about him Fulcun noticed that he stared out from under half-lowered eyelids like a sleepy, sullen hawk. Fulcun heard him speak once to an older man beyond him; it was to contradict sharply something that the other had said, and then he laughed. "That's what all you old men think," he said.

He turned then on Fulcun. "Who are you?" he says, staring Fulcun up and down under his sullen lids.

Fulcun told him, "Fulcun Geroy." He did not ask the other's name simply because he did not want to know.

But, "The Geroys are no friends to my house," says the black-haired man.

Fulcun sometimes would be blankly indifferent to this kind of thing. He looked, then turned away and said nothing, good or bad, and watched the man with the gray beard take a collop of meat from a spit, slant his mouth under it so as to catch the gravy, and pop it in.

The black-haired man spoke again; his voice was different now and much more pleasant. "I am cousin to Rogier of Montgommeri," he says. "I am Mauger of Fervacques."

Fulcun said nothing to that either, but he nodded.

Mauger of Fervacques looked at him for a second, then he smiled; it was an unexpected smile that lightened his heavy face, but still there was a kind of bitterness in it, as though the man could not help but be sour.

"Well," he says, "I don't think I love Mabille of Belesme any more than you Geroys do, although my cousin married her. If she were my wife," he says, and his big fist shut tight on the table, "I'd beat her to within an inch of her life. I'd not let a woman master me—no, nor try to."

After telling Fulcun that, he turned away and did not speak to him again. Fulcun had nothing to do but eat and drink and listen to the noise in the hall that was no more intelligible than the noise of the rain that for a while drummed with an extraordinary hurry on the roof and then suddenly ceased.

When supper was finished the duke came down through the hall with his hand on Robert Geroy's shoulder. As they came near to Fulcun he heard Robert say, "There he is," and he beckoned. So Fulcun followed them out. It was all sun and blue sky now, and the glitter of rain on the grass. A company of geese was feeding, necks down, in the steep sloping yard that ran up to the great rocks where the tower stood—it was a stone tower, new and very white.

The duke went a little aside of the door and then faced about. Says he to Fulcun, "Sire Robert here says he will do me homage for Gandelain, and you for Montgaudri."

Fulcun tried not to look confounded, but Robert gave a great laugh.

"Ho! Fulcun," he says, "you think I ought to have spent a month bargaining. But I'm not a Jew."

Guillelm says, "It will be no loss to you Geroys to have me for lord." He said it greatly, like a king, but it sounded to Fulcun as much threat as promise, and Fulcun saw Guillelm's look, close and watchful, the look of a man who has learned to trust sparingly.

Guillelm says, "Well?"

Fulcun looked from him to Robert's square, open face that for all its lines and its strength was a boy's still. He thought,

"Just like Robert to throw all away because he likes a man," and he loved Robert for it. Robert smiled at him.

"I'll do as my uncle counsels," says Fulcun to the duke.

Guillelm nodded. "Good," and then, "Come, Robert, we'll find our wives." He said nothing to Fulcun, only tipped up his chin to bid him come too.

They went up through the yard. All the men had come out from the hall now, and beyond, under the rocks of the tower, there were women who had come down after supper to take the air, so the great yard was full and gay with colors. As the duke and Robert went through, with Fulcun behind, the duke says:

"Is he married?"

"Fulcun?" says Robert. "No."

"I might find him a match," says the duke, and Fulcun, because he was reminded by that, began to watch the women. Two young maids, walking together with their gowns lifted off the wet grass, passed close by him with the pretty, gallant insolence of young things. Fulcun was not especially vain, but he thought that they saw him better than their bright indifferent eyes seemed to do. He wondered who they were. He wondered if Duke Guillelm had in his mind any women among all these.

Someone told the duke that Dame Mahalt was on the tower top, so they went up and came out after the dark stair, again into blue air and sunshine. There were perhaps a dozen people there—Fulcun saw Dame Aelis, and the man he had sat next to in hall, Mauger of Fervacques; he was listening to an old woman with a high-bridged nose and thin lips. Beside them, leaning her back against the parapet wall of the tower, stood another woman, a young one, in a gown of young summer green; her arms were spread out and her hands lay on the top of the wall—it was almost a boy's pose, but it showed her a true woman, deep-breasted.

That was as much as Fulcun saw, because Robert called him over and he had to kiss Duchess Mahalt's hand. Fulcun thought little of her except that she had a sensible, kind face. She was a Fleming, and though her hair was hidden under her veil he guessed it sandy by her fair eyebrows.

After that Guillelm drew Robert to a corner of the tower and began to talk to him. Fulcun heard them say "Mayenne" and "Martel," so he knew what it was about. Dame Aelis and the duchess and another woman were telling each other what was best to do when a child was cutting teeth.

Fulcun drew away from them and went and leaned on the wall and looked over at the crowded yard, and the steep town, the near fields beyond the town, and then the woods and over the hills to the horizon. The thunder had gone by, but over to the east a great wall of white cloud stood up into the air; it seemed a wall of snow mountains; and like mountains it had a wash of level cloud floating between the shining peaks and the darker flanks below. It was very high, remote, and beautiful. He turned from it and found himself looking at the woman in green who was still leaning against the wall. He let himself look at her.

She was not beautiful; her features were too blunt for that; but he liked her face. He saw the ghost of a smile come and go, more in her eyes than on her mouth, at something that the old woman said to Mauger, and he liked that too. When she was not smiling, her mouth had a sober cheerfulness. He turned hastily away then, because her eyes met his. They were very straight, clear, and kind.

He did not look round again till he heard Mauger say, "Come along, wench," and then he turned. Mauger had the green-gowned woman by the arm, and they went away together down the stair. Fulcun thought, "She looks happy. I don't think he beats her," and he was glad—as if he had anything to do with the pair of them. He thought of Mauger's big fist on the table; he remembered that there were many very black hairs all over the back of it. "No," he thought to himself again, "she is happy. He is fond of her—that sullen, sour fellow. He doesn't beat her."

Soon after, Robert and Aelis went, and Fulcun with them. Aelis was very pleased that Robert would do homage for Gandelain—he and Fulcun were to get their seisin tomorrow. As they went through the crowd in the yard Fulcun did not look about at any of the young women there. He thought, though he did not even wonder why, that there could not be any among them that was worth her dower.

Next day in the hall Robert and Fulcun put their hands between the duke's hands, and he kissed them and gave them each half of a sod that had been cut from the yard outside. So they were his men for Gandelain and for Montgaudri, and while they were in Falaise, the Geroys would do one night in every week gate-watch, and Fulcun would, every second week that he was there, watch armed, for three nights, at the duke's chamber door. Guillelm said to Robert that he would not ask him that service, but a young bachelor might well do it; and they laughed.

It was that season of the year that the huntsmen call the time of grease for red and fallow deer, and two or three times a week Duke Guillelm rode out hunting from Falaise and as many with him as liked to come. Some of the married women rode with their husbands, and Fulcun, the first day he went out, saw Mauger's wife riding beside him on a big bay. He did not come near to Mauger at the hunt, but up at the castle after supper Mauger came and sat by him and talked for a little. When Robert and Fulcun walked down the hill to their lodging at the tanner's house, Robert said:

"That fellow—Rogier of Montgommeri's cousin—they say he's a quarrelsome man."

Fulcun laughed. "He tried to quarrel with me the night we came."

Robert growled. "I don't know why one of that house should seek out one of ours. Montgommeri and Belesme—it's all one now."

Fulcun said nothing to that. He could not dislike Mauger of Fervacques.

It was about a week after they had come to Falaise that, when they were out hunting beyond Trun, Fulcun broke a stirrup leather. When he had mended it the silence of the woods was only just broken, and that sweetly, by the distant sounding of the horns. He cursed and rode on after them at a great gallop; he was thinking, as he drew up level with a clump of dark hollies, "I'll be up with them soon," and then as he passed the clump, he pulled up and swung his horse about.

Mauger's wife was there, with a servant, and two horses. One stood drooping and shaking, and she and the servant were staring at the fore hock.

She looked up from the horse's leg, and so did the servant too, but she said:

"Oh! It is you!" Fulcun did not think it a strange thing to say because it spoke the thought in his own mind.

He got down and joined them, and just then the servant said, "You can't ride on, lady. We'll have to go back."

"I'm going back too," says Fulcun, and he saw that she was pleased. He was pleased too. He forgot to regret the hunt. He mounted her on the servant's horse, and they turned and went through the woods with the man behind, leading her horse.

He turned his head when they had ridden for a few minutes, and found that she was looking at him. She smiled.

He said without meaning to say just that, "What is your name?"

"I am Mauger of Fervacques' wife."

"I know that," he says.

She told him then "Alde," and he said it after her, "Alde," and then bowed his head as if he thanked her.

She said, "I know your name. I asked it when I saw you on the top of the tower the other night."

He looked round at her and smiled because there was so much pleasure in his mind. It did not seem at all strange to him that she should have asked then, or should tell him now; or if it were strange it was only as any great, common, and inevitable thing is strange. As he looked at her he saw, and part of his mind remembered after, that her hair where it showed under her hood was a rich, sultry, unshining sunburned gold.

She said, "I am of Flanders, like the duchess. I came with her when she came to Normandy to be married." Then, "Are you married?" she asked him.

He said simply, "No."

"Why not?"

He only shook his head and smiled at her.

Then she said, "They gave me to Mauger of Fervacques when I had been in Normandy a year," and she looked away from him. Fulcun thought, "She loves that queer fellow." He was sure of it, because he was sure that she must be very happy.

"Tell me," she turned to him, "have you sisters or brothers?"

He said, "One brother. Geroy; he's younger than I am—and much more comely." He smiled at her.

She looked at him gravely. "I would not have you any other than you are," she said, and because of her gravity and her steady eyes considering him, he did not think that strange either.

Then she began to tell about Flanders, and about Thierry at home there. "He's my brother. He's as tall as you. He stammers." She looked beyond the horse's ears and Fulcun saw her mouth close soberly, almost, he thought, in pain. Then she turned quickly to him again. "I always hope Thierry will come to Normandy someday. But he sends me messages and gifts when the chapmen come to Guibray fair. I may hear word from him any day." She looked at Fulcun, smiling doubtfully, as if she wished him to promise it to her.

He said, "Perhaps when we get back—"

She nodded. "You know," she told him, "I used to cry so often to be home in Flanders." Yet she was smiling.

He said, "But now?"

"Now I am glad I came to Normandy." She frowned at him.

He thought, "Of course—Mauger," though he did not know why she frowned and spoke as if she challenged him.

They came from the woods, and in sight of the town pale, and there was a company of mules and donkeys loaded with packs that waited at the gate.

Fulcun looked at Alde. She cried, "Oh! Go and ask them— ask them for word of Thierry of Ardoye."

He rode forward and asked them, but they were come from Poitou and knew nothing of Flanders. He came back to her.

"They may be here tomorrow," he said, and she nodded.

He brought her up to the castle, and they found Duchess Mahalt there with some of her women; they had just been gathering windfall apples from the orchard and carried them in baskets. Fulcun stayed talking a little, and when he left, Alde thanked him, more, he thought, than she need, but he thought too that she spoke differently now. She seemed almost a different woman from the woman who had talked to him as they came home. She seemed older, statelier, more a stranger.

Chapter 4

My love is of a birth as rare
   As 'tis, for object, strange and high;
It was begotten by despair
   Upon impossibility.

Andrew Marvell

I

Mahalt of Normandy was a great giver to God and the saints, and very devout in observance besides. She did all she could to compensate for the one sin that she could not give up. She could not give up her husband, and he would not give her up, but they were too close cousins ever to have been married. So on the morning of the feast of Saint Anne she rode out of Falaise with a silk purse containing a gold mark, to offer it on the altar of the little church of Saint Anne at Guibray. Alde of Fervacques rode with her, not so much because she liked hour-long kneeling in small churches, but because she and Mahalt were both of Flanders and had always been friends. They trusted each other as surely as man ever trusts fighting man.

They rode slowly down the rough, steep street from the castle gate, with the horses sliding and clattering on the loose stories; two servants came behind them with bills over their shoulders. It was early and the streets empty. The air, after last night's thunder, was fresh, as if the world had been renewed.

At the foot of the slope there was a small open space of grass and a well in the midst of the grass. Beyond the well there was a wattle-and-daub house, with a thatched roof, and an outer staircase leading to a gallery that ran the whole length under the thatch. A small boy was standing there and a tall man in a faded gray-green kirtle cutting at a stick with a knife. He looked up, saluted them, and watched them as they went by. When they were past they heard the child cry, "Go on, Fulcun! Go on! I want my whistle if you please, Fulcun."

Alde smiled, a very small, tender smile at her horse's ears. "I want my whistle if you please, Fulcun," she said after the child, almost under her breath.

The duchess heard, and turned to her, smiling too. Then she said, "I wish you had borne Mauger sons, my girl."

Alde did not answer. She was not thinking of any child at all. She was thinking, only the thought was in the dark places of her mind, "I am doing him no harm. I am doing nothing at all. But I must be happy a little."

She was indeed doing almost nothing, only turning, as flowers turn toward the south, to Fulcun, so as to be happy a little.

They came back by the same way an hour later, and out again into the little space of grass before the tanner's house. But as they came abreast of it this time there was a clamor from within. Someone shouted, "No! No! Oh! You scoundrel!" with a shout of laughter, and they heard Robert Geroy's voice: "Ful-cun! You—" and quick on that a stampede of feet, and a man who ran out from the upper room, vaulted over the balcony, and landed in the road. That man was Fulcun: another charged out after him and shook his fist over the gallery rail—he was young Guion of Courville, with his hair drenched and dripping.

Mahalt had reined in, and Alde; and Fulcun, turning, saw them. The duchess was grave, but Alde threw her head back and laughed; Mahalt laughed too then.

By that time Robert Geroy was on the gallery, and when he saw the duchess he came down the steps. Guion Geroy followed him, shaking water out of his hair like a dog. Dame Aelis came from the house too, and down into the road, and asked the duchess to go up and break fast. She would not, but they stayed talking—Aelis asked pardon for the young men. Robert gave a great laugh and said, "It's the Heron; I tell you he's mad these days!"

But Fulcun had moved from them. He came and stood by Alde's horse, and laid his hand on its neck. He asked her how the other horse was—the one that had torn a tendon in the hunting. She told him it was mending.

Then she said, "What did you do to him?" and nodded at Guion, smiling only with her eyes. Her voice was as it had been when they rode in from hunting the other day, and made him happy to hear her; it was as if, when they spoke only to each other, they went back together to the candor and the confidence of children.

Fulcun says, "I soused a crock of water over him," and he looked at her, not laughing, but with the sparks of laughter in his eyes.

His hand was still on the horse's neck. She laid hers there too, just above Fulcun's, so that her little finger was a couple of inches from his.

"How different they are!" she said, leaning forward and staring at them as if hands were strange things. He stared too at hers—it was square and brown—almost like a young boy's hand.

When the duchess and Alde of Fervacques had gone on, and Robert and Aelis in again, and Guion to dry himself, Fulcun sat down on the steps. He picked up the stick that he had been cutting into a whistle for young Robert, began to work on it and then forgot it, and sat still with his hands hanging between his knees. The whole world that morning was simple, fair, friendly, and full of light.

That evening was the first of his nights of guard outside the duke's great chamber. He went up to the castle, supped there, and afterward walked in the yard with a young man called Drogo of Ecouis, while all color died out of the sky and all the light went back to it from the darkening earth, filling it with a strange, intensely clear, unshining brightness, against which the top of the walls, the roof of the hall, and the great west tower stood up black and sharply edged. Then at last the horn blew and they went into the tower, and to the guardroom. Fulcun armed there, for it was his watch first, and waited for the second horn.

The door of the duke's great chamber was shut, for the duchess and her women had gone in and now were laid in bed waiting for their men. In a few minutes these began to come up. Two men Fulcun did not know went through first, then Hue of

Grandmesnil, who stopped a moment and spoke to Fulcun, for they were cousins, then Mauger of Fervacques, who nodded as he went by. Last of all the duke came, and when he had gone in and shut the door, Fulcun moved in front of it and stood, leaning his two hands on the quillons of his sword, watching the little hanging lamp that burned steady in the shuttered, still air and, as all noise ceased and fell away into a great silence, listening to a mouse rattling by under the planks of the floor.

In his mind there were no clear thoughts, only a drift of changing recollections and a steady anticipation of something good, as though joy must come in with every morning. When the sands of the glass were run through he woke up Drogo, unarmed and lay down on the mattress, and fell asleep at once.

He wakened late next morning. Someone was opening the shutters; they clattered back and the light burst in, dulling the lamp flame to a pale stain in the bright air. Fulcun scrambled up, stretching and yawning; Drogo hailed him across the room, and Fulcun stopped whistling to answer.

Just then the door of the great chamber opened, and Hue of Grandmesnil came out. But he dropped his sword as he stepped over the threshold and stooped to pick it up, and in that second, as the door stood open, Fulcun saw past him into the room.

The shutters there were closed and the room dark except for the light that came through the door and the flame of the lamp. The green and white curtains of the duke's great bed were still drawn, but Fulcun could see two men standing up in the room, getting into their shirts and hose while their wives lay yet on the pallets, waiting for them all to be gone.

Fulcun saw that, and then one other thing. In the daylight that slanted through the half-open door he saw a loose, curling tress of sunburned, unshining gold that lay, wreathed like an eddy in water, on the floor just beyond the doorway. It was barely more than a handsbreadth from Hue of Grandmesnil's heels.

Then Hue shut the door.

As Fulcun went hastily down the hill from the castle to get breakfast, he was seeing that eddy of hair again and again as if it meant something. Alde had lain all night just inside the door, on the pallet beside Mauger. That was the fact, but Fulcun did not know what it meant; he was neither glad nor sorry, and yet the earth moved under him. It was as if he had seen, lying at his feet within the duke's great chamber, and near enough for his hand to touch, the high-riding, silver winter moon.

That day the duke was riding out hunting again, but when they had all gone out of Falaise, with crowding and clatter and the long clamor of horns, none of the Geroys were with them. For that morning Robert of Saint-Céneri had gone down into the lower part of the tanner's house, where now the horses were stabled and the tanner and his family lived along with a few hens and a pig and one cow. Robert had gone to look at the gray gelding's fetlock that Fulcun had said was swelling, and young Robert went with him. But as his father stooped over the horse's leg, young Robert, ranging about, came on a hen sitting in a dark corner. The hen, scared, flew off, and Fulcun's black stallion, which stood next the gray, being scared too, let out with his hooves. One of the irons struck Robert. He went down, and young Robert yelled aloud. But before Fulcun and Ranof Badger came in, Robert had crawled clear with no worse than a broken ankle, only it was a bad break.

Dame Aelis, when they carried him upstairs, was very tender to Robert, but young Robert she cuffed and sent to bed, to stay fasting till next day. And Fulcun knew that she would have liked to cuff him too, because the stallion was his. He said, "I'll go up to the castle. They say the duke's farrier, Solomon, knows well how to set bones." Robert says, "Good lad—yes, go," and grinned hardily at Fulcun.

Fulcun started off up the hill in a great hurry. He noticed, as he went, a big company of mules and pack ponies standing at one inn. They must belong to chapmen come to Guibray fair. He thought, "Are they from Flanders with news?" He hoped so. They must just have come in, for though the packs were off, the animals were still patched dark with sweat.

When he got there the castle yard was empty, except for a few lounging house serfs who did not know where Solomon was, so Fulcun tried the stable, but neither was Solomon there; he came out and stood a moment trying to think where the fellow might be, and in that moment he saw Alde come down the steps from the tower.

She held her head up and stared straight before her. She stared at him and he knew she did not see him. At the bottom of the steps she turned sharply and went over to the little wattle-and-daub chapel that stood against the wooden pale of the yard. The door stood open. She went in and shut it behind her.

Fulcun was at the door and his hand on the latch before he thought what he was doing. He pushed the door open and went in. He turned and fastened it, and only then he looked at Alde.

She stood, a few paces away from him in the small dark place. He did not know if she had seen who came in, but now she was turned away from him. She was not looking toward the altar either, but stood very still with her hands at her sides, dumbly staring at the mud-plastered wall.

"Alde," he said. "What is it?"

He was close to her. She did not look at him, she did not seem to wonder that he was there, but answered low and slowly:

"They told me—those men—my brother . . . is dead."

"Your brother?" Fulcun repeated stupidly, because he was thinking only of her.

She said, "Thierry . . . at home . . ." Her voice did not shake, but suddenly she turned her head sharply from him.

What he did then he did of necessity, because he must have her close to him. He put out his arms and drew her near, so that her shoulder was against his breast, and held her so. She did not turn to him, but stood still, her head down, only she caught his left wrist in both her hands and gripped it hard, and they stood there together for a moment without a word. Then he felt something fall on his wrist, and on the back of his hand. She was crying.

He cried out, hardly knowing what he said, "Dear—my dear—don't! Alde—don't—"

He could feel the tremor of each sob as he held her, but he could feel too how her whole body stiffened against it, and all the time her fingers strained on his wrist. He stared down at her head, tightening his arm about her. It was a pain unknown to see her hurt like this.

He muttered, more to himself than her, "What can I do? What can I do?" but he knew he could do nothing.

They had seemed so strangely close, talking there by the tanner's house, or here in the hall, or in the orchard when Dame Mahalt went out to look for early pears. But now he knew there was a wall between them; he knew that, but in the deep, aching disturbance of his mind he had no time to know what the wall was.

She ceased after a while and stood quite still. Then she lifted one hand and wiped it clumsily across her eyes and put it back on his wrist, all wet.

She said, "Chapmen came today from Champagne fair. They told me."

Fulcun, staring at her bent head, could find no words. He wanted to wrench his heart out—his heart . . . to comfort her. But how could that comfort her? He could not get at her to comfort her. His thoughts ran confused and hasty as floodwater.

"So I shall never go home. Nor Thierry come," she said, as simply and hopelessly as a child.

"You've your husband," Fulcun cried at her then, out of a blind, bitter dark.

"Yes," she said in the same voice.

He asked her through his teeth, "Alde, is he kind?"

She waited a minute and then answered him. "Sometimes. He's angry often because—I do not want him. And sometimes he finds another woman, and then he does not care."

Fulcun did not wonder if that hurt her. He knew. He had looked into her, like a man looking down into a well. There is a square of brave blue that no one can see through, but that is the mask of the well; below it, the pure clear water lives in darkness.

He cried in his helplessness: "If I had been born your brother!"

She shook her head, and said, "No!" urgently, but he did not wonder what she meant. His mind was groping blindly along the wall between them. He could find no way to come at her to comfort her. He was in despair.

She moved, drawing away from him. He let his arms drop, but she still held his left wrist, and now her fingers moved on it as if they spoke to it. She looked up at him, for the first time since he had come there, and her face was puckered and strange with crying.

She said, "You are kind," and then very low, "I have you."

He was staring at her face. If he heard her, he could not think of what she meant. When she took her hands from his wrist and turned away toward the door he did not move, but stood looking down at the place where her fingers had held his wrist. He put his hand over it, but he did it without thinking, because all his mind was taken up with that sight of her hurt, unhappy face. He heard the door shut behind him. She had gone.

After a moment he lifted his head to stare at the altar. But he did not pray; unless it were in a single sharp, wordless cry, not directed to any place or person, but wrung from him by his necessity. He went out of the chapel knowing only one thing. She was in need of comfort and he could not give it.

It was only when he found himself striding down the hill again with the stones spinning out from under his feet that he remembered why he had come up to the castle. Robert Geroy was waiting still for Solomon. Fulcun turned about and ran back. He found Solomon in the corn store and hurried him down the hill.

II

That afternoon a high cloud, whose crest had at first been only a sharp-edged white hill beyond the trees to the southeast, reared itself up into a hot blue, and towered, and leaned over half the sky, its foundations dark and ragged and spreading, its summit still clear-rounded, shining, and beautiful. Before sunset it hung overhead, ready to topple and fall in ruin upon Falaise, a white stone tower on a white cliff, dwarfed now to a tiny thing by the heavenly tower above it.

Yet the storm that was in the cloud did not break. The hot lull of the afternoon changed to a dark, fell evening. No sky was left anywhere, only a fierce welter of gray above, like waves of a wind-beaten sea, and along the horizon, heavy swollen clouds, brown and sullen. There was thunder far off, and from the gate of Falaise castle you could see that the storm had broken over toward Trun, but here—the world lay still and waited.

Fulcun, coming up for his second night of guard, stood a moment in the gate looking at the distant storm and wished that it would break over Falaise and have done with it. He did not know why; he was like a swimmer who feels and does not yet understand the undertow of a great current. He was restless and ill at ease; but he was not quite afraid.

It was not till after dark that the thunder that had lurked about Falaise for the past weeks gathered and advanced upon it. First the wind came, rattling the shutters and groaning through the chinks and knotholes in the pale till it had collected its strength and, with a roar like the sea, could fling the full flood of rain against the tower. Then, when there was a lull, the thunder wakened, and broke up the sky, and sent it reeling in a huger downpour and fiercer strife of wind.

Duke Guillelm, asleep in his curtained bed, did not wake at the first crash of the storm. But as he lay with every muscle tight, sweating in the dark, it was not in the great tower of Falaise that he thought himself, nor was it Mahalt who was beside him. It was some other place—it was years and years ago, and yet it was tonight, and once more Osber slept beside him under the bearskin. Then Osber stirred and sat up. Though Guillelm knew that it was dark, yet he could see Osber's face quite clearly, and his eyes were staring. "Listen!" said Osber, but for a minute Guillelm could not think of listening nor of anything but of the knife that stood now in Osber's throat, and the blood that sprang from about the blade and ran down his bare chest, and onto the feeble, fumbling hands that tried to pluck the thing out.

Then Guillelm heard that shout outside that he had heard in sleep often enough the last twenty years since the night he had heard it indeed. "Beat in the door!" they shouted, and then came the first shattering crash of an axe on the wood.

Guillelm heaved himself up in bed and tried to shout, but the cry was choked and feeble as Osber's had been when he went down on his knees clawing at the knife.

Then he woke.

For two great heartbeats he thought he had awakened to that night of fear twenty years ago. The clatter and crash was a real noise. It was black dark too; there was no chink of light showing beyond the bed; and something moved across his groping hands. Then he knew where he was—in his great tower at Falaise, with Mahalt stirring and sighing beside him in her sleep, and the open shutter of the window hurling itself back against the wall while the wind came in with a wild spatter of rain and swept the bed curtains inward across the bed. It was the wind too that must have blown out the flame of the lamp that hung from the rafters beyond the curtains.

But for a minute Guillelm could not move or call because he had been so lately a little lad again, and Osber the seneschal had only just gone down in front of him, bleeding and choking. Then he heard someone move in the room.

"What's that?" he cried, and woke Mahalt.

She started up. "Sir?" She caught at his arm.

Alde's voice answered them from the dark. She spoke through her teeth.

"The shutter. I have shut it once. But I think the latch is broke."

She struggled a moment and the rush of the wind quieted; the bed curtains sucked back across the bed; there was silence in the room.

"There," says Alde. "It is shut again, but it won't hold long."

"Sir," Mahalt asked, "shall she call whoever keeps the watch to make it fast?"

Guillelm said, "Aye. Tell him bring the lamp in from there first to light this one again. Do you hear?"

There was no sound. She did not answer. He pulled the curtains and looked out, but he could not see Alde and she did not move.

Then from the pallet by the door Mauger cried out, "Where are you, wench?"

"Here, sir," she answered him, and then to Guillelm, "I will call."

Fulcun, standing guard while the others slept, had jammed one shoulder against the wall and gripped the hilt of his sword till his hand ached. He had heard the growing rumor of the storm outside and it mingled with the storm that was in his mind. Now and again at a fiercer buffet of the wind against the tower he would turn his head restlessly. This rage of all heaven and earth made it harder to think—made him more afraid.

For he was afraid. Something was coming upon him so great that it filled the world as this noisy wind filled the night, something strong that moved toward him clothed in darkness, that would snatch at him soon and carry him like a dead leaf: and yet the strength of it was his own strength; the strength of body, his soul, his will, his utmost self.

Once he raised his head and laughed silently and crazily. Today in the chapel he had not known what was the wall that stood between him and Alde. He knew now. His shoulder was against it, and on the other side of it Alde lay beside Mauger. Two yards from him, beside Mauger—Alde that he could not live without. At that the thunder was on him; it was in his brain.

He straightened himself suddenly. The latch of the door beside him lifted. He turned; he did not know what it was that he expected.

What he saw was Alde standing in the doorway with a dark cloak huddled round her and trailing. Her hair was all trussed up under the cloak as she drew it tight about her throat, and in the dark folds he could see her arm, white and bare.

He thought he stared at her for a long moment, and she too, though she saw in front of her against the faint light only a tall man with his shield like a great wing on one shoulder and his face all shadow under the rim of the helmet and the jutting nasal, forgot time. She knew it was Fulcun.

Then she said, speaking very quick, "Bring in the lamp." She could not say more.

He jerked his eyes away from her and lifted off his shield and put it down against the wall.

"The lamp—" He repeated the words as he went over to fetch it.

It was a small lamp hung by three chains from the beam of the guardroom. The lamp itself was a little iron pot half full of water with fat on top and the wick stuck into that, burning smoky and feeble.

He took the pot and carried it into the great chamber, shielding the flame with his hand and looking at nothing but that little fluctuating lake of light within his fingers.

Only when, beyond his hand, he saw a dark shadow, he stopped. It was Alde standing in front of the curtains of the duke's bed, just under the extinguished lamp.

She moved back, and pointed up at the lamp above, and then held out her hand.

"Give that to me," she said.

He understood what she meant in the tumult of his mind as if he distinguished one small near sound in the midst of a great din. He put the lit lamp into her hands and reached up for the other.

But he was slow over getting it from its chains, because she was so close to him that he could smell her hair, warm with sleep. The iron pot clattered against the rim as he fumbled with it, and Duke Guillelm thrust out a hand and hairy forearm, pulling the curtains aside.

"Have you done'?" he cried.

"No." Fulcun did not look round. He had the lamp in his hand now and he reached out to take the burning wick from the other one that Alde held cupped in her palms. All that he could look at was her fingertips that the light shone through, red-rosy.

There was a sudden bursting clatter. The shutter flew open and the wind flung through again, and the rain. The flame in Alde's hands leaped, streamed, fluttered, and went out, and the room was full of noisy darkness.

But for Fulcun there was nothing—nothing in all the world but the touch of Alde's wrist that his fingers met, by pure chance, as he started at the noise. They stayed, because he could not take them away. His hand followed his fingers, open, most gentle. It encircled her wrist, closing on it, then slid higher, hungry, thirsty like a starved mouth. All his awful want was in his hand as it moved up her arm till it met the rough touch of the cloak. He dared not move it farther.

He heard her draw a deep sudden breath, but she stood dead still.

"Splendor of God!" cried Guillelm. "Fasten that cursed shutter, can't you?"

What happened then Fulcun barely knew. There were people stirring in the room, and he was at the window with the rain on his face. He slammed the shutter to and drove his knife into the frame to hold it. As he plunged to the door he ran into someone who swore loudly, then his shoulder met the doorpost.

Duke Guillelm cried again, "Splendor of God! Can no one light the lamp," but Fulcun was halfway across the guardroom. He said, for any that might hear, "I'll fetch light."

He went down the stairs anyhow, careless of falling. The bower below was dark, and the hearth seemed dead, but the white ashes when he stirred them had a heart of fire. He had the lamp still in his hand though there was little left of the fat that was not spilt. He held the wick to the glow; it sputtered, flared, and steadied.

When he came back to the great chamber the curtains of the bed were drawn again, but he heard the duke's voice speaking very low to Mahalt.

Rogier of Montgommeri was sitting up on his pallet; he lay down again as Fulcun brought in the lamp. Fulcun hung it in the chains and turned and went out. But as he went he could not save himself from seeing, just inside the door, Alde's head as she lay. She was turned from Mauger. Her eyes were open; her face was not a yard from his feet.

Chapter 5

MACBETH.   I'll go no more;
I am afraid to think what I have done.
Look on't again I dare not.

Macbeth, Act II, sc. ii

I

That great wind blew from dark to dawn, and so passed over Normandy to the east. It had torn up some trees and beaten much barley down and shaken off many green apples from the boughs. Cloudless weather came after it; shining blue days waking out of golden mist, and nights of peace with moon and mist and faint stars.

On the second day after the storm, at evening, Hernaut Geroy of Echauffour stood leaning on the rail of the footbridge over the brook at Echauffour—Blackbrook they called it. Hernaut Geroy was more like his mother, Fulbert Beina's daughter, than he was like any of the Geroys. He had a heavy, plain face with very steady eyes that looked at things intently and without hurry; when he had to make up his mind about a matter he took his time, and once it was made up he did not readily change. His hair was bright brown and thick, not exactly curling but nearly so; his wife, Emma, who, with the best will in the world, could not think Hernaut comely, loved his hair as a precious thing; waking on summer mornings before he woke, she would lean over him looking at it, seeing with extreme pleasure how strong and bright it grew, and how rough it was with sleep—just like a little boy's hair. Emma had two real little boys, Guillelm and Rainald, and this other, her husband, and ten years older than she was.

Hernaut looked downstream, but the orange glare of the sun was in his eyes. He turned round so that he could lean his back against the rail, and hooked his elbows onto it. He did not want to go back to the tower yet—Hernaut had a taste for solitude that none of the other Geroys except Fulcun had, and he only by fits and starts.

Over in the fallow old Fulbert and two or three wenches were milking, crouched under the sides of the red cows that glowed in the low sun a burning color. One of the wenches, swinging an empty pail, came over to a cow close by the brook; when she began to milk, Hernaut could hear the low drumming noise of the milk on the wooden bottom; it changed in a minute to a softer, higher note, like a sleepy, hissing purr, as the bucket filled. The cow turned its head and looked along its flank at the girl, and swung its tail and shifted its weight on its feet. From the woods came the voices of the children, halloing shrill and sweet to each other, and high and low.

And then all those quiet sounds were quenched by another, loud and discordant. Hernaut stood up and swung round staring up at the tower. The watchman on the top was blowing his horn. He blew it three times and had no breath for more. There was a silence. Then in the tower a woman screamed.

Hernaut had started to go toward the castle when someone in the meadow shouted, "Look!" and just then the watchman, having got his breath, began to blow again. Hernaut went back over the little bridge to meet the man, who ran, slowly and stumbling, along the line of apple trees beside the barleyfield.

Hernaut met him at the corner and caught his arms and held him. For a minute the man gasped for breath, his head hanging. Then, "Merlerault," he says. "Burned . . . the Frenchmen!"

Hernaut let go his arms. The fellow went down on his knees, then rolled over and sat, looking up stupidly at Hernaut. Hernaut left him there. He could get the rest of the news better in a while. He turned and ran for the castle. On the outside stair of the tower he stopped a moment and looked back. The cows were coming in, with Fulbert and the women shouting and whacking them on. From the edge of the woods the first of the children ran out. Hernaut dived into the low door and raced up the stairs.

From the top of the tower he looked west toward Merlerault, over the summer woods, very still and ready for sleep. Almost under the sun's setting there was a cloud of dull smoke. It rose and spread and for a moment was bright with a redder gleam than the pure gold light of the sky. Merlerault was burning this quiet evening, and beyond it there were other fires. He counted four.

Then he looked down at the near woods, and the stream running by the willows to the mill, and the big field of barley where the harsh ears were already crooking over and paling with ripeness. It would be a good harvest this year—if ever it were carried. He leaned over the pale and began to shout orders to the men down below in the yard.

⚜

Next day, and almost at the same hour, but in the duke's castle at Falaise, Mauger of Fervacques came on his wife sitting in one of the windows of the tower that looked over the yard; there was no one else there; the duchess was in the orchard, and those that were not with her were on the top of the tower in the cooler air up there. Alde was not looking out, neither was she busy. She sat with her head bowed and her hands in her lap; Mauger was not the man to notice that her hands were clasped tight together.

He went up to her and put his hand under her chin and tipped her head up. She tried to draw back, but her head was against the wall and she could not; he held her so, just roughly enough to make the caress an indignity, and to show her that he knew she had tried to withdraw.

"What is it?" she asked him, looking full at him as she did at everyone; but he would not let her meet his eyes. She grew angry at that and at his hold upon her chin, and she lifted her hand and tore his away.

"What do you want?" she asked again.

He sat down by her on the bench so that his knee touched hers. After a minute, "You know what I want," he says.

She sat very still. "Well," she told him, as if she were tired of this, "you have me when you want."

He did not answer, and she turned her face away and looked through the window, and then her heart jumped and stood still. Fulcun of Montgaudri was walking along the roundway that went along the inside of the pale; he was just below her. He turned sharp about and tramped away, his chin on his chest, and then with another sharp turn began to come back again.

The first thing she did, and she did it without thinking, was to stiffen her whole body so that she might, very slowly, draw herself away from the touch of Mauger's knee. She could not bear it if Fulcun were to look up while Mauger touched her. Then, as she watched Fulcun still, she began to be afraid at the fierce aimlessness of that hasty tramping.

Mauger spoke suddenly in a strange voice.

"I have you, have I? Much good you are to me! Do you think a man wants a woman like a wooden saint in church?" He stopped short and cried, "What are you staring at?"

She had strength enough not to turn her head quickly. "Nothing," she told him, and then, lest he should look out, "Go to another woman then that will please you better."

He got up. In his heavy face she could see nothing except anger; indeed she did not try to understand his face; it meant nothing to her, just as he himself was nothing but a hard and unloved master.

He said, "You don't know how to love. I thought at first . . . But you'll never know. You haven't got it in you to know." He laughed, but not at all happily. "I'll do as you tell me," he says. "Only see you don't complain of it."

He went away then. When she could look out of the window again Fulcun was gone from the roundway.

⚜

It was just about this time that Hernaut Geroy came to the gate of Falaise and pulled up his horse as the gate-ward set a spear across his way. Hernaut felt the horse shake under him; he got off its back and then stood a minute holding to the saddle. He had not slept since he left Echauffour; he had ridden for the last eight hours without a pause; and for an hour of that time he had ridden for his life.

He said, and his voice croaked, "They told me at Trun that the duke was here." He did not wait for the gate-ward's "Aye, he is," but began to go on, not having breath to waste. "Take me up to him," he said.

So, leading the horse that clattered and stumbled on the narrow stony way, Hernaut went up beside the gate-ward. They came to the gate of the castle. A man Hernaut did not know met them there. "What is it?" he asked and stared at Hernaut.

Hernaut did not lift his head. He had let go the bridle of the horse and stood now leaning his weight on his spear.

"Where is the duke?" he said.

The man told him, "In the chapel— There— Look. He is just coming out," and he put out his hand to take the spear from Hernaut's hands. Hernaut held to it for a minute, because he was dazed, then he gave it up, and without a word began to go across the yard, walking slowly and clumsily. He did not see anyone else of all the crowd but only Duke Guillelm moving away from the open door of the chapel. He was glad when Guillelm turned and saw him and stopped.

Hernaut stood in front of him, then he began to go down on his knees stiffly, but the duke stopped him.

"What brings you like this, Hernaut Geroy?" says he.

Hernaut's throat was dry. All he said was, "News."

Mahalt was at Guillelm's side. The duke turned to her. "Go on—I will come after." And to Hernaut, "We'll be private in the chapel."

They went in there. Hernaut backed against the door, shutting it with a clang, and leaned on it. The duke stood in front of him, holding his chin in one hand, and the other stuck into his brown leather belt.

"Now—the news," said he.

Hernaut told him. The Frenchmen burning all through the Hiesmois, right up to the gates of Argentan and on toward Trun. They had passed within ten miles of Echauffour. Hernaut had followed them to beyond Trun, then turned and come hard for Falaise.

"They're moving fast," he said. "Toward the Bessin I think."

The duke heard him out; then he turned and spat on the floor. He swore, "Splendor of God," very softly, and then so suddenly loud that the short echoes rang in the little chapel. "Get out of the way," he says curtly, and when Hernaut moved, pulled open the door and went past him. Hernaut heard him shouting, as he crossed the yard, for Rogier, and Hue of Montfort, and Gilbert.

Hernaut came out from the chapel into the yard. His horse was still at the gate, its head hanging. He began to go toward it, but halfway across someone shouted, "Hernaut!"

It was Berenger, Geroy of Courville's younger boy—a fat, jolly, careless youngster with no more sense than a boy should have.

He wanted to know all the news. Hernaut told him shortly, and then asked for Robert. Where was he? Berenger says, "Laid up with a broken ankle." "Where, up here?" "Why no—down in the town at a lodging there. But Fulcun is here—he keeps watch these three nights. He's in the stable." He tipped his head back over his shoulder.

Hernaut says, "I'll go to him," and turned to go.

"He's in a black temper," cried Berenger. "I brought up his horse for him this afternoon, since he's to keep guard tonight, and then he clouted me on the head for doing it without telling."

Hernaut was going on. "I expect you deserved it," he says. Berenger put his tongue out at Hernaut's back; he was a good-tempered lad, but Fulcun had hit hard and unjustly.

Hernaut came to the stable door and leaned with one hand on the post. "Fulcun!" he shouted. "Fulcun!" He looked in. The long low shed was dark; he could see only the hindquarters of a few of the near horses, a bay, a white, two chestnuts; but nowhere Fulcun's black—if he was riding that ill-tempered black stallion still.

Then someone moved at the far end, and a buckle rapped sharply on wood.

"Fulcun!" Hernaut cried again. But there was no answer.

Hernaut looked over his shoulder for Berenger. Was this one of that lad's silly tricks? But Berenger had made off. Hernaut waited a second and then went in and along between the horses. There certainly was someone in the stable.

And it was Fulcun. He stood in the last stall with his hand on the rump of the black horse, quite still. The animal had its bit and bridle on, and the saddle was across its back with the girths not fastened but trailing. Fulcun was armed but for his helm, and that was on the post of the stall. His shield and spear leaned beside it.

"Death of God!" cries Hernaut at him. "Why didn't you answer?"

Fulcun looked at him. "It's you?" says he very slow. "I didn't know who it was."

He stood there, not moving. He did not welcome Hernaut nor ask why he was there, but Hernaut, without waiting for the question, told him.

Fulcun heard, and again was silent for a second. "So I cannot go. I was going," he said heavily, and then, in a quick, sharp voice, "Now, I cannot."

"Go! Where?" Hernaut asked him, but before Fulcun answered they both turned to the door and stood listening. A horn was blowing outside, long and urgently.

Fulcun turned suddenly and lifted the saddle off and tossed it upon its peg.

"What are you doing that for, you fool?" says Hernaut. "That horn is blown to saddle up to ride."

Fulcun said, as if he were only half listening, "Of course, I forgot." He reached the saddle down again and flung the girths under and caught and made them fast. He worked very quickly.

Hernaut turned away. "Where does Robert lodge?" he asked. "I'll go and eat there and borrow a horse. Mine is beaten out."

Fulcun, stooping under the black, told him, "Down the hill, turn to the left at the forge and the house beside the well." But he led out his horse and caught up Hernaut at the door. He had his helmet in his hand, and Hernaut, seeing him clear for the first time, saw how his black hair lay damp and close on his brow under the leather coif.

"You have been sweating," says Hernaut.

Fulcun said it was hot in the stable.

"Well," says Hernaut, "if you're saddled up, come down with me."

Fulcun went with him for about a dozen paces. Then he stopped. "No," he said. "There's a thing I must do before I come."

He turned back without any more than that. Hernaut looked after him, and then, too tired to be curious, plodded on. The yard was crowded now and busy, men were coming from the buildings round about, leading out horses, and carrying bundles of spears. When Hernaut turned again at the gate to look after Fulcun, he could not see him in the press.

Fulcun had gone straight over to the steps of the keep. He slipped the horse's bridle over the post of the handrail there, leaned his shield and spear, and set his helm on the ground. Then he began to climb up, quickly at first and then slower. He had been quite sure that he must come here, but now that he was near the door of the keep he did not know and could not think what he would do.

But he went on. He must go on. There was little time left now before they would start; little time and less chance. He went in at the door.

Voices above him, and the sound of men coming down, with their shield points scraping on the stone, drove him down instead of up. There was only a corn store and the well in the dark chamber below, but anyway he could get a drink there—he was parched with thirst. After that he would have to go out again and mount and ride—without having seen her.

It was twilight dark on the stairs down here, and cool. The door of the well chamber was open. Did it mean that there was someone there? He knew before he went in that indeed someone was there, and who it was. He went in and saw her, and for him the cool quiet was full of thunderous noise.

She was coming to the door, carrying in her hand a water pot for sprinkling the floor of the duchess's room that was choking everyone with dust after all the hasty passing and repassing. She stopped when she saw him, and went a step back, and the hand she held over the hole of the pot to keep the water in went up to her breast. The water began to dribble fast through the rose. He took the earthen pot from her and set it on the floor, because next moment she would have dropped it.

She had drawn back behind the door and stood now close to the wall. He came in and kicked the door half shut with his heel. Then for a moment they stood still, and neither knew how to move or speak.

She said, "Fulcun!" at last in a whisper, but it seemed loud in the hollow silence. And then there was no space between them;

he pressed her against the cold stones of the wall so that he crushed his own hands that were about her. He leaned against her there, wanting only to be closer yet, and for a pause in time there was nothing for either except that urgent contact and the fierce starving pressure of his mouth on hers.

The sound of voices above dragged Fulcun away, but she stumbled toward him and put one arm about his neck and clung to him. She did it partly because, without that support, she was afraid of falling, and partly because she could not lose the touch of him all at once.

She said, breathless and hardly audible, "Fulcun—a minute."

But he took hold of her wrist and pulled her arm down from his shoulder. He was gripping it harder than he knew, but the pain helped her, since she had to stiffen herself to bear it.

"I was going away," he said, low and harsh, as if he were angry with her. "But now—I shall come back."

He dropped her arm, but he still stared at her while he groped behind him for the door. His fingers found it; he swung round, away from her, and out, his head down. She heard him going up the stairs outside, heavily and fast.

II

Duke Guillelm halted his small host next noon in a wood beyond Conteville. He had little more than a hundred knights with him, for the great court was over and most folks gone home; and besides these such freemen of the countryside as he had been able to call in to the ban as he passed. They came along, some mounted on shaggy ponies, but most on foot, armed with bows, or knives, or swords; here and there one would carry an old axe with a blade that had come into Normandy on the long ships with his father's great-grandfather.

Duke Guillelm had found the Frenchmen's trail soon after dawn that day; it was at Rouvres, and the Frenchmen's mark was a smoking farmstead and the drifting hot white ash of the hay-stacks. After that it was easy to follow their road from burned village to burned village with here and there a dead serf tumbled in the ditch or sprawling on the road.

They were catching up the Frenchmen too. At Vimont they saw before them, against the hill beyond, the first puff and trail of a new fire. That was just before noon. Three miles farther on, beside a wood, Guillelm halted. He did not want to catch the French too soon.

Fulcun was with Hernaut in the middle of the wood. They ate their bacon and some moldy rye bread—all they had been able to find in Vimont village. Then Hernaut hitched his sword round and rolled over and lay on his side with his face on his arm. He had snatched what sleep he might in the halts of the march, and in the short night that Guillelm allowed them. Now, in the pleasant light shade of the trees, and at ease on the deep pale late summer grass where last year's leaves rustled, he was sound asleep in a moment.

But Fulcun could not sleep. For a while he stared at the blue and white banner that hung down from under the leaf-shaped blade of his spear as it leaned against the trunk of a small oak, beside Hernaut's spear with Hernaut's blue banner.

The day was so still that not even the fringes swayed with any breath of air, and yet the wood where they were was near enough to the sea for the treetops to be brushed all one way like windblown hair.

Fulcun got up after a minute and put his hands to the spear shaft. He lowered the blade to look at it; it was dark and smooth as broken flint and unreflecting, but like flint, it held a somber light. He moved his palm over it and then, lifting it, drove the iron-shod shaft of the spear down into the soft turf. But at once he wrenched it out again, and drove it deeper.

When that was done, there was nothing more to do. He stared at the ground for a minute, and then went off to the edge of the wood, and stood in the sun, and felt the sweat run down his neck under the leather gorget as he looked out across the empty land, heavy and pale with heat; the noonday sun had sucked up all the colors, and the only bright thing was a clump of scarlet poppies on the bank beyond the track.

He shut his eyes and clenched his hands and tried, for one second of time, to be once again in the well house at Falaise, and to feel her mouth against his, and her body close to his body.

Almost he felt it. But then he opened his eyes and knew that between him and that moment there were miles of wood and hill and hours of time. All he had done was to make sharper the ache of his hunger.

He turned and went back through the wood, stepping over men here and there, but he could not find Hernaut again. He must be too far to the left. He edged round between some horses and a bramble clump and then he stopped dead.

A group of knights lay sprawling there; they were all asleep except for one who had his arm over his eyes and whistled noiselessly to himself. But the man whose head was almost at Fulcun's feet was Mauger of Fervacques.

He lay on his back with his helm off and his coif pushed back for coolness. Fulcun's eyes went over him; he did not want to look at him, but he could not look away. Mauger's face was blank with sleep, and his mouth open; his hair was rumpled and damp with sweat. He had a hauberk of small iron scales that overlapped each other like dull, harsh feathers. One hand lay on his chest, and the hairs on the back of it showed black and shining in a patch of sunlight spilt through the leaves.

Fulcun looked from that hand to Mauger's mouth and back again. His hand was harmless enough now, empty and inert as a dead man's. And his mouth was open and slack. But that was the hand that might touch Alde, and the mouth that might kiss her as it willed.

He stood a moment looking down at Mauger in the sunshine-dappled shade of the wood, and as he looked he raised his own hand to his teeth and bit on his fingers. These thoughts couldn't be borne. But they had to be borne.

The man who was awake yawned and stretched and sat up, but before he could look round Fulcun had gone quietly away.

That evening, just after sunset, Guillelm of Normandy caught the Frenchmen, when the chill was rising from the sodden marshland that bordered the windings of the little river Dives.

Half an hour before that, the first of the French had reached the ford over the river below the green slope that goes up to Bastembourg. As they came to the ford—Berenger's ford the people call it—the clean round of the sun dipped beyond the low hills toward Varaville, and slid, rolling and sinking sidelong, behind the sharp little distant trees that edged the skyline there.

The Frenchmen went over the water. The ford was almost up to the stirrup irons, but no one troubled to go by the bridge except one young knight who did it for curiosity. He found holes in the planking and thought that some of the timbers looked rotted and ready to fall.

With those that went over at sunset there was a tall old man that wore a gold crown about his helm. He had very bristling white eyebrows under the gilded rim and a long red face. It was King Henri of France.

He and the knights with him were near the top of the slope, in sight almost of Bastembourg tower, before the rest of the Frenchmen came down to the little river. These could not move fast, for they were driving cattle and leading carts piled up with sacks of grain and flitches of bacon and other household stuff. Only here and there among them a group of knights kept together and rode in order, a little clump of slanted spears above the crowd.

They came down to the ford and crowded all together, and a couple of knights went down first into the water. It rose to their stirrups, and over, and the horses threw up their heads and backed, and then trampled on again, plunging against the spurs. Then one slipped and went down, and the rider cried once and not again as his horse dragged him under the water of the quiet sullen Dives that was flowing now not seaward but inland, with the full salt flood of the rising tide.

It was then that Guillelm and the men of Normandy, with no more than one trumpet blown, but with a great sudden shout, came over the brow of the hill and down the long slope from Varaville.

Fulcun rode on Hernaut's left in that charge. He could see out of the tail of his eye Hernaut's shield, the cowhide cover painted dark red, and a blue dragon on it eating the iron boss. But he did not look round at Hernaut, only straight ahead, as they went downhill like a loud and swift flood. He was gripping the shaft of his spear and gritting his teeth and waiting for the shock when the blade should meet leather or ringed steel; and for the drag and wrench that came after.

And then, when they were close to the bank, and going slower and with a heavier stride because of the sodden land, the horse in front of Fulcun checked and swung aside and left a space in which, half a spear's length before his stallion's hooves, Fulcun saw another horse down and rolling. Beside it, right ahead, a man lay groveling on his face, his hands clutching the grass, his helmet torn off. The man was Mauger.

Fulcun shouted, he did not know what, and felt his horse stagger. He saw, as he went by, the flying iron shoes of the fallen horse swing close to his stirrups, shining white like water. Then he was past them and on, and his spear had found its mark in a man, and the tough ash strained and bent and held. He wrenched it out and hurled on again. There was no time then to think.

They had been at it not more than five minutes when, with a crack and sudden silence, and then a shout, the old bridge broke and sagged and crashed into the river, and the crowding men and horses on it went down with a horrid great cry.

The fighting did not last long after that. Duke Guillelm drew his men back out of range of the spears that the Frenchmen who had got over cast at them from the other bank. Between the Norman line and the Dives, brimming now to the level of the clean green sedges, there was an untidy jumble of fallen men and horses; where sometimes something moved in the deepening twilight; from which came strange choked voices and now and again sharp cries.

Fulcun had lost Hernaut in the fighting, but he did not care, though now he was wedged knee to knee with strangers, and not among his own kin, as a man should be. The black horse had got a long gash in its shoulder that showed dark, deep red in the faint light. Fulcun himself had his sword in his left hand and laid across his knees, and he sucked at a cut that ran up his right forearm and spat the blood out of his mouth without knowing that he did it, or even that he was touched.

All his mind was fixed on that one least instant of time when he had seen Mauger sprawling on his face, and had felt the black swerve, stumble, and recover, and then go on.

He must remember. He strained to force his mind back. He could remember seeing Mauger's hands clutch at the rank meadow grass. He could remember that some of the scales of his hauberk stood up stiff like ruffled feathers. He could remember the way Mauger's helm hung by one thong and jerked as Mauger lifted his head.

But he could not remember whether he had dragged at the bridle of the black to swing it clear. That was as dark as the valley was growing now—he could see nothing in his mind when he tried to see what he had meant in that instant. He could not even see beyond that blank so as to understand why it mattered that he should know what he had meant.

It was dark night, without moon or stars, when Duke Guillelm bade them sound the horns and cry out to go back up the hillside. The French were gone on; the tide would not be low enough to cross until midnight, so they would camp, and eat, and sleep. For the last half-hour there had been men moving and stooping among the fallen French by the river, stripping the dead, till now the tumbled bodies showed faint white in the dark, like linen laid to bleach.

When the Norman host drew off Fulcun did not go with them. He sat in the saddle holding the stallion still as they jostled by him. In a little while he was alone, with the trampling and the talking and the creak of leather and the rap and jingle of iron all gone from him into the night. He set his teeth and began to ride slowly down the slope of the hill.

Here, though it was quiet, it was not silent. He could hear the dry whisper of the reeds as the wind touched them, and the mutter of the Dives that began now to run again toward the sea. Then a weak voice cried out and trailed into a thin scream, and suddenly a man almost at Fulcun's feet began to say, "The flail—it's all bloody—look out—your head!" and then the stallion shied from something that moved before its hooves.

Fulcun pulled up and peered into the darkness. He dreaded to go on among those naked dead, and among those not dead, but he must find Mauger, because he knew now, what, in that minute, he had meant. Yet how could he, in this black dark, find any man? He got out of the saddle and then stood still and could not move because now utter fear had caught him.

If he found Mauger, he would not know him, for Mauger's head would be smashed; there would be no face left to recognize. But Mauger would know him—he would know it was Fulcun Geroy who had ridden him down, who had not pulled his horse aside because he wished him dead. If he went, stooping and peering among the dead, Mauger might laugh at him suddenly out of a maimed mouth, and catch him by the throat, and—

He almost screamed because something touched his wrist and hand, moving smoothly and slowly down it. He snatched it up, and only then realized that it was his own blood running down from the gash upon his arm.

He wheeled round at a sound—or was it a movement? Nothing had moved. But it had. It moved again. One of those pale things, neither quite alive nor quite dead, was creeping toward him. It was a man spending his last strength to get to the water to drink, but, for Fulcun it was Mauger who came after him.

"God defend me!" he cried in his throat, and then knew that there was no defense for him, because he had killed Mauger.

He grabbed at the saddle as the black stallion threw up its head and danced aside, and then he was on his back, crouching in the saddle, and spurring. If something neither dead nor alive moved and cried as the horse went over it with a long stagger, Fulcun did not know. He had killed Mauger, and he was afraid. He did not remember now why he had ever wanted Mauger dead. But he had wanted it—he had wanted it in the bright noon sunshine of the wood, and tonight before dusk he had killed him.

Hernaut, sitting wrapped in his cloak among the men from Saint-Céneri, looked up and saw Fulcun standing in the red glow of the dying fires that lit the branches of trees in the wood where the host camped, and left the sky beyond blacker and denser than ever.

Fulcun was standing by his horse, and that was shaking, but he himself was very still, and it was as if the dark night had wiped life and understanding out of his face.

"Where have you been?" says Hernaut, staring at him.

Fulcun said nothing. He only shook his head, because he had to keep his teeth clenched to stop them chattering. He sat down suddenly beyond the Geroy men, as though he were broken, and put his head down on his knees.

Ranof Badger says, "Blood of God, Fulcun—" and Fulcun jerked his head up sharply and stared, but not at Ranof. He was listening.

Someone nearby was saying, "God! Mauger, *you'll* die an old man in your bed. When I saw you go down I never thought—"

Hernaut stirred Fulcun with his foot. "They've water for the horses over there," he says.

Fulcun turned, stared, and then got up.

As he led off the black horse he remembered very well why he had wanted Mauger dead. Because of Alde. But Mauger was alive.

Chapter 6

I wanted to be with you as dust with its ashes.

Li Bai, translated by
F. Ayscough and A. Lowell

I

They came back to Falaise in the last colored light of a clear evening. Five miles out the first shouting lads met them, for the news had come faster than they. After that they moved between lines of folk who waved their hands and threw down flowers and green branches for them to tread over, and turned about and went with them in growing crowds.

Inside the gates of Falaise town, in the open space there, Mahalt the duchess and her women waited, and behind, crowded on the steps of the houses, men with viols and drums and horns, all making the most noise they could. The green space filled till there was no room to move a foot.

Hernaut did not like the noise and the crowding. He edged his horse through the press and came clear, through the fringe of children, to the open streets, and so to the tanner's house by the well.

Robert of Saint-Céneri was in the gallery, and at his great shout Aelis came out, and little Robert. Little Robert raced for the stairs and down and caught Hernaut's bridle to lead him in.

But before Hernaut dismounted Robert called to him from above:

"Where's Fulcun—and the rest?"

"All safe—they'll be here soon," says Hernaut.

When Dame Aelis had gone to get ready plenty of hot water for baths for them, and young Robert had run off to meet and hasten the others, Hernaut sat down by Robert in the gallery, where a pair of swallows came in now and again, with a swift clean dive under the thatch, and a flutter and murmur inside the mud nest.

Hernaut was turning about in his hands the horn of wine that Aelis had fetched him, drinking now and again, and telling Robert how they had caught the French.

"And all our folk sound and whole?" says Robert.

"I've a strained shoulder," Hernaut told him, shifting it gingerly. "But Emma has a balm will cure that. She used it last year when I put my knee out. And Fulcun got a slash on his right arm, but it's nearly healed already."

Robert nodded. For a moment neither said anything.

Then, "Sir," says Hernaut, frowning at the dark shaken surface of the wine, "what is wrong with the Heron?"

Robert looked at him sharply.

"Nothing. Is there? Why?"

Hernaut says, "I don't know." And then after a minute, "After the fighting at the ford, I lost him. He came up when we were camped. He looked—he looked—" Hernaut had no gift for description. "Scared," he says at last. "No—mazed."

Robert laughed. He sounded relieved. "That's nothing. He may have taken a blow on his helm."

Hernaut said, "Perhaps," and then, after a minute, "I think he ought to marry."

"Of course he ought," Robert took him up crossly. "And I've heard of a marriage for him."

"Good?"

"Not so bad—one of Raol of le Torp's girls."

Hernaut thought about that for a moment; then he frowned.

"Sir," he says. "Where was Fulcun going to that day I came to Falaise with the news?"

"Going?" says Robert. While Hernaut told him how he had found Fulcun in the stable, he listened, and he was silent when Hernaut had done.

Then he said suddenly, "Fulcun's mother—she was a Breton lass. Fulcun is like her. It's his eyes, the gray color, and the shine in them when he laughs—he's like her—" He stopped.

"She ran away?" says Hernaut.

Robert turned and stared at him and through him, frowning.

"Fulcun—the Heron's father—he always said that she ran away with a scoundrel horse coper from Avranches. But—"

"Didn't she?"

Robert looked from him, and down the street.

"They're coming," he says, and then, "Fulcun isn't there."

He brought his fist down on his knee and scowled at it.

"If I knew where she ran to," he said in a voice that sounded angry, "I might know where Fulcun may run, one of these days."

❧

When Fulcun came in sight of the tanner's house there were several horses standing there, their mouths dripping after being watered. In the gallery above he could see the top of Robert's head with its fair, crisp hair; and young Robert astride of the rail; and Hernaut leaning on it, unarmed, in his shirt and breeches. There were several other men there, besides Neel and Ranof, and the two Geroys from Courville.

Young Robert saw him first and shouted, "Fulcun!" Fulcun got off his horse at the outer stairway. He was in no hurry to go up, and anyway the visitors were just coming down. He waited for them. They were three cousins of Rogier of l'Aigle's—all brothers. One of them—Herluin the Bearded—said to Fulcun as he passed, "Robert says he has baths hotted for you and Hernaut, but not for all of us," and he laughed and mounted his horse and went off after his brothers.

Then Fulcun must go up. So he went and kissed Robert, and little Robert, and Dame Aelis, distantly, just under her eye. Then he sat down and tried not to be noticed.

He had come into the town behind Hernaut, but he had not seen where Hernaut went and had not cared. He knew that somewhere ahead of him, among the crowd of women that he caught sight of now and again as one of the knights ahead dismounted, Alde was waiting. He dreaded to see her, and could not try to get away before he had seen her. But he could not see her; neither could he see Mauger.

Someone thrust by him, and the black stallion, startled, swung half round, and then he saw them—Alde and Mauger together, not six paces away.

Mauger had dismounted, and a lad was leading off his horse. Alde stood waiting, staring level; she was facing Fulcun, but she looked at nothing but Mauger's throat—no higher than that.

Mauger put his arms round her and his face went down to hers. Fulcun could not shut his eyes.

Then he heard her give a sort of cry. She pulled her face away, and Fulcun saw on her cheek the patch of red where the iron nasal of Mauger's helmet had hurt her, and her face was smudged with the dust and grime that was on Mauger's face. Mauger laughed and kissed her again, and this time she did not cry out, because in that second when she dragged her head away, her eyes had met Fulcun's eyes.

When Fulcun had pushed his way out of the crowd, and he did it roughly and suddenly a moment after, he did not go straight to the tanner's house, but by the longest way round and yet in a great hurry.

He had thought he knew the worst—that parting in the well house; the sight of Mauger sleeping in the wood. But there was worse yet. While they rode after the Frenchmen, Mauger had been from her as much as he, but now, Mauger had come back.

Sitting in the gallery of the tanner's house, with the others all talking round him, Fulcun held on to the solid wood of the bench he sat on, because he felt like a swimmer who has learned the strength of the tide that has caught him and is afraid of the fear that beats in his throat.

Quite soon Dame Aelis came up and called away Guion and Berenger to help carry the water for the baths. Ranof and Neel Crooked Nose went to see to the horses. Fulcun and Hernaut and Robert Geroy were left alone except for young Robert riding the wooden rail.

Fulcun began to fidget. Hernaut was bending down unstrapping his spurs, but Fulcun thought he was being watched.

He asked Robert quickly how his ankle was mending. "Well," says Robert. Then Fulcun wanted to know where that boy Berenger was. "I want to unarm," says he. But Berenger did not come when he shouted, so Fulcun looked across at young Robert and says, "Come here then. You shall unarm me."

Young Robert got off the sword with its belt, and took the shield, and laid them carefully in a corner. Now, breathing hard through his nose, he stood in front of Fulcun, who knelt down to let him reach the thongs of the helm.

Hernaut said, stretching and yawning, "When we've bathed we must go up to the castle, Fulcun."

"No," says Fulcun.

"Why not?" Hernaut was staring. Fulcun thought he stared too hard, as if he knew something. He pushed the child's hands away from his throat.

"What in the devil's name—" he began, and little Robert went back a step from him at the sound of his voice.

Robert said sharply, "Fulcun!" and Fulcun shut his mouth.

Then, "Come on! Come on!" he told the child, and when young Robert hung on his heel, he was ashamed of his anger and smiled at him. Young Robert grinned back, and came.

Robert said then, cheerfully, "Well, Fulcun, I've heard of a marriage for you."

Fulcun's head jerked round. He looked at Robert as if a strange thing had been said.

"Raol of le Torp's girl," Robert told him.

Fulcun said nothing, but Hernaut asked, "What goes with her?"

Before Robert could answer Fulcun says, "I've no will to marry."

Robert held his tongue, but Hernaut was not so wise.

"You ought to."

"Why 'ought'?"

"It's that," says Hernaut roundly. "Or a man goes whoring."

It was lucky that just then Guion ran up the steps and spoke to Hernaut.

"Sir," he said, "the bath is ready."

The others were all glad. Hernaut got up and went with Guion. Robert put out his hand and drew to him the chess-board that lay on a bench by him and rattled the pieces together. Fulcun hitched up the skirts of his hauberk and stooped and bade young Robert, "Now—pull."

When he came out into the light again, with his hair all ruffled, while young Robert dragged the heavy iron coat rattling along the floor, Fulcun had forgotten his anger. He stood up, took the hauberk from the lad, shook it out, and told him to hang it over the rail.

Then he turned to Robert.

"What is she like?" he says. "If I do marry—" He was staring at Robert, frowning. If he married . . . It sounded so simple. Was marriage something he could clutch and hold to, and save himself from the tug of the strong tide that was trying to carry him away? That tide was so strong and so resistless that he thought he would snatch at anything.

Robert said he didn't know what she was like, but Fulcun could have a look at her. Then he said, more gravely than he generally spoke, "It would be a good thing, I think. We Geroys—we need sons."

Fulcun was looking down at young Robert, who knelt, undoing his spurs. "Hernaut has two already, and Emma is big again," he says. "And there's Guillelm and Geroy in Apulia—and—this thing." He pulled young Robert's hair as the boy got up.

"Not enough," says Robert. "There were seven of us, and only two left now—and one a monk."

When Hernaut came up flushed with his bath and dressed for the feasting, Fulcun did not linger. He went down with little Robert to the washhouse under the gallery where the wooden bathtub stood steaming. Dame Aelis and Jueta, her old cousin who was her waiting woman, undressed him, and he stepped in, and whistled at the heat of it, and sat down, and felt it clutch him fiercely and then comfort him. Little Robert leaned on the edge and dabbled his hand in the water, and splashed it at Fulcun's chest, till Fulcun lifted a wet arm, and sprinkled him, and he dodged off shouting with laughter. Dame Aelis, with a towel tied over her gown, scrubbed Fulcun's back, and Jueta brought more herbs and strewed them on the water, and stirred them in, so that the steam that rose and curled sidelong across the roof beams was scented.

Fulcun, very much at ease after all the weariness and sweat of riding, was thinking, as Dame Aelis smeared ointment on the half-healed slash on his arm, that indeed he need not be afraid of any tide. He would marry, as Robert said, and there would be nothing to fear. It seemed to him that a person called Fulcun—who was himself, but not afraid of anything—might do very well at Montgaudri with a wife. He did not, it is true, think of her—she was a blank patch in the picture in his mind. He thought instead of riding out to hunt (having said good-bye to her), on autumn mornings when the bracken was on fire, and the milk-white, slim trunks of the birch trees were warmed to a faint rose by the sun that shone through their showering red-gold leaves; mornings when the deer went by with the sunlight and soft leaf shadows rippling over them like moving water gleams, and the horns blew up clear, with a merry noise, in the sharp, shining, blue air.

When he was dried and dressed in Raol Malacorona's scarlet gown and blue cloak, he went to the door to go up. Young Robert ran after him and said he wanted a ride, and Fulcun took him up pick-a-back, though Dame Aelis said tartly that his feet would soil the cloak.

So Fulcun told the boy, "Kick your feet out behind, or the duke will say to me, 'You've a dirty cloak on you, Fulcun Geroy,' and send me back without any feasting," and then he ran out, and up the stairs, and shot young Robert off at his father's feet.

Robert and Hernaut had a lantern by them on the bench, for it was dark now, and they were playing at tables.

"Who is winning?" says Fulcun.

"I am," says Robert.

Hernaut laughed. "I should think he was!"

They were all very friendly together as relations are when they have disagreed and want it forgotten. Fulcun sat down and watched the game. It was pleasant to be with them; he felt safe.

He got up after a little while and went to the rail and stood looking out. There was a large star in the sky, very bright and low, and beside it rose the black bulk that was the castle rock, and above that again, a darkness against the sky, the tower of Falaise. It was as though it stood higher than the stars and looked down on them.

He started at the sound of a horn blown, it seemed, in the sky. It blew three times. It was the summons to the feasting. He caught the rail in his hands and gripped it.

"Come on, Fulcun," Hernaut said behind him.

They went off together. Hernaut put his arm through Fulcun's; Ranof and Neel and the rest came behind; they walked lightly in the dark, and carefully, because of the unevenness of the street. At the turn they looked back and called out good-bye. Robert answered them. They could see him in the lit gallery, and Aelis too; she seemed to be looking straight at them, and Fulcun raised his hand and waved it in the dark.

"Come on," says Hernaut again, and pulled him on.

In that pause Fulcun had wanted to stop, to go back to the light there, and sit all evening, safe, beside Robert and Aelis. For he had learned, when the horn sounded over the town, how brittle a thing was his security. The horn had blown, and his heart had leaped to his throat, because Alde was up at the castle and he was going there. Another woman instead of Alde? There was no other woman. There was in all the world no real thing but her. The flood that carried him had widened till it had no shore.

II

They had eaten their fill and now the dogs were cracking the bones under the tables, and snarling, and getting kicked when they started fighting among folks' legs. The hall was very hot by the time the drinking horns began to go round, one serving man carrying the horns to each table and another going after him with pitchers of ale and thin Norman wine. The windows all stood open on the dark, and men had laid by their cloaks in respect to the duke, but great gusts of warm air came in from the kitchens, and with so much crowding everyone was overhot, and like to be hotter yet for drinking.

Fulcun could not see Mauger from where he sat between Hernaut and Ranof Badger; but he could see the door. All the time they were eating, though he knew he need not begin to watch yet, he was watching for the moment when Mauger would get up and go out.

When the drinking horn came round he was glad. He thought that if he drank he would care less when that moment came. But as he drank he grew the more afraid. He could see in his mind Mauger, drunken, lurching out, stumbling across the yard, shouting for her to come down to him from the tower where the duchess feasted with her women. And then in some room, under a small burning lamp—

He turned to Hernaut, because Hernaut had spoken. He caught the words that were lingering in his mind and answered them.

"No," he said. "My shield is lime. I like it better than ash. But ash for spears."

"I like apple for spears," someone cried, and Fulcun made himself join in the dispute that followed; anything was better than thinking; but he shook his head when they brought the horn round to him.

After a while someone noticed that—it was Baudri of Boquenci's son Wiger. "Fulcun is a poor drinker," said he.

"Well, you're not," says Hernaut. Wiger was pretty drunk.

"I've finished drinking now," Wiger said, and then he laughed. "Now I'm for my wife," and he stood up.

Fulcun got up suddenly. "I'll come too," says he, and Ranof laughed, and they all laughed, and shouted at him, and hammered on the table.

"Hark at him!" cried Herluin the Bearded, who sat opposite. "It's not many that tell a man they're coming along to cuckold him."

Fulcun shouted, "Hold your tongue," but even Hernaut was laughing at him, and Fulcun laughed suddenly himself, with the sparks in his eyes that Robert had said the Breton girl used to have.

When Fulcun had turned away, with Wiger holding to his shoulder to keep himself straight, Hernaut held out his horn for more wine. He thought, "The Heron is all right."

But he had not seen Fulcun's face as he went down to the door. Before he was halfway to it Fulcun had remembered that if he went now he would not know the moment when Mauger should go to Alde. All the night he would be thinking, "Is it now? Is it now?"

When they got outside into the cooler air Wiger broke away and was sick. Fulcun waited for him. The black bulk of the big keep stood above them at the top of the steep sloping ward. On the second floor of the keep the windows were lit with a bright warm yellow, and when the clamor in the hall behind them dropped a minute, he could hear the high shrill note of the women all laughing together. The yard was empty and dark, but beyond the gate, which stood open tonight, there was a brightness in the air over the town, for the common folk were feasting down there about the great fires that had roasted sheep and boars and oxen.

Wiger came back. "That's better," he says, but he was still very unsteady. He put his arm round Fulcun's neck and pulled him up the slope toward the keep. But when they got to the steps that led up to the door, Wiger sat down on them and began to laugh foolishly.

"Fulcun," he says, when he could stop laughing, "be a good fellow and go up and fetch me my wife. Or I may fall, and take a broken leg, and get no pleasure this night at all."

Fulcun stood still for a moment. He had come out from the feasting so as to go quickly away. He must go away. The gate was open, and once back in the tanner's house with Robert he would be safe for tonight at least. Then he stepped over Wiger and began to go up. Alde was up there. If he went up the stairs he would be going a little nearer to her.

And yet he went slowly. He knew most clearly that here was a choice, he knew that he must choose to go away. He must turn and go down and go away.

At the top he found a man that had been left on guard, but he was dozing with his head on his knees, and a lantern on the planks beside him. Fulcun put a hand on him suddenly and shook him. "Get up!" he cried at him, suddenly fierce. "Go up and say Wiger of Boquenci is waiting for his wife."

The fellow jumped up, dazed and stupid.

"You're not Wiger of Boquenci," he dragged out, "you're—"

"I'm Fulcun Geroy," Fulcun cut him short. "Wiger's below."

The man began to laugh. He too was very drunk. "Ho! well!" he cried. "I suppose all the cocks will be treading their hens tonight."

That was too near the brutal coarseness of the truth. Fulcun reached out, caught the fellow's collar, shook him soundly, and then kicked him. The man landed stumbling on the stairs, caught at the rail, and hung there.

"Now, go up as I bid you," Fulcun told him. But the fellow was already halfway down the stairs. "Go up yourself," he called, and then Fulcun heard him fall over Wiger, and the things they said to each other.

As he went into the doorway and up the twisting stairs in the wall, groping in the dark with his hands before him, he thought, "I had to come up."

❦

He had crossed the empty first-floor chamber and had started to go up the stairway above when he heard something move sharply beyond the turn of the newel post. The next two steps brought him in sight of the faint lightening that an arrow slit made in the thick dark. He could see nothing on the stairs, but he knew that someone was standing just above him.

"Who is it?" he says.

There was a long silence. Then "Alde," her voice answered him.

He could not speak for a minute, and when he did, it was harshly. "Wiger of Boquenci wants his wife." He stopped, and then said, flinging the words at her, "He's drunk," but it was Mauger he was thinking of.

She knew it, and she jerked her head aside in the dark as if he had struck her in the face. In her simple mind she thought, "He was kind. Now he is angry—like Mauger. It is not my fault that I am Mauger's." But he had piled pain on pain for her, so she laughed sharply, and said, "I suppose the men will all be drunk tonight." At least he should not know how he had hurt her.

Fulcun says, "Well, haven't you women drunk too?" He barely knew what he meant; the words had no more purpose than the cursing of a wounded man.

But she answered after a second, in a strange, scared, hurried voice:

"I? No—I haven't drunk. I could not."

It was her voice more than the words that spoke to him. He stood a minute, still as the stones of the tower; then he moved, but not to touch her, not even to lay so much as a finger on her. He put his hand on the wall and leaned his forehead on his hand.

"Alde—" he said. "Alde—my dear."

Just for that moment all the fury of jealousy, the fever, the disgust, the heart-shaking desire that had been mounting in him, dropped and lay by. He knew then that far beyond all passion he was hers—solemnly, gently, rightly, inevitably hers, as inevitably as night leads to dawn and daylight to the dark.

Her fingers groping out, touched his neck. He caught her hands and thrust them away.

"No," he cried, and nothing more. Her touch had reminded him that soon Mauger would come for her. He could not touch her now.

He turned and went down the stairs. He had gone perhaps six steps when he remembered Wiger waiting in the yard. He shouted up to her, "Send Wiger of Boquenci's wife," and went on.

But in the chamber below he slackened, and hung on his heel, and then stopped. He had pushed her hands away and cried "No!" at her. He had thought only of his own necessity. He had not even tried to comfort her, but now he thought his heart would break with pitying her.

He could not go on then. He moved very softly back to the wall by the stair and stood there waiting. He would let Wiger's wife go down, and then he would run upstairs. Perhaps Alde would come out again. Anyway he must try; he must go back in case she came out again; he could not go away leaving her uncomforted.

Wiger's wife went by him. He held his breath. He heard her gown trail on the rushes, and then the rustle ceased; she had lifted it to go down the next flight of steps.

He turned and went up, as quiet as he could, feeling with his hands; his hands touched Alde before he knew she was there. She gave a little gasping cry, but she stood still.

He said, instead of all the impossible things he had wanted to say, "You came out again."

She answered him simply, "I hoped you would come back." And then she told him more. "I came out the first time when you found me, because I had to think of you, Fulcun, for a little while . . . before . . ."

Her voice failed, and suddenly, though she made no sound, he knew that she was shaking all over and twisting her fingers together.

"Oh!" she cried, "I ought not to have come. I ought not to have come out again."

Fulcun tried to say what he had come back for. "Alde," he began. "Forgive me—I didn't mean—"

Then someone below on the stairs shouted:

"Who's that up there? By God—"

They knew it was Mauger though they did not know his voice.

Alde's hands gripped Fulcun's shoulder in the dark. After one breathless, silent second she murmured, "Stay here!" and made to pass him. "It is Alde, sir," she said, "I am coming."

Fulcun caught her. "No," he says urgently, and Mauger shouted:

"Who's that man there?" He was just below them; they heard the rasp of his sword as he began to lug it out, but the hilt ground on the wall of the narrow stair and he swore.

Fulcun says, "Keep your sword in. It's Fulcun Geroy," and then he saw Mauger's face, a blur of gray in the blackness as he came level with the arrow slit. And there was a gray gleam on the sword blade; he had got it out.

"Fulcun Geroy?" says Mauger, and then he cried, "I'll see you burned for this, you whore!"

Fulcun says to him, "Take that back!" and to Alde, very sharp, "Up—up—get you up." He had his own sword out now and lifted.

Mauger shouted, "I'll have you down," and cut slashing at Fulcun's legs.

Fulcun leapt, striking downward; he heard Mauger's sword jar under his feet, and he had time to think, "If I miss, or fall on the point—"

Then he was tumbling, with a voice muttering in his ear, another body below him, and his hands clutching a rough throat and a man's arm.

When he picked himself up there was nothing but darkness and silence. He bent forward and his fingers touched Mauger's foot. He went down a step, still feeling with his hands. Mauger was all over the next step below. Fulcun felt about him till he found his head; it was resting against the wall and it moved limply as he touched it and his fingers found warm blood. He tried to feel, fumbling hastily, if Mauger's heart beat still, but he could find no pulse at all.

He stood up then, and a thought came into his empty mind, "I have killed him." That seemed silly at first. He was just beginning to get used to it when he heard someone above muttering, "O Christ!" and remembered Alde. She was coming down.

He said, "Stop where you are!" and went up to her. Her hands found his shoulders; she clutched him as he stood on the step below; she pulled his head to her breast and held it there. "I thought—I thought!" she said, and began to shake, with her teeth chattering. Fulcun put his arms round her and held her to him. "I think he is dead," he told her, and for a moment they stood close, clinging together, hardly knowing anything except the necessity of touch in their confusion.

Then Fulcun said, "I must go. I must get out of Falaise," but he did not move. Through the arrow slit just below them came clear the long trailing hoot of an owl. The sound moved through the dark; it had been here, now it was there, and now far away. When it ceased Fulcun said, "I can get out. I can get out tonight for it is the Geroys' night at the gate."

At the words her hands clutched him, and he remembered that to go, was to go from her. He tightened his hold about her, dragging her to him so that her feet slipped from the step and she hung in his arms, but clinging to him. He held her, and with his mouth on hers he tried to be satisfied. He put out all his strength; this was the last. Now he must let her go.

He loosed her till she was standing again, but very close to him, for the steps were narrow; she leaned against him, catching her breath because he had hurt her. He put both his hands behind him and caught one wrist with the other hand so that his arms should not go round her again.

She said, with her hands feebly wandering over him and clutching at his gown, "Fulcun, don't go. Take me with you. Take me too."

"Take you?" he cried. "How can I?"

She said, "If you leave me and he is alive he will have me burned—or his kin if he is dead." Then she muttered, "But I should not care—" and then her fingers came up to his face and touched his cheek. She spoke in the faint, choked voice of a child that has cried its fill, "Oh! Fulcun," she said. "Must you leave me?" He snatched her hand and held it hard against his mouth.

"I can't leave you," he said.

Chapter 7

CLEOPATRA.   Pardon, pardon!
ANTONY.   Fall not a tear, I say, one of them rates
             All that is won and lost; give me a kiss.
             Even this repays me.

Antony and Cleopatra, Act III, sc. ix

I

When they were outside the castle gate he took her hand, and they ran down the hill. As they ran, she stumbled, and he held her up, and she felt his strength thrill through her; but he was thinking what good luck it was that tonight the Geroys kept the gate. It is the truth that he thought of that as a piece of great good luck.

But all the same, when they came out by the tanner's house, he pulled up. She said nothing, for she had no breath. He muttered to her, "I don't want Robert to see us," but even then he did not think why.

He went over to the door of the lower room where the horses were stabled and the tanner's family slept. "Stay here," he says, and left her standing by the door. He saddled the black as quickly as he could (he pulled a face in the dark when he felt down its legs) and led it out. Alde stood just where he had left her. He did not notice then, but he remembered after, that she had not asked a question or spoken a word since he had lifted her across Mauger's body in the keep.

He said, "Stay here—I must get my arms," and then they both held themselves very still. Some men were coming down the road from the castle, walking briskly. They came abreast of the tanner's house. Fulcun had pulled Alde close to him, and now he shifted her a little so that his sword was clear.

But the men went by. They were talking about a smith that lived in Poitiers—a very good smith who lived near Saint Johan.

When they had gone, Fulcun says, "We must be quick. And you'd best come up."

In the room that opened on the gallery, where they all ate, and where all but Aelis and Robert and little Robert slept, the lamp still burned. On the table was Robert's chessboard, with the chessmen tumbled upon it, and Robert's horn with the gilt rim lay by it. The room had the look that a room gets the moment it is left alone, of having been abandoned for hours—as though the day that was over was very far away. By the wall the light of the lamp shone on the blade of Fulcun's knife. He had lost it this evening, and there it was. But he could not believe it was only a couple of hours since he lost it.

There was no time to think of these things. The mail coats hung in a row along a bar; he lifted his own down and rolled it in the leather coat that went under it. There was no time to arm. His helm was above. He lifted it off and then turned. Alde was by him. She took the mail and helm from him. He went over to the corner where the spears leaned; felt for and found his own;

then he picked up his shield, slipped the strap over his head, and tossed it on to his back.

"Now," he says. He put his hand on her arm, a hard grasp; they were almost at the door of the gallery when the inner door opened.

"Who is there?" Robert Geroy cried, and came out, limping, with a big red cloak wrapped about him and trailing down to his bare feet. He looked at them for a long second, and in that second he guessed a great deal. He said:

"What are you doing, Fulcun Geroy?

Fulcun said, "I have killed a man. I am going."

"Who is that by you?"

Fulcun could not say anything. Robert gave a sort of laugh.

"No need to tell me. Who is the man?"

Fulcun said, "Mauger of Fervacques."

"That will make Montgommeri love us." As Robert spoke Fulcun found him a stranger. He knew Robert's anger, but not this mockery. "And what now?" Robert asked.

"It's our night at the gate. I can get away."

"God above!" Robert cried suddenly. "You think only of getting away!"

It was his voice that spoke to Fulcun, that, and all the things he left unsaid. It kept him dumb for a minute. Then—

"Robert—" he began, and stopped, because the door behind Robert was open and Aelis stood there, dark and fierce and bright-eyed, with her hair all loose and an old gown on her.

"I have heard," she cried, with her eyes on Fulcun.

Robert turned to her. "Go in!" he said. She did not move, and he lifted his hand and struck her with his fist. She caught at the door as she stumbled back, and stood holding to it, her face dead white except where a trickle of blood ran down from her lip. She never looked at Robert, only at Fulcun; the blow went down to his account along with the rest. She went in and shut the door.

Robert stood still, halting heavily on one foot; his head was bent and he was biting on his fingers.

"Robert—" Fulcun began again, and again stopped, for what was there he could say? Then, "I cannot help it!" he cried.

Robert lifted his head quickly. "Heron," he said, and now they were not strangers, but again, as they had always been before, close in blood and in affection, "Heron, stay here and stand your trial. I swear we'll see you through—all we Geroys."

Alde moved suddenly and dragged her arm away from Fulcun, who held it still, but he hardly noticed what she did. His eyes were on Robert.

He could not say what he must say. He was silent, and then he brought it out. "No. I must go."

Robert said, after a silence, "Because of her," and Fulcun nodded.

Robert moved. He limped across the room till he stood in front of Alde. He said, "I'll have a look at you, since it's you we shall all suffer for."

Alde bore it for a moment; then she hid her face from him in her hands. Robert laughed.

But Alde turned slowly to Fulcun—he could see her eyes, but not her mouth, for her hands were clenched against it. She said to him in an empty, dead voice, "He is right. You must stay here. I will go back."

Fulcun made one stride to her. He threw his arm over her shoulder and dragged her away from Robert.

"By God, you shall not!" he cried, and then to Robert, "Out of my way!"

Robert stepped back. Even in that moment Fulcun thought, "Did he think I could have touched him?"

Robert said, "Go on then, bastard!"

Ranof Badger and the Saint-Céneri men opened the gate for them. Ranof did not understand, but Fulcun left him no time to think. Least said was best. The black stallion moved out, and Fulcun tightened his hold about Alde, sitting before him in the curve of his shield arm. Behind them they heard Ranof cry, "Now—with a run!" and the gates came to, crashed on the post, and stood still, shaking. The bar went trundling back through the sockets. They were free of Falaise. Fulcun let the stallion feel the spur. They plunged forward into the night.

They had gone perhaps three miles with never a word, when Alde raised her hand and touched his cheek.

"Fulcun," she whispered. He did not know it, but his silence, after Robert Geroy's words, had made her frightened of him.

His head came down to hers. His mouth moved over her face, but he was not kissing, for his lips were closed and his teeth clenched, and in that strange caress sudden violences alternated with sharp withdrawals.

He pulled away after a minute.

"Oh! Fulcun," she said in a sigh, and then, when his head did stoop to her again, "I thought you wanted to go back."

The jerk and tightening of his arm answered her; she cried, "I hated him when he called you bastard."

Fulcun did not look down at her. "I am," he said.

"What do I care? I hated him."

"Oh! Hush!" says Fulcun sharply. He wanted not to speak or think of Robert, since certainly he could not hate him. All that Robert had said was just, and far more that he had not said. And yet, again and again in Fulcun's mind, the only answer he could find was the answer he had given Robert, "I cannot help it." As for Robert's last word, its bitterness was to Fulcun nothing else at all but the measure of the affection that he had wounded. But again he could not help it.

He pulled up a little while after, and said, "I must arm. They may send after us."

As he armed, hastily in the dark, with Alde doing her best to help him, he was wondering whether they had found Mauger, and if the guard would remember that Fulcun of Montgaudri had gone into the keep, and if, supposing they came asking for him at the tanner's house, Robert would tell them that he had gone out of Falaise. He only spoke to Alde to tell her what to do, and she said as little. He mounted again, lifted her up, and they rode on.

But they did not ride far.

Alde said, "Fulcun—sometimes I think I can hear horses."

He reined in, and they sat, listening. It was that hour between dark and light when the shape of things shows, but no feature of them, and the stars were very close and bright in a graying sky. When the regular beat of the stallion's hooves ceased, for a second all seemed silence; then they heard what Alde had heard, the trampling of horses behind, and not so far behind either.

Fulcun got down. He took Alde and lifted her over the saddle to the crupper. "You must be behind me for this," he says, as he swung up again, "I daren't risk you in front."

They rode on again; he was looking for a good place to turn about; there was a village before them and there might be a narrow place there; the less room the better, for him. They reached the first buildings of the village. There was a long barn on one side with a duck pond at the foot of its wall. On the other side of the road there was a stack yard with a paling round it. This place would do.

He went a score of yards farther and then turned, and as he turned, saw, for the first time, the men behind. There were four of them. It was just light enough to see their faces but not to know who they were. They shouted, and one of them cried, "Stop—you dog of a Geroy!"

Fulcun said quickly, "Keep your arm tight round me and your head below my shoulder whatever you do." And then, before she could think or speak, she felt the muscles of his body tighten, and the horse moved along the road toward the four. They shouted suddenly, and Fulcun struck in with his spurs and shouted too—

"Hoi! Geroy!" The cry was like an axe lifting and coming down; she felt the strong vibration of it within her arms.

Then she was lost in a tumult of speed that ended with a swerve that all but shook her off, and a shock and a crash that jolted her head against Fulcun's shoulder blades; his body seemed as hard and unmoved as a tree.

He had caught one spear in his shield, but his own had gone clean through the man's thigh. Luckily it missed the wood of the saddle behind, and he wrenched it out and heard the man go down as they swung by. Of the others, two had gone past up the road, having missed him by that swerve, but the other had lingered, and now he was almost on Fulcun.

Fulcun had not speed enough to meet his charge; he did the only thing he could, he shortened his spear in his hand and threw it. It went under the shield, and the man toppled, as his horse shied off. Fulcun shouted again then.

But the others were there and coming down on him. He wheeled about and got his sword out. The first man—it was Ruald of Saint Pierre, Mauger's own brother—came on slowly; he had an axe. When the horses were almost breast to breast he lifted it and struck. The blade bit into the shield rim and through to the limewood, but that held, and the axe hung a minute and would not be dragged out.

Fulcun took his chance; he slashed down at Ruald's shoulder, missed it as Ruald got the axe clear, but caught the arm, and shore it all but through—Ruald of Saint Pierre was a one-armed man after. Fulcun was not content with that, but drove on, and though Ruald snatched at the saddle to steady himself, Fulcun's horse caught him and jostled him down.

But it was that moment that the last of the four came on with a shout. His spear struck Fulcun full and fair on the shield against the upper arm and bore him down in the saddle backward and sideways. For a second he thought the stirrup leather or the girths would go, and that would be the end.

But they held. He pulled upright, wrenching at his shield and twisting it with all his strength. The spear shaft strained, then broke short below the socket. Fulcun had his sword out and he had time for three blows before the other got his clear. The first two were caught on the shield rim, the third found the shoulder and bit deep; the man bowed over his saddle and his sword dropped. Fulcun struck the horse with the flat of his sword; it reared, swung about, and bolted; the rider had no other thought now than to keep his saddle.

That was the end, but for a moment Fulcun must fight to get the stallion in hand again, for it was blood mad. As the beast reared and backed Fulcun could see the man whose thigh he had run through sitting on the grass gripping his leg with both hands. The second one with the spear through his body lay still. Only Ruald of Saint Pierre was on his feet; his right arm was dangling, but in his left hand he had a spear. Fulcun shouted at him with a yell of laughter, as the stallion swung about.

They plunged on and again Fulcun shouted. And then, as they went, he saw in the gray twilight the spear that Ruald flung come flighting low beside his stirrup. But there was little strength in the cast; it fell on the road and they were gone beyond it almost before it lay still.

Alde had given a gasp and clutched him as the spear dropped, clattering. Fulcun laughed. "Hoi! Geroy!" he yelled again and lifted his sword and shook it high above his head.

They swept on with the wind rushing past their ears in a roaring flood; Fulcun felt the stallion's neck like iron against the bit, and drove in the spurs again, for he was mad too. So he rode, shouting, a bare sword in his hand with the blood beginning to dry and turn brown on it, and a hacked and gaping shield on his arm. He had forgotten Robert Geroy, he had forgotten his fear of the strong thing that had mastered him. When, after a little, the horse dropped to an easier pace and Fulcun, putting up his sword, reached round and dragged Alde back to her place before him, he had almost forgotten that it was Alde. His hand was hard on her. He remembered now only his own strength, and that she was his woman, won by the sword.

II

They came, in the strengthening light that set the bounds of the empty world wider every minute, within sight of a town. There were hills on the left hand and the morning lay beyond them; the sky above was coldly brightening, but all the hither slopes were dark yet, and there was mist to right and left of the town hanging low over a river.

"That is Argentan," says Fulcun, and swung the horse away over to the right. They had to skirt the great field because the corn was not reaped yet, and the wattle fence stood round about it. Beyond, in the common, rabbits slipped away, little gray shadows with white scuts; and the dew on the grass was leaden gray. They crossed the Orne above the town—there was not much water in it—and found the Mortrée road beyond.

It was when they had passed Mortrée and Fulcun bore up south toward the high woods of Ecouves that Alde said, "Where are you taking me?"

"To Montgaudri."

"Is it near?"

"Not yet," says Fulcun, and then, "Bear up, girl!"

She said, "I am all right."

He did not answer, but as they drew near to the hills he was thinking that all the time she had done simply what he had told her, without word or question.

The woods, when they entered them, were chill with the morning shadow and very silent. But when they climbed higher to the long eastward-facing rampart of the forest, where the road runs along just under the crest, they could see, as they looked out above all the crowded treetops of the steep slope below them, the pale and cloudy east barred with faint color. Then the trees thinned for a little and they were riding through a scattered holt of bushes where gray rocks cropped out, and where there were sweet-smelling herbs in the long, fine upland grass. It was there that the first gentle, suffused beam of sunlight touched them.

Fulcun pulled up. When the horse stood, the silence was as wide as the world.

He said, "We'll rest here awhile," and threw his leg over the saddle and dropped to the ground. Then he turned and put his hands to her waist and lifted her. He said, "There, girl!" as he set her down, but she cried out, and stumbled, and almost fell.

She told him, trying to laugh, "My foot—that spear got it."

Fulcun cried out, "You said nothing."

"We had to get away," she answered. It was the truth, but she did not tell him besides that she had welcomed the pain because it came to her through him.

He lifted her then and carried her to a tree and put her down so that she could lean against it; he went down on his knees at her feet, but she pushed him away.

"No," she said. "Go—go and see to the horse."

She was so urgent that he went. When he came back she had her shoe off and she was tearing a strip of linen from the long shift under her gown.

He knelt down again and took her foot in his hands. He took no notice of anything she said. He looked down at it; it was soft to touch and of a strange shape to him, delicate and small, not at all like a man's foot. And it was hers. And then as he looked the blood welled out again along the gaping lips of the long tear.

He put his mouth down to it. He was kissing the blood from it in a sort of madness when she cried out, "Fulcun! You hurt me!" That stopped him.

He sat back on his heels, his mouth stained with the blood. He was shaking.

She began to speak hastily.

"You've—you've drunk my blood. That's like as when men swear the oath to be brothers and loyal forever."

Fulcun wiped the blood from his mouth.

"It is forever. I swear it."

She said, with her eyes on his, "I swear it too."

"Then," says Fulcun, very eager, "you must drink my blood." He lifted the flap of his hauberk and pulled out the knife from his belt. "Cut my arm there," he says, and held out the knife to her, and when she took it, his wrist.

But she cried out, "Fulcun, I cannot. I cannot. I could not hurt you," and she covered his wrist with both her hands as if to keep it safe.

He looked down at her hands and then at her face.

"Then I am sworn to you, but not you to me." She lifted her head and looked at him. "You know that I could not change," she said. He saw her eyes, and he believed.

He bound up her foot as well as he could, and then he went and sat by her. He slipped his arm behind her and drew her to him. He had meant only that she should rest on his shoulder, but her nearness made him forget that. He pulled her closer, straining her to him.

She pushed him off in a minute. "Your hauberk—it hurts me," she murmured. She leaned against the tree with her eyes shut.

He jumped up. "I'll take it off." He got his helmet off and tossed it down on the grass. Then he struggled out of the mail, wrenching and twisting, in a great hurry.

Yet, when he was out of it, and had unlaced and pushed back the coif of the leather coat, and felt the air cool on his head, he stood a minute. The first delicate clear morning sunshine was on the hillside, and overhead the sky was pure sharp blue; the morning stillness was as intense as any sound.

He looked at Alde, and then he could not look away. Her eyes came up to his and dropped.

He said, jerkily, "The grass is softer over there. And there is shade." He went close and stood over her. When he held out his hands she put hers into them and he lifted her up.

Yet, when she was on her feet, she pushed him away and limped on by herself. He went after her in a great perturbation. She let herself down on the grass; the bracken grew high beyond, fresh smelling and fresh green yet.

He stood staring at her for a moment, then he flung himself down by her and she was in his arms again.

But she drew away, and again he could not understand and cried out, "Alde!" She did not answer. She had dragged herself from his shoulder till her weight rested on the curve of his arm; her head fell back and he saw her eyes glimmer under half-shut lids. She was heavy on his arm; her weight was dragging him toward her. He let himself go, and they sank down together, his arm below her shoulders. His breast touched hers.

He understood then, or he thought he did, but he must make sure, so that his bliss should be complete.

"You meant—this?" he whispered.

"Yes—this," she murmured, and he felt all her body tremble.

His last thought before all thought drowned, was—

"She is hungry to give." His heart reeled.

❦

When he woke the sun was high. Alde sighed in his arms; he felt her breath on his throat, and he lifted his head cautiously so that he could look at her sleeping. Her hands lay against his breast. He took them softly into his hand; they were cuddled close together, powerless and warm. He let his head sink down again and shut his eyes, only he moved so close to her that, when he pouted his lips, he could just touch her hair. Then he lay quiet, in the most utter, still content, thinking of nothing, but aware, as his eyes through his eyelids were aware of the light, that she was with him.

She woke without moving, and said, "Fulcun!"

They got up soon, and they realized then that they were very hungry.

Fulcun says, "Can't we snare a rabbit?" They were both gay, with a high, exquisite gaiety, as if the world had been new-made that morning and all for them.

"Oh, Fulcun!" she cried. "And eat it raw?"

They laughed, and then he turned from her, listening.

"Do you hear that?" he says.

"That clinking of little bells?"

"They must be sheep bells!"

She said, "I don't think they sound quite like sheep bells," but she was really intent on watching his face as he listened.

Fulcun said he was sure it must be sheep, and they would go on and find the shepherd and get food from him. So he armed except for his helm and lifted her up and mounted. He put his face down on her head when he was up and muttered, "God! Alde—" and no more. As for her, she was dumb with joy.

The track led still along the edge of the ridge; the sound of bells came from below, through the thicker trees down there. They were both thinking, "That's no place for sheep," when the way began to go down the hillside, a steep, rough track deep in gritty sand, with juts of rock breaking it, and all splashed over with sunshine and shadow. Fulcun pulled up and got out of the saddle to lead the horse, and then he stood, listening.

From below them came the sound of the clinking bells, nearer now, and besides that there was the noise of wheels grinding and jolting on the road, the creak and complaint of the wain timbers, and now the sound of footsteps.

And then, moving slowly through the many many shadows and lights of the wood, a dozen men came trudging on foot, and after them the oxen that dragged the wain, swinging their heads and whisking their tails. On either side of the wain itself went a man, one old, the other hardly more than a lad. Each carried a bell in his hand. Between them, on the wain, lay a long bundle, wrapped in a scarlet cloth; and now and again when the wain jolted and swayed over a stone, the old man put his hand on that covered thing to stop it sliding; for a dead man cannot fend for himself.

Fulcun stared at them as they came on with the shadows crawling over them. They were coming by, and the way was too narrow for them to pass. He could feel the warmth of the sun on his neck, but there was a chill on him that could not be warmed.

He jerked the bridle so that the startled horse threw up its head, and Alde had to clutch at the mane. Then he dragged it off the track into the deep bracken and wheeled it about, trampling and terrified, till it faced the slow procession again, and then he let it stand. He flung one arm over Alde's knees as if to keep her safe. She felt the hard pressure of it, but she could not see his face.

She did not see it till the wain, and the barefoot, shaggy serfs that came after it, had gone by out of sight and almost out of hearing; only the sound of the bells came faintly still.

Then he looked up at her, and she did not know his face.

He said hoarsely, "I stayed there alone down by the Dives river. They were all round, white like sheep in the dark. I thought he was there, dead and naked among the rest." He stopped. "Now he is dead," he said.

She did not try to argue, she only put her hands behind his head, and with all her strength dragged him toward her. But he pulled her hands apart and held her wrists, staring at her with that same look of horror.

Then she saw his face change as if he had been lost and had seen at last some known landmark. He threw his arm round her and buried his face on her knee.

He said in a moment, without looking up, "He had his sword out on the stairs. I had done him no wrong—then."

She told him, "He would have killed you."

She felt him shiver. "But God is angry," he muttered.

Again she did not try to argue. She cried, "Oh, Fulcun, forgive me!" and then almost in a whisper, "I could not be in the world and be without you."

He raised his head then and stared at her. That was the truth; it covered everything, though it explained nothing.

He said, "Let's get on," and he mounted. Before he tightened the reins he kissed her, not fiercely, but solemnly, as though the touch itself were far less than the meaning it carried.

Chapter 8

Et molt lor amentoit sovent
L'ermite lor delungement.
A Tristran dist par grant desroi,
"Que feras tu? Conselle toi."
   "Sire, j'am Yseut a mervelle,
Si que n'en dor ne ne somelle.
De tot an est li consel pris:
Mex aim o li estre mendis
Et vivre d'erbes et de glan
Q'avoir le reigne au roi Otran.
De lié laisier parler ne ruis,
Certes, quar faire ne le puis."

Béroul, Tristan, v. 1397–1408

I

It was late afternoon when they came to the brook that bounded Montgaudri manor on the north. The black horse splashed through the clear and shallow stream over round, golden-brown stones. Then it heaved itself up on the quaggy bank.

Fulcun said, "That was the boundary of Montgaudri land—that brook."

She answered very low, "Then we are come home."

As they rode on and across a clearing in the woods—a hot pool of light, bright with tall willow herb round the stumps of felled tree—he knew that what she had said was most true. To be with her was for him indeed to have come home. He found it surprising that he had never known, before he saw her, that he was a stranger in a world of strangers. But now he was come home to her.

They saw at last, through the trees, the sloping cornfield of Montgaudri that ran up a third of the hillside; above the field the hill rose more steeply, broken only by a sandy warren and three old thornbushes halfway up; on top, crowning the steep southern end of the hill, they could see the pale, and the thatched roofs of the town, and the wooden tower of the castle.

The corn was all reaped on this side of the field, and the garbs were piled into stooks; but beyond, on the slope of the hill, it still stood deep, a sheet of red-gold, smoldering with ripeness and smudged here and there to a fiercer color, as though the sun's hand had touched it and it had burned under the intolerable heat. Along the edge of the standing crop the reapers moved, naked to the waist and burned as the corn, stooping, reaching, and swinging; after them went the women to gather and to bind.

Fulcun rode out from the trees to the open field, and some of the children, playing tig among the stooks, saw the armed horseman and ran screaming. Fulcun laughed, and put the horse to a round trot, and rode on past them to where he saw Osmunt standing staring under his hand. Fulcun shouted to him, "Ho! Osmunt, God save you!" and pulled up by him. The reapers and the women and all the children came crowding round. Fulcun changed suddenly from laughing to stern.

He lowered his shield arm so that they could all see that he had a woman—a woman in a rose-red gown and a white veil, sitting on the black horse's withers in front of him.

He said, looking round at all of them with his eyes hard and ready—

"Listen, you men of Montgaudri! This is your lady. See that you do her courteous service."

They stared in silence, waiting for more, but that was all they got from Fulcun. He thought, wryly, "They'll get to know soon enough." There was an empty pause, and then he said to Osmunt—

"Sound your horn. Let them eat now."

Osmunt looked up at the sun that stood over the heights of Perseigne forest. "It's early," he says.

Fulcun says, "Sound it!" He could see that Osmunt was staring at Alde, and he did not like that.

When Osmunt had blown the horn Fulcun wheeled his horse to go up to Montgaudri, but Alde spoke.

She said, "Sir—I am so hungry. Could we eat with them?"

He looked down at her, caught most of all by that word *sir*. It was the first time she had used it, and it was as if she were already and indeed his wife—as if he had just led her home from Cortilly church with flowers and branches strewn under the stallion's hooves. Then he thought of what she said. She would eat with the reapers—she was not afraid of their staring and their whispering. He said, "Brave wench," and she lifted her eyes and looked at him, and he saw she did not understand—she simply did not see anything to fear. That reassured him, though it was not his own serfs that he was afraid of.

So they ate with the folk under the wild cherry trees that stood in the corner of the field. There was black bread, and goat's milk cheese, and garlic, and cresses from the stream. Osmunt sent a lad up to Montgaudri to fetch butter, and he came back very hot, carrying a wooden dish covered over with a cabbage leaf, and in it the butter, golden, sweating cool salt-white water. Fulcun cleaned his knife on his sleeve and spread butter on the black bread for Alde and for himself.

When he had finished eating he got up and went over to Osmunt, who was looking at one of the sickles that he held up against the sky.

"The teeth of that blade are all broke," says Osmunt.

Fulcun took it and squinted up at it. "Where is Lord Geroy?" he asked.

Osmunt says, after a second, "Up there," and nodded toward Montgaudri.

Fulcun was thinking half of Geroy, and half of how much he should tell Osmunt. He decided to tell him nothing yet. He turned back and looked at Alde.

The women had gathered round her, and a small boy had brought wild raspberries from the woods and held them out to her. She took them now, smiling, and there was the same fearless, friendly gaiety in her eyes that Fulcun remembered at Falaise at the beginning. Once again he was surrounded by a flawless happiness.

He did not go back to her until Osmunt had blown his horn again, and the reapers and the women had tramped off across the drying stubble. He wanted her to be with his folk. Now that he had seen her with them he was quite sure that there could not be a creature in the world, still less in Montgaudri, which was his part in the world, who would not love her. He went back at last and found her lying in the shade, asleep.

He did not wake her. For a minute he looked down at her and could not understand why just to watch her tired out and fast asleep should hurt him so with pity for her. But it did hurt him strangely.

He beckoned two little girls who were prowling about nearby, sent them to tear bracken fronds from the ditch under the trees, and then bade them sit by Dame Alde and keep the flies from her. And tell her, if she waked, that he was gone up to Montgaudri to see things set in order for her, and he would be back soon. He left them, squatting on each side of her, slowly waving the bracken, and staring at her solemnly.

Then he caught the black stallion and mounted and rode for Montgaudri.

The town was empty, since everyone had gone down to the reaping, and so was the castle yard when he came to it. He stabled the black himself and gave it a full feed of oats. It had carried him and Alde. He laid a hand on its shoulder, sticky with sweat and dust, and said, before he left it, "I'll not part with you after this day, my lad."

He went up the steps of the tower and stood a minute at the top before he went in, because from here he could see the cornfield where the reapers worked, and the line of cherry trees, and Alde's rose-red kirtle. The planks of the tower smelled pleasant and sharp of resin, for the sun was baking them. The whole world was full of warmth and peace as the day drowsed toward evening, just as, in these August days, the summer turned, slow and burdened with riches, to the autumn. Fulcun ducked his head under the low doorway and began to climb the stairs. A starling had got in somehow and built its nest, and the dark steps were littered with twigs. He thought, "I must get a wench to sweep this, while Alianor and that woman of hers fettle up the great chamber."

He came out in the light of the hall. It was empty.—No! At the far side, just by the door of the great chamber there were two women. They were bending down with their heads close to the door. When they heard Fulcun they jumped away.

He went past them and opened the door. As he opened it young Baudri shouted, very shrill and loud,

"I don't care. I'll bite her again if she clouts me. She is only a serf wench."

And Alianor's voice said, "No, you shall not touch him."

Fulcun shut the door behind him, and put his back to it, and there was a silence.

There were four people in the great chamber. Fulcun saw Geroy first; he had a whip in his hand. Facing him Dame Alianor stood with one hand on Baudri's shoulder, and the child had hold of her arm in both his hands. Alianor looked round at

Fulcun as he came in, and he saw the face that had kept Geroy off, white and pinched, venomous with fury.

Beyond Geroy, sitting on the bed, was another woman, with straight, black hair and darkly flushed cheeks, in a very fine bright gown of golden yellow; but she sat cross-legged, holding her scarlet-shod feet in her hands, as if she were any wild young colt of a serf girl. And she was. It was Custance.

For a long moment no one spoke or moved, then Fulcun pulled open the door.

"Stand outside!" says he to Baudri, "and keep those wenches off from it." He pointed his finger to the two women who were nearer than they had been when he came in.

Then he shut Baudri out.

It was Geroy who spoke. He had thrown down the whip.

"Where have you come from?" But Fulcun did not answer him.

He pointed at Custance, who had put her feet to the ground and was scowling at him.

"Are you keeping—that girl—up at the castle?"

Dame Alianor screamed at him suddenly, "Aye—he has her in your bed—" and she pointed at it.

Fulcun looked at Geroy, and Geroy says jauntily, "Well, what of it?" but his eyes went away from Fulcun's.

Fulcun said, "I'll not have her here." He had, for those few seconds, forgotten that Alde was asleep in the cornfield below. He remembered now, and he thought of her in this room that seemed full of lustful ugliness. Without knowing what he was doing he went over to one of the windows and tugged open a shutter that had swung to. He must let in some sweeter air.

Geroy says, very sulky, "If I do send her away it won't bring me back to that old scarecrow there." He pointed at Alianor, and she cried out.

Fulcun says again, "I'll not have her here," but when Geroy growled, "Why not?" he was silent.

Then he told them, very curt, with his eyes on Geroy.

It was Custance who laughed suddenly, the wild, loud, ungoverned laughter of the serf. "Oh! And he'll have me out to make room for his woman!"

Fulcun looked at her. "Hold your tongue!" he told her, and she said no more and stopped laughing.

Geroy swore, "Blood of God! You cuckold a man, and kill him, and bring off his wife, and then you say you'll not have my wench under your roof."

He went over to the bed and dragged Custance up by the arm.

"Come on, wench," he says. "Get you in and make that bed ready for us, since better folk than you and me must have the great chamber now." He gave Custance a shove toward the door of the room that he and his wife had used to sleep in.

Alianor started after her. "And where shall I?" she cried and stopped.

Geroy laughed. "Oh! Where you will, so that it's not with me."

She looked at him, and then at Fulcun. She said, "Sorrow that I ever saw one of your cursed house!" and she turned and went out from them.

Fulcun stood still with his back to the window. He kept his eyes down on the ground because he dared not look at Geroy for the rage in him that could not break out.

Geroy says, confident now, "And who is she, Fulcun?"

Fulcun told him, "The man was Mauger of Fervacques."

"Fervacques?"

"Rogier of Montgommeri's land."

"Oh!" says Geroy, "Normandy! But we hold of Mayenne."

"No. I'm the duke's man now for Montgaudri," Fulcun said. Geroy must know.

"God's Death!" Geroy shouted. "You fool, then! You've brought Rogier down on us, and he's viscount in the Hiesmois."

Fulcun says, "He'll not move. We're too near the March of Mayenne for them to meddle with us for a dead man's sake."

Geroy was frowning and tapping on his teeth. "Well," he muttered, "I suppose you can always patch it up by sending her off again," and looked up to meet Fulcun's eyes staring at him.

"God forbid," says Fulcun, very hard and quiet.

Geroy laughed rudely, "Oh—God? D'you think he will like to see me snug in there tonight with Custance and you here with your wench?" He swung away past Fulcun to the door. "What's her name?" he turned to ask.

"Alde," Fulcun told him without looking at him.

When Geroy was gone he did not move for a bit, except to turn his back on the room and stare out through the window to the open sky and the hills below.

He felt sick—sick with the anger that he had no right to show. And he was sick too with bewilderment. Geroy and Custance—he and Alde. It was the same thing. And it was a thing utterly different. He thought of God looking down on them this morning on the hillside, in the still, early sunlight. God had seen that, and that was the same. But then he thought of God looking into the blind dusk of his mind, and seeing there a thing he could not clearly see himself. It was a dumb aching want, a fettered desire, a need—but of what? He could not tell, only it seemed to him that the thing that moved there in the darkness was love. But what was love? A faint memory stirred. Someone had said something to him once that would tell him. Who had said it? What was it? He could not remember.

He went to the door and shouted in the hall for folk to come and make ready the chamber. When they came in, and while they were sweeping and strewing fresh rushes and laying on the rushes two red deerskins from the chest at the bed's foot, Fulcun sat on the edge of the bed watching them, and trying to understand what it was that the thing in his mind needed so painfully, and to remember what it was that someone had said.

The first question, had he known it, was easy, and he answered it himself. He sat for a while fidgeting on the bed, full of discontent. He would have liked to help to strew the rushes, or spread the skins out, if it would not have made him look too much of a fool. In the end he got up and flung open the big chest and rummaged there. He pulled out at last a steel mirror wrapped in a bit of soft kidskin and polished it fresh on the skirt of his gown. He found a comb there too and laid them both on the lid of the chest. Then he sat down a little satisfied, because he had been able to do something for her.

❦

That night as he came up from the reapers' feast in the yard, he was again trying to make himself think of the thing he could not remember, because he was almost afraid to think of her as he would find her, in the great chamber where the lights were lit and shone warm yellow to the night.

He went in. Richereda, Osmunt's wife, was holding up the mirror for her. Alde stood, in her long, white, crumpled shift, and her hands were busy in her hair, loosening one plait; the hair leaped in her fingers and shone as she shook it free.

Fulcun took the mirror from Richereda, and she went away.

Alde said hastily, "I should have been ready."

Fulcun dropped the mirror on the bench. "Never mind your hair," he says curtly, and laid his hand on the bed curtains and ran them back, clattering the rings along the bar.

It was when he wakened in the dark and lay holding his breath so that he could hear Alde breathe beside him that the thing he had tried to remember came suddenly into his mind. The words were Robert Geroy's words as they sat together in the sunshine by the sheep-dipping pool.

Robert had said, "A great kindness . . . and care . . . Very great."

Indeed it was very great. He felt Alde stir, her fingers touched his hand. He knew then, though obscurely, that it was even greater than he had yet learned; a care as heavy as the weight of the round world, a kindness as sharp and wounding as a sword.

II

Fulcun had thought, when he had found Geroy and Custance in the great chamber, and Dame Alianor, desperate as a cornered rat, that it was unthinkable Alde should be brought into such wretched company; or, since she must be brought, that they would live all together in Montgaudri tower in a miserable state of war. But it was not so. For one thing there are few dark and unpleasant places that the habit of kinship cannot cover over, for a time at least, with a thin flooring of planks to make all decent. For another—Alde was Alde.

Fulcun watched her with Geroy. Geroy greeted her that first night, as she came limping into the great hall, with a courtesy that was sharpened to insolence by his grin and his stare. And she had met him with her straight gaze; first an intent, serious look, and then a smile as frank as her voice.

"Sir," she says, "I know you are my lord's brother. Will you be good friends with me?"

Geroy stared more, stammered, and said he would; if he was not that, he was always pleasant to her. It seemed to Fulcun that he even went out of his way to try to make her think well of him. As for Dame Alianor, she was irreconcilable, but they saw little of her. She went about alone among the folk, a small, bitter shadow, speaking to no one, and answering nothing if she were spoken to. Baudri, after a day or two of awkward defiance, and one sound cuffing from Fulcun, came round altogether. He followed Alde about like a dog, stared at her only most of the time he was supposed to be waiting on them all at table, and made a very pointed difference between the way he brought her the bread or filled her wine cup and the way he served Custance. Geroy grinned at that. He liked to plague Custance, and she lost her temper easily.

She did not have a chance of using it against Alde, for Alde treated her with a sober, delicate, serene courtesy that was like a wall with no gate in it. Custance, stormy, resentful, passionate serf wench as she was, had no chance against the high certainty of Alde's utterly unconscious pride.

Alde was sure—that was what Fulcun loved to watch her for—sure of herself and of other people. One day he overheard a brush between her and Richereda. He was coming across the hall to the door of the great chamber, and he heard Richereda's voice, "What? Cook boar's chaps so? That's no way to cook boar's chaps."

"It's my way," says Alde, quite cool and easy. "Do it so."

Richereda said something that Fulcun lost, and then he heard Alde's voice say, "Come here!" in a different tone, and then the sound of a hearty slap. "If my lord heard you say that," Alde says, "you'd get a beating."

He was at the door then and went in to them. Richereda had her hands up to her ears.

"What did she say?" says he to Alde, his face very dark. "I'll have her beaten."

Alde only shook her head. "No—you didn't hear it," she told him, and he saw her eyes shine and knew she was laughing at him.

It was things like these made him very happy and made him worship Alde in a kind of wonder. It was strange and exquisite delight to know that the creature he so loved was in plain truth a thing so lovable. And when he thought of the love that she gave him, which was as strong and simple as she was herself, it was a marvel to him. He grew humble in his thoughts those days, for he set her very high above him—and higher yet because of her submission.

Once, when they were in the orchard together, he could not keep that growing passion of humility dumb any longer. It was a still evening, with a sky empty of cloud, and the sun, shining low, lit up the red lamps of the Duke Richart apples till they burned like fire and gave the pears a sunset glow of gold and a flush of rose.

She said, "It's too late for the bees to swarm again this year, isn't it?" and she looked away toward the row of hives, each with its little doorway facing the morning east. He did not answer, and then he cried suddenly, "Alde! Oh, Alde—and I'm a bastard!" but he meant far more than that.

She looked at him then, intently, as though she did not understand; and indeed she could not, but she guessed a little. She caught his wrist in both her hands and held it hard and said with her eyes straight on his, speaking urgently, "You're my heart."

He was looking at her, but his face darkened. She could have thought he had not heard what she said. He had heard, but he had hardly time to mark it, beyond the pang of joy it gave him, because another thought had come.

He said fiercely to her, "It was my fault. All my fault. But I tried to go from Falaise. I should have gone, only Hernaut came." He stopped and then muttered, as his thoughts went back to those days, "I did not know I loved you till that night it thundered."

Her hands were firm about his wrists. She said, "I loved you long before that. The first time I saw you—on the tower—I was watching you."

His face cleared. She had not answered his trouble but she had thrust it away. He asked her, "Truly, Alde?" and she nodded at him half smiling; but the smile was a caress.

He smiled again at her, and then suddenly he jerked his head back and his hands caught her arms and held her.

"Alde!" he said, and she saw his face strange with pain or fear—she did not know which.

"What is it, sir?" she cried to him.

"I could not give you up." His own voice and the words themselves startled him. The thought had come into his mind, but how he did not know, nor whence. Only it had fallen like a dropping arrow out of the air and now lodged, quivering.

"I will not. I could not!" he said between his teeth as they stared at each other, she understanding little but that it was Fulcun and in pain, and he trying to bar his mind against any understanding.

He saw her distress. He laughed suddenly and put his hand over her eyes. Then he pulled her veil away so that he could set his lips on her throat. There was nothing he could not forget when he let passion run full flood.

The harvest was all in and the hedges down so that the cattle strayed where they liked through the stubble fields, and the geese were fattening up for Michaelmas. Very soon the villagers would be gathering the grapes from Montgaudri's one vineyard, and after that, men looked forward to plowing and winnowing and to the winter.

One morning Fulcun was in the stable with Osmunt looking over the sorrel horse. Osmunt had said that there was a swelling in the fetlock of the near hind leg. Fulcun squatted now on his heels and lifted the hoof. Osmunt stood behind him.

"Ho!" says Osmunt, who was staring out of the door. "Here's Herfast the priest."

Fulcun was feeling along the sorrel's leg; for one long second he did not move his hand. Then he says, "You're right. He mustn't be ridden today."

He got up and went out of the stable and across the yard. The wind, which drove big bulging gray clouds across a paler gray sky, snatched at his gown and switched his cloak across his face. He caught Herfast up at the doorway of the tower.

"You're welcome," he says to the priest, and went before him into the hall, calling to someone to bring ale and cakes.

He set Herfast down at the high table and, while they waited, talked to him about the harvest so that Herfast should not say anything. But when one of the women had brought a horn of ale, and cakes on a beech-wood plate, Fulcun turned to Herfast.

"Priest," he says, "what is it that you've heard?"

Herfast was drinking. He stopped and wiped his hand over the bristles round his mouth.

"Sire," says he. "That you've stolen another man's wife."

Fulcun said, with his eyes hard on the priest, "He is dead. I killed him." Best to have the black truth out at once.

But Herfast looked relieved. "O!" he says, and took another pull at the horn. "That's very different. Then there's no adultery."

Fulcun was frowning at him. He had not thought of that. But—yes—it must be very different. He had never set much store by Herfast, but after all the man was a priest. He had the right to speak with authority, and it was Fulcun's duty to believe him.

So he said, "What shall I do now?"

"You're sure he's dead?" Herfast was peering at him with his dull blue eyes as he crammed a cake into his mouth.

"I struck him on the head with my sword. I felt jagged bone in his hair, and blood. I felt at his heart—I couldn't find any life in him. It was in the dark." Fulcun did not like this talking, but it must be done.

"Well," says Herfast, "if he's dead you must do penance and make offerings, and then I'll marry you both—if you're keeping her."

Fulcun looked at his hands on the table. It was a long time since he had thought that the world could be so easy a place. "When will you marry us?" he asked.

"I'll confess you if you come to Mass on Sunday. And then, since the business is like as it is, I'll cry your banns, and then I'll marry you. That's a month." He looked at Fulcun and saw him frowning. "That's not long—and what with one thing and another," Herfast says, "I daren't do more for you."

Fulcun nodded and drew a deep breath. "And then," he said, "God will leave off to be angry with me?" He asked Herfast as if he should know.

Herfast says, "Aye, when you've done penance—and made offering."

Fulcun jumped up. "I'll make offering now—something." He stood a moment thinking, and then hurried off to the great chamber. Alde was there, darning a tear in the bed curtains. He only glanced at her and went over to the bench were his great drinking horn lay; it was a white horn capped and rimmed with silver, and the rim was chased with a pattern of slim leopards slinking low after a deer and a fawn. There was a little wine in the curve of it, for he and Alde had drunk out of it this morning (now that she was at Montgaudri he used all the finest things he had), and as he shook it out on the floor he was glad that somehow she shared with him in the gift. He went hastily back to Herfast and pushed the horn into his hands. "And I'll bring a mark of silver for the altar when I come to Cortilly," he said.

Nor was that all. When Herfast went away that afternoon, he went mounted, though he had come on foot. Fulcun watched him from Montgaudri gate. Herfast was riding the black stallion, the horse that had brought Alde and Fulcun from Falaise.

On Sunday, which was a softly drenching day, they rode out early. Fulcun had the mark of silver in a bag at his belt. Osmunt's youngest son came with them, riding a spear's cast behind. Halfway to Cortilly, when they were going through Little High Wood, the rain left off, though while they were still among the trees there was a constant irregular mutter of water dripping and sometimes a scattering of heavy big drops falling down on them from the leaves. But when they came out on the hillside above Cortilly the clouds were rolling up together into soft floating mists and the sun was warming the hillside through them. The horses' flanks and their own cloaks began to steam, and the pale sunset-colored bents were all bowed down and hung with clustered drops of silver as if with heavy rime. Young Herluin behind them sang to himself as he rode.

Alde was gay too, and Fulcun, listening to her talking about Ardoye, and the dogs that had been at home, and the horses, was cheerful. They were going to confess, and then he would make his offering, and do penance—any penance. And afterward God would cease to be angry. Herfast had said so.

The bell in the wooden tower of Cortilly church began to swing. They were so near that they heard the creak and rattle of the beam. Then the bell rang, a harsh note with a humming aftersong that the sound of the clapper caught and drowned.

Fulcun pulled up, and pushed on again, but his face was stony. This was the same bell that he had heard that evening on the hillside waiting for Custance, and it spoke the same monotonous, merciless refusal. He rode on now, because, having come so far, he must go on, but he had no hope of pardon, or only so much as a man's mind can always get by a desperate self-deception. All the time the bell rang he was answering it monotonously, "I love her. It is good. I love her. It is good."

But when they knelt in the dark church with Herfast fumbling and muttering at the altar, and when the priest put the bread on Fulcun's tongue, Fulcun knew that God said to him, "You must not have this woman," and he answered, "I love her."

That was all, but it was everything.

That night Alde wakened and knew that Fulcun had stirred. A thin sliver of light came from the hanging lamp through the curtains, where they gaped apart at the top; it was an unsteady blinking light, and Alde remembered that she had not had the lamp filled yesterday. She raised her head from Fulcun's arm to look at him. His eyes were open, and he was staring at her. Just then the lamp flared and went out.

He did not move to pull her close as she expected, but said in a low voice, "Alde, I've been thinking."

She whispered, "Yes," not knowing why she was frightened.

He waited a long time before he spoke again, and then he turned his face sharply away and spoke to the curtains of the bed.

"In your mind," he said, "is this sin?"

She said, "No," and felt his body relax. She only knew then how tightly strained his muscles had been.

"Are you sure? Quite sure?"

She said, "Quite sure—" and then added, "When the priest has married us," and when he said nothing, "He is dead— Mauger." It was the first time she had spoken that name, and he knew it, and they lay silent for a while.

She moved at last and caught his head and held it to her breast. She thought he would forget that way, but he drew back and almost pushed her from him.

That drove her to cry out. "Fulcun," she said, "I don't care. I don't care if God hates me . . . if . . . if . . . if you do not."

He knew she was crying; he had seen her cry only once before, and again, just as that other time, she was holding herself rigid, fighting against her tears.

He took her in his arms then and was very tender with her. But when she had fallen asleep, he lay awake, staring into the dark. He was not afraid that God should hate Alde; it was not possible for him to conceive of anyone hating her. But again and again, and clearer every time, he had heard God's voice condemning this thing that was too great and grave to be called love—this care and kindness that were good and, being good, could have no home but with God himself. God had said, "It is sin." Fulcun knew that it was sin and knew too that it was holy.

Chapter 9

If thy hand offend thee, cut it off. . . . If thine eye offend thee, pluck it out. . . . It is better for thee . . .

Mark 9:43–47

I

The fair weather that had held all September broke suddenly toward the end of the month. One morning it was very bright and clear at sunrise, but the wind got up as the sun mounted higher, and brought white, quick-sailing clouds, and gathered them, and filled the sky till it was all one gray. Then the rain came, blowing in gusts and blotting out the outlines of the hills. In the hall and the great chamber the shutters of the western windows had to be barred, so that the rooms were dark, and whenever the door to the kitchen opened, the smoke came beating in.

Fulcun was busy at the perches with one of his hawks, a young brancher that would not take its meat, when Alde came in. Her cloak was wet with the rain and her wet veil clung to her hair. She took both off and dropped them on a bench. Then she came to Fulcun and stood near him.

He turned. "What is it?" he says.

"Sir, we want for barley flour. There's none for the folks' puddings."

"We have plenty of rye."

"Yes, sir, I know. But that is no use for puddings. It makes them all soft so that they run about the platters."

"There's barley threshed," says Fulcun. All yesterday the courtyard had resounded to the clatter of the flails. "But we can't winnow in this rain." He was frowning at the young hawk that would not eat.

He picked up the lump of raw meat and went over toward the window to toss it out into the yard. It was that window that looked out over the town; the window from which he had watched Custance go out. Now, as he moved across the hall, he heard Custance in the great chamber. She was shouting. Dame Alianor must have come down, for it was her thin voice that answered. Fulcun frowned darker.

Alde says, "Sir, you are angry with me."

Fulcun turned, with his head at the window.

"Alde!" he said. "No!" speaking deep and quick in the way that made her heart stand still in surprise at what love was. He tossed the raw meat out, thinking only of going to her to make her sure he was not angry, but even as he was turning he glanced through the window, his eye caught perhaps by something that moved out there.

He stood quite still for as long as it takes an apple to fall from a tree, and then he was leaning out of the window, both hands to his mouth, shouting with all his strength into the gusty rain.

"Ho! there! The town gate! Shut the town gate! Shut the town gate! Up with the bridge!"

The Montgaudri horn that Osmunt blew every morning to send out the serfs to work and every evening to call them home hung by a leather strap from a hook on the wall. Fulcun reached it and wrenched it down so that the leather snapped. He was at the window again in two strides, and blowing it, and then shouting again. "Shut the town gate!"

Out in the midst of the rain, along the hillside, moved a clump of riders coming steadily toward the open gate of Montgaudri. Their spears were all slanted forward, and the drenched banners, dark with rain, danced with the pace of the horses.

Fulcun was out of the hall and down the stairs. He had his sword bare in his hand; there was no time for arming. As he ran out of the hall, he saw Geroy come in, and shouted to him, but Geroy shouted back, "I'll arm first—" Fulcun left him to it. As he ran out of the castle with other men following him from the stables and brew house and barn, there were four of the Montgaudri serfs at the town gate. They strained at the bridge ropes, heaving and stamping back. The bridge came up, slowly, faster, till it stood upright, and checked with a rattle. When Fulcun reached it there were a dozen fellows about the gate. The two halves swung to, jolting and grinding. The bolts were rammed in, and the great bar shot. It was done in time, but only just in time. A horn blew up outside the pale, and everyone stood still in the silence that followed.

"Who comes to Montgaudri?" Fulcun shouted.

The answer came, "Rogier of Montgommeri—" and in Rogier's own voice. "Fulcun Geroy," he cried. "Bid them open me the gate. I bring the duke's summons."

Fulcun laughed. "I can hear well enough with the gate shut. You'll not get it open that way."

Rogier neither laughed nor grew angry. He says, very courteous still, "Come up to the pale then, so that I can give my message."

"I'll do so much," says Fulcun, and turned to go up the wooden roundway that went along the inner side of the pale, not quite a man's height below the top. But first he told the men with spears to get up on the walk, and those with bows to get under cover, "Or your strings will slack in the rain," he says.

Rogier was just opposite to Fulcun on the edge of the ditch, and behind him there were perhaps threescore mounted men. But Fulcun looked only at Rogier. He was a thin man with a hooked nose and a blue jaw. He had a stiff way with him, always stately and courteous and unbending, so that men spoke to him as if he were older than his years. His voice was the best of him outwardly, for it was deep and musical.

Fulcun laid his naked sword along the top of the pale and leaned both hands on it, his right on the hilt, and the other across the blade.

"Now, Rogier of Montgommeri," he said, "give me the duke's summons."

Before Rogier could speak, some of the knights behind him shouted and pressed on. "There he is," one yelled. Fulcun thought he knew that voice, but there were many shouting. He shook his fist at them all. Rogier's horse had danced aside at the noise and he cried to his men, waving them back, but now he brought his horse again to the very edge of the ditch and held it there. The rain was drenching down between them. Fulcun felt it soak through his kirtle and drum on his shoulders like small fingers. It ran down Rogier's helmet and hung in a row of great drops along the worked copper brow band above his eyes. Rogier raised his hand and brushed them away now and again so that he could see Fulcun clear.

"Hear the summons then, Fulcun Geroy," he said, and he gave it out. He gave it very well, for he was a good lawyer. Fulcun Geroy of Montgaudri was in the duke's mercy for life and limb and goods, because he had drawn his sword and struck one of the duke's men, in the duke's castle, and within seven days of the return of the host. And also, to that, he had done rape upon the wife of the man, Mauger of Fervacques.

Fulcun says, when it was finished. "I have heard you, Rogier. Now you can go back."

A man moved behind Rogier—it was a man in a great green cloak; Fulcun saw his arm jerk up, but someone caught him back, and just then Ruald, Mauger's brother, pushed out.

"Not till we have the woman," he shouted. "Put her out of the gate to us. You'd best, you Geroy swine!"

Fulcun turned to look at Ruald. He began to smile, and then the smile died. The man in the green cloak had come up alongside; he had a broad heavy face; you could hardly see his eyes for the shadow of the helmet and the eyelids that drooped over them.

He cried out now, "Curse you! Give her to me. By God, you shall!"

Fulcun looked at him, and then looked, slowly and wood-enly, at all of them, as if they should deny that it was Mauger of Fervacques, who rode with them, a living man, not dead.

Then he turned to Mauger.

"I'll die first," he said.

Mauger had his spear lifted, but Rogier of Montgommeri saw it, and he beat the shaft down with the blade of his own. "Back, Mauger," he cried, and then turned to Fulcun.

He said, "Mauger is my man. You know me, Fulcun Geroy?"

He stopped and waited. Fulcun did not know what he was driving at, so he waited too, saying nothing.

"Would you trust in my sworn word?" says Rogier.

Fulcun said, yes, he would.

"Then if you put the woman out to us, I will be her surety. Neither Mauger nor any of Mauger's house shall do her harm for this. I swear it to you—on the cross of God," and he lifted up his sword and put his hand on the cross quillons. "They shall answer to me," he says, "if harm is done her, hurt for hurt."

Fulcun stood still. Mauger cried out, "If he will not?" He pushed his horse close to Rogier and caught Rogier's wrist in his hand. "I'll not leave her here. If you'll not help me take her from him, I'll stay alone. But you're my lord and my blood cousin. Will you see me shamed and the Geroy laugh?"

Rogier bade him, "Keep silent!" but Mauger's kin behind muttered at that, and someone cried out, "We'll not leave you, Mauger."

Fulcun had not moved. Now he turned slowly from them all and looked up at the tower, but he did not know why he looked.

When he turned back his face was empty. Rogier thought that in a moment he would say, "Take her then." Rogier wanted it settled quietly so that they could get back to Séez tonight. He did not want to try to burn down Montgaudri to get the woman; that would be to break the duke's peace; but Mauger was his cousin, and blood is a strong obligation.

He said, "You'd best, Fulcun Geroy. Your own house has disowned you. Robert Geroy of Saint-Céneri stood up before the duke and cast you out from them for all suits and quarrels."

Still Fulcun did not answer. He was gripping the top of the pale with both hands. When the fingers of his left hand slipped on the wet wood he gripped the naked sword blade and did not know till afterward that it had cut him to the bone.

At last he said, "I will not give her up for God himself."

Rogier of Montgommeri tossed up one hand to the dull sky, as though he called witness, and in that second there was a shout from Mauger, "There then, bastard!" and a spear went flying level.

Fulcun ducked down behind the pale. His sword fell clattering on the planks of the roundway. The spear had gone close over his shoulder, and now it jarred and leapt on a stone in the path behind, and fell.

"Throw!" yelled Fulcun, and leapt down after it. He caught it, and using it as a staff, vaulted up again, and threw it. There were many spears flying in and out of Montgaudri town for a minute, and then all the Montgaudri men shouted aloud. Rogier of Montgommeri had gone down out of the saddle with a spear through his shoulder. They shouted the more when they saw his people draw off a little way, carrying him with them; they did not think that his fall was their own undoing. With Rogier down, Mauger and the rest were neither to hold nor bind.

Fulcun picked up his sword from where it had fallen, and shook it high in the air against them. He laughed. He was hugely angry, and merry with it.

Then he remembered who it was, alive, among those fellows out there, and the laughter was wiped off his mouth.

He turned from the pale, and saw Geroy armed, leaning on his spear, just below the wall. He said, "Stay here with half the folk, while I and the rest go up and arm."

He went back beside Osmunt. Osmunt told him that he had sent out three carts to Great High Wood this morning to fetch the faggots that had lain cut there since July. And there were men working down in the valley.

"I cannot help," says Fulcun. "They're out. They must stay out." All his thought now was to go straight to Alde.

Osmunt guessed it. He thought of Montgaudri, and of his own sheep that were with the flock outside. He spat in the middle of the road, "Curse the bitch!" he said to himself.

When they came to the yard Fulcun stopped short. "Osmunt," he says, "go up and fetch my arms. I'll not come up. There are things I must see to here. And bid Dame Alde keep the women from the windows for fear of arrows."

He knew that he could not bear to see her now. He turned off to the big barn where they kept the grain, and when he got in he pushed the door half to, so that he moved in a dusty twilight among the sacks. He went from end to end of the rows three

times, counting and recounting, because each time he forgot
what the number of them was. All his mind was full of one
darkness—Mauger was alive, not dead.

He went out at last and saw Osmunt coming down from
the tower with his arms. He thought, with a sudden clenching
of his teeth, that he would keep that darkness to himself. Alde
should not know.

It was evening before he could go up again to the castle. Half
an hour after their first coming Montgommeri's men were at the
ditch again, but with them they had three oxcarts, and carried
high on the blades of spears, five round things—the heads of the
men that had gone off this morning, sitting on the shafts of the
carts, and swinging their legs, and whistling.

At the best of times Montgaudri town ditch was not very
deep. But when it was full of bundles of the faggots from Great
High Wood there was an easy way over to the pale. And besides
the faggots Montgommeri's men had brought a great ash trunk.
They drew off from the ditch now and were busy about it.

Osmunt turned to Fulcun. There were men sprawling on the
far side of the ditch, and one hung by his leather coat from the
edge of the piled faggots, but for all their labor the Montgaudri
men had not been able to keep the ditch clear.

Osmunt says, "We must burn that wood."

"Too wet," says Fulcun. The rain had not lifted all day.

"Try."

"You may try." Someone fetched a brazier of hot coals and
tipped it over the pale on to the faggots. They hissed, spat, crack-
led faintly, and then the little flames fluttered and went out.

Montgommeri's men came on again. They had made slings out of the harness from the oxcarts. The ash trunk made a very fair ram.

Geroy, on Fulcun's left hand, said quickly, "The pale won't stand that. We must get back to the castle."

Fulcun turned on him. "They mustn't get to the pale," he says, and shouted for men to be ready.

The arrows began to go up again from both sides, leaping up and dropping like fishes, and the long spears flying level between them. Montgommeri's men came on. They trampled across the faggots, staggering and plunging. The ram took the timbers with a jar that shook the pale. It swung out and in again with another crash, and another shiver of the wood. Fulcun caught the top to steady himself as the roundwall rocked. He heard in all the din the groaning of the strained timbers.

He turned and shouted at Osmunt, "Go up through the town and drive anyone who's there to the castle. This is too hot. We—"

He stopped. Osmunt had clapped his hands to his face and bent double as though something had stung him. The shaft of an arrow stuck out through his fingers; the barb had gone in at the midst of his black beard. He toppled off the roundway and lay on his side on the ground; his legs moved as though he were trying to climb up a steep stair.

Then Fulcun saw Geroy going off up the street. He was shouting. He had no shield nor spear. A few of the men at the pale jumped down and ran after him. Fulcun yelled, "Stand to it! God!" and the wall rocked again under the blow of the ram.

They stood to it for ten minutes more, and then the pale went. Fulcun felt the boards of the roundway heave and tilt. He leaped, came down on all fours, and was up again.

"Back to the castle!" The men bunched about him and they began to go back. "Steady!" he shouted. The ram came through the pale as they got into the street between the cottages, and when it drew out Montgommeri's men came through the great gap.

They fought all up the street. Fulcun, who had got no worse than a bleeding gash across his cheek, labored away like a smith's man. He had dropped his shield and worked with a bill in his left hand and his sword in his right. He was near to madness, thinking that they might not get back to the castle gate—remembering that he had not gone up to Alde this morning, and that now he might never go up to her again.

They came to the castle ditch and made a stand there, and then there were shouts from behind them, and they heard the strings of the bows twang sharp and the arrows go past with their shrill wailing hiss. The crowd of shields and swinging swords in front of them melted away. Fulcun stood a minute and then turned, and trampled in over the bridge after the rest, and felt the timbers leap and spring under his feet.

They got the bridge up, and shut the gate, and then stood ready. But it was dusk, and Montgommeri's men had had enough. When Fulcun had set a guard he went across the yard. Geroy was by him.

"We saved you then," says Geroy.

Fulcun looked at him. "Yes—" he says, then hastily, "Yes—you did so." But he was not thinking of Geroy at all.

⚜

Fulcun came from the hall into the light and warmth of the great chamber. The brazier there was lit; it was the first fire of the autumn, and made the room, with all the shutters barred, seem to be a place of quiet security, of shelter and peace. Alde got up as he came in. She took a step toward him, "You're hurt," she cried, but he shook his head and she stood still.

She said, "I sent them away. I have got a bath ready for you."

He saw the bath steaming behind her, and a lump of black soap beside it on a wooden dish. He dropped on one of the benches and let his head go down on his hands.

"I don't want a bath," he says, and knew he had hurt her, but he was almost glad because of his own pain.

"Come here," he told her. He did not know what he would do when she came. He had a black thought that if he could make her cry out it might ease him, but he was ashamed of that.

She came close and stood by him. Without lifting his head he could see her green gown and her red shoes—they were the shoes she had come to Montgaudri in; he could see the place where she had stitched the leather that Ruald's spear had slit.

He leaped up suddenly and threw his hands wide so that they should not touch her, and pressed them, palms open, against the wall, leaning back on them.

Then he said what he had meant not to say.

"Mauger is not dead."

It was out. He waited for horror to come to her face, but her eyes were steady on his. She was slow.

"He is alive?"

"He is outside," Fulcun told her, and still she stared at him; then her face changed, but to fear, and not to horror.

"Fulcun!" she cried.

He did not move, and she could not come near him while he stood so still and with that look on his face. She whispered, "You are going to give me back?"

"No!" Fulcun cried, as though the word was wrenched out of him.

They looked at each other, dumb for a moment. Then Fulcun said, "He is alive. It is mortal sin."

She murmured vaguely, "Sin?" as though she did not know what that word meant. Then she lifted her head; she stretched out her hands to him, but still she would not touch him. "Fulcun!" she cried. "What do you mean? I could not live without you."

He flung himself off the wall then and caught her. As he kissed her, harsh terrible kisses, he muttered—she did not know what. He only knew what were the words that were crushed on her lips and eyes and throat—he was telling her that he could not live without this—this. And she should never go—never.

II

Alde wakened next morning out of a deep peace and turned to Fulcun—but he was gone. That brought all of yesterday back. Montgaudri town was lost; Mauger was alive; Fulcun had said "It is mortal sin." All that came into her mind at once and snuffed out the light in it like a candle flame. The only thing she knew in the darkness was that Fulcun was gone out and might not come in again.

She sprang up, pulled on her shift and her gown, put her shoes on bare feet, and veiled her hair without pinning it. She must go to him—quick. It could not be true. It could not be sin to be with Fulcun. She was in an extremity of terror.

There were a great many people in the hall, all women and children: not only the house servants were there but women from the town, and it was dark, for the shutters were barred round about. She went through the crowd, and the women made way for her. As she passed she heard one say, "Aye, that's her. It's because of her," but she did not then think what that meant. She must get to Fulcun.

He was in the yard. He stood with his feet apart, leaning on the sheathed sword that he had not yet belted on, as he watched the men who were carrying out spears from the store, and fresh arrows, and rolling stones nearer to the wall so as to be handy for throwing if they should lack arrows.

He saw her. "Alde!" he cried, and then, "You must not come here."

She said, "You went while I was asleep." Her eyes were on his face. If she could only watch his face that she loved so, she need not think. She said suddenly, because she must touch him, "Sir, let me do on your sword." She went down on her knees and had it out of his hands before he could answer, and her arms were about him.

"Alde," he cried, "you must go in. You're not safe here. If you were killed—"

She said, with her face against him, a thing she had not thought to say, "I should be glad to be dead." It startled her. But he did not hear it.

He caught her suddenly by the arms and lifted her.

"Run! Run in!" he shouted. A shadow ran down out of the sky and became an arrow. It struck slanting into the ground a dozen paces from them. Another fell just beyond.

"Fulcun!" she cried. She thought, "If one should strike him."

"God!" he shouted at her and pushed her fiercely. "Run in!"

She turned to obey and then saw something that stayed her. A fat, naked two-year-old lad was staggering across the yard. He must have slipped out from the hall and climbed down the stairs. Now he ran unsteadily, with his elbows up, toward an arrow that stood in the ground beyond the well. He reached it and tried to haul it out.

Alde cried, "Come here!" and began to run to him. He looked at her. He was frightened at her voice. He dropped the arrow and stumbled on.

Someone began to scream from the steps of the tower and went on screaming as she came blundering down. It was the child's mother, a red-haired woman called Eremburge.

Alde did not scream, but she ran. She was nearly within reach, her hands were stretched out to catch up the little naked lad; then she checked, jerking her head back, as if from a blow.

A slim black thing came down through the air before her eyes. She thought, even as she checked, "It has missed him," but it had not missed.

Without a cry the child fell, and the arrowhead stood out beside its backbone.

Alde staring at it, could for a second think of nothing but the size of the arrow and the smallness of the child. The long shaft of tough, waxed wood, stubbed with harsh feathers and barbed with iron—it was far too big a thing for the soft, small body.

She stooped and lifted it, and that moment Fulcun was on her, and the mother.

Fulcun snatched it from her and thrust it into Eremburge's arms.

"Here," he cried, "take your brat," and then to Alde, "Get in! Get in!" His eyes were blazing. She turned and ran.

At the tower door she waited for Eremburge who came laboring up after her, sobbing, with the child clutched to her.

Alde said, "I tried to catch him."

Eremburge went by her with a blind look. As she climbed up the stairs she cried out in a wail that was shaken with sobs, "If you'd stayed with your wedded man there'd 'a been no need." She blundered on and into the hall, sobbing and screaming.

Alde went up slowly after her. When she passed through the hall they made way for her again, but this time she heard the words they said, and understood them. She even understood their silence. She went into the great chamber and sat down there. They had lit the lamp and a couple of candles. Custance was there, and Dame Alianor. Dame Alianor spoke.

"Well, mistress, how do you like your handiwork in Montgaudri?"

Alde turned a blank face to her but she did not speak. Custance stared under her black brows from one to another.

For the rest of that day, till the darkness came, Alde sat with the other two women in the candlelight, listening to the shouts and clatter outside, and the great dunting shock of the ram on the castle pale, or went out into the hall to wash and tend wounded men that came dragging themselves up, or were carried in, with their hands and feet trailing. They ate in the hall and sent down food for the men in the yard, and now and again someone brought them news. But all the time, and whatever Alde did with her hands, within her mind there were heavy millstones that slowly turned and ground. She had to keep them turning though the effort to move the weight of them was a huge pain; and yet, while it was she herself that must turn them, the tortured thing between the stones—that too was herself. Because she was simple those millstones were too plain thoughts. Because she was slow it took all day before the work was done. Because she was honest she could not stop.

A little naked brat spitted by a long arrow— That could not have happened if she had not done mortal sin. Fulcun had spoken the truth. It *was* mortal sin.

Just before dark the noise in the yard grew louder. Alde stood up. Custance ran out into the hall. Dame Alianor sat still, gripping the bench with her hands and thrusting hard at the floor with her feet.

Then the women rushed in at them screaming. In all the confusion Alde heard "Fire!" "The pale down," and last, "Lord Fulcun dead." They laid their hands on her, not in anger now, but in pure fear. She pushed through them and into the hall, and there she stood, waiting, with no thought in her mind except that if he were dead, nothing mattered. Now and again an arrow struck into the shutters with a sound like a great gout of rain.

But Fulcun was not dead. After a little the noise slackened and dropped. Soon there was a sound of trampling on the stairs. The men began to come up. Fulcun was among them.

He saw her, he took her hand in his left hand—his sword was bare in the other—and led her back to the great chamber. He told her not to be frightened. The pale was broken through, but they had beaten back Montgommeri's men twice and would again tomorrow. He said, "They'll soon have had their belly full."

In the great chamber, as she unarmed him and Custance did the same for Geroy, Fulcun caught her by the wrist and dragged her down and whispered to her. She turned her face away. He cried, "What? Alde!" His voice was angry, but still she shook her head. He said no more then, but she saw him watching her, and she dreaded the night.

Yet, when he had gone to sleep at last, she would have given all the world to have even that awful time over again, because it was the last time—the last.

She lay in the dark forcing herself not to move closer so that she might feel the touch of his body. She had refused him; he had struck her, and still she had refused him. She had expected another blow, but his hand dropped, and instead he looked at her with such a wounded face that she thought she could not endure.

He had laid himself down then and been so quiet for a while that she thought he was asleep. But he spoke, "Alde, did I hurt you?" His hands came out to her and touched her, but she did not move. He said, "Won't you forgive me?"

She cried, "Yes," but she did not turn to him, she dared have no mercy, and after a minute he drew his hands away. She lay still and knew that never—never would his arms be about her again.

It seemed an age of agony till he was sound asleep, and yet the time went far too soon, since still for this little while she was beside him. The noises in the tower dwindled; she kept her eyes straining in the darkness, staring toward the place where, every night, Fulcun hung the key of the tower door on the post at the foot of the bed.

She dragged herself up at last, and when she sat upright she shook as if she had torn her flesh in that movement. There was only one comfort, and that was a killing sword: she had kept herself, tonight at least, for Mauger.

When she stood by the bedside she looked back once. She could see in the faint lamplight Fulcun's dark head and the thin curve of his cheek. She did not even think to pity him. Her mind was fixed only on the one necessity—to do right. Like an intolerable glare of merciless uncolored light it blinded her, and still she would not turn from it. She pulled the curtains to and shut Fulcun from her.

Montgommeri's watch outside the castle pale heard the sound of voices talking low inside the yard. The large moon stood in the west, and it was not dark. He cried out, "Who's there?" and his fellow farther along heard and joined him. They went together to the edge of the ditch where the faggots had been tossed in during the fighting. Someone was stumbling across them.

"Stand there!" the watch cried, but whoever came did not stand. The watch leveled his spear. Then, "God's Death!" he cried. "It's a woman."

She stood with the spear at her breast; her face was gray in the moonlight as if she were dead. He said, "What are y' doing here?"

She said, "Take me to Lord Mauger of Fervacques."

"Why for?"

"I am his wife."

"God!" says the fellow. "Are you that strumpet?"

"I am," she answered. She was past all hurt of words.

He said, "Well, I never!" and took her by the arm. She stumbled as he led her down the street to the barn—it was Osmunt's barn—where Rogier lay nursing his wound, and where he and a dozen of his knights slept. The fellow knocked at the door with the butt of his lance, keeping hold of her all the time, then he opened it and cried—

"Lords! Lords!" A man within stirred and groaned.

"What is it?"

He told them.

When someone had brought a torch Rogier says, "Bring her in," and sat up, leaning on one elbow.

They brought her in, and the men there stared at her. But she only saw Mauger. He stood in front of her.

He said, "You—come back," and his voice cracked. "Tired of your wantonness—Come back?" he cried.

"Yes, sir," she answered him. Mauger looked round as if someone might tell him what to do.

Rogier says, "Did he put you out?"

"No." Alde did not take her eyes from Mauger. "I came—he . . . does not know," and then she cried suddenly, "Oh! Sir, take me from here. Take me from here."

Rogier said, "Did he bring you here against your will?" He could not understand.

But she could only wring her hands and cry, "Take me away, sir—" She was near the limit of her endurance, for she had remembered that, though Fulcun was as far from her as the living from the dead, yet a cry would have reached his ears.

Mauger said, "By God, we'll burn him out of this place first."

She thought then that she was falling into a gulf. She went down on her knees, and on her hands to hold herself up. "Mauger," she cried, "sir—I pray you—" The old, dark, binding conjuration came out of her darkness, "Mauger, by God, by the earth, by the grass of the earth!"

Rogier of Montgommeri heaved himself up from the pile of hay he lay on and began to go unsteadily toward the place where they had hung his hauberk, shield, and helm.

"Come on, Mauger!" he says. "You've got her back. We'll go. It's light enough to ride with the moon, and the dawn isn't long."

Everyone moved then, glad to forget Alde, crouching on the ground with her hair trailing down over her hands.

Chapter 10

Scissors cannot cut this thing;
Unravelled, it joins again and clings.
It is the sorrow of separation,
And none other tastes to the heart like this.

By a descendant of the founder
of the Southern Tang dynasty,
translated by F. Ayscough and A. Lowell

I

They rode into the yard at Fervacques and the horses came to a stand as men ran from the outbuildings and crowded round. Mauger said to one of the house serfs, "Lift her down!" and pointed his finger at Alde. So it was Turstin the cook's man who lifted her from the saddle and set her on her feet, while Mauger and Rogier and the rest dismounted all about. After that she realized that Mauger was speaking to her. "Go in!" he was saying. "Go in! Go in, you—" She turned and went across the bridge and up the steps of the tower. She was glad to be inside the door because she knew that all in the yard watched her go.

Upstairs in the hall there were only a few women; everyone else had hurried out to see Lord Mauger come home. Alde looked at them and they at her. The door to the kitchen stood open and the fire was great and hot ready to cook the dinner. At the end of the hall someone had been busy at a table over a heap of cabbages. One of them had fallen and lay on the floor. Alde stooped and picked it up and felt the firm, fat, green leaves creak under her fingers. As she put it back on the table, with the women watching every movement, Mauger and the other men came in.

Mauger saw what she did and he shouted, "Let that alone! Put it down," as if a cabbage at Fervacques were a thing of price. His voice was high and harsh, and Rogier of Montgommeri turned his head and stared, and moved to lay a hand on his arm; he thought, as he had thought more than once, that Mauger, since that blow on the head at Falaise, was sometimes not quite a sane man.

But Alde did not think of that. Her mind was too broken to see strangeness in anything. She was here at Fervacques— Fulcun was at Montgaudri, miles away—that was all. When Mauger cried to her, not now quite so fiercely but still angry enough, "Go up and wait for me till I come to you," she did just what he bade her.

There was no one upstairs; she was glad of that. She sat down on a stool to wait; she said aloud to herself, "Mauger—*Mauger* is coming soon," because she must not think of Fulcun. She dared not think of Fulcun because that was an agony too great.

After about an hour Mauger came in. He had a whip in his hand, and he ran the bolt across the door. She stood up and faced him. Her eyes were caught and held by a mark just above his forehead, a gray patch where the hair did not grow. She did not think what it was, nor how it had come there, only she could not take her eyes from it because it was strange.

He came to her and put his hand on her shoulder. His fingers hurt her. She said, "Are you going to beat me?"

"I am," he answered her, and then shouted, "Yes, I'm going to beat you."

But he did not begin. He looked down at the whip, and said, quite quietly now, "I wanted to bring a stick to you, you wanton, but Rogier, he says no. He wouldn't let me use more than this on you." He looked at it still, and still clutching her shoulder; then he dropped it on the floor.

"But I can strangle you with my bare hands," he said. "Rogier didn't think of that."

He had her by the throat. She stared up into his face—dark and heavy, with the heavy jowl and drooping lids. She remembered in one single thought, as she saw him so close, all the years of her marriage; the loneliness, the causeless, cureless enmity, the captivity. And then it leaped to her mind, "He is going to kill me. I can think of Fulcun now."

Mauger's hands were tight about her throat, but he was not hurting her much yet; she had one clear instant to remember Fulcun. She shut her eyes. She saw him in her mind as he had sat one day on a stool by the fire working at a wooden bowl with a knife—he was very clever with a knife, her Fulcun. She had come in and stood close behind him, and he had thrown his head back and let it rest against her side as she stood. She saw his face looking up. She smiled.

Mauger's hands closed. She tried to scream, but the scream was strangled. And then she was free. She opened her eyes and stood, shaking now and clutching her throat.

"You—you smiled," Mauger whispered to her.

She could only look at him dumbly. The fear she had not felt was on her now.

"Why did you smile?"

She shook her head and said nothing, but she saw that he had guessed.

He stared at her, chewing his lips—it was an old trick and it was strange to her to see the familiar thing, here in the familiar room, after so long—a lifetime it seemed.

He began to talk, not in his usual slow, heavy, grudging way, as if he dropped his words for her to pick up, but fiercely, unsteadily, staring at her all the time with an intensity that was as strange as his speech.

"I can't understand you," he cried. "I never could. You seem kind—you're a woman . . . You've breasts . . . but no kindness. None—never for me—"

He came nearer, and for all she could do she shrank. His face peered into hers. "You never had—not even at the first." He waited as if she might deny that, but when she stood dumb, he turned away and began to ramble aimlessly about the room.

"If ever—ever you'd cared the worth of an egg . . . for me—" he said, staring down at the whip that lay among the stale rushes on the floor. "It was your fault—your fault I ever brought in that wench—the miller's girl." He kicked fiercely at the whip and then turned again to her.

"You don't know how to care. You don't. You've left that fellow in the lurch now—you said so— Or did he turn you out? Which?"

She said, and found it strange that she could speak of it in words, "I left him—" Such small words too for so immense a thing.

For a long minute Mauger said nothing, only stared at her; she must meet his look. She was afraid that he saw in her eyes the thing that her eyes saw, and that was Fulcun lying in bed turned from her just as she pulled the curtains together and shut him away from her.

"So you don't care for him either—no more than for me."

"Oh!" she cried, and clapped her hands over her mouth, because she had broken silence and was afraid of what might burst through after that cry.

"You do? That Geroy—that black-faced scarecrow?" he shouted at her, and flung off again, roaming away through the room. He came to the bed, and pulling the curtains apart looked into the shadows. Her eyes had followed him till then, but at that she turned her face away. She did not know where he was till he was beside her again.

"I meant to beat you," he said. "I thought when you came back to me, 'I'll beat her—I'll make her sorry.' But there's no use. It won't make you care for me—if you don't care." After a second he cried, "But why did you come back?" And when she did not answer, "You're just the same. Dumb, sullen—no kindness—none—none for me," and suddenly she saw his head go down and his hands come up to his face.

Then he was at her feet, his face pressed against her, his hands trying to find her hands; she snatched them away and put them behind her. He clung to her knees instead; he cried; the sound and quiver of his sobs was horrible to her; for a minute it was nothing but that, horrible and monstrous.

He stopped crying. She felt him tugging at her gown and realized that he was wiping his face on it. That small thing, like a cold knife, pierced through her dullness with a two-edged pang of pity and disgust. For the first time in her life she pitied him, and that pity made her sick. She thought, "I ought to do something to comfort him. I ought to put my hand on his head." But she could not. It was all that she could do to stand still, because the head that pressed against her knees was his and not Fulcun's.

He said, "But why did you come back? You must have cared for me—you must—a little—"

He waited, and the silence was awful. She thought, "I can't say yes—I must say yes—but I can't." She was silent, and then someone knocked sharply on the door.

Mauger lifted his head. "Get away!" he shouted. "Get away. Stop that!"

"Mauger!" It was Rogier of Montgommeri's voice, but there were more men than one outside. "Let me in!"

"No!"

"I'll break down the door," cried Rogier, and beat on it with his fist and his foot.

Mauger buried his head again in Alde's knees. Among the clatter she heard him cry—

"You must care—a little," as if the noise made it more urgent that she should answer.

She looked down at him and found he was staring up at her. His face was broken and strange with tears, and again she saw the dent above his forehead and a pulse beating in it.

But this time she knew what the mark was, and how it had come there. It was the mark of Fulcun's sword. And Fulcun was not only Fulcun; he was her lover, and she was a woman whose lover had tried to kill her husband. That was how her slow brain began to apprehend the truth of what she had done.

As the thought filled her Rogier thundered again on the door and shouted; that added confusion and hurry to the distress of her mind and yet it helped her. She opened her lips and answered Mauger at last:

"Oh!" she cried. "Yes—yes— If you like— Yes." She was as near distracted as he.

And he became suddenly calm. He got up. "I knew it," he said, and looked quickly at her and away. "But if that fellow comes near you again," he said, "I shall kill you." He went to the door and slid back the bolt.

Rogier of Montgommeri came in, and Ruald of Saint Pierre, and two or three more. They stared at Alde, at Mauger, and about the room.

Rogier's eyes went from Mauger's tear-blubbered face to the whip on the floor. "God!" he thought, "the man's crazed. I thought he might have done her a mischief—but he's been crying."

Rogier would not look at Mauger again. He spoke to Alde.

"Dame," says he, "see that you're a good wife now to my cousin." He stared hard at her. She had been a comely woman he thought—but not now; her face was dull, strained, old.

She answered him, "Yes, sire."

It was only when Rogier had taken Mauger and the rest away that she could begin to think. But then, clinging to the windowsill and staring blindly into the dull and muddy clouds, puddled here and there with cold light, her mind went back to the work of understanding the thing that she had done. The fact, hard, heavy, and relentless, pressed upon her like a cope of lead; she could think of nothing else—of nothing else but this new Mauger—her handiwork. She had unmade him to this strange man; she had broken him, unloosed him, till his sullen reserve had melted to his open ruin.

And she was his wife; that meant, she knew now without argument as before she had rejected without argument—that meant that she was bound to him; she must have pity on him. As the light faded it was pity filled her mind—pity, and the awful quailing of the senses that goes with pity when there is no love. Her punishment and her purgation began that afternoon though she was too simple to know that it was so. She was only utterly drowned in the horror of it—and she must not admit into that horror one thought of the light that lay like a colored, clear sunset all about Montgaudri. Fulcun was there, but here in Fervacques she was in a different world.

II

For Fulcun there was no colored sunset light over Montgaudri, no light at all, or if there were it did not lighten his darkness. He had wakened that morning just about the time that Rogier of Montgommeri and his folk crossed the Orne. He wakened with a start, and in the same start sat up. The curtains of the bed were open, it was broad day, and people stood staring in at him, but silent. There was Geroy and Richereda and Custance and, peeping from the end of the bed, young Baudri.

"What's wrong?" Fulcun cried at them, staring at their faces, and his hand wandered to find Alde's shoulder so that she should not be frightened. But his hand could not find her, and he looked down and saw that the bed beside him was empty. He did not know then what it was that he feared, but a huge fear kept him dumb.

"They've gone," says Geroy at last.

"Gone? How?" Fulcun dared not ask the other question that filled his mind.

They were watching him still. Geroy muttered something about, "Lucky for us that they're gone."

Fulcun could not hold that other question back any longer—

"Where is she?" he cried, keeping his voice steady. "Where is—Alde?"

Geroy said, "She went—" and then stopped because of the look on Fulcun's face. But Fulcun said nothing, only stared. When he did speak it was to himself—

"It's all right," he muttered. "She can't."

He broke off and stared again at Geroy. Geroy was watching him. They were all watching him. His heart in his breast went small, hard, and cold. He knew the thing was true before he believed it. He said to Geroy, speaking carefully, "Don't tell me such a lie."

Geroy cried, "It is no lie—I was there by the breach, an hour before moon setting, because I thought the guard might be asleep. I heard a noise and she came down. She said she must go out to them. She said they would go away from Montgaudri when they had her. And so they did."

Fulcun looked away from Geroy, turning his head slowly till his eyes were on the empty bed beside him. He put his elbows on his knees and his face in his hands. The fact was too impossible—too huge to understand. In his mind's vacancy he had even time to wonder why he was not more moved by it.

"You let her—" he muttered, and Geroy said, "Aye—why should we keep her to our sorrow? She wanted to go." But Fulcun did not hear him. He was beginning to see something in his mind. It was—Alde going out to them in the low moonlight—Alde alone—at their mercy.

He jerked his head up. "She can't have gone," he shouted, so that Richereda clapped her hands over her mouth. "You lie, Geroy—" and then in a whisper, "Why should she go?"

Geroy caught Custance's eye and it put an answer into his mouth.

"I suppose you weren't hot enough for her," he says, and laughed. He was thinking that he knew better how to manage women than Fulcun did.

Then he went back from the bed, because with a shout Fulcun had leapt up. He had his hand on the sword that lay at the bed's foot, he pulled it out, a naked blade in the hand of a naked man, while Geroy could do nothing but stare and Richereda screamed and Custance let out a cry.

Geroy put up both hands as if they could ward off the steel and went back again before Fulcun. His mouth was open and his eyes saw nothing but Fulcun's mad face. The blade swung up, then down, but it fell short, bit into the planking, and stayed swinging, as Fulcun stumbled back with little Baudri clinging to him. They all stood still then, watching the sword till it stood still too, without a quiver.

Then Geroy said, "You'd have killed me but for the lad." He looked at Custance. She was looking at Fulcun, and in his fear Geroy hated her that moment. It was the child that had stopped the blow—Alianor's child—his own lawful child. He turned his back on all of them and went out.

Fulcun took Baudri's wrists in his hands and pulled them apart. "Let go," he says, in so flat a voice that Baudri, with a child's sensitive vanity, thought he had made a fool of himself and began to cry because he had been so frightened.

Fulcun took no notice of him or anyone. He dressed, armed, lugged the sword out of the floor and ran it into the sheath. Then he went down to the yard, shouting for his horse.

He came back a little before the early twilight, drenched, spattered with mire, his clothes torn, the horse limping. The folk were all at supper. He went up through the hall and sat down in his place. Baudri brought him meat, bread, and wine. He ate, resting his head on his hand because he was so weary.

As he ate he was not thinking, but only seeing in his mind the dull sodden fields through which he had ridden all day; and the empty woods where in the still air the leaves came sifting slowly down; and the trampled tracks of many horses that had churned the grass to black mud, and the mud to black, puddled water. He had ridden, his eyes always on those tracks, until he came to a place where at last, since in some place he must turn, he pulled the horse up and round, and turned his back on Alde.

Geroy had drunk more than enough and went on drinking. He had Custance by him on the other side from Fulcun, and he kept romping with her, more roughly all the time. At last he took her and lifted her on to his knee, and then, laughing loud, thrust her down, so that her head rested on Fulcun's arm, and held her there.

Fulcun looked down into her face, and she looked up at him. She had been laughing too, but she stopped laughing and stared at him with her mouth still open. He got up, pushing her off, and tramped away to the door of the great chamber. As he went, Geroy laughed again and pulled Custance to him again; but he had to take her by the chin to turn her face from staring after Fulcun.

Fulcun went into the great chamber and shut the door. The only light there was the red eye of the brazier, and all the rest of the room was a warm glooming darkness. He stood and saw the glow just reach the curtains of the bed; he looked at them and could not turn away his head. His heart did not burst; he went on being alive and enduring the same unendurable pain that neither diminished nor destroyed him.

He jerked his head aside at last from the sight of the bed where she had lain in his arms and where now he would lie alone. He went slowly to the wall under one of the shuttered windows and sat down on the floor there. He hugged his knees to him as tight as he could; he gripped one wrist with the other hand, straining at it; his hands were damp with sweat and yet he was very cold.

Alde was gone. he did not need now to ask anyone why she had gone; indeed he had never needed to ask, because there was only one reason possible. She had gone because she was honorable, true, loyal; because she must do right.

"But oh! Alde—" He had put his head down on his knees and clenched his teeth together. She had gone from him in a cruel silence, as if she were his enemy for the sake of right. For a minute he almost thought that she did count herself his enemy, and that thought was like the cold draft of death against his lips.

Then he knew—he knew that it was not so. He could not understand her, but he knew that she loved him. And she had gone out into the night, with a desperate courage, and given herself back to Mauger.

He caught up his hands to his teeth then and bit on his fingers, because this fear was unendurable. How had Mauger dealt with her? How, this minute, was he dealing with her? He crushed his knuckles against his eyes so that they should not see the things that his mind dared not.

It was no use. He lifted his face at last, and cried, but in a whisper, "God! God!" God must keep her safe; she had done right. After that he was silent, staring up into the red darkness of the rafters, but in the silence he clamored to God, most like a dog that howls at the moon, to hear and keep her safe.

It was a few days later that Fulcun came down into the yard one morning and found Geroy there, with five or six of the men, cutting loose the broken knee-timbers of the pale and digging up the shattered logs so as to drive in new ones. Fulcun came from the stable leading his horse; he had a couple of dogs with him and their collar bells sounded merry.

Geroy left his work and went over to meet him, but he did not lay down the axe he had been working with; he carried it on his shoulder. Fulcun stopped and looked at him as he came up.

"Do you know what they say now?" says Geroy.

"Who? No."

Fulcun's face was blank, and Geroy grew angry. He fingered the haft of the axe on his shoulder. He wasn't afraid of Fulcun; he went close to him. He would tell him that now the wanton was gone he must make his peace all round, and smartly. But when he came to speak he was not so blunt.

He says, "The duke's summons is out against you. He'll put you out of law next."

Fulcun said he knew that.

"But it's not all," Geroy shouted at him. "Now they say that Herfast cried you excommunicate in church at Cortilly yesterday. That's the first time of the three, so you've a fortnight to make your peace with Ivo at Séez."

Fulcun stared at him for a second, then he dropped his eyes, but he said nothing at all.

Geroy grew braver, because he had seen fear in Fulcun's eyes. He said, "She's gone. You've only to go to the bishop and do penance and say you repent and renounce all your traffic with her."

Fulcun was looking down at one of the dogs that stood waving its tail and gaping with impatience to be off. He said, without lifting his head, "I'll not do that."

Geroy lost his temper then. "Well, when you're excommunicate and outlaw don't count on me to stand by you. I've not forgotten that you'd have killed me but for the lad."

Fulcun had forgotten it—or almost. Now he said, "I was mad then. Forgive me, Geroy."

But Geroy shut his mouth. He wasn't going to forgive. Fulcun did not press him; the thing sank out of sight in his mind, where there was nothing but one blackness. He got up into the saddle.

"Where are you going?" cried Geroy.

Fulcun told him, "I don't know," and left him.

Geroy still stood there a long time, biting at a splinter in his palm and staring over it at the round black-edged gray scar on the grass outside the gate that the campfire of Rogier of Montgommeri's people had left, and the bones and fells of the sheep that had been cooked at it. He wished, and he growled the wish into his hand, that, wherever Fulcun had gone, he would never come back.

❧

Fulcun rode out of the town gate and turned down the hill without thinking of where he was going. In a fortnight he would be excommunicate, God's outlaw. What use then, since God was his enemy, to cry to him to keep her safe? It could be none at all.

But Geroy said, "Renounce her." As if he could! She had gone from him and so had ended their sin, but he could never repent that he had loved her, and loved her now; never in this world or in eternity could his heart renounce her, turn away from her, forsake her.

He was riding along the edge of the Montgaudri vineyard; the rows of vines ran up the hill from him, regular as plow furrows; the twisted stems looked tortured, blasted, hopeless of any future harvest. Below him the grass of the hillside was tufted and lank, pale drab in color, and the dry, brittle haulms of what had been golden ragwort stood up among it. It was November and the year was nearly dead.

He pulled up at the edge of the woods; through them Alde and he had gone to Mass at Cortilly. At Cortilly Herfast had cried the excommunication last Sunday. He was dirty, ignorant, drunken, but a priest. Perhaps Herfast would know what Fulcun could do, for indeed he did not know himself. He turned and rode along the woods; he could not bear to go through them the way he had ridden that soft, drenching morning with Alde riding by him.

He found Herfast digging in his garden. A great heap of rubbish burned sulkily with a lot of smoke behind him, and a robin sat on the peak of the thatch and now and then spilled out into the dull air a song as clear as dropping water.

Fulcun got down from the saddle and leaned on Herfast's garden fence. But he could think of no way of opening what he had come to say.

Herfast drove his spade deep and leaned both hands on it. He did not look at Fulcun after the first glance. All that had happened at Montgaudri was a small thing compared with his own trouble.

He said with a big sigh, "These are bad times."

"Aye," says Fulcun, thinking of Montgaudri—empty. And then a thought went through him—a new thought keen as a knife. Alde had been gone from him for five whole days, and not all his life, nor eternity after it, could restore to him those hours that he had lost with her. And yet—the sharp pain widened into an ache as of homesickness—and yet she was somewhere, though not here—she was in some place, and people there could see her, hear her speak—Alde—the real Alde. At that, the close-embraced thought of her that was always in his heart thinned and wavered like smoke. It was only a thought; but somewhere, where he could not be, was Alde herself.

He wakened out of that pain to hear Herfast's creaking voice—"And he said it was his last word to me. He's a hard man, that bishop; 'Herfast,' says he, 'you'll turn that woman away or lose your priesting!'" Fulcun heard now what he was saying.

"But if I did turn her off, I'd be alone," says Herfast. Fulcun heard him, and what was more he knew what it meant.

Herfast saw that in his face and forgot that it was Fulcun of Montgaudri, one of the great Geroys. He came close to the fence, his feet sucking out of the heavy clay.

"Bishop Ivo, he says it's sin," he cried. "But . . . but . . ." and suddenly tears rushed into his small eyes, blurring them. "But if it is . . . how can I turn the wench away? What'd she do?" He caught Fulcun's wrist in his dirty hand. "Would you turn her out of doors . . . tell her to go . . . and lie alone in bed and not know where she was . . . not know?"

Fulcun tried to drag his hand away. He could not stand this. "Don't ask *me!*" he cried.

Herfast kept tight hold on him with one hand; with the other he wiped his eyes and left smudges on his cheeks.

"Would you shut the door on her," he mumbled, "because the bishop said it was sin . . . and let her fend . . . and not know where she was nor how it went with her . . . ?"

"No!" Fulcun shouted, and wrenched himself free. He snatched at the bridle and was up in the saddle before the priest could stop him. He spurred the horse and it leaped forward. He spurred it again.

Herfast stood there at the fence. Fulcun was riding like mad, stooping over the neck of his horse. There were wide pools in the mud of the village street; the horse trampled through them, tearing up the dull, flat water and flinging it apart in ragged splashes. Fulcun went the way he had come. In a few minutes Herfast lost sight of him.

Chapter 11

Homeless am I, O Lord: whither shall I turn?
A wanderer in the desert, whither shall I turn?
    I come to Thee at last, driven from every threshold;
And if Thy door be closed, whither shall I turn?

Tahir, translated by Robert Bridges,
The Spirit of Man

I

It was the day Herfast the priest had cried the excommunication of Fulcun Geroy of Montgaudri for the second time that Geroy came upon his wife as she was warming her hands at the fire in the hall. Dame Alianor's thin face was pinched and white with the cold, and her nose was red. She saw Geroy, but she kept her eyes on her hands, stretched out above the fire.

Geroy said, "Wife, why not come in to the fire in the great chamber?"

Alianor looked at him then, and he smiled, but his smile could not outlast her stare. "I don't like the company," she answered him, and looked again into the fire as though he were not there.

Geroy recovered his confidence when she was not looking at him.

He came nearer. Says he, "And I'm weary of it." She did not give him even a glance. "See here," he said, and rubbed one finger down her sleeve in a sort of casual caress. "If I send her packing will you be a good lass and forget it?"

She stood very still. Her face was turned away from him. He laid his hand upon her shoulder, and then he felt her begin to shake. "God!" he thought, "tears! This is easier than I thought."

A small strange sound came from her. She turned and he saw that she was laughing. Her teeth shone in the firelight, sharp, white, and pointed.

He cried out, "What are you laughing at?" And she told him, "You."

"The devil you are!" he says, and flung away from her, but he could not go quick enough to miss her words.

"I know," she said, and she gave a fresh titter of laughter. "You think, with Bishop Ivo so stirring, that a lawful wife'd be safer for you."

He slammed the door of the great chamber on her then, but she had said all she meant to say. She stood by the fire a little while longer, smiling at the flames. She thought, "I wouldn't be that doxy of his, now that he's weary of her—and frightened . . . The coward!" she said to herself, and her lips drew tight.

After that, she took care to watch, and for one who watched there was plenty to see. For one thing there was Custance's pinched face—the wench, heavy with her child, had little comeliness now. She was fretful too and cried easily when Geroy teased her, and that was often. Dame Alianor, watching, let Custance see her thin smile; she herself had never cried.

A week before Christmas, Herfast, in Cortilly church, cried Fulcun excommunicate the third time. They heard next day at Montgaudri that it had been done. Geroy said nothing to Fulcun, but he gave little Baudri a licking and twisted Custance's arm when she was sulky with him. She cried out with an angry wail, and Fulcun got up from his place by the fire, dropping the wood he was working at, and the knife, anyhow into the rushes, and went heavily out. He did not come back till suppertime.

At supper Geroy drank more than he needed, and he would have Herluin, the new steward since Osmunt had died, to drink horn for horn with him. Herluin was Geroy's choice for steward; Fulcun did not like him; he was a rat-faced fellow with bad teeth; Fulcun wondered if there were anyone that he told the truth to.

Toward the end of the meal, as Geroy reached across Custance to pass the horn to Herluin, she cried out that he bore too hard on her with his arm.

He says, "Oh! Do I?" and drawing his arm back jerked her harder with his elbow, gave her a push, and told her to get away back where she belonged if she weren't satisfied.

She got up then, sobbing and clutching her side, and went away from the table, and Geroy laughed. At the door of the great chamber she lingered an instant and looked round. Her eyes met Fulcun's in a fixed stare; it was such a glance as might be utterly vacant or charged with some passionate, fierce meaning; whichever it was, Fulcun did not even wonder. He saw her with his eyes, but her look did not come to his mind.

When he got up from the table, leaving Geroy drinking with Herluin, he had forgotten that Custance had gone into the great

chamber. He shut the door behind him and crossed over to the brazier and stood staring into it; it was full of glowing charcoal, played
over by the smallest flames, too thin even to be colored, almost
invisible, the very essence of heat. Then he sat down on his faldstool
and fumbled about in the rushes for the wood and the knife he had
dropped. He was always very busy these days whenever he must be
indoors, cutting out boxwood bowls or knife handles or the like.
Now he was whittling fresh arrows from thin, straight ash staves,
and waxing them, and feathering them with the feathers of an eagle
he had shot last lambing season on the hill.

He found the shaft and the knife, sorted them from the
rushes that came with them, and rubbed his finger down the
smooth, fresh-cut wood. Then he looked round because someone in the shadows had moved.

Custance was standing at the foot of the curtained bed; her
hands were clenched at her sides, and tears were running down
her flushed, thin cheeks. She said, in a choked voice, as his eyes
found her, "He will kill his child. But he doesn't care."

Fulcun stared, for a moment at a loss. Then he said, "You're
with child by him?"

She gave a sobbing laugh. "The seventh month," she told
him. And he had not noticed.

He began to work on the arrow shaft again. The little delicate white chips of wood fell into his lap like flakes of apple.
After a few minutes, because he felt her eyes still on him, he
said, "Well, I can't help you, can I?"

"No," she said, but she meant "Yes," although she did not in
the least know how he could have helped.

That was cloudy in her mind, just as her thoughts of him were cloudy and all confused with her thoughts of the child she carried; as though, that hot summer afternoon on the hillside, Fulcun had not let her go; as though she had never gone on and seen Geroy stooping over his horse's hoof, prizing a stone out of it with the knife from his pouch.

Fulcun kept his head down, and anger mounted in her, a desolate, hopeless, aching anger. She remembered that woman—the woman with the clear, fearless eyes that made you silent and afraid of showing yourself a common peasant wench. And he loved her—Custance had watched them and seen love; she knew now what it was like. But the woman was gone; she had run away from him, left him—left him like this, with a dull face, and his head bowed, and lips always set.

Her hands went up to her mouth. He was in torment. She could see it. He was as lonely and desperate as she herself, but with him it was because of that other woman. For a moment she could not tell whether she were glad of it or very sorry. "Let him be in torment," she thought, and then nearer to the truth, "So long as I can comfort him on my breast."

Suddenly she knew what she must do. She must have him there—she must. And oh! Why not? It was where he had wanted to be, so short a time ago.

She was at his feet and leaning against his knees. Her hands were at the neck of her gown, dragging at it. She cried to him, "You wanted me before ever you saw her. Oh! I'm the same. Come here! Come here!" The brooch that held her gown tore out and dropped on the floor. But he caught at her wrists and held them. "No," he muttered through his teeth as she struggled. "No, you shan't!" It made him sick to think of what she had meant; he thought for a second that she must be mad.

She cried, "Let me go! Let me go!" pulling herself away from him; and just then Geroy opened the door. He opened it softly, peered in, and shut it softly again. Fulcun did not hear it, and Custance did not care.

Fulcun loosed her. She got up and went from the great chamber to the room where she slept with Geroy and shut the door. Fulcun went on working at the arrow shaft. His mind turned very soon from Custance and fixed itself on Alde. His heart reached out to her, straining to come at her somehow by means of his longing, his fearful care.

He thought, "Where is she now, this minute? Oh God! Is she safe? Or is she—?" He cried in his mind, "Is he hurting her? Oh God!" But then again he remembered that it was no use crying on God for her sake, because God was his enemy. And he had no friend.

Next morning, when the tardy light came, there was nothing to be seen from any window of Montgaudri but the blank white of mist. The great hill and forest of Perseigne were drowned in it, as though they had sunk into the earth overnight; even the houses and orchards of Montgaudri were all fallen away into the same nothingness, until, at about nine in the morning, they began to come back, first as pale shadows, then as things that had bulk but no features, and at last clear and solid enough under a thick, pale sky where the sun was a sickly smudge of yellowish light. But down in the valley, and halfway up the hill, the mist lay, dead heavy, not even crawling before the motion of any wind.

Before dinner Geroy rode out with Herluin the steward. He came first to Fulcun, who was looking out of one of the tower windows with a face as vacant as the fog.

Says Geroy, very grudging, "I suppose you've not thought to have Masses for Osmunt and the others that died in the siege?"

Fulcun says, "No—but—"

Geroy told him impatiently that it was time to do something. "I'll ride over to Cortilly and bid Herfast see to it," he says.

"No, I'll go," said Fulcun—a little eager since it was a way to pass a few hours of one of these livelong days.

Geroy took him up quick. "You can't, seeing you're excommunicate."

"No—I suppose not," says Fulcun, and turned again to the window.

So it was Geroy and Herluin who went with money for the Masses in Herluin's pouch.

Soon after dinner Fulcun went out. He found a dreary humor in the fact that he must go because Custance was in the great chamber. The mist was coming up again and drifted in now at the windows, making the room very cold. Custance sat crouched over the brazier. She looked up at him when he went toward the door and gave a sort of laugh and said, "You needn't be afraid of me." Her eyes were hard and hostile.

There were few folk stirring in Montgaudri castle or town. Fulcun saw shapes moving, indistinct through the mist, but no one close to, until he came to the town gate. There was a man on guard there and Fulcun nodded to him as he went out, and saw, from the tail of his eye, how the fellow spat after him and crossed himself. But in a few paces Fulcun was cut off even from that much of human company. He moved down the track in a gray-white blindness and silence, quite alone.

That was the very truth. He was alone.

He pulled up at that knowledge and stood for a minute. The almost total extinction of sight and sound made it more intolerable. He could not endure it. He went on again, hurrying along the track. Geroy and Herluin would be coming back this way; he would meet them. Little as they wanted his company, he thought, he must have theirs, because a man simply could not be alone as he was alone.

And yet, after a few minutes, as he tramped on staring into the mist, it was not of Geroy and Herluin that he was thinking. He was alone because God had shut the door on him and left him alone. If he could only beat on that door!

He raised his head as if to cry out, "Open! Open!" but he dropped it again. He could not. If the door should open a voice would cry, "Do you renounce your sin? Do you renounce the woman with whom you sinned?"

As if, he thought once more, with a sweet pang of tenderness in his mind, as if he could renounce her. He held her tighter, closer in his heart.

"My girl!" he whispered to her. "Not I! Never!"

But the sweetness died. The truth was that she herself was—not in his heart—but in Mauger's hands. It was that knowledge that kept on roweling him like a spur, driving him frantic with fear. What could he do? Nothing—nothing.

He had come to the valley now; he saw the wet dull grass tussocks at the edge of the road that ran north to Séez; beyond the woods began; when he crossed the road the drenched branches were above him, shining very black in the white mist and hung with cold, bright drops. He climbed over the ditch and bank into the woods. The world was less empty here where he could see the trees than in the open.

He had forgotten Geroy and Herluin. But now, hearing the sound of horses, he stopped, listening. And, in those few seconds, as he listened, his thoughts cleared suddenly, as though someone had spoken in his mind, telling him what was there.

He knew that he needed one thing—to go to God at Séez. He needed it because he was alone—but far beyond that, he needed it so that he would cry out on God, importuning him to remember her danger. And he could not go because, when he went, and when he beat on that door imploring mercy, he must renounce her.

He moved back through the wood. He could not go, so Geroy and Herluin were his only refuge. They were almost abreast of him on the road. He could just see the looming shapes in the mist. He stood on the top of the bank and called out, "Ho, Geroy! Is that you?"

The horses stopped. There was such a silence that instead of jumping down into the ditch, he stayed where he was. He thought, "Perhaps it's not Geroy."

But Geroy's voice answered him. "Who's that?" He sounded scared. Then suddenly very sharp, "Who's that?"

Fulcun laughed. "It's me," he says, and again meant to jump down, and again did not because of the silence those two kept.

Geroy cried suddenly, "Where are you?"

"Why, here!" Fulcun answered him.

"That's a tree," Geroy says, as if he were talking to himself. "Where are you?"

"Damn you! Here!" Fulcun shouted at him, and then leaped suddenly aside, missed his footing, and crashed down among the sodden leaves and fallen, brittle twigs. A spear, very solid and swift in the impalpable still whiteness, had come flying at him. It went close by over him and lodged its blade deep into the soft ground.

"You got him!" That was Herluin's voice.

Fulcun lay still. Luckily for him he had hit his head on a root as he fell, and it kept him dazed long enough to prevent him scrambling up.

Then Geroy cried out, "Herluin, I got him!" He sounded horribly afraid.

"Well," says Herluin, "he is excommunicate and as good as outlawed. And you say he was at your wench already?"

Geroy did not answer that. "He hasn't made a sound," he said. "I must have got him in the throat."

Herluin says, "I'll make sure." But Geroy cried out then, "No—no—come on. Come on!" And then as the horses moved, "I don't believe it was him. It was some stranger—an outlaw. He never told us his name . . . did he . . . when I asked him?"

When there was silence again Fulcun sat up, put his hand gently to his head, which was sore, and got to his knees. Then he stayed still.

Here he was; where should he go? He had been going to Geroy because he could not be any longer quite alone. He turned his head and looked at the spear. It was little use to go to Geroy.

He covered his face with his hands. He could go to That Other . . . But—Alde? No, he would not go, because he would not forsake her.

He would not go. He struggled for one instant longer; for her sake he would not turn, with his eyes shut, without thought, condition, or reserve, just because he must, from utter need. He would not, and yet—

His strength broke like a snapped stick. He cried, his hands crammed over his mouth, "O God! Forgive!" because he could not endure. And then, because in that cry he had forsaken her, "O God, keep her safe!"

He did not know then what he had done—whether he had betrayed her or not. But he knew that he was going to Séez. He got up, pulled the spear out of the ground, and started off, using it as a staff. Once on the track he stopped again, unclasped his shoes, and kicked them off. He would go to Séez barefoot.

II

The gates of Séez had been shut at sundown. Soon after moonrise they had to be opened again after a great deal of shouting from both sides of the ditch. It was a woman's voice that did most of the shouting from the outside. She was very peremptory; she threatened whippings all round if the lazy hounds at the gate didn't hurry; she swore at them too as they opened. The bridge had barely fallen, and the echoes had not died, when she put her horse at it and rode over; after her came a small boy on a piebald, and then forty knights and half as many men-at-arms and servants behind. Last of all, and unnoticed in that great rout, a man limped in on foot; he was glad to be in, but he did not wonder what he would have done if there had not been that imperious, sharp-voiced woman to get the gate open; he was too tired. He followed the riders through the dark streets; the large moon lurking behind the boughs of the orchard trees showed through the branches like a lamp. In the open space near the cathedral it stood clear in the sky over the houses, as yellow as a cheese but not quite round.

Bishop Ivo of Séez—Ivo count of Belesme—yes, he thought sometimes, he was that till he died, however Mabille might grudge it him—Ivo of Belesme, bishop of Séez, was climbing up to his bedroom. He went slowly because he was heavy, old, and rheumatic. The boy who carried a candle before him knew exactly how slow the bishop was, and he had a habit of running quickly up three steps, then standing, then running up another three. But tonight, as he waited, he turned his head, listening. "There's one come up after you, sire," he says, looking down on the bishop's broad, pale face with its wide forehead and square jaw and the haze of white hair about the tonsure.

The bishop grunted and turned about, and the man who followed caught them up. It was a young knight of the bishop's.

"Sire," says he, out of breath, "Dame Mabille is at the gate, and the steward has gone down to open and I came to tell you. They lost their way," he says, summing up shortly and inoffensively what Mabille had said at great length.

Bishop Ivo said, "Tckh!" It might have meant sorrow for his niece's wanderings and probable fatigue, or, just as well, a wish that, as she had not come betimes, she had continued to wander and let him get to bed in peace. He turned and began to go down again, one hand on the wall and the other lifting his gown from off his feet.

"How many did you say she has brought with her, Gualtier?" he asked.

Gualtier had not said, and could not say now for certain, but he thought close on a hundred. Bishop Ivo says, "Tchk!" again, and there was less doubt as to what that meant, but Gualtier took no notice, because the bishop, though a simple, was also a stately old man.

Ivo, bishop of Séez and count of Belesme, was the one good branch of a bad stock, excepting only for his own bastard, Oliver, the Alençon weaver's daughter's child, once a knight and now a monk at Bec. Bishop Ivo was Guillelm Talvas's brother and daily prayed, without much hope, for dead Guillelm's soul; but there was nothing alike in the two. Mabille, Talvas's daughter, Rogier of Montgommeri's wife, could never feel one touch of kinship between her and her uncle; nor could he in her for that matter; he thought her worse, because a woman, than her dead father, poor old Guillelm, or than her scoundrel brother Arnoul—dead too—God have mercy on them both!

Bishop Ivo met Mabille in the midst of the hall. The servants were running about setting tables and rolling up the pallets that had been spread for the night. They did not stop for their master's coming, so Mabille, who had by the hand a heavy, sullen, sleepy lad, went down on her knees for his blessing among a great deal of trampling and confusion.

Bishop Ivo gave it to her and to the lad, young Robert, her eldest son. But he was more concerned, as he stared over their heads, with the preposterous number of her men-at-arms, still crowding and shoving about the door, than with any blessing upon the two of them.

Mabille got up quickly when he had finished, and the child too. Says Bishop Ivo, "They'll set supper in a few minutes. You're welcome, niece."

"I don't want any supper," says Robert; he was almost whimpering.

Mabille loosed the lad's hand and cuffed his head. "Hold your tongue," says she, and when he yelled she cuffed him again.

Bishop Ivo put his hand on the boy's shoulder and said, "Come, Robert." He disliked the lad, who was liker to that fellow Arnoul than it was right for any child to be, but at the moment he disliked Mabille more.

They went to the high table. The bishop insisted that Robert should sit down and sup with them, mainly because Mabille would have had him wait. Bishop Ivo caught Mabille's stare, hard, bright, sharp as a knife; he saw the anger in it and guessed her thought, "Curse the old devil! But he hasn't long to live." Then he saw her eyes grow blank as dark broken flint stones, and she smiled at him. He liked her even less smiling.

She talked while she ate; she was always talking. She was amusing enough too, in a sour way, but as he listened Bishop Ivo was thinking, "Her eyes are never still. I don't like women with such black hair and black eyes. And all the while she talks you know she is thinking things she doesn't say."

She glanced from him, in her restless way, down the hall, and suddenly he saw her stare fix. She sat very still. Then she raised her hand and pointed.

"Who is that?" she said, but more as if she asked herself.

Bishop Ivo says, "Where?" He could not pick out one stranger among the horde she had brought with her. Then he saw the man she meant.

He was very tall, with a dark thin face. He was not sitting with her men at the tables, but leaning against the wall, his arms folded, staring down at the ground. Who was he? Bishop Ivo thought, just as Mabille was thinking, "He's like someone, or I've seen him before—"

Then Mabille cried, very loud, "Guillelm Geroy!" She had remembered.

She had remembered Guillelm Geroy as she had seen him come out of the guardroom by the gate at Alençon, trying to walk steady, holding himself straight, but groping with his hands. It was years and years ago; she had been a child then, and she had screamed and hated him, as he turned his face toward her, for the ugliness of his horrid red eye sockets, and the way he shook his head to get the blood away from his mouth. She had been taught to hate Geroys before that, but she had never needed any teaching since.

That name, heard through all the noise in the hall, wakened Fulcun. He heaved himself off from the wall and came up through the crowd. Bishop Ivo, who was an old man, a priest, and a great lord, watched him as he came. This Geroy went barefoot and his feet were bleeding; and the look on his face— Bishop Ivo had seen that look before.

Mabille stood up beside him and beat with her fist on the board, "I know," she cried, and pointed again. "It's Fulcun Geroy of Montgaudri. Take him! Take him!"

Fulcun turned at that. The men-at-arms were getting up from the tables. He put his hand to his side, but there was no sword there. He looked over his shoulder at Mabille, knowing her and hating her—Talvas's daughter. Then he saw Bishop Ivo heaving himself up, slow and heavy and huge like a white bear.

"Get back!" cried Bishop Ivo. The men-at-arms stood, moved, and stood again.

"Who are you?" says Bishop Ivo. "What do you want?"

Fulcun turned his back on the men. He looked only at the bishop. "I'm Fulcun Geroy," he said. "I want pardon."

"You are an excommunicated man," says the bishop.

Fulcun said again, "I want pardon."

Bishop Ivo called a little, dry, withered priest who took Fulcun up into the tower and opened a door.

"Go in," he said.

Fulcun went in and down two steps. It was not dark, for the moonlight came in through two windows and he could see that this was a chapel.

"There's no room anywhere tonight," the priest said, "and you should want to watch and fast."

He shut the door and went away.

Fulcun moved toward the altar. The moonlight slanted down upon it and showed a white, carved wooden crucifix hung just above it.

Now that he was here, Fulcun could for a minute think of nothing clearly. Things went by in his head but had no meaning—the mist, the flying spear; the miles of road between Montgaudri and Séez; Mabille, Talvas's daughter, with her black eyes. He looked up from the spilt patch of moonlight, through the window, to the moon itself; it rode high now, and the darkness of the night sky was misted over and awash from end to end with its gray dimming light. There was such great emptiness there that his mind emptied, and in the quiet he remembered why he had come.

He had come to find God at Séez, and here he was, upon the cross. He stood looking at the crucifix; it was an ancient one, the head of the Christ was round like an egg, but flattened; the arms were very thin and the hands large, with long, straight fingers. And one of the arms had been broken once and was now mended, for there was a nail driven through the flat wrist to hold it to the cross. It was a real nail; he could see it quite clear against the white wood; it was a big, round-headed, rusty iron nail.

He stared at it for long, and then he went down slowly on his knees. It was a real nail. And on one real night, perhaps a moonlit night like this, Christ had hung dead upon the cross. For Christ was real, as the nail was real.

He whispered, "Christ!" and from his knees went down flat on his face. He turned his head so that his cheek touched the cold tiles, and he spread out his arms like the arms of the cross.

He did not know why that little thing that he had seen should make so huge a difference, but now he had no fear at all. The earth that bore up his body was not more close nor real than God that bore up his strengthless soul. And now, without question or even thought, he knew that he had not forsaken Alde. It was as if he had brought her here, swaddled in his love like a child in its bands, and laid her on the step of the altar for God to look to.

Lying there, in peace, he slept. He slept so sound that he did not wake when the door opened.

Bishop Ivo came in, and the small priest carrying an earthen lamp, and the young knight Gualtier behind them.

Bishop Ivo came quite close and looked at Fulcun, chewing sidelong like a horse in the way he had, as he thought what he would do. Then he turned and swept the other two out of the little chapel with his arm.

When he had shut the door, he locked it and pulled the key out. He spoke to the priest and the young knight ponderously in a whisper.

"He is here as a penitent," he says, "even though he is a Geroy and an outlaw and the rest." He showed them the key. "He'll be quite safe there," he said. "He can't get out."

Gualtier, who had a particular dislike for Mabille, put up his hand so as to be able to smile behind it. "Nor can that woman get in," he thought.

Next morning, it was he who, being young enough to make a game of the risks of life and death, told one of Mabille's knights that that Geroy fellow had got out of Séez in the night. Mabille heard it very soon, and while the winter sky was still full of the colored clouds of the dawn she got to horse with all her people in the yard at Séez.

It was their stir that wakened Fulcun. He scrambled up, stiff and cold, and went to the door. It was locked. He remembered then that this was a very nest of the Belesme and that he was swordless.

As he stood, knowing that he was caught, he heard a woman outside shouting "to make haste or we may not catch him." He knew it was Mabille. Then there was the noise of a horn blown, and her voice again, "If he's gone home, and not Alençon way," she cried, "he'll find Lord Rogier sitting at his gate when he gets there." The horses' neighing drowned any more there might have been. Fulcun wondered who it was she was after, and then began walking up and down and swinging his hands to warm himself.

When Bishop Ivo came in Fulcun was ready for anything to happen. What did happen was simple. It took less than an hour, and before noon he was going out through the gate of Séez. The little priest had laid on with a scourge, while another repeated the penitential psalms; the bishop had admitted him again into the peace of God and the church; and a serving woman had bathed and bound up his feet and brought him a pair of untanned cowhide boots. Before he left he had asked Bishop Ivo's blessing and got it, though not a fervent one. Bishop Ivo could not love any Geroy, though he had done his duty by this one.

It was evening when he came to the foot of Little High Wood. It rose above him, quite bare now of leaves and full of purple-brown shadows. The dark would be early tonight because the sky was heavy with clouds. He climbed up through the wood and out on to the open top. Quite soon he would see Montgaudri over the swell of the hill. He thought now of Montgaudri only as a place where he could lie down and sleep.

He had been tramping on with an almost vacant mind when he pulled up short. That glow above the hillside—he had been thinking it, if he thought at all, to be the sunset. But that was due south, not west at all. The sun set behind Perseigne forest.

He stared at the orange flaming blur low down over the hillside. It was not the sunset. Then it was a great fire. He saw now how it leaped and suddenly spread wider. And Montgaudri lay that way. He broke into a stumbling run.

Chapter 12

Even for the space of a flash
Of lightning
That flashes over the corn-ears
Of an autumn field—
Can I forget you?

Anonymous,

translated by Arthur Waley,

"Japanese Poetry: The Uta"

I

Fulcun opened his eyes and shut them again, because even the dull gray light was intolerably glaring. He did not know what had happened, nor where he was; he tried to think but could not because his head ached outrageously. And something very heavy, or someone very strong, was pressing upon him so that he could not move.

He opened his eyes again and saw a chaffinch fleeting by just over him with a fan-flash of white feathers and a flight like the leaping of a small boat against a fresh sea. He put his hands flat on the ground on either side of him, gathered all his strength, and heaved himself up. The heavy weight slipped as he moved till it lay not on his body but across his legs. He looked down at it and saw what it was.

It was a man, but the man had no head. But he was wearing Geroy's scarlet kirtle.

It was just then that a charred beam fell in the gutted tower, and the wind brought a stronger, stinging whiff of smoke. It was with smoke in his eyes and nose and throat that Fulcun had gone down, and the smell of it brought all back to him now.

He remembered how he had blundered into Montgaudri from the hill; how he had run through the empty town, and seen old Ingulf the farrier lie on his back in the street with his beard pointing up at the sky; and there had been a dead dog by him. He remembered the man, doubled up and groaning, by the smithy, who had tried to hold on to the sword that Fulcun tore out of his hand. He remembered coming in sight of the open castle gate, and how the tower had blazed with a long, drifting flag of flame and smoke and showering sparks. He had heard men shouting then, and caught so much—"St. Foy Montgommeri!" and he had run at a crowd of them that were bunched together about the stable door; the stable roof had just come crashing down, and the flames leapt up high into the gray air.

Their backs were to him. He struck and struck again in silence, and surprise and luck brought him through them. Then he found that in the midst, with his back against the doorpost, Geroy stood, unarmed but for a sword, his face blackened with smoke.

For the least fraction of an instant their eyes met, and in that instant Geroy lifted his sword again. Fulcun had just time for a thought, "He's mad with fear," before the flat of the blade came down on him like a flail. That was all that he knew about it, but as he went down on his back one of Montgommeri's men drove at Geroy and got him in the leg. Geroy stumbled forward to his knees, and as he groveled over Fulcun's body, another man shore down at him with an axe, a slanting, woodcutter's blow that caught him on the neck.

They took his head up from where it lay and carried it, dribbling blood all the way down Montgaudri street, to where Rogier of Montgommeri sat in his saddle just outside the gate. They were sure it was the Geroy's head, for the man it had belonged to had been dressed in scarlet, embroidered very fine. The other fellow, in the torn and muddied gray gown and the plowman's shoes, they did not think anything of.

Rogier looked at the twisted face and said, "No, that's not Fulcun Geroy." He glanced quickly over his shoulder to see if the woman sitting on the edge of the road had seen it too. She had, and she was looking at it, but without any expression at all in her face; she was looking at it as if it had been of no more worth or moment than a turnip. Then Dame Alianor dropped her eyes to her hands folded easily in her lap.

Little Baudri was staring at it too, but his eyes were wide with horror, and his round face grew white and sick. Everything today, since the moment they had heard the shouting and the horns in the town, had gone from strange to horrible. It had been strange when his mother had caught him by the arm and hurried him out of the castle gate toward the shouting men that swarmed beyond it. It had begun to be horrible when he saw Salomon the Thatcher run out of his cottage and up the street, and then leap into the air and fall and roll with a spear through him just above his brown leather belt. And now this was the most horrible—his father's face dangling from the hand of a man whose fingers were twisted into Geroy's dark hair, the face all grinning, and below the face— He covered his eyes with his hands and sat down suddenly on the ground.

Rogier of Montgommeri bade blow up the horns to draw out of the town till the fires had burned down. He was not minded to leave Montgaudri though. He thought that he would set all to work to build a new pale, and he would leave men to hold it. Then, if he chose, Duke Guillelm could keep it against the time when there should be trouble with Mayenne.

Fulcun got out of Montgaudri castle over the charred timbers of what had been the pale. He carried the borrowed sword in his hand; anyway he had no sheath for it. As he climbed down into the ditch he was grinning foolishly and thinking that there was one good thing in having your pale broken down—it was easy for you to get out.

It was twilight, and there was no one on this side of Montgaudri hill; he went down the steep slope; there was a smell of frost in the air. He came to the edge of the cornfield—what had been the cornfield last summer, but this year it would lie fallow. That thought came to him, and on its heels another, so strange and daunting that he stopped short to face it. Would he see the corn come up sharp green and grow to its tall crowding of spears in Montgaudri fields again?

Montgaudri tower was a tumble of burned timbers. Geroy was dead. Alianor? Little Baudri? Custance? The folk? He did not know. But he did know that what had been Montgaudri was in the hand of Rogier of Montgommeri, the duke's viscount, and that he must go away. And then in the dimming twilight he looked toward the bare cherry trees at the edge of the field and remembered that hot harvest afternoon when he had brought Alde here, and they had eaten with the reapers, and he had looked down at her lying asleep under those same trees. He must go away from Montgaudri, where she had been with him. It seemed to him that he had come to the heart of all his loss.

At the foot of the hill he took to the woods. They were safer for him than the open road; besides, if there were any Montgaudri folk to be found he would find them here. When he saw, through the darkening trees, the bright flicker of a fire, he made for it; he was sure that he had found them.

He came out in a little clearing. He saw half a dozen women and as many men sitting about the fire; they started up, and though he called to two or three of them by name, they bolted into the undergrowth like rabbits.

He called again and came on, thinking he would wait till they came back, and then he realized that they had not all fled. Half lying, half leaning upon a felled trunk, there was a woman with dark hair straggling over her shoulders. A very young child nuzzled at her breast. It was Custance.

She said, in a thin, small voice, almost as weak as the whimper of the child, "If they dare come back they will kill you."

Fulcun did not answer that. He stood looking at her, leaning his hands on the quillons of the sword. "What has happened?" he asked her.

She told him, "Rogier of Montgommeri has got Montgaudri," but he said, "I know that. How did he?"

The babe cried more shrill and she bent over it, and only when she had quieted it answered him.

"They came this morning. The folk didn't get the gate shut quick enough. I was near, and when they were in, I ran out."

He asked, as if it mattered, "With the child?"

"I bore him here in the woods," she told him, and then said, "It is a lad," as if she said, "It is wonderful," and her head drooped again over the little thing that stirred and wailed still at her breast.

Fulcun sat down. He remembered now that he was very weary. He laid his sword across his knees and held out his hands to the blaze. Once he spoke to ask Custance what had become of Dame Alianor and Baudri, but she did not know. After a while he glanced at her; he thought she had forgotten he was there, but she looked up and met his eyes.

She smiled, a strange, distant, languid smile. Her face, he thought, was different; she was not like Custance at all; he thought suddenly that she looked as if she might die.

She stared at him for a minute. She wanted to say something to him, yet hardly knew what it was she wanted to say. Only she was happy now, because this precious thing in her hands needed her, and so she needed now no other creature in the world. She would have liked to tell him that, and yet did not know why, nor how to say it. She bent her head again over the child; after all it was the only thing that mattered for her now.

But a while after she looked up again. She was not smiling now. Her face was puckered.

"I have no milk for him," she cried. "Look, he wants it! And I can do nothing for him . . . I can do nothing. And I'd die for him."

Her head slipped back against the log. "I shall die," she said in a whisper so low that he could barely hear her.

He cried out, "No!" but he knew that she spoke the truth.

She lay quite still a few minutes, and he saw tears begin to slide over her face and drip down on to the sodden ground. She turned her head a little so that her eyes would find his.

She muttered, hardly moving her lips, "You must take him. Get milk for him." And then after a minute in a whispering cry, "I must let you take him. I must let him go."

Fulcun reached out his hands and put them about the small creature—just a bundle of stuff and a puckered, querulous red face with an open mouth but her hands did not loose it; she clung to it closer.

"Oh!" she cried sharply. "No!" and then, "Yes!" She lifted her eyes to Fulcun; they were wide open, very bright, full of meaning. She looked at him steadfastly as though they two shared some secret that did not need words. Then she said very slow, "Take care of him. Keep him safe." He thought she was going to say something more, but her face changed. He saw her eyes dim as though a light faded, her hands slipped from about the child; her head rolled more aside. He knew that she was dead.

❦

When he had laid her down, shut her eyes, and crossed her hands, he took up the child again in one hand and the sword in the other and left her. He knew the other folk would come back to her when he was gone.

He did not see any of them as he went through the darkening woods, though he thought that some of them followed him for a while. But they did not come near, and when he left the woods and heard no more of them he forgot them.

He was going to Saint-Céneri. He must go there, for there was no one in the world but Robert Geroy to whom he could take this smallest son of the house. He would go to Robert and give him the child, and then— He did not know what then. He was a landless man now except for the little alod at Caharel by the Breton sea.

The child piped, sudden and shrill, and he peered at it in the deep dusk. When it stopped, his thoughts went for a moment to Custance. He remembered that he had not yet said a prayer for her soul, so he stopped and kneeled and said it. But when he got up and tramped on his thoughts went home again to Alde; his heart hung over her as Custance had hung over the child. Above the black, crouched backs of the hills the night sky was filling with stars, frosty bright. He lifted his face and muttered to it: "O keep her safe. O take care of her."

II

Every Christmas Day, when the priest had sung Mass at the church in Saint-Céneri town, he went to the little chapel of Saint-

Céneri in the meadows by the Sarthe, where that young but very holy man had long ago built his mud-and-wattle oratory. Many of the Saint-Céneri townsfolk went out too, and others came in from the essarts and the lonely huts scattered through the woods and up and down the banks of the Sarthe.

Robert Geroy of Saint-Céneri always went; and he had taught young Robert that this was a thing that must be done on Christmas Day, because it had always been done by the lord of Saint-Céneri; and also that you never rode there that day but must always walk.

It was a fine, frosty morning when they set out; the sharp pale blue of winter was above and white rime underfoot; but where a bank of hollies threw a shadow on the rime there was a cloudy gloom of another misty blue, delicately hyacinthine, as though the ghost of summer lurked there. As they tramped across the open meadow the crusted grass crunched under their feet; it was so stiff that even the dogs' light footsteps rustled in it, and so chill that when the dogs stood after running, with their red tongues hanging, they stood in a white steaming cloud of their own breath. Young Robert always liked this going to the chapel at Christmas because the thin winter woods were not empty or quiet that day, but full of the sound of voices and footsteps and, now and again, of singing.

It was he who came first to the foot of the open slope and to the road that ran down from the gate of the town. Robert Geroy and Neel Badger and Guion were not far behind, but young Robert was alone when he lifted up his eyes and saw the man who was coming very slowly along the path that led from Perseigne forest. It was a tall man who went stooping and stumbling a little; his face was gray-white except where it was marked with brown, dried blood; his kirtle was gray, and that too had a great patch of dull brown right over the breast of it; in his left arm he carried a bundle and in his right hand a naked sword.

Robert stared, gulped, and ran at him, snatching out his knife.

"Stop! Go away!" he shouted. "Go—!" and stopped short, while his heart pounded. It was not a dead man, as he had thought at first, nor a thief—it was Fulcun.

Fulcun stood still. He put the point of the sword down into the frosty grass and leaned on it.

"Where is Robert Geroy?" he says, and then he saw, over young Robert's head, Robert and Guion and Neel Badger. He did not look at the youngster again, but only at Robert. Young Robert stepped aside, feeling a small child among men. Robert Geroy came and stood in front of Fulcun.

Fulcun began, "Sir—" but Robert stopped him. He stepped close and laid his hands on the lacing of Fulcun's kirtle. "What is this?" he says sharply.

Fulcun pushed his hands away.

"Not my blood," he says, with a sort of laugh. "I've only my head broke."

"What's happened?"

"Montgaudri's lost. Geroy's dead." He must be brief. He held out the bundle toward Robert. "Will you take this? It's his . . . ," he said.

Robert says, "A child?" and Fulcun nodded. Robert bent over the bundle.

"It's dead," he says.

Fulcun cried out, "Oh!" peering at it. Then he said, "I didn't like it at first. It was so ugly. But then, I thought it would grow into a man . . . Now—it's dead." He stared down at it, and Robert stared too at the small thing, a seven-months child and only two days old, whose life had slipped into death as invisibly as a drop of water into a clear stream and left no empty space at all in the world because it was so small.

Then Fulcun said, "I brought it to you. I didn't know where else to bring it. I thought you would keep it. It was Geroy's, not mine." He stopped and then muttered something about ". . . hadn't done you any harm."

Robert took the dead child suddenly from him and put it down on the grass. Then he laid his hands on Fulcun's arms.

"Oh! You fool! You fool! You fool!" he cried at him.

Fulcun put his head down on Robert's shoulder. It was most comforting to hear Robert's big voice swearing close by his ear. He began to laugh, but Robert shouted, "Stop that!" and Fulcun stopped and bit his teeth together.

Even Dame Aelis was kind to Fulcun that day. It was Christmas Day for one thing, and for another, a spent man with a broken head, though he were Fulcun, was so like a boy that she must be kind. But after that day she did not trouble to pretend to be glad of his coming.

Young Robert was glad. He told Fulcun so when he brought him a wooden bowl full of steaming broth that same evening. He leaned against the bed, staring hard at Fulcun with his blue eyes, and then he said, "I didn't know you. I thought you were a dead man walking." Fulcun smiled at him over the bowl that he held in his hands. He thought what a brave brat it was to run at a dead man walking.

Just then Robert Geroy came in and sent the lad off. He said the very same words, "I'm glad you're back," and then sat down by Fulcun's feet and crossed his arms over his broad chest and said, "Now tell me what has happened."

Fulcun looked at him and then down at the bowl. "Have you heard nothing?" he asked.

Robert stared at his feet thrust out before him. "Adam the Peddler came in for the winter three weeks ago. He told us that Rogier of Montgommeri had come to Montgaudri." Robert slowed, picking his words. "And that he took away with him," he says, "the wife of Mauger of Fervacques . . . Was it so?"

Fulcun said, "Yes." He was glad that he need not try to put that immense blank into words. He began to tell Robert how he had gone to Séez.

They did not once use Alde's name. Fulcun was afraid to have it on his tongue; it was too dear a thing, and it hurt too much to say. Robert wanted to forget that he had ever heard it spoken. So, when Fulcun had finished talking, Robert says, "It's the Belesme behind the duke. But we'll not let 'em keep Montgaudri to laugh at us. We— But go to sleep now."

He took the empty bowl out of Fulcun's hands, and as he went to the door, he says, without looking again at Fulcun,

"You're a fool, Heron, but I'm glad you're back."

❦

One night, more than two months after Fulcun had come back to Saint-Céneri, as Dame Aelis lay in bed and Robert stood in the middle of the floor pulling off his shirt, she said,

"Sir."

Says Robert, "What is it?"

"I think Fulcun Geroy means to be a monk."

Robert stood perfectly still a second; then he whisked his shirt over his head and threw it down on the floor. "No," he cried. "No. Nonsense." His voice was angry.

He came to the bed and lifted the coverlet and got in beside her, growling again, "Nonsense!" Then he said, "Why do you think so?"

"You know I had to go down this morning to help with that girl Johane in her labor?"

Robert says, "What's that to do—?"

"Wait a minute. The moon hadn't set. I looked out of a shot window as I went down. He was going across the yard—Fulcun Geroy." She paused, but Robert did not speak. "I thought," she said, "'Perhaps it's a wench,' but he went in at the door of the chapel."

"You stayed watching him," Robert told her.

"Why not? But that's not all. When the girl was delivered I came by the chapel. The door was open and I looked in. I could see him in the moonlight, down on his knees and his hands out—like that." She thrust out her hands, locked together. Robert turned his face away from them.

He began, "You shouldn't have—" and stopped. When he spoke again it was to swear.

"What's the matter?" she asked him.

"I was thinking . . . All the best of us Geroys get shaven heads."

She cried, "Chut!" She did not think so well of Fulcun. Sometimes she hated him. Then she said, "I'm content with mine."

He rolled over and caught her under his arm. "Aelis!" he says.

But she pushed him off because she was so angry with Fulcun. "Go to sleep," she said.

Robert did not go to sleep. He lay thinking about what she had said. It was only too likely to be true. He had been very glad when Fulcun came back—he had never thought of this. He wished he could ask Fulcun point-blank if it were true. But he couldn't.

But he did. It was the very next day, one of those sweet, bright, tender February days when the sap begins to rise, and men to feel the stirring of the spring, and even the wine is troubled in the wineskins. Robert was going across the yard with dogs at his heels—he never went far without dogs following him—and he turned and saw Fulcun coming stooping out of the low doorway of the chapel. He hung on his heel and then went over to him.

"Where have you been?" he asked.

"In there," says Fulcun, tipping his head back where he had come from, and then, with that needless, useless question asked and answered, they stood silent. One of the dogs jumped up at Robert's knee, but he pushed it down.

Then Robert came out with it, "Do you mean to be a monk?" he says with a hard, frowning stare on Fulcun's face.

Fulcun says, "A monk? No, Robert."

Robert should have been content at that, but he was not. There was something in Fulcun's face, and his voice, that he could not let pass. Here was—he thought—more of the Heron's madness—but what was it?

"What for do you go there then?" he says, and when Fulcun did not tell him, "Listen to me, my lad, if you're thinking that a man must go on with . . . that kind of thing after he's made his peace in church—"

Fulcun shook his head.

"Then what in God's name is it?" cried Robert.

Fulcun looked hard at him. After a minute he said, "You told me yourself, you told me . . . loving . . . was to have a very great care and kindness." His eyes were on Robert's while he spoke. "That is it," he said.

Robert took an instant to understand. Then he spoke, not loud but very angry:

"That wanton still!" he cried. Fulcun lifted his hand, but Robert went on, "Do you pray God her man should die? Is that what it is?"

Fulcun said, in a difficult, low voice, "No," and Robert felt more ashamed than really he had need to feel, because, however hard Fulcun tried not to see it, his mind would keep on showing him, as if it had been a glimpse through a window, four candles burning in a dark church, and between them a dead man lying, and the dead man, Mauger. Robert muttered at last, "Well, I can't understand. It's all over—"

Fulcun said, "No," again, and Robert stared, then grew angry again.

"If I were lusting still after another man's wife," he says, "I'd be afraid to go in there," and he nodded at the chapel. He swung away from Fulcun and then stood still, but without turning back, because Fulcun spoke:

"Robert," he says slowly, "it is not like that. I—" Then he stopped. Was it not like that at all? "I can't stop loving her—I can't want to stop," he says, desperate of finding anything nearer the truth than that.

Robert stood a second longer, biting on his fingers; then he said emphatically, "I call it sin," and went away.

When Robert had gone up into the tower Fulcun went out of the town. He crossed the full river and climbed up into the woods. The sun was just past its noon height and shone down into them, making the mossed trunks and branches as clear a green as any summer leaves. The sky was blue beyond them, and when a few rooks went by above, their shadows slid and flickered and dodged from trunk to green trunk.

At first he thought only how far Robert had been from the truth. Sin was it, to love her? Not as he loved her. Over, was it? Never so long as his soul should live. Should he fear to go into the chapel to move God to keep her safe and make her happy? He almost laughed. And then, striding on through the bright empty woods he found, as most men find, the barb of the argument lodged in his mind.

But the bare doubt, that to love her might be sin, was too deadly to face. He turned from it to think of her. He remembered in an agony of tenderness her head, smooth and shining with the dull gleam of sun-burned gold. He ached to take her head between his hands; he ached to wrap his love about her like a cloak, to hold her safe and close—but it could never be close enough. The thought of holding her sent a jar of life running through all his body. He held her, and she lifted her lips to his, in that full, frank kiss of hers.

He jerked his head back as if from her actual mouth. That was the sin that Robert had told him of.

And yet, as he tramped on, he knew that this love and the other were all one. Soul and body, she was Alde, and how could he love her body without her soul, or her soul without her body? Nor could he say to Robert, or to God himself, "I will not love her," because there was no part of him that was not wholly hers. There was no fragment of him that could deliver up the rest to God, if it were sin. He was all—all—all hers, and she was his—he was sure of that . . .

It was twilight, with the fringe of the bare trees showing intense and fine against the pale edge of the sky above the hills, when he came again to the river. Down here it was dark, and as he crossed by the stones he lingered a moment watching, where, in one of the deep flashes, the reflection of a star floated, hardly shaken at all or distorted by the smoothly running water. He was not eager to go up, because Robert Geroy was angry—justly angry, and yet Fulcun could do no other than he did now.

But when he was come to the hall and took his place at the table, Robert called to him across the others and sent Berenger along with his own horn of wine. Like Fulcun, he had found a barb sticking in his mind. It was the Heron—he was mad always. And if he went into the chapel by day and by dark, perhaps there was some queer good in this crazy love of his—and very likely it was all the woman's fault too. Robert was glad when he thought of that, and promptly shoved everything else out of his mind.

One evening in mid-March as they sat at supper with the last of the daylight showing very blue through the open windows beyond the yellow glow of the torches in the hall, a man came up from the gate of the town to say that lord Rogier of Montgommeri and his company were asking lodging for the night on their way out of Mayenne.

Fulcun had both his hands on the table as if he would have got up, but Robert saw him.

"No," cried Robert, loud enough for half the hall to hear. "I'll have whom I please at my board and under my roof. Sit still, Fulcun Geroy."

Aelis cried out at that, "He's an outlaw. Why stir trouble?"

"He's a Geroy," says Robert very blunt, and then to her, "Go in, and take the maidens with you. Montgommeri and his folk are no friends of mine."

Aelis had to go though she was very angry, since she counted Montgommeri, Duke Guillelm's friend, enough friend of the Geroys to sit at meat with the women of the house.

Rogier came in, dark and very fine in woodland green and a great cloak of marten skins. But Fulcun looked beyond to the knights behind him. When he saw that Mauger was not there he did not care much for Rogier. Robert stood up, and as he spoke to welcome the guests he pulled Fulcun toward him by his wrist.

Rogier, with his foot on the steps, paused. His eyes were on Fulcun, and he lifted his hand and pointed at him.

"You've an outlaw beside you, Robert Geroy," he says.

Robert looked him between his eyes.

"He's a Geroy," he answered, as he had answered Aelis.

"You have disowned him."

"I have taken up his quarrels again. So I have quarrels against you, Rogier of Montgommeri—Montgaudri taken and a Geroy dead."

Rogier took his foot from the step. "Shall I go?" he says.

"Go or stay," says Robert, "whichever you will, in peace—this time."

Rogier looked at him for a second. He liked plain dealing and he himself could be very plain, though he was far more discreet than Robert Geroy. He says, "Suffer me to stay tonight in peace."

Robert bade him then, "Come and eat."

But as they ate, Robert turned to Fulcun. The ends of his big mouth were twitching.

"Pledge me, Fulcun Geroy," he says, as he took the horn from Berenger.

Fulcun lifted up his knife and held it over the table while Robert drank. He guessed that Robert was teasing Rogier of Montgommeri, and the thought was in his mind, "Robert's always a boy, even when he's angry." Then Robert says, "Now

I'll pledge you," and gave the half-empty horn into Fulcun's hand, and held up his own knife with the point toward Rogier. As Fulcun drank Robert turned his head away and looked at his guest and laughed, his great, sudden shout of laughter.

Rogier stood it very well. He went a little red, but he says to Robert, "Who will pledge me?"

"How can I tell that?" says Robert, grinning at him.

Next morning Robert himself brought a horn of wine, and cake to sop in the wine, to Rogier when he was mounted in the yard. Robert could be a great lord when he chose, and this morning he did so choose; the service he did made him seem all the state-lier. Rogier took the wine and cake; as he handed back the horn empty, Dame Aelis came out of the tower and down the steps, so Rogier greeted her.

She says, "Sir, carry my greetings to my cousin the duke."

Rogier said he would, and then, farewell. But he stayed a moment when his knights had moved on.

"Listen to me, Robert Geroy," he says. "If you want the duke's love, you mustn't keep his enemies here," and he nodded at Fulcun. "I speak friendly," he added quickly.

But Robert did not care for that.

"Must I not?" he says, and flared. "I'll not then. I'll bring him with me to the duke's court to get justice—if there is justice for any Geroy where there is track of the hooves of Belesme."

Rogier answered only, "There is justice," and jerked his bridle and went after the others.

Robert turned about to Fulcun, but Fulcun was leaning against the post of the tower steps, his chin on his chest, staring at the ground. Robert knew that Aelis's eyes were on him, and he turned to her instead.

He said, "We'll have justice at the duke's hand. We'll get Montgaudri again."

She looked at him, and said nothing. Then she turned her eyes on Fulcun.

"This is your doing," she says, and went past him up the steps.

That evening at supper she was very silent. Robert knew well what her hard, shut mouth meant, and her eyes that kept so much to themselves that they would never meet his. He turned his back on her. It was the easiest way.

He talked for the most part to Ranof Badger across the table. They disputed half the mealtime as to whether a man must have wildware leather for his arming thongs or no. Ranof said that well-worked calfskin would do, but Robert maintained stoutly and even angrily that it must be wildware of the deer. He turned to Fulcun at last and says, "What do you think?"

Fulcun was sitting looking at the table. He did not turn his head. Robert nudged him. "What do you think?" he says again.

But Aelis spoke before Fulcun.

"Look at him! Look at him!" she cried, not very loud, but in a voice that made everyone at the table look where her hand pointed—at Fulcun.

She turned on Robert then—

"You'll go to the duke? You'll make an enemy of Guillelm of Normandy to get Montgaudri back—for him—?"

Robert brought his fist down on the table.

"Silence!" he shouted at her, but she only laughed.

"Oh! Strike me again if you like. You've struck me once before for his sake!"

Robert, who had had it in his mind to strike her, let his hand drop. "Then hold your tongue," he muttered and turned his shoulder on her.

But she laid her hand on it, dragging him about.

"You fool! You fool!" she cried at him. "Listen to me. You care more for him than for me, more than for your own only son. D'you think he cares for you?"

She shook him, nearly frantic now. "Look at him!" she cried again. "He doesn't care for you. He doesn't care for Montgaudri. He doesn't care for a thing in all the world but that wanton wench that is another man's."

Fulcun stood up then, but it was Robert who spoke.

"Go!" he says to Aelis, and she knew she must.

She pushed her chair back and went toward the door; but even now she stopped and half turned.

"You've forgotten now how he played you false," she said. "You'll remember when he does it again." Then she went.

Robert pulled Fulcun down again. "She's only a fool of a woman," he says. "Never mind her."

He thought hastily, "She never liked Fulcun. She always wants her own way. She's only a woman," and did not know what doubt his mind was answering.

Fulcun says, "Oh, Robert, let it be."

He would have said more, when Robert swore at him. It was on his tongue to say, "Robert, it's true," but that was so hard a thing to say to Robert, knowing that he would never understand.

Robert cried, "Death of God! I won't leave Montgaudri to the Belesme. What do I care for the Bastard? I'll not see Geroys killed and reived while there are spears in Saint-Céneri!"

That was what he said, but he thought too—"And if I get him Montgaudri again, he'll have to remember I did—whatever happens."

Chapter 13

"Ah, traitor untrue," said King Arthur, "now thou hast betrayed me twice. Who would have weened that, thou that hast been to me so lief and dear?"

Malory, *Le Morte Darthur*, book 21, chapter 5

I

They set out for Caen, where the Easter court was held, on a stormy spring day with sun, wind, and big clouds. They were going first to Echauffour, where Hernaut and many other Geroys would be ready to ride with them, for Robert had called all out that could ride. It was blowing a slanting, cold shower when they left Saint-Céneri; a bitter weather for parting, and Dame Aelis was as unfriendly. Even Robert got only a cold kiss, though, to part so hurt her even more than it hurt him; and Fulcun got no kiss at all. They rode out of the town gate, heads down against the driving rain, and what thoughts any man had, he must perforce keep to himself.

But an hour or so later they were riding in warm sunshine, with all the pools in the soaked, bright green fields as blue as the sky. The great cloud that had rained on them was gone by and now showed snow-white above, although rain was falling in the distance from its dragging dark skirts.

Robert, who had been riding half his horse's length in front of Fulcun, dropped back and began to talk to him. He said that by now Engeler would be at Caharel, and he could soon set the alod to rights. Engeler was one of the freemen of Saint-Céneri, and when Robert had found out from Fulcun that he had got no dues from Caharel for the last two years, he had said, "Engeler Over-the-River is your man. He's got too many brothers at home; he'll be glad to go; and I'll be glad to see the back of him, such poaching as he does in my forest." Now, as they rode together, Robert says, "Engeler's a good man—except for poaching—for all he talks so wild; and a bundle of badger skins and five deer skins are good rent enough for that little alod. You'll get them next year for sure, when the chapmen come with the salted salmon from the bay." Fulcun says, "Aye," as if he were thinking of something else, and for a while Robert was silent.

At last he looked sidelong at Fulcun—a quaint, boyish, guilty look, and then he chuckled.

Fulcun turned to him half smiling.

"I was thinking," says Robert, "Mauger is sure to be at this court—I was thinking—I'll be glad to see you laying on at him if he claims a duel in this suit against you."

He stopped short there. Fulcun was not smiling now. Robert looked away from Fulcun's eyes, frowning with his big eyebrows. "Aye," he says obstinately, "I'll be glad to see you paying him for the harm he's done us."

He glowered at his horse's ears for a minute. There was something unsatisfactory in that thought—yet it had seemed right enough till he had met Fulcun's look. He frowned fiercer. What was wrong with it? If Mauger claimed duel, that was his own lookout. And Fulcun was only fighting for Montgaudri. So it was all right. Robert put the whole thing out of his mind.

But Fulcun could not. Robert had spoken the thing that he had been shutting out of his thoughts, and now the doors were broken down. He was going to Caen. In three days perhaps he would be in the field between the town and the river, facing Mauger, with his sword out and shield up. And the day after that Mauger might be lying quiet between four tall candles burning steady in some dark church.

He did not dare look aside at Robert. He did not dare even to look up from his own hand clenched on the reins. He had to shut his teeth hard and summon his strength to contain the huge swell of life that rose up in him then.

For if Mauger lay still between those candles, then he could go to Alde, and even to think of that was life after being dead.

He raised his head now. He wanted to shout aloud. A swift movement caught his eyes; a flock of pigeons was flying above the field to the left; they wheeled and swung about and flowered suddenly into white against the blue sky. Then they turned again and the white was quenched. Fulcun dropped his head.

For the rest of that morning, and beyond it, he rode in silence mostly, because he was at war. That hope he must deny; he must not look at it. He fought, but the more steadfastly he shut his mind to it, the more surely the very sound of the horse's hooves told him that there might soon be nothing between him and Alde but a stretch of road like this road.

❦

They came to the gate of Caen on Maundy Thursday, in the morning. As they drew near a dozen horsemen rode out; they had hawks on their fists and dogs ranging after the horses' hooves. Among the first of them, on a tall white mare, went Guillelm himself.

They met a stone's throw from the gate. Duke Guillelm held up his hand for his people to stop, but he came on a few paces. Robert Geroy did the same; when his horse's nose was almost at Guillelm's knee he gave the duke greeting.

Guillelm did not answer it. "You ride with too many spears, Robert Geroy," he says.

Robert answered in his big, brave voice, "Not a one too many while you have a Belesme by you."

Guillelm scowled at him. "That's as I choose," he said, and then, very harsh, "I do not welcome you. What have you come for?"

Robert looked at him between the eyes. "For justice," he says.

"Justice?" cried Guillelm. "You'll get it, full measure." He looked beyond Robert, one glance, and then his hand went out, pointing straight at Fulcun among all the others. "There's the man shall have my justice," he says.

His eyes came again to Robert's face, square, blunt, with the grim mouth and the heavy lines that told both of laughter and old pain. Robert stared back at him, then his eyes began almost to twinkle. He did not say, but he looked, "You'll have to get him first."

The duke said, "He broke my peace, he failed my summons. If he'd been wise he'd have dreaded to come now," but his voice was not so angry.

Says Robert, "Why should he dread? I'm his surety." His eyes were certainly smiling now, and the corners of his big mouth twitched. "And the spears," he says.

Guillelm turned from him, frowning. Then he said curtly, "Well, he shall stand his trial. I'll give him equal justice. But if he fails in his proof, Montgaudri is forfeit, Robert Geroy, say what you will."

"He'll not fail," says Robert, and he laughed. The duke shot a dark under-glance at him and rode on.

That day they pitched their tents outside the town in an apple orchard, and there they stayed, all through the feast. Robert would not have them lodge, nor even go up into the town except to church on Good Friday and Easter Day. So they waited. No message came to them from the duke, nor any welcome, nor gifts such as a lord gives at great feasts. They stayed there, almost as if they were besieging the town, only that the gate stood open to them to go in if they chose. The days were long to all of them, but longest to Fulcun. He watched the pale, the gate, the road from the gate. Was Alde there—so near to him? His heart and almost his reason rocked at the thought. He could think of nothing but that, that and Mauger; Mauger in the field by the river, Mauger lying quiet between four tall candles in some dark church.

Sometimes he dreaded that Mauger was not there, and could hardly endure to wait, lest these days of terrible hope should end in blank futility. Sometimes he was sure that Mauger was there, that they would meet in the field and he would kill Mauger. He would be sure then that this was meant; he was being carried to it, helpless and choiceless; he need only wait and it would come to pass. He said in his heart then, "It is the will of God. It is his hand," and was the more adread.

Three days after Easter Day, and just after noon, Gueroult, the duke's seneschal, came out to cry the assembly of the duke's court for an hour before sunset. So in the clear and still light of the spring evening, with thrush answering blackbird all about the orchards where the apple blossom was brightening to a strange beauty as the sun shone lower, the Geroys, unarmed except for their swords, went, close on fifty strong, through the town of Caen, and up the steep street to the castle. Those of them who were the duke's homagers went first—Robert and Hernaut, with Fulcun on Robert's left hand, and old Engenulf of l'Aigle, and the two brothers from Merlerault, and squat, scowling Gui Bollein. The rest came after; they would not sit in the duke's court, but they would come in and listen to the judgment and let all the barons of Normandy see what force the Geroys had.

They came to the doors of the hall and from the sunshine passed into twilight. Those who were not homagers fell back, the others went on to the benches set at the upper end of the hall, where already the court sat, and where men turned and watched them as they came. In the midst, on his seat of state, with the scarlet cushion latticed with gold thread, and the carved lion heads, sat Guillelm. He had his sheathed sword unbelted and upright in his hand, resting against his shoulder.

Fulcun looked at him and then away. It was not Guillelm his eye sought for among all that were here. He thought for a moment, "He is not here," and then, as he sat down, he saw, right over against him, beside Gerard the butler, Mauger of Fervacques.

Mauger was staring at him, and for one moment, in all that crowd, they were alone, eye glaring to eye. Then Fulcun looked away. He had to, or the hate and rage and agony of loss would have torn him; for Alde was Mauger's. He could not look at Mauger and think of that.

He heard in the dark confusion of his mind, a sudden silence. He lifted his head. Mauger was on his feet. Fulcun could not look away again.

Said Mauger, pointing his hand at Fulcun, "I accuse Fulcun Geroy of Montgaudri." He stopped, as if he must steady himself. "He has broken the duke's peace in the duke's castle of Falaise within seven days of the return of the host. He has raped my wife. He has failed the duke's summons. I claim my proof. I claim duel for my proof." He stood there, one hand shaking on the grip of his sword, the other pointing still at Fulcun, and that shook too.

"Answer," says the duke's voice, and Fulcun got up with a jerk. He turned away from Mauger, because he could not answer right if he saw him. Then with his eyes on the green leather and silver plates of the duke's scabbard, he denied the charge, carefully, word for word against Mauger's words, as the law must have it. Then he sat down and heard Robert chuckle beside him. But he only knew that he would fight Mauger tomorrow.

The rest of it was all swamped in his mind by that knowledge. He saw Mauger go to the duke and put a glove into his hand. He went himself, stepping carefully over Hernaut's feet, and stood in front of the duke's chair. He held out his glove in his clenched hand at the full stretch of his arm and let it fall into Guillelm's hand. Mauger's glove lay on the duke's knee—a brown glove thonged with scarlet. After that they went out into the yard, and the benches were set for him and Mauger, and Richart of Avranches went to and fro between them, carrying the defiance. Fulcun did not try to look at Mauger then. He could wait. He looked down at his own hands, and thoughts went through his brain as wild as windblown fire. He must hit down at Mauger's helm . . . one old wound makes a man dread another in that place . . . Was his sword well sharpened? . . . If Alde were in Caen, Mauger would not be going to her tonight because of the vigil . . . And tomorrow night—

Those racing thoughts went with him to the very door of the church where he and Mauger and two priests to confess them were to watch through the night. He halted in the porch and saw, as if he had not known him, Robert Geroy beside him.

Robert stood with his feet apart. He stared hard at Fulcun, frowning. Then he said, with a cheerfulness that went ill with his look,

"Mauger's big, Heron, and a crafty fighter, but don't you forget you need only hold him till the first star, and then he loses his suit . . . And you get Montgaudri. Don't you forget that."

He seemed very anxious that Fulcun should be sure of it, for he stayed staring at him.

"Do you hear?" he says.

Fulcun turned to him. His face, except for his eyes, was blank, but they burned like fever. He says, quickly and impatiently, "Yes—yes—the first star," as if he were thinking urgently of something very different.

Robert had to leave it. He clapped Fulcun on the shoulder and kissed him. Then he went away.

Fulcun pushed open the door and stepped into the church. It was dark, quiet, and cold, after the streets. Mauger knelt already at one altar and a priest sat near him on a stool. The other priest beckoned to Fulcun. He must go up to the high altar itself. He went, and as he went every thought fell away out of his mind and left it empty of all but a blind dread.

In the morning the priest heard Fulcun's confession, shrived him, and said, "Wait here."

Then he went away, his shoes clapping on the stones of the pavement. Fulcun looked round. Someone else was coming up behind. It was Mauger. He knelt down in a line with Fulcun but not near. The priest came back, vested. He said Mass, laid God first upon Mauger's tongue, then upon Fulcun's. When it was finished Mauger got up and went away.

Fulcun stayed a minute. The dark was over, and the emptiness of the night. The sunshine came fresh through the unglazed windows, and with it the scent of moist earth and young, growing things, the scent of spring. Behind him he heard Robert

Geroy's voice speaking low to someone. But he stayed. Now that the light was come, and the daytime, he must know what to do—he must be able to see.

He covered his face with his hands, crushing his eyeballs with his fingers.

"O God," he cried to his hands, "Show me! Show me!" He waited for an answer, for light. Then he got up. His mind told itself that there was no certain answer, but in those dark places far below the floor of the mind, where a man's self resides, he knew that there was no need even to ask.

II

A few minutes before the bells in Caen rang for None next afternoon, the Geroys went down, armed and horsed, to the river. Fulcun rode between Robert and Hernaut. None of them said anything, except that when they got to the ground Robert says, "The sun will set clear. See that you keep it behind you."

Fulcun nodded, but that was all.

Duke Guillelm came down soon, and Rogier of Montgommeri riding at his right hand. Mauger was on his left. When they had come to a stand Robert turned to Guion who held his rein.

"Take his horse!" he says very sharp. Guion went and took Fulcun's bridle. Fulcun got down. He looked up into Robert's face for one second and Robert nodded at him. "Go on," he says, and with that one word and no other Fulcun went out into the space between.

The sun was going down clear in the west over the flat marsh and the distant woods beyond the river. The high arch of heaven was dappled with light cloud, but clear again over the eastern horizon. Except for the slight, restless jingle of bits and bridles, there was such quiet in the open green space that Fulcun could hear the sound of the river sliding by between the flat banks.

Mauger had dismounted and came out now from the crowd of men and horses opposite. He had his sword drawn. Fulcun lugged out his own and shook his shield down on his arm to a better grip. He went toward Mauger until they stood perhaps six paces apart, and then both stood, weighing their swords in their hands, watching eye to eye, and waiting for the duke's herald to sound.

He blew a sudden blast of noise that sent up a couple of herons that were feeding lower down the river. The watching men leaned forward on their horses; the proof was begun.

It was Mauger moved first. He stepped sidelong toward Fulcun, then swung about with his sword up, and brought it down. It was a great blow; Fulcun caught it on his shield and countered, but Mauger had stepped off again and the sword found Mauger's shield rim only a handsbreadth from its point.

Robert muttered to Hernaut, but never taking his eyes off the fighting, "That Mauger—he's fierce as a fox. And stout." He gritted his teeth for a minute and then said, "If the Heron doesn't wake up—"

After that stroke they fought open for a long while—slow work. It was clear that Mauger was feeling his way and waiting to choose his time. "But God knows," thought Robert, "what

Fulcun is doing. He'll get caught yet at one of those recovers if he's not quicker."

They went in again, and for a few seconds the quiet was broken by the dunting of blows on the wood or the iron shield rims. Robert, sitting very still on his horse with a grim face that told nothing, was thinking, "It's my fault. I told him to fight a waiting game." He jerked young Guion in the back with his foot, but without taking his eyes off Fulcun.

"You keep watching for the first star. Never mind the fighting," he says, and when Guion did not answer, being intent on the fighting too, "Do you hear, you young fool," and jerked him again and harder. Guion, used to Robert's sudden claps of temper, was astonished by his fierceness. He did what he was told.

When they had been at it close on an hour, and there was a trampled patch in the young moist green where they had circled about each other, Mauger, drawing back, but with his shield well up, says to Fulcun—

"Shall we draw off awhile?"

"Aye—if you will," says Fulcun.

It was the first time they had spoken; they had fought all the while in silence, except that each could hear the other's hard, controlled breathing when they closed.

Mauger went away toward where Rogier and the duke were, and sat down, and leaned his head on his hands, but Fulcun stayed where he was, leaning on his shield point and jabbing at the grass now and again with his sword. After a while Mauger got up again. They went at it once more, but fighting open for a while.

Then Fulcun struck out; it was a slicing blow, aimed at the shoulder. Mauger lifted his shield and crouched his back, the blow glanced down the shield rim harmless, but Mauger, from under the shield, thrust up, right at Fulcun's throat.

Robert Geroy shut his teeth and said behind them, "God!"

But Fulcun was not down. The point had missed his throat though it caught his cheek and tore flesh and leather gorget and the lacing of the helm. He stumbled aside, bleeding, and Mauger came after to get another blow in that would be the end.

Fulcun turned. He saw Mauger's face, he saw the sword lifted, and then he sprang. His sword swung and met Mauger's, the sparks leaped and spat. He struck again, careless of Mauger's blows. He shouted, he did not know what, but Robert, hearing it, swore aloud and bit his fingers. For it was not the cry, "Hoi! Geroy!" but "Alde! Alde! Alde!" with every blacksmith's stroke.

Mauger went back. Fulcun saw his face whiten and his eyes stare. He struck and struck again, and Mauger caught the blows on his shield, on his blade, but Fulcun knew that soon one would go home.

Mauger, with his shield hacked and blood running down from his nose from a dunt that he had got on the head with the last of a glancing blow, staggered clear a moment. Fulcun let him go. He spat blood out of his own mouth and watched Mauger stand with his head hanging. Then he drew breath and lifted his sword. Mauger turned his head away and back, he raised his shield but it jerked down again. Fulcun knew that he had only to strike once. He took a step toward Mauger and stopped.

Robert Geroy felt someone's hand tugging at his knee. He struck at it. His eyes were on Fulcun.

But young Guion caught hold of him again. He was crying, "Look—look—up there. There's a star!"

Robert Geroy turned, looked down at Guion's finger, and up where it pointed. There was a star, a faint white speck in a space of clear pale sky among the dappled clouds.

"Count Guillelm! Duke Guillelm!" he shouted, but his voice was drowned in a greater shout. He stopped short, staring at the field.

Fulcun was on his knees, his helm torn off, his head down, and Mauger, rocking on his feet, beat blindly on his head and shoulders with the flat of his sword.

Then the duke's herald sounded his horn again and someone ran out and got hold of Mauger and led him off. Fulcun rolled over till he sat, leaning heavily on one hand, his head hanging.

Robert cried: "What—?"

Hernaut answered him through his teeth. "Fulcun went at him and Mauger got his sword up. Fulcun stopped. Then he threw his sword away and Mauger caught him a buffet on the head—"

Robert looked again at Fulcun. His sword lay in the untrodden grass a dozen paces from where he had gone down.

When the duke had given judgment Robert went across the field. His horse stepped daintily across Fulcun's sword, and stared aslant with wide eyes at Fulcun, and snatched its head aside at the smell of blood. Robert stopped and looked down, and Fulcun looked up and wiped his hand over his mouth to clear off the blood.

He said, "Robert—I—couldn't kill him. I thought I could—then—"

Robert cut him short. "Aelis was right," he says, and rode on.

That same evening Rogier of Montgommeri came to the duke in the treasury of the castle. The duke had a clerk with him, and a pile of tallies lay on the table between them. Guillelm looked up.

"What of Mauger?"

"He'll live," says Rogier. He went to the window and stared out. "But he's a broken man," he says. "He fell from one fit to another. He must have got a blow on the old blow—where he was trepanned. He's asleep now, but I doubt when he wakes he may be an idiot."

Guillelm said, "Tchk!"

"When he can," says Rogier, "he'd best go back to Fervacques—to his wife. Let her mend what she's married." He broke off then to curse her. Guillelm had never seen Rogier so moved.

"Well," says the duke, to comfort him, "Fulcun Geroy is locked up, and he'll stay so till the Geroys give me surety for him. If they'll not, I'll pack him out of Normandy and let him beg his bread in France."

Rogier says, "It won't help Mauger," but he sounded glad to hear it.

"And for Montgaudri," Guillelm had his eyes hard on Rogier, "for Montgaudri, I am selling it to Robert Geroy. He offered me a price and paid me some of it at once. He'll come to court at

Pentecost and pay the rest. He'll not take up that nephew of his again I think."

Rogier, for a minute, said nothing. Then, "You ought to keep Montgaudri. You know that."

Guillelm says tartly, "I know Mabille says so. But I like Robert Geroy. Besides—" He stopped, looking under a frown at Rogier, and was silent. Pentecost was not yet.

In a small room at the top of one of the towers of Caen castle Fulcun Geroy stood, three paces from the window, looking out. He could not go any nearer, for he stood now at the full stretch of the chain that tethered him by one ankle to a ring in the wall. It was a gray day with a steady gale blowing, and in the sky the seagulls leaned their shoulders against the wind, turning high and strong on their sharp sickle wings and crying desolately. From here he could see nothing but that, the gray sky, and the gray, wheeling seagulls.

He turned his back on the window and went four steps across the room to the pile of straw that was his bed and sat down on it. He had been here ten days; he knew that by the nicks he had made with his knife in one of the planks of the floor. At first he had lain most of the time between sleep and waking, with the pain of the wound in his face enough to keep thought away. But now his cheek was healing well, and his strength had come back, and now he could do nothing but think.

Aelis had spoken the truth. He had cared nothing for Robert; nothing for any creature in the world but Alde. He could not help it. Compared with her, Robert was—just nothing; but Fulcun put his head down on his fists then and groaned, because Robert was, after all, so much. But before, at the beginning, that night at Falaise, he had thrown over Robert's kindness for her sake and failed him. Now he had done it again, and if again he were to have the choice, again he would do the same.

As he sat there watching the bits of straw that moved with a restless uneasy hiss over the floor as the draft shifted them, his mind floundered into a slough of despair. He had failed Robert, and he would do it again. Another man would have been able to keep out of his mind the thought of Mauger dead. Another man would have known how to repent of his sin and yet keep that continuing love that he knew was holy. Another man would not have fought, or if he had fought he would have remembered that he need only hold Mauger till the first star showed; he would not have first tried to kill him and then thrown his sword away.

But he was not that other man; he was Fulcun Geroy. He smiled bitterly at the name as if it had a hateful sound, and then the smile died on his lips, and he sat quite still, not daring to move, because of the terror of a new thought.

He was that Fulcun Geroy. Did he really think that Alde—*Alde* could love him?

After a still pause, like the seconds before a felled tree reels and falls tearing and crashing through the other trees of the wood, thought on thought came crowding on him. She had gone from him willingly. That night, when she knew Mauger was alive, she had denied him. She had gone back to Mauger, and now it was months since she had gone. If she wished to forget it would be easy for her to have forgotten by now. And was it likely that she wished to remember—Fulcun Geroy?

He got up and began to move about the room, but the chain kept jerking at his ankle and nearly tripping him in his hasty pacing, till he stood still in the middle of the floor and put his fists to his teeth to prevent himself screaming out curses. He made himself be quiet, but his heart was hammering. What could he do? For he must do something.

Then he knew what he could do. He went back, stepping carefully, and crouched down by the pile of straw. With his hands locked together and shoved between his knees he began to say behind his clenched teeth, "Take care of her! Take care of her!" again and again.

And then, dumb with the growing force of an urgency that went beyond words, he cried in silence to the silence of God, to take his soul and life for hers—to break, destroy, torment—to turn his pity away, so only that he pitied her. He pushed himself to the last limit of endurance; he thrust his soul out into the dark till he was afraid that it might fall into some empty gulf of space and never return to him. But he could get no answer.

He lifted his head at last and stared at the wall. It was of wood on this inner side and there was a row of old nails in it; he counted them—eight. His face was drained altogether of life and he knelt there, counting and recounting the nails to keep his mind from the greater dread it had stumbled on.

But he could not. It was God's kindness that he had reached out and clung to, now, as in the chapel at Séez; God's kindness that was like Robert's, only greater by more than a man could think. And that kindness—the only kindness left him now—if ever he had to choose, to weigh it against Alde—that kindness—

He dared not think out that thought, but he had no need to, he knew the end. He knew too that someday God would make him weigh the one against the other.

Chapter 14

Gentis homs fu, moult l'aimoient si chien.

Garin le Loherain

I

Duke Guillelm held his Pentecost court that year at Rouen, the feast falling early, on the 23rd of May. Robert Geroy of Saint-Céneri, with Dame Aelis and young Robert and a great company of knights and servants, rode across Normandy, a week before, through a green country that seemed snowed over with the may, while the air was heavy and drunk with the scent of it. Dame Aelis was very well satisfied with everything as it was just then; Robert had bought her silk for a new gown from a chapman who had it from Sicily—it was a silk as green as the young woods and woven with a pattern of palm trees and birds, milky-white like the may blossom. Besides being pleased with the gown, she was glad to be coming to court; she hoped that she would be able to prevent Robert paying more than he need for Montgaudri; she thought he was no match for the duke when it came to a bargain; he would not haggle, as he called it. But best of all, though she did not dwell on it, was the knowledge that Robert had done with Fulcun Geroy. He had never spoken Fulcun's name after he had told her shortly what had happened at Caen, and he had been angry with young Robert for asking about Fulcun. She thought,

"How could Robert ever forgive him now—Robert that doesn't know how to be disloyal?" and she looked at him riding beside her, staring straight ahead, with his heavy mouth set, grim but cheerful. He turned and smiled at her, and her heart filled with a pride in him that made her, for a moment, humble.

That journey was pleasant; the Pentecost court was not. Robert came back from the duke biting on his fingers and frowning. Guillelm would not talk about Montgaudri till after the feast. Robert said to Aelis that he didn't see there was anything to talk about; the money for the price of Montgaudri was here, in the leather-covered chest with the Spanish locks; it had only to be paid, and seisin given. Dame Aelis thought, and looked as though she thought, that she could have managed Duke Guillelm better. Robert scowled at her and went away.

When the court was over and most men riding off to their lands again, Robert Geroy still stayed, waiting for the duke to talk about Montgaudri. Then one morning he and Aelis were awakened in their lodging by a great noise of horses' hooves and shouting men in the streets. When Robert went down he heard that the duke had gone to Caen. A messenger had come in overnight telling Guillelm of trouble there between the men of Cabourg and the viscount, and he had ridden in haste—Dame Mahalt had gone too with her husband.

Robert came back and said to Aelis, "Truss up all the gear. We'll go to Caen."

They came to Caen about two hours after the duke and found the town crowded and very busy. Guillelm and most of his folk were lodged up at the castle, and that meant that rooms had to be cleared for them. So there were men carrying down loads of arms and wheeling carts loaded with ale and wine casks and sacks of corn. Robert found lodgings in the town, and they took up all their baggage, but when Aelis would have undone the saddlebags he said, "Let them alone. I shall ride for home today." It was past noon then.

She cried out, "What? Today! And without Montgaudri!"

He says, "No," and left her.

He had to pass by Saint Savior's Church. He turned his face from it and looked the other way because that was where Fulcun had kept vigil before he fought with Mauger. Robert could avoid looking at the church, but he could not avoid his thoughts. It was in his mind as he went into the narrow alley beside the church, "Aelis knew he would be untrue. How did she know? I couldn't see it in his face." He thought, "I'm a fool and growing old. I don't know how to tell if a man is untrue."

He lifted up his eyes and stood still in the midst of the lane. A couple of men with spears were coming toward him. In front of them walked a bandy-legged fellow dangling a bunch of keys in one hand and holding the end of a rope in the other. Between the spears there was a man whose hands were tied behind him by that same rope, and it was Fulcun.

Robert had time to see the new scar that puckered Fulcun's cheek beside his mouth, and time to see his face change from dullness to life, and change again to pain. Then he stepped aside and shouldered past them, his head down, biting on his fingers.

No use to stop, or speak, or remember. The Heron . . . Fulcun Geroy . . . was not a man a man could trust. That was all.

All the same, when they had gone by, Robert stopped again, and swung round, and stood watching them. They had stopped too, and the bandy-legged man was unlocking a door in the building opposite the flank of the church. It looked as if it were a corn store. Then Robert saw Fulcun stoop his head and go in under the low lintel. The spearmen stood outside, the old man went in.

Robert turned away. He supposed that, just as there was no room in the castle for the flour and the arms and the ale, there was no room for Fulcun Geroy, so they had brought him down here. Well—it made no difference. Nothing could make a difference if you could not trust a man. Robert went on heavily.

In a room of the great tower at Caen Duke Guillelm sat on his fald-stool. No one was with him now except Rogier of Montgommeri, but cushions lay about the floor where the viscount had sat, and Gerard the butler, and the seneschal and the rest, as they had taken counsel in the matter of the men of Cabourg.

Guillelm sat with his chin on his hand, staring and frowning straight before him. He looked far older so than his thirty-one years; he looked an ill man to quarrel with; dark, secret, dangerous.

He said at last, not looking at Rogier, "I shall have their right hands off ten of those men and put the rest out of my law." Then he stretched his arms out with the fists clenched and drew his breath sharply through his teeth. "After, we'll go to the Anjou border and see how they keep Ambrières."

Someone knocked at the door then.

"Go and see," says the duke.

Rogier got up, opened it, and put his head out.

"It's Robert Geroy of Saint-Céneri," he says to Guillelm.

"Let him wait," says Guillelm, so Rogier shut the door again but did not sit down.

Guillelm turned his overcast, frowning stare on him. "You were right," he says, "as to Montgaudri. I shall keep it."

Rogier said nothing, and Guillelm cried at him, with a black, fierce look, "Have men been so loyal to me that I should be loyal to anyone?"

Rogier did not answer that either. It was a hard question to answer. He dropped his eyes.

Guillelm said, "I like Robert Geroy. But he's a fool. It's time he learned—what I learned when I was a child."

Still Rogier said nothing. He did not like Robert Geroy, but he would have kept his word to the devil.

"It was what you wanted me to do," says Guillelm, and then, "Let him in."

Robert came in, and Rogier shut the door and stood against it. Robert went on till he was before the duke; then he stopped and stood with his feet apart and his fists on his hips, the way he would stand watching the reapers, or listening to Ansgot the steward, or talking with any of his knights.

"Sire," he says, "I have brought you the rest of the price of Montgaudri. Take it, and give me seisin, and have my homage, and let me go."

Guillelm met his look with a dark, lowering stare.

"I will not, Robert Geroy," he says.

Robert said nothing for several seconds. Then, "You promised it. And it is law. Why not?"

"Because I shall keep Montgaudri. Ask Rogier why."

Robert swung about. "Is this your counsel?" he cried.

It was hard to say yes or no to that, so Rogier did not answer. Robert stared, then threw back his head and gave a great angry laugh.

"I know—" he says. "Not yours—Mabille's of Belesme."

He turned back to the duke, "By God's Son!" he cried, "this is a seemly thing. So it should be when Talvas's daughter takes a hand with the tanner's grandson."

In the silence that came after, the clack of the duke's finger ring, as he drove his hands down on the arms of his chair, sounded as loud as a door slamming. He leaped up and stepped toward Robert Geroy and stood a sword's length from him.

"Splendor of God!" he said, low and hard. "Splendor of God! Splendor of God!" He put his hand to his sword and jerked it half out of the sheath. Then he rammed it in but stayed staring into Robert's eyes, and Robert gave him back just that equal stare of a man watching for another to strike; his hand was on his hilt too.

Guillelm turned away at last. He put up his clenched fists to his mouth and bit on them. Neither Rogier nor Robert could see his face. When he sat down again in his chair it was set like a stone.

"If I find," says he, speaking very slow, "if I find one man of your rebel Geroy blood in Caen tomorrow morning, I'll hang him from the tallest oak in the Virgin's Wood."

Robert says, "You'll not find one."

He stooped and caught up a handful of straw from the floor and took it in his two hands.

"Hear me, Duke Guillelm," he says, "and bear me witness, Rogier of Montgommeri—Normandy has broken faith with me." He lifted his knee and laid the straw across it and wrenched at it. It strained and parted. He threw the torn stalks down at Guillelm's feet. "I break my faith sworn to you," he said, and pointed his finger, "as that straw is broken."

He turned his back on Guillelm then and went to the door. Rogier moved aside, and he opened it and went out.

Robert went back to their lodgings. They were empty except for the servants and young Robert, who was playing marbles. But the saddlebags had been unpacked and even the painted canvas hung up round the walls, and Robert's silver plates and his drinking horn laid out on a bench.

"Where is your mother?" he says to young Robert.

"Gone to the duchess, sir."

Robert went to the door. "May I come?" cried the lad, and left his marbles.

"No," says Robert. "Go off and find the knights. Bring them here and tell them arm and saddle."

He went out, shouting to the servants to pack all up.

Back again in the castle he went to the great chamber and knocked on the door. A lad opened it for him. Robert saw Mahalt beyond, sitting on a cushion, and Aelis with her. Aelis was laughing. Mabille of Belesme was by her.

He went in, pushing the boy on one side, and straight on till he stood over Aelis. He reached out his hand to her.

"Come on, wench," he said to her.

But she did not take it.

"What's amiss with you? Don't you see the duchess?" she cried.

Robert caught her wrist and pulled her up. He turned to Mahalt, holding Aelis still.

"Dame," he says, "I take no leave of you. Duke Guillelm will tell you why."

Then he looked at Aelis. "Come," he says, and let go her wrist and moved to the door. She followed. She had heard in his voice and seen in his face something that made her fear him as she had not feared since the first days of their marriage. She was astonished and hugely proud of him.

On the stair she cried out to him, going down in front of her. "Sir—what has happened?"

He told her. She caught his wrist. "Oh, Robert!" she cried.

He turned to her, his face somber. "It's the base blood in him . . . in him too," he said, and then stared at her. "You're not his cousin that side."

"Oh, Robert!" she cried again, "you don't think that I—"

He only said, "Come on," but she heard him mutter as they crossed the yard, "I don't know how to tell when any is false."

It was not quite sunset when they were mounted, but above, the lights were kindling already in the castle. Ranof Badger says, "It's dark early tonight. They'll be shutting the gate."

Robert heard him. "They must open again if they shut before sunset hour," he says.

Neel Crook-Nose said that he would be glad to be out of Caen. "And the Bastard can hang whom he likes in the morning."

Then he turned on his horse and pulled up, because Robert had stopped.

Robert said, "Go on. Go out through the gate. I must go back, but I'll follow you."

Aelis cried out, "No—no—you must not go back. Why do you go?"

He told her harshly to be silent, and she obeyed. "Wait at the ford of the Laize," he says. "Wait till moonrise."

Ranof Badger said, "I'm coming back with you," but Robert bade him, "Do what you're told," and Ranof knew he must.

Robert said no more then but lifted his spear to them in the narrow street, swung his horse about, and clattered away from them back along the street, the banner jogging heavily against the slight wind. They did what he had said. They rode on and out of the gate. The men were getting ready to shut it. It was Neel Crook-Nose, a crafty fellow always, who pulled up and told the gate watch that Sire Robert was coming and would be very angry if the gate was shut, for it wasn't sunset hour yet. "And I wouldn't be in your shoes," he says, "if you keep him waiting when he does come."

Fulcun, lying with his cheek on a pile of sacks in the half-empty corn store, with his hands bound behind his back by the rope that tied his feet neatly together, watched the daylight fade till the dusty small place was almost dark. He was hungry, for, since they had shifted him here to make room for the duke's folk, they had been too busy to bring him food. He was stiff, for they had bound him tightly because there was no place here for a chain to be fastened. But beyond those weary discomforts there was worse in his thoughts. He has to think of Robert, staring into his face and turning away.

He heard the key rattle and turn in the lock. Then he thought he heard a sound like a cry, and something fell against the door. But after that there was silence. When the door opened Fulcun did not raise his head. The man who looked after the prisoners in Caen castle was talkative, and tonight Fulcun did not want to talk.

The door shut to, and the key turned again in the lock. For a second Fulcun thought that someone had only looked in and gone again. Then he knew that there was a man with him in the little room.

He wrenched himself up so that he sat, and peered into the dark. He saw in it a long gray gleam. The man had a sword in his hand.

"Where are you?" It was Robert Geroy's voice. "Where are you, Fulcun?"

Fulcun says, "Here!" with a gasp.

Robert Geroy laughed. "I didn't think it could have been so easy," he says.

⚜

He did not tell Fulcun what he had done, nor how he had done it, till they were outside the gate of Caen, with Fulcun running along beside Robert's horse, his hand on the stirrup leather.

Then Robert told him, sometimes laughing to himself, and then suddenly very curt when he remembered that the man running beside his heel was Fulcun Geroy that he could not trust.

He had come back from the gate, not knowing, he said, what the devil he should do. He had hidden in the church porch opposite the corn store, hoping that someone would come along and open the door. Sure enough, the bandy-legged man had come. Robert had stepped out and hit him on the head with the flat of his sword. "I let him set in the right key first, though," he says, and chuckled, and then fell abruptly silent.

It was Fulcun who spoke, not even looking up at Robert, who was only a shape in the dark.

"You shouldn't have done it for me," he says, and no more, partly because he had no breath to spare, and partly because the load of despair that lay on his mind made words difficult.

Robert quickened the horse, then, remembering, pulled back. He said, speaking roughly, "The Bastard and I had words. I broke my homage, and he swore he'd hang any Geroy that he found in Caen tomorrow morning."

Fulcun said nothing to that. It was all he could do, after his weeks in prison, to keep up with the horse. But Robert brooded on it. After a while he spoke, not so much to Fulcun as himself—

"I *couldn't* have left you there for him to hang," he says, and his voice was troubled and angry.

At last they came down through the scented air of hay meadows to the ford of Laize. There was a paleness in the sky just over the low hillside beyond; the moon would soon be up.

Someone shouted from a clump of trees, "Who rides there?"

Robert answered, "Geroy!" and the man came out, and a woman cried, "Robert."

In the dark, just by the way down into the murmuring water of the ford, Aelis and the Saint-Céneri folk came about them.

Fulcun drew away from Robert's stirrup, but Aelis pointed a finger at him.

"Who is that?" she cried.

Robert says, "Fulcun Geroy," and nothing else, nor did she dare this night to make any answer. Robert said, "Mount him, one of you," and turned his horse to the ford. He went over first, the rest followed, and Fulcun last of all on one of the servants' horses, with the fellow running at his stirrup as he had run beside Robert's.

They rode so all that short night and the next day till evening, through a land where it was high summer. The moon daisies floated in the young hay as though in half-translucent green water; when they halted at a village a whitethroat sang to them from an oak tree, and, black in the clean blue above, the swifts towered up, wheeling, and fell with a rocking sheer and a golden gleam of polished feathers against the sun.

When they got down in the castle yard at Saint-Céneri all the dogs came out to welcome them. They barked and leaped round Robert, and then found out Fulcun and did the same by him. But when Robert went in with the others to the hall he whistled to the dogs and they went with him, jostling each other about his heels, so that Fulcun was left alone.

II

What began that day for Fulcun went on through the summer and autumn. Once, quite soon after he came back to Saint-Céneri, he stopped Robert, who would have gone past him, in the yard.

"Sir," said Fulcun, "if you give me leave I'll go away—to France or—"

Robert said, "I'll not keep any man against his will," and went by without once looking at Fulcun. So Fulcun stayed.

All that autumn men kept riding into Saint-Céncri from the south. Robert welcomed them; they ate in hall; but after, they would go off with him to the great chamber and talk there behind locked doors, with one of Robert's knights on guard outside. Everyone in the castle, though, knew pretty well what it was. Robert was making a league with Mayenne and Anjou.

Aelis knew for certain, because Robert told her. She did not like it, but now she said nothing. She was meek these days with Robert, obedient and very serviceable. If he was sharp with her, and he was more so than ordinarily, she gave him no back answers; she wished in her own mind that he would be really harsh, partly so that he should see how cheerfully she would bear it; partly because she wanted him to be eased somehow of his trouble; for watching him in an agony of angry pity she knew that he was troubled. He was troubled because of Fulcun Geroy.

Not that Robert had anything to do with Fulcun. He did not try to, and she snubbed young Robert so sharply that he did not go on trying. But she was very sure that Fulcun was the cause, the whole, only cause of Robert's fits of brooding, his short temper, his troubled, puzzled look, that more than anything went straight to her heart because it made him seem so like a boy, and yet made her realize that he was growing old.

Then, a little while after Christmas, one suppertime, a knight came in from Echauffour. Fulcun, who never sat now with Robert and Aelis, but at the far end of the knights' table below, saw him talking very earnestly with Robert. He saw too how still Aelis sat, except that once she put her hand to her breast. He thought, "I suppose Hernaut is trying to make him break with Anjou—if he has joined with Anjou." It couldn't be bad news, because Robert laughed.

But it was bad news—Hernaut had sure warning, through Robert of Grandmesnil, Avice Geroy's son, who was abbot now of Saint-Évroult, that the duke was at Alençon, in the Belesme land, and even now gathering a host to fall on Saint-Céneri.

In the great chamber that night Aelis was quickly undressed and in bed. Robert talked a lot; he was much cheerfuller since Hernaut's news, but to all of it Aelis said never a word.

But when he stood by the bed ready to get in she cried,

"Sir, send him away. Oh! Sir, send him away!"

Robert did not even ask whom she meant. He said, angrily, "I will not," and then, more kindly, for her face was so unhappy, "There's nothing to fear now that we have warning.

And it's not for Fulcun. Duke Guillelm is after me. It's for this business of Anjou."

She did not for a moment believe it. It was Fulcun, always Fulcun. She sat up suddenly in bed and stretched her hands out to him. Her face shook and she stared at him for a moment without a word. Then she cried again, "Oh! Send him away! Send him!" and broke into a passion of weeping.

He was amazed. This was not like Aelis. But he comforted her very tenderly and found himself comforted somehow at the end of it.

In three days Duke Guillelm came, but the gate of Saint-Céneri was shut, and the frosty sunshine winked on spear blades as men ran shouting along the roundway of the town pale. Then Duke Guillelm's horns blew up, and the horns and drums from Saint-Céneri tower answered them. It was a brave thing to see and hear on that bright morning.

The first two days Guillelm's men were busy building huts and breastworks from the trees they cut down in the woods. Then the rain came, and for two days the mire was too deep for them to bring up the ram or do anything much but cast in spears and shoot arrows. But the fifth day they came on, and the fighting at the pale was pretty hot, but Guillelm's men were soundly beaten off.

Next morning Robert had had the gate opened and the bridge let down, and rode out with twelve knights and twice as many afoot. They fell on the flank of the duke's men as they were trying to ram down the pale near the river and for a few minutes fought hand to hand.

In that fighting a chance spear got Robert's horse in the throat. He was well in front of all, and he went down among Duke Guillelm's men, and there was a great shout. But those of Saint-Céneri pressed on. Robert, rolling over, saw someone stride his body—a man with a quilted coat who swung an axe and shouted, "Hoi Geroy!" When he scrambled up and got his sword again, he was shoulder to shoulder with Fulcun.

"Thanks, Heron," he says as he struck, and did not know what it was he had said; but Fulcun knew.

It was that same evening in the yard that Robert came on Fulcun sitting on the well coping staring down at nothing. He slackened, hesitated, stopped, and Fulcun looked up.

For a moment they looked at each other, neither able to find a word. Then Robert said, as if he were angry,

"You need more than a leather coat. Aelis shall get you out a hauberk from the chest."

Fulcun did not answer nor did his face change. Then at last he said,

"Robert!" and stopped, and again, "Robert—Robert—" and was dumb.

Robert dropped his eyes. He stared fiercely at the ground for a moment and then he said, hastily and uncomfortably as though he were to blame for everything, "I pushed you to the duel—I would have you go. It was my fault."

"Robert—" says Fulcun, with so keen a pain in his voice that Robert looked up and then away.

"No," Fulcun said. "It was all my fault. It . . . I . . ." He stumbled over the words, and then said in a rush, "There is no good in me—none."

Robert kicked angrily at a stone. "There's no sense!" he said.

Fulcun let that pass. "I'd time in Caen to think," he says. "I have thought. All I did . . . it was wrong, wrong from the beginning, and yet if I had to do it again, I could do no other. I meant . . . right . . . but . . . it was no use. Because there is no good in me . . . nothing to trust."

Robert, staring fiercely at Fulcun's head, could not think what to say. This was so like what he had let himself think all these months. Now, though for no reason at all, he knew that it was pure madness—the Heron's usual madness.

He stamped his foot on the ground. "Stop talking like that," he told Fulcun. "And I won't have you eating down in the hall with the knights. You're a Geroy. Come up today."

Fulcun says, "No!" but Robert shouted at him, "By God you shall! See that you do it," and swung away and left Fulcun sitting there.

Aelis, standing at one of the windows of the tower, watched him go. It was a moist, still day, and the shutters all stood open. She had looked out, and seen them together, and then she had stayed. She could hear voices, but not a word of what they said till Robert shouted. She thought then that they had quarreled, and when Robert had gone she stood there still, her eyes on Fulcun, watching him, letting herself hate him.

But at suppertime Fulcun came up the hall and sat in his old place. Robert passed him the horn and grinned cheerfully at him. Aelis looked down at her hands clenched tight in her lap. After supper, Robert got hold of Fulcun's arm and made him come along to the great chamber. Robert talked that evening of Anjou, and how the duke would draw off soon, and Fulcun said a word now and again. But Aelis sewed in silence, which was the woman's part.

Next morning when she woke Robert was gone. She heard, in the distance, the sound of shouting—so they were at it already—Duke Guillelm was battering at the pale betimes; he was a terrible enemy. She sat on the edge of the bed for a long time, shivering, in nothing more than her shift, and chewing at her finger ends—Robert's trick she knew, and the thought went through her with a pang of tenderness.

When she was dressed she went to the loft where they kept the apples. In the dim light they lay in hundreds; dull green, red-cheeked, russet. She moved between them, going very softly, and when she heard a mouse rattle by under the flooring she stopped and waited, listening.

She was there perhaps a quarter of an hour, yet when she came down again she had only four apples in her hands. But she had been very careful in choosing them. They were all Duke Richart apples, three of them had still a leaf clinging to the stalk, a pleasant reminder of summer; the fourth had no leaf on it.

From the apple loft she went down to Robert's treasury, and there, when she had locked the door, she dragged out a dusty, small, iron-bound chest. It had been Raol Malacorona's, who had been so skilled in medicine that in Palermo only one woman had been his equal, and at home in Montreuil people still talked of how he could raise from the dead. She opened the chest. There were bottles inside, and little boxes, and knives, very fine and sharp, and pointed things of steel. She took out the boxes one by one and opened and smelled at them. Her hands had been shaking up in the dusty, dim, apple-smelling loft, but now they were quite steady.

All that day the fighting was very close. The men did not once come in while the daylight lasted but ate at the pale what the servants carried down to them.

So, when it fell dusk, and the duke's horns blew to call off his men, everyone came back very hungry, and in hall the knights sat long over their meal. Robert left the table before any of them and took Fulcun with him. The great chamber was empty when they came there, for all the women were busy these days with the wounded and with work that the men had now no time for. But when Robert had sat down on his cushioned seat, and Fulcun on the floor, staring into the fire, Dame Aelis came in with some apples in the lap of her gown and sat down opposite Robert. She began playing with one of the apples, twirling it in her fingers. The other three, lying in her lap, had each a faded, gray-green leaf still clinging to the stalk.

"Do you want an apple, Fulcun?" she said, looking down at them.

Robert laughed. He said, "You think Fulcun's a lad still to like apples."

She looked at Fulcun and she smiled. "He always did."

"I do still," he says, and Robert, extraordinarily pleased, said, "Toss him one, girl."

She took one up from her lap and tossed it to Fulcun, he caught it.

"It's a Duke Richart," she said. "That's the sort you like." She could not take her eyes from Fulcun. He had the apple in his hands and now he nipped off the withered leaf and rolled it between his fingers.

He said, "Are these from the tree down in the orchard corner?" and lifted it to his mouth.

She could not answer for watching him. But he only sniffed the fresh scent of it, then took to dangling it by the stalk between his knees.

"Yes—yes I think so," she said then hastily.

Robert got up suddenly, and she started and sat staring at him as he came over to her.

He put out his hand to the apples that lay on her lap. "I'll have one," he says, and only then she moved sharply. She dropped the one she held and snatched at his hand. "No!" she cried.

He laughed. "But I want one. O, greedy!" His hand was fumbling among the apples as she struggled, trying to push it away. Then he caught her wrists together in one of his hands, and while he held her, snatched one of them, and stepped back.

She sprang up after him and seized his wrist, but he fended her off, laughing still, with his other hand, holding the apple above her head.

Then she loosed him. That apple had no leaf on it. "Well, you shall have it," she says, and tried to laugh too. She stooped quickly and snatched up the others that had fallen and threw them into the fire. "Those are bad," she said. "The wasps must have got at them."

She found that her knees were shaking. She could not stay here any longer lest she should cry out. She muttered something about fetching more and left them. She did not look again at Fulcun playing absently with his apple.

When she was gone Robert sat down again and there was silence. Robert began to eat his apple moodily; he was not laughing now. He said suddenly to Fulcun, "Have you heard about Raol Malacorona?"

"No." Fulcun asked no question. For no reason at all he did not want to know.

Robert shifted his feet among the rushes and, stooping, pulled out a withered head of flowering sedge and began to slap his knee with it.

"He came to Saint-Évroult last summer when they made Robert of Grandmesnil abbot. But now," he said, "Raol . . . he's a leper."

Fulcun looked up at that.

"They say," Robert told him, "that Raol thanks God for it . . . says it has been granted him . . . that he asked God for it."

They turned away from each other then and stared into the fire, but Raol was in both their minds, a dark shadow for Robert, for Fulcun, a dread.

The apple dropped out of Fulcun's hand as he sat playing with it. He reached out for it but it had rolled too far. He let it lie. After a long time he spoke.

"I went to Séez," he said, "and I did penance there, and I repented of having her. But I can't . . . Robert, I can't repent of loving her."

He jerked his head up and stared at Robert. Robert had been angry before; he had said that this was sin. But now, as Fulcun tried to understand his face, he could find in it only kindness and trouble. So now he could turn to Robert for help against the dark fear that at Raol's name had stirred and wakened.

He looked again into the fire; he tried to find words to tell Robert how in Caen in his darkness he had groped for, touched, and clung to no less a thing than the enormous kindness of God. But he could find no words, and so he went on leaving it unsaid.

"But when I pray," he cried, "I fight him for her sake. And, Robert, I know if one day God should say, 'Forsake her, or forsake me. Choose!' I . . . I could not forsake her."

"And I am afraid," he said in a whisper.

Robert spat out the last of the apple into his hand and threw it, with the core, into the fire.

"Ugh!" he says, "I should think the wasps have got at that," and for a long time he said no more. Then at last he turned to Fulcun.

"I can't understand," he says, and he frowned, "but I don't believe he'd ever want a man to forsake anyone."

Fulcun turned sharply. Was that true? What did Robert mean? Was it only that he could not forgive disloyalty and could not think that God would either? Or was it something far beyond that? Was it something that Robert did not understand, but knew?

"What do you mean?" cried Fulcun. "Robert!"

Robert was frowning at him. He put his hand over his eyes, and when he uncovered them he looked about the room.

"I don't believe—" he began again, and stopped.

"What is the matter with the torches?" he says. "They're burning . . . burning . . ."

He stood up and began to go toward one of them, but half-way across the room he seemed to change his mind and came toward Fulcun. His foot caught the apple that Fulcun had dropped and sent it rolling, and then Fulcun jumped up and grabbed at him.

"I . . . it was your apple . . . under my feet," says Robert, pulling away, and then without a pause, "I'm so thirsty—I can't see—what is the matter?"

There was a sound at the door. Fulcun, still holding Robert so that he should not fall, turned about and saw Aelis standing there. He had never seen a human face so utterly changed with horror.

"Robert!" she cried, "it hadn't a leaf on it. It hadn't any leaf."

Chapter 15

I cannot come to you. I am afraid.
I will not come to you. There, I have said.
Though all the night I lie awake and know
That you are lying, waking, even so.
Though day by day you take the lonely road,
And come at nightfall to a dark abode.

Anonymous, written 718 BC,

from *Lyrics from the Chinese,*

by Helen Waddell

I

Fulcun could not believe that Robert was dead, not even though he was by the bed in the great chamber when, after five days of that heartbreaking babble, and the restless tossing, and the crying for water, Robert stopped talking suddenly and turned on his side and then lay very still.

Aelis was there too, and little Robert, silent and white, staring first at one and then another of the grown people, and then again at his father. When that silence came, Jueta, Aelis's old waiting woman, leaned over and put her hand on Robert's chest. They watched her, but they knew before she spoke what it meant, for Robert's voice for the last hours had been only a dry whisper that went on and on.

Jueta turned her face to Aelis, and at that, with a sudden movement, Aelis sprang up and struck her hand away from Robert.

"Don't touch him!" she says. "Out—all of you! Out!"

The other two women and Jueta went back toward the door. They were afraid of Aelis that moment. Fulcun did not move. Young Robert jumped up from his knees. He stood at the end of the bed, his feet planted well apart, frowning and biting at his fingers.

"He's . . . not dead?" he says, looking at his mother, and then, "What must I do?"

She laughed at that, high and wild. He was a child, but he was Robert's child, standing Robert's way and speaking as Robert might have done. He was so like as to be unbearable. She came at him and, without a word, struck him in the face.

Young Robert took it in silence. He looked at the bed, at Fulcun; then he turned and went after the women. Fulcun followed him, but at the door he stopped. Aelis had cried out to him, though it was no word that she said.

She was standing beside the bed. She looked down at Robert, then turned her face to Fulcun. Across the great chamber she spoke to him.

"I have killed my soul," she said.

He went out and shut the door. He sat down outside it on the stairs. He heard no sound from within. Presently young Robert came up again and sat down by him in the dark. They did not say anything, and the boy kept very still, holding Fulcun's thumb hard.

Two of the Saint-Céneri men were sent out to try to slip through Duke Guillelm's host, and, by different ways, to reach Echauffour and tell Hernaut that Robert Geroy was dead. One of them did it, and five days after Robert died, in the dark of a moonless night, Hernaut rode into Saint-Céneri with twenty knights. The first that Duke Guillelm's watch knew of their coming was the shouting at the gate of the town as the bridge came up again after the last horseman had passed over; they had come by the cattle path up from the river, and the guard was not well kept on that side.

Hernaut asked no questions of any as he rode up through the street by torchlight. He went straight to the castle and to the great chamber and found Aelis there. In the middle of the floor there was an empty bier, and at each corner of it four half-burned candles, snuffed out now. Yesterday Robert, who had lain there four days with the candles burning and folk watching round him, had been wrapped about in a cloth of blue silk, then stitched into a deer's hide, and all at last lapped up in lead. Now he lay in the dark before the altar of the little chapel across the yard.

There was only one torch burning in the room, and it gave no great light. Hernaut saw Aelis standing by the bed. She came to him.

He said, "How did he die? The fellow you sent said poison."

"Deadly nightshade," she told him, whispering.

"By whose hand?"

She lifted her hand and looked at it, then thrust it out at the full length of her arm for him to look at too. "Mine," she told him.

He thought she was mad. He went away, leaving her there between the bed and the bier, both empty. He found Fulcun in the hall, and after some trouble got at the rest of the truth from him. Hernaut said at the end, "There's nothing but to keep our mouths shut and let be. We can't bring Robert back." He began to ask Fulcun how the siege was going, were they short of arrows, and how about food, and fodder for the animals.

For nearly a fortnight more Duke Guillelm laid siege to Saint-Céneri, but the place was too strong for him, and the February weather too bad for great siege works. At last he sent Hue of Montfort to the gate. Hernaut spoke to him from the roundway but he did not come within the pale. Next day they let the bridge down, and Hernaut rode out. But, before the bridge was up again, Hue of Montfort went in to Saint-Céneri to be Hernaut's hostage.

That afternoon, when Hernaut came back, he told Aelis and Fulcun what were the best terms he could get from the duke. They were together in the great chamber. Fulcun stood leaning against the wall, his chin on his chest. Hernaut was on Robert's faldstool, and Aelis, sitting by the fire, kept her eyes away from him.

He told them that the duke at first would not hear of anything except that Saint-Céneri should be in his mercy. "But," says Hernaut, "I told him it was a strong town and not yet taken. The end is he will give it to my hands—Saint-Céneri, and Gandelain, le Pooté—all of it, so only that I hold it of Normandy."

Aelis turned her head toward him. "There is—" she said, "there is . . . his son." She would not say young Robert's name because it was Robert.

Hernaut told her. "He would not give him the land even if I did not take it. Robert is to go to court, and you too. He said, 'She is my cousin.' And, for the land, this is the only way to keep it Geroy."

She did not answer or protest but looked again into the fire.

Hernaut turned to Fulcun.

"He'd have had me give you up, but I said no."

"Oh," said Fulcun, "I'll go from Normandy. Never mind for me." He did not care for himself just now.

"No," says Hernaut, "we need all the Geroys there are. If you will come, I'd have you go with me to Echauffour."

"As you will," says Fulcun.

They set out three days after that. Aelis and young Robert came with them, for in the midst of all their company, laid on a hay wain and covered with his great red, gold-threaded mantle, went the lead coffin that held Robert Geroy's body. He was to be buried in Saint-Évroult Abbey because he and Raol and Guillelm Geroy had, long ago, given lands and tithes, serfs and mills and fisheries to the house when it was founded. After, when that was done, Aelis and young Robert would go to the duke.

They buried Robert Geroy in the monks' cloister at Saint-Évroult on a dark February day with a touch of frost in the air, and left him there, without any of his own folk, or the dogs, alone with only monks.

Next morning—she would stay no longer—Aelis and young Robert went away. Hernaut sent ten knights with them, and

Fulcun said he would ride with them as far as the ford where the river went over the Carentonne. He did it because he had come that morning on young Robert standing watching while the servants were loading the two baggage horses. Robert looked up at Fulcun and then down at his feet.

"Can't you come with us—a little way?" he says in a small voice.

"I will," says Fulcun.

"Thank you." Robert stumped away from him then.

When Fulcun pulled up at the edge of the brown, swirling eddies of the river, Dame Aelis did not even turn her head. Her horse went on and down, picking its way carefully.

Fulcun stooped and kissed Robert. "Don't forget me, nor any Geroys," he said, "for the Bastard and his folk."

Young Robert burrowed his head against Fulcun's breastbone.

"By God, I'll not," he said in as near as might be to a sob, and pulled away and spurred his cob at the ford, and got over somehow without mischief.

So they were gone, Aelis and Robert's young Robert. Fulcun turned and started to ride back, but along the riverbank this time because he was not in any hurry to be again in Echauffour.

The valley narrowed then widened. The grass by the river was a quick, vivid jewel green; above it had the yellow look of winter, and above that, the near, bare trees were all warm purple brown. Far down the valley the distant woods hung like a glooming cloud against the flanks of hills that were flat, clean-edged, and blue as steel.

Fulcun heard a sound and looked up. A man in a monk's gown was swinging an axe at the edge of the wood; he turned his red, round face toward Fulcun and let his axe rest for a minute as he called out a greeting. Beyond him, and nearer the river, a new stone chapel stood, and a wooden hut beside it. There was an orchard round about, and a patch of newly dug and planted ground. From close by the chapel came a little bright brown stream that ran down to the river talking to itself among the thick dank grasses. As Fulcun crossed it, he heard, mingled with the sound of it, the quick rattle of a wooden clapper—a leper's clapper. He knew then where he was. Here was the chapel and hut that Abbot Robert of Saint-Évroult had given Raol Malacorona.

He spurred on along the riverbank. He was afraid and did not know of what, only he knew that he must not see Raol. He had almost reached the trees when the horse checked and shied off toward the water. He pulled it up with a long slither on the sodden ground and sat, staring at the man who stood in the path, who had no face but a mask of linen cloth with holes for the eyes.

"Are you afraid of the leper?" says Raol Malacorona, and though his voice was changed by the disease there was the old harsh note in it still.

Fulcun told him, "No!" but there was fear in his face.

Raol stared through the holes in the linen. Fulcun could see the glint of his eyes, no more. "Then you are afraid of God," said Raol.

Fulcun faced him in silence. At last he said, "I love her. I can never leave loving her."

"What?" Raol cried. "Do you still lust after that woman?"

Fulcun lifted his eyes from the linen mask and looked beyond into the open wood. The low sun touched it now; the fallen leaves made a fire-bright floor, and the green-lichened branches were netted in a checker-work of their own light shadows.

"I love her . . . with my soul," he said.

Raol came closer, and Fulcun's hand jerked on the bridle so that the horse swung aside, but he brought it back again.

"It is not wrong that way," he said.

Raol answered him. "It is worse wrong. What's the body but a dying thing? The higher you love, the more he loses."

Fulcun said through his teeth, and not to Raol, "I must love her."

"Will you lose your soul for a woman?" Raol cried.

For a long second Fulcun was silent, then he answered, "I would do that for her."

Raol knew from his voice that the words were as near the truth as words may come. He crossed himself and moved away from the road as if it were Fulcun who was the leper. "Are you not afraid?" he cried. "Afraid to say that, lest he hears? Are you not afraid of his anger?"

Fulcun stared at him with a set face. His thoughts went back to another time and place. In the little church of Saint-Céneri Raol and he had stood together, and Raol had talked then of God's anger, but Fulcun, groping in the dark places of his mind, had found that the thing that he dreaded should forbid him human love was not God's anger but his love itself, which greedy, bitter, insatiable as any hate, would allow no other object but itself.

Today Raol talked again of anger, and again Fulcun feared, not anger, but love. But now, just as he knew more of the human love he had craved for, so also he knew more of God's love that he dreaded. It was not bitter, nor greedy; it was as patient and as kind as the earth under his feet. But still it stood opposed to the other, and he between them, afraid.

He said at last what he had said before, "I must love her," and remembered, as if it were a trembling uncertain light seen in utter dark, Robert's words, "I don't believe he'd have a man forsake anyone." But the dark swallowed the flicker; he did not know what Robert had meant.

Raol lifted his hand, and as the sleeve fell back Fulcun saw how it was dreadfully eaten with leprosy, and he could not take his eyes from the finger that pointed at him.

"You do not dread his anger now," said Raol. "But you will dread it when he takes from you all that you will not forgo."

He turned away then and went limping slowly up the slope toward the hut. He did not say any word of farewell, nor did he look back to see when Fulcun tightened the reins and rode into the wood.

Fulcun did not go again by the little chapel and the hut beside the Carentonne. He stayed at Echauffour till it was close on Easter, and then Hernaut would have him come to the duke's court, which was at Bernay this year, and at which Hernaut would get seisin of Saint-Céneri and the rest. Fulcun did not want to go because Bernay was near to Fervacques, but Hernaut insisted. The Geroys must show a bold face these days.

II

Mahalt of Normandy was in the orchard of the abbey at Bernay. The orchard lay on the west side of the abbey and was bounded on one side by the monks' fence and on the other by the long line of thatched stables. The fence was higher than the height of a man, but not so high that passersby on foot outside could not see how the monks' fruit trees bloomed; first a scatter of white plum blossom like snow among bare boughs, then the flushed and paling apple flowers, then the cream-white of pear and the pearl-white of cherry. And any monk who worked there, unless he rigorously turned his back on the fence, could be refreshed and diverted by the sight of the head and shoulders of every horseman who went by along the road.

Now, for it was only the end of March, was the time of the plum blossom. The leaves of the other fruit trees were opening, and the apple buds were bunched and swelling, but the orchard was an open airy place where the spring sun of a fair day was most pleasantly warm. Duchess Mahalt and her women had been out here for the last hour. It was good to think that in another month winter would be done with and Maytime almost here. This afternoon, with all the birds singing in all the orchards of Bernay, it was almost possible to believe, if you shut your eyes, that summer was come already.

Mahalt was sitting on the edge of an old stone pig trough that lay in the grass, and Hue of Grandmesnil's wife was with her and Eve of Montfort and a few more. They were talking, but for the most part the duchess was silent, or if she spoke it was briefly. At last, in the middle of Dame Eve's story of how she had caught her girl Clarice kissing a young puppy of an esquire— and what could one do with girls nowadays?—Mahalt got up suddenly and, as the others made way for her, went through them and away.

She came, walking quickly, to the side of a woman who stood neither alone nor yet quite among a group.

"Alde," says the duchess. "Come with me."

Alde of Fervacques turned, looked for a second into Mahalt's eyes, and then moved away with her between the trees.

But the duchess did not speak. They went the whole length of the orchard and halfway back before she turned again and looked at Alde, and with one consent they stood still.

Mahalt said, "I did not give you any welcome when you and Mauger came."

Alde made no answer to that. From her face no one would have known whether she had cared. She looked straight before her, her mouth shut firm, over Mahalt's head to the orchard fence.

"Guillelm," says Mahalt, "told me I did wrong. He said that no one knew if Fulcun Geroy had not carried you away against your will, since of your will you came back to Mauger."

Still Alde did not speak, and Mahalt, staring into her face, could learn nothing there except that the light that had always lurked behind the sober serenity of her eyes was not there now.

"Did he force you?" says Mahalt.

Alde's eyes came to her. "No," she said, and it was as if dark water was shaken by a stone that left no trace except the widening, silent ripples.

Mahalt cried out, irrelevantly, "If you had only told me!"

Alde understood. She and Mahalt were Flemings, alone among these Normans. They had been friends, and they had trusted each other.

She said, "I never thought to tell you. I never thought of you at all. There was no one, nothing, nothing in earth or heaven, those days, but only—him!"

Mahalt was struck dumb by that sudden cry of truth after the silence. She looked down at the grass between them.

"Why did you leave him?" she says after a minute. Then, "No—don't tell me." She could not bear to hear Alde confess the dwindling of that passion, whose only justification was its immensity.

But Alde said as if she had not heard the last, "Mauger came. So . . . we . . . knew he was alive."

"You thought Mauger was dead?"

"*I* never could. But he did . . . he . . . Fulcun did," Alde said, and looked down suddenly into Mahalt's face. "I tried to think he was dead. But even if I had known he lived I should have gone . . . with Fulcun. I tell you," she cried again in a desperate low voice, "there was nothing but him—nothing. I could have died, but I could not have let him go."

There was a change in Mahalt's eyes. She turned away. She had remembered something that she was almost afraid to remember. She had remembered how, years ago, Guillelm had told her that their marriage was no marriage—the apostle at Rome bade him put her away because they were cousins. As he told her, he had held her wrist so tight that she could not distinguish the pain of her body from the pain of the awful fear that came on her. Then he had said, "I shall not. I could not. And we're not close akin. But," he had said, and she remembered his voice and his face and could never forget it, "if you were my sister I could not let you go." She had cried out then with a different fear and flung herself on his breast because she would not let him brave God and the saints alone.

"God forgive me," Mahalt whispered, "I know what you mean." She caught Alde's wrists in her hands. "Oh, my girl!" she said. She was thinking how she had never had to choose. Lanfranc of Bec had brought arguments, Guillelm had spent money, and in any case, they were not close akin.

But then she remembered—Alde had left him.

"Why did you leave him?" she cried, and now it was almost a reproach.

Alde drew her wrists away from Mahalt's hold. She said, "Why do you want to know? . . . I had to—it was right."

"But you loved him less?" says Mahalt.

Alde did not answer that, and there was no answer to see in her face. "I had to," she said again.

Mahalt stared at her a moment, trying to understand her, who did not understand herself. Then she dropped her eyes.

"God forgive me," she muttered. "And I thought you should be ashamed."

"I am ashamed," Alde said.

The duchess did not look up, and Alde, looking out above Mahalt's head to the orchard pale, kept herself perfectly still. A company of men was riding past. She stood as rigid as one of the old apple trees. She saw Hernaut Geroy, she saw Guion Geroy of Courville, whose face she knew though not his name. She saw Fulcun, riding on the far side of Hernaut. So they had come at last.

Mahalt said after a minute, "Alde, take Mauger home. He will go now he has touched the relics here. Take him home. I ought to have told you. The Geroys are coming to this court."

"No," said Alde, and kept herself from speaking quickly, "I knew they were coming. No, I shall not."

For a long moment Mahalt stared at her, less able than ever to understand. Then she turned and began to walk again. She began to talk to Alde too, as she had talked to her times without number in the past, asking now what she should do with a hawk that had lost her courage. Alde was skilled with hawks. This one, when she was cast at a bird, would fly awayward as if she did not see it. Alde said, give her beef steeped in oil of Spain, and clear wine, and the yolk of an egg. She told Mahalt carefully how to prepare all this; she did not seem to be in any haste to be gone, but when the duchess called to all the women to come indoors and eat some of the hot roots that the peddler said came from the east beyond Jerusalem, and they trooped into the monks' guesthouse again, Alde, hanging back, did not know how she had breathed, let alone spoken, for this last quarter of an hour. Her heart was beating in her breast, in her throat, in her head, it seemed. She knew now that she had waited for a year and a half—and three days—and a quarter of an hour, and the quarter of an hour was the worst. But now she would not have much longer to wait. As she went cautiously across the stable yard she did not try to think of what she was doing. Had she meant to do it? Or had she fought not to do it? She did not think of that either. She knew only that Fulcun had come to Bernay. She had seen him, just a glimpse, but she must see him again, and speak, and touch him. That was all. She must.

That afternoon, as Fulcun stood watching Guion Geroy of Courville try the paces of a mare he thought of buying, a lad came and pulled him by the sleeve.

"Is your name Fulcun Geroy?"

Fulcun says, "It is."

The boy held out a muddy hand, and there, in the palm of it, was a tuft, no more, of hair of a dull sultry gold. "There was a woman," says the boy, "at the abbey, that gave me this and told me to come to you and say, 'Holy Cross Church.' And she gave me a penny and said you would too."

Fulcun says, "Give that to me." He could not let it lie on the lad's dirty palm a second longer. Then he gave him a silver penny and stood watching him go, because he could not move nor think yet. He must wait a minute till this amazement passed and changed into life—new life. And yet it was new life already, but like the blood running into a cramped limb, it hurt. Then, before he knew that he had moved, he was crossing the yard to the stair at the top of which Hernaut stood talking to one of the men.

Hernaut turned as Fulcun went up, and the man ran down past him. Hernaut said, seeing Fulcun's face, "Well?"

Fulcun had his fist clenched tight about that small bit of hair, and he kept his arm stiff at his side. He said, "She says, 'Holy Cross Church.' I'm going. I don't know when I shall be back."

Hernaut stared, then cried, "Who the devil? What?"

"Alde," says Fulcun and turned, "I am going." He said it as simply as he meant it. He was going. There was nothing else conceivable.

But Hernaut came down and caught his shoulder. "See here, Fulcun," he says in his ear. "I'll not stand by you if you get us again into trouble. No, by God's Son! I'm not so patient a man as Robert Geroy. I'll see you hang first."

Fulcun took hold of his hand and pulled it off.

"I shan't," he said, meaning anything Hernaut liked to think. "She has sent for me," he explained, and went away down the steps.

Fulcun came to the porch of the wattle church of Holy Cross that stood in a narrow small road opposite a carter's yard. He put his hand on the door latch and pushed it open. He would have said that he felt nothing that moment—everything in him, thoughts and feelings, seemed suspended or dead. But when he shut the door behind him, and looked round and found the church empty, a cold pang like death went through him, for that suspension had been feeling at too high a pitch to know itself. He stood a minute, waiting and listening, but there was no sound. He began to breathe again. This was the life he knew—the empty thing without her—not that dizzy height of impossibility coming true. Then he remembered that he had only to wait—it was not impossible. It was truth.

He went up toward the altar, but before he got there he dropped down on his knees because he could go no farther and must hide his face. He put both arms up, and with one hand tugged at his hair so that he might hurt himself in a way that a man could bear; so that he should not split and founder in the deep waters of this tide of gladness.

"God," he cried out in a whisper, "God, this is you." He went on saying that for a long time. He was very sure now that not only was Raol wrong, but that all his own fear was idle, foolish, almost a thing to laugh at. God was like this; he was giving him Alde again.

Yet all the time, through all his thoughts, he was listening, waiting, his heart ready to leap up and silence thought. But still she did not come. The light colored in the narrow slit in the west wall and then faded. An old priest came in, half blind he seemed, fumbling, and feeling his way with a stick. He said Compline and went tapping out. Fulcun stayed where he was and heard him lock the door, and his heart, which had been trembling with impatience, fear, hope, must become still. She could not come tonight. He wrapped himself in his cloak and went to sleep on a bench in the belfry.

She did not come till close on noon next day. Fulcun, sitting on the step of the font, lifted his head as he had lifted it at every sound of the latch. The door opened; a woman came in; Alde came in.

He stood up. He did not know if he was a living man. He might as well have been a log. But he found that he was shutting the door. She turned to him. They saw each other plain. If he had any thought it was simply that they were close now, together now, and that was as right as it was terrible. Then they were closer yet; he felt the truth of her lips, her body in his arms, no dream, no aching memory, but the truth. For that one minute he knew bliss.

When it ceased and he saw her again, but still within his arms and clinging to him, he said, "Is—is he dead?" It was the thought that he had managed to keep under his heel till now, but now he could not. And what lesser thing could have brought her back to him after the terrible cruel courage of her going?

She said, "Mauger? Dead? No—" After a minute she said, "But I had to come."

That was enough for him then, for he did not understand—he did not even try to understand the stunned pain of his mind. Mauger was not dead. Then why—?

She was leaning against him. He tightened his arms suddenly as a new thought came.

"Alde," he cried. "Did he—? Is he . . . ? Oh, Alde, how did he deal with you?" He took her chin in his hand and stared down at her face as if he could read it there, and his mind was sick with fear of what her answer might be.

She said, "Mauger . . . he . . . he is very kind—always. Even when he is angry . . . he is not angry with me. He has not even struck me—not once."

Fulcun said nothing because he could not.

"And he is a sick man now," she went on, and seemed to be in haste to make him understand. "That is why I could not come yesterday. I thought he might fall into a fit. So I stayed. And when he slept, Dame Mahalt sent for me. I could not tell her no; so I could not come."

She looked into Fulcun's face and understood nothing of his thoughts. Hardly indeed did he understand them yet, but her words were blow on blow that he would feel the pain of later. She had stayed lest Mauger should need her. Mauger, that was nothing to Fulcun but the sword of God set between them, was to Alde a man—a man that needed her. And she would not tell Mahalt, so could not come to him.

He said at last, "Come and sit down. There's a bench over there."

They went, stepping over the curved tail of the bell rope, and sat down on the bench. She had his wrist in her hand as they went, and when they sat down she pulled his arm round her and pressed her face against his shoulder.

"Fulcun," she said, and her voice was strange, smothered, and shaken, "Fulcun—I had to come. Oh, Fulcun."

He had not meant it, but feeling her in his arms, he could do no other. He drew her close, held her, kissed her so that she cried out and he himself was frightened of himself and of the beast within him. Then he let her go, and they sat still, both of them shaking.

"Alde," he said after a minute, "I can't let you go back. Not now. I can't."

He said it as if it came from a fixed determination, but actually it was no more than the flying scud of the wave that had passed, forgotten as soon as he had said it.

She moved sharply, then sat very still.

"I must go back," she said in a hard voice. "I must do right."

He did not cry out, as the hurt nerves of his mind cried, "Why did you come, to go again?" He said after a long time, and very humbly—

"Can't I see you again?"

She turned then and clung to him. She put her face to his. "Yes, Fulcun," he heard her say, and knew that another woman would have been crying. Then she said, "Fulcun, I love you—I love you. You know it?"

He told her, "Yes, Alde, I do."

She stood up and turned her face away. He stood up too, and he did not touch her.

"Can I see you again, Alde?" he asked after a minute.

"Yes—I'll come tomorrow at the same time," she said.

She turned her face to him then, and said, "Kiss me, Fulcun." He kissed her, and while he held her and waited to master himself, so that he might kiss her again, she drew away. "I must go now," she said. "They mustn't miss me."

When she had gone and would certainly not come back again, he sat down as he had sat while he waited for her, on the ground by the font. And there he let himself be overtaken by the thoughts that had gathered like wolves and now pulled him down and mauled and devoured him. She cared for Mauger—perhaps it was only kindness, but Fulcun had kindness only for her. She was ashamed to love him; Fulcun would have cried out his love in the face of the sun.

Still, he would see her tomorrow, and she loved him. He knew that, and he went back to the Geroys' lodging thinking steadfastly of those two things.

Next morning Hernaut came to him with a very dark face.

"I think," he says, "we'd do best to ride for home. The Bastard talks too much with Montgommeri and the Belesme. And Odo of Bayeux made a mock of Abbot Robert" (he meant Robert of Grandmesnil, abbot of Saint-Évroult) "in open hall. Odo that is the tanner daughter's son by Herluin of Conteville—" He spat in the yard.

Fulcun said, "If you ride early I can't come. But I'll follow later."

Hernaut looked at him. "Fulcun," he says, "I have liked you well enough. I've never counted you a bastard Geroy. But if you don't ride with us, you can ride where you will, but not after us."

Fulcun said nothing for a moment, then, "I can't help that, if it falls out so," and left him.

An hour before noon he went to the church of Holy Cross. He had forgotten Hernaut and forgotten to think where he would ride if not with Hernaut and the Geroys. He would see her again now, and this time they would not hurt each other, "For," he thought, "I hurt her too when I kissed her like that and when I said I could not let her go." He waited. Noon passed. The spring sunshine, which had been bright, dulled and faded as clouds came up, and the afternoon darkened.

He did not know what time it was when the door opened. But it was Hernaut Geroy who came in.

He shut the door behind him and said to Fulcun, who had not got up—

"Are you coming? Your woman rode out of the gate three hours ago. Her husband went in front in a horse litter. She was last and only servants with her. She saw me but she said nothing. Will you stay longer for her?"

Fulcun got up. He went out after Hernaut in silence.

Chapter 16

When Sir Lancelot was brought to her, then she said . . .
Through this man and me hath all this war been wrought . . .
for through our love that we have loved together is my most
noble lord slain. . . . Therefore, Sir Lancelot, I require thee and
beseech thee heartily, for all the love that ever was betwixt us,
that thou never see me more in the visage.

Malory, *Le Morte Darthur,* book 21, chapter 9

I

As they were riding next day, somewhere between Chamblai and
Montreuil, Hernaut came up alongside Fulcun. He had been
thinking over this affair of the woman from Fervacques—and he
had decided that he was glad he had gone to fetch Fulcun from
the church yesterday and was bringing him back to Echauffour,
because you couldn't help liking the mad old Heron. He was not
sorry though that he had spoken as he did . . . or if he was sorry
it didn't matter now because the whole business was over; quite
clearly the woman had tired of it. Hernaut's duty now was to
make Fulcun see sense. But he would not be too abrupt.

First he talked about Abbot Robert and Odo of Bayeux,
and how swollen with pride that fellow was. Then after a pause
he said, not unkindly, but with his rigorous candor, "Y'know,
Fulcun, all women change. It's as they're made."

Fulcun turned to him with no expression in his face. "I suppose so," he says in a light, empty voice.

Hernaut left it at that, and after another awkward silence went on talking about Rogier of Toeny; he thought he'd be in trouble soon with the duke.

Fulcun rode on beside him. He heard what Hernaut was saying, and he answered when it was necessary, but far away from that and the sounds and movement of the journeying, his mind was contemplating one word—the word that Hernaut had said.

Change. She had changed.

After a long time, however, he found out that that did not mean the common, trivial thing it meant to Hernaut—"All women change." That was not it. His mind, stunned yet, and fumbling, found another word that was truer—the word was *different.*

That was it; and he could see clearer for it, and feel more keenly too it seemed. Alde was different. He remembered, not because he wanted to but because he must, Alde that night at Falaise as they stood on the stairs of the tower with Mauger lying huddled a few steps below them. *She* had said, "Take me with you." She had said it. And in the wood, next morning, on the hillside facing the rising sun . . . she had offered herself. But now—she was different.

He tried to understand how she was different, for even yesterday she had clung to him; she had said, "You know I love you," and that moment he had known it. But still, she was different. She had come to him by stealth—Alde who was like clear daylight. She had been ashamed to come; she had been afraid that Dame Mahalt should know that she came. Alde . . . who had said she did not care if God hated her.

She loved him, but she loved him differently. That was all he knew, and he knew it more in his heart than in his mind; but both his mind and heart were in darkness.

They came to the woods of Saint-Évroult when it was close on sunset, and as they rode through the village the bell was ringing for Compline in the church here, and through the evening stillness the sound of the greater bell in the abbey church three miles away came faintly and intermittently.

In the middle of the village street Fulcun pulled up and listened. The others went on past him. They had not gone beyond the last croft and the alehouse opposite, before Fulcun turned his horse and rode back toward the church. He tied the bridle to the paling of the churchyard, and then, inevitably and blindly as a crying child runs to its mother, he went to the door and in. There was help for him here, though he had forgotten in his darkness that there was help anywhere.

Emma was walking in the meadows by the stream while Rainald went poking and prying along the bank like any terrier dog. Emma had her youngest, little Geva, in her arms, and Petronelle, who was close on three now, plodded on ahead, gripping, and occasionally biting at, a honey butty that she had got from the kitchen. Guillelm, the eldest, was racing in circles through the meadow like a horse, very flushed and serious.

Emma had an eye on the children, but she was thinking not of them, but of Hernaut. Hernaut had come home today; he was home again. That was the great solid fact. But the thought that lurked at the back of her mind was that when he had kissed her and patted her shoulder and talked to her a bit, telling her the news—amongst other things about Fulcun Geroy and that woman—he had gone off at once with Goulafre the steward to learn how things went in the manor. Now, he would be busy till it was bedtime. Well, she would have him then, she thought, and warmed; and then chilled and turned from the thought because it hurt. But it was foolish to be hurt—things—that is to say men, were like that.

Rainald was calling out something. She turned and looked across the brook and saw Fulcun Geroy riding slowly down to the place where the stony spit gave good foothold for crossing. She did not like Fulcun Geroy; the things he had done were things she must be afraid of, and she had not been pleased when he came with Hernaut to Echauffour. So she turned to go up to the castle, and then stopped because she saw Petronelle was standing in the way of the horse, staring at Fulcun.

"Come out of the way," Emma called to her. "Silly girl!"

But Fulcun had pulled up in midstream, and now he got down from the saddle and waded out through the water leading the horse.

Petronelle took a blundering step toward him and came up against his leg. He stood quite still, only he stooped, and with one hand set her straight again. She went on without looking up at him, as if he were no more than a tree, and then stopped to take another bite out of her butty.

Fulcun looked at Emma, and he smiled.

She did not smile, and after a second she dropped her eyes from his face.

"You'll spoil your shoes and hosen," she said. "They're all wet."

"They'll dry," he told her casually, and went on.

That was all, but as he went she turned and watched him. She had not liked Fulcun. No, but she liked the way his hand had touched Petronelle. And the look that was on his face? She tried to think what it had meant. All she could make out, though she could see it clearly yet in her mind, was that this evening he looked very happy, but somehow as if he were happy at such a height that it was frightening; though he did not look frightened.

She was still thinking of him as she came up to the gate and through the yard, and as she passed the stable she heard a man singing very softly to himself—there was hardly any tune and yet he was singing. She had never heard Fulcun sing, but she was sure that it was he—the hushed, half-fearful, difficult happiness of it made her sure.

And she was right; it was Fulcun. He took a long time to unsaddle and water and feed his horse, because he kept doing things wrong, and stopping doing anything at all, so that he could be still a moment, and contemplate, and again feel that assurance he had come upon in the church in Saint-Évroult village.

It was just that—assurance. As though God had audibly, and in the presence of the witnessing priest, sworn by his own self that there was nothing to fear; that Alde was, somehow, not different; that nothing was broken, diminished, nor lost, nor should be ever. So now, as Fulcun trusted God, just so might he be sure that Alde loved him.

He had come out of the church with his mind full of a light like the light of the gold sunset he rode into; it was so triumphant a shining that he dared even to think again of that short, dreadful, precious time in the church at Bernay, and to try again to understand. And at once, without striving, he found an answer to all his fears, and in one word. She was good. She had not come again—because she was good. She cared for Mauger with a pity like God's pity—because she was good. And she loved him.

He thought then, with the perennial blind confidence of a man in his own immutability, that he could remain without fear in this assurance. In the long months that followed he learned otherwise, but still, though the assurance might fail, he kept and clung to the trust. And sometimes with a shock of surprise that sent his heart up like a lark from the field, he would remember, as if it were a new thing and strange, that he was the man that Alde loved.

Once that autumn, before the roads grew too bad, Hernaut went to the duke. He was away a week; when he came back he rode to the abbey of Saint-Évroult to see Abbot Robert there. What had happened at court, or what he and Robert of Grandmesnil had talked of, he told no one at Echauffour. After that they all went to Montreuil for a while, and Hernaut spoke of going to the duke's court for Christmas; but first they would go back to Echauffour.

In November one of Rogier of Montgommeri's knights came. He spoke with Hernaut in private and went away again. Hernaut said nothing of that either. Who, after all, was he to talk to? Emma? She was only a woman. Fulcun Geroy? He was a bastard Geroy, and besides— So all he said was to the steward, who asked was he going to the duke's court at Christmas. Hernaut says then, "No."

One day soon after Christmas, Emma asked Fulcun to ride to l'Aigle, for Fulbert Reina's widow, Hernaut's grandmother on the spindle side, had promised to let her have some cloves. So Fulcun went out on a fine, cold morning, without frost but clear and sunny. The whole day was fair, and as he came back in the afternoon the looming colors of winter, veiled yet intense, like the colors of uncut precious stones, were everywhere. The plowland, sticky and heavy and still, with its huge, latent potency, was purple against the west; the mist that blurred the outlines of things was of a keen blue; the cold green of the resting fields was at once startling and soft. The bare branches of distant trees whose trunks were dipped below the horizon seemed to float up against the uncolored light of the sky like seaweed in clear water. Everything was still, quiet, closed in the winter peace that sent men in, not unkindly but in friendliness, from the cold, dimming world, to the fires at home.

When he came into the castle yard Fulcun knew that something had happened and that there was no peace here. Servants were hurrying about; in the stables two men with lanterns were saddling up the horses; they did not know why, only that it had to be done. Fulcun fed his and watered it, and left it harnessed while he went up into the tower.

An hour ago up there, in the great chamber, Hernaut had found Emma.

"Come, girl," he says, "we must pack all up and go. The duke has put us out of law."

She stood up, her face pale and her child's eyes round with fright, but she did not cry out.

"Help me to arm," he said. "I must ride first to Saint-Évroult. After, you can see to the packing." He went over to the presses where the mail coats hung.

She said then, without moving, "Did you expect this?"

"I guessed," he told her as he opened the press.

"You told me nothing."

"You? You're a child."

"I'm a woman enough to bear you children," she says.

Hernaut did not answer that. He did not think it made much difference, and he was in too great a hurry to find it strange that she could speak so at all. He shoved into her hands the mail coat, hung out like a scarecrow on its wooden bar, and then the helm.

She clutched them to her, and felt them as cold and heavy as her heart. He lifted out his shield and dropped it on the floor; it rolled on its iron boss, then steadied. She could see beyond the iron rim, smeared with bear's grease and soot to keep it from rusting, a bit of the red-painted hide that covered the wood, with the blue serpent pattern on it.

When he was armed he turned away from her and went without more than, "I shan't be long."

It was dark when they were ready to start. Emma, standing a moment in the door of the great chamber, looked back. The chests were all open, and what stuff was left in them tumbled anyhow. The candles were flaring with long smoking wicks, for no one had time to snuff them. It was bedtime, and there in the far corner was her bed and Hernaut's, but she was going out in the dark, out of Normandy, and did not even know where.

That homelessness, and her weariness, were not the only things, though, that made the dark journey the wretchedest thing that she had known yet. As they rode with a half moon giving light enough to go by, she was thinking, a small thought almost drowned in the dark, that a man's need of a woman stopped when daylight came, but a woman went on all day needing something—something different. Then she cried shame on herself, for Hernaut was good to her. But still, she wondered, stupidly and hopelessly, what is loving, really? Is it his way or mine? And why was love made? Was there any use of it except to make children?

She looked round for Hernaut. He was not near her, and it happened to be Fulcun who rode by her. She bent again over Geva who lay, swaddled, in her arms, but after a moment she turned back to him.

"What . . . what was she like to look at?" she asked, and blushed fiery hot for mentioning her.

"Who?" says Fulcun.

"I don't know her name," Emma told him.

He was silent for a moment, and then he said, "Alde. Bigger than you—a lot. Her hair—it's dull gold . . . not yellow at all . . . She smiles with her eyes often."

Emma cried after a silence, with extraordinary fierceness, "I hope he will die!"

Fulcun said nothing at all to that.

Next morning, quite early, they came to the gate of Courville on the western edge of the great plain of Chartres. They were clear out of Normandy, and Geroy of Courville would shelter them. As they rode into the castle someone shouted from a window. It was young Guion Geroy. He came racing down in nothing else but a kirtle to welcome them in, and especially Fulcun, for sometimes, at home at Courville, he was homesick for Saint-Céneri.

II

At the end of January Abbot Robert of Saint-Évroult came to Courville. He had two monks with him, no more, for he had fled in as great haste from the abbey as Hernaut had fled from Echauffour. He sat over the fire with Geroy of Courville and Hernaut and Guion, who was a knight now, and told them how things were going in Normandy. Rogier of Toeny had fled, Hue of Grandmesnil, Abbot Robert's brother, he had fled too. The Geroys and their kin and friends were down, and the Belesme mounted up; it was all the doing of Rogier of Montgommeri, and of Mabille, Talvas's daughter, who had poisoned Rogier against the Geroys as Rogier poisoned the duke.

Geroy of Courville, who was a big, plain, slow man, kindly and a little stupid, said, "Well, we shall have our day again if we wait."

Abbot Robert, who was not patient, looked at him with scorn, but Geroy missed the look. Robert picked up the tail of the cord that went round him and took to whipping his palm with it. Then he turned to Hernaut.

"Will you sit down here and wait for that?"

Hernaut said first that of course he was grateful to Geroy for keeping them. Geroy shook his head, "Oh no—" he began, but Hernaut went on.

"I shan't sit still though," he says. "I'll take any that will ride with me, and we'll burn and waste in Normandy where we may. Then, when the Bastard wants to go against Anjou, or Maine, or France, he'll call us home again to keep us quiet."

Abbot Robert swore by the Son of God, "You're a crafty man, Hernaut!" Next morning he went on his way. He was going to Rome to the apostle. He said to Hernaut, "That's my best hope of plaguing the Bastard."

From time to time, all that spring and summer, Hernaut rode into Normandy to do the same thing in his own way. Winter stopped him, but next April, just before Easter, he began it again. They rode out of Courville ten knights, Hernaut, Fulcun, and Geroy among them, and as many mounted men-at-arms. At Mortagne they met Gui Bollein from the Corbonnois. He brought three more knights with him and a dozen men-at-arms. So they were in good force, and all Normandy before them. It was Echauffour itself that Hernaut was bound for. He knew very well that round about there they would find friends to shelter them as well as enemies to plunder. So, only turning aside to burn a mill and a grange at Soligny that belonged to Rogier of Montgommeri, they came, one dark evening of low clouds and driving rain, within sight of the lights in Echauffour tower. A man in Sainte Gauburge had told them that the duke had put in a garrison of fifty men or more, and therefore, says Hernaut, it was no use trying the castle itself. They would make a circle about, burn the mill and the barns that lay beyond the river, and then go on and sleep at l'Aigle, where Engenulf would welcome them.

But as they rode on in the gathering dark Fulcun pushed up alongside Hernaut's horse.

"What is it?" Hernaut asked him.

Fulcun says, "They're in the hall of the tower. There aren't any lights up above."

"Well what of that?"

Fulcun laughed. "If you and I and two or three more got in and raised a shout and a din, and the rest fired the peat stack outside the gate and shouted too, and blew the horns, then—" He laughed again.

Hernaut laughed too. "By God, Heron!" he says, "it'll be better than bird's-nesting." He was thinking that this was the Heron like the Heron used to be, madder and wilder and more unexpected than any of them.

It was better than bird's-nesting, and not much more difficult. One of the serfs in Echauffour house, seeing a man drop down inside the pale, would have given the alarm if he had been quick-witted enough to shout. But he stood staring long enough to recognize Hernaut. After that it was easy though risky. They crept up the stair beside the door of the hall itself, where everyone was inside, eating. Then, up above in the great chamber the fun began. They shouted, stamped, lifted and threw the chests on the floor, and stood and shouted again. In a minute they were breathless with it all, and with their own smothered laughter, and they stopped and listened to the horns outside and the shouting there.

But there was another sound now below stairs—more shouts and the stampede of feet. Hernaut ran to the door of the great chamber. "Down now, all of you," he yelled while he waved them back. "All but a score. Cut them down!" The rest joined them in the shouting, and heard below the trampling of men racing down the stairs, stumbling and cursing.

In less than ten minutes Echauffour was in Hernaut's hands, and having barred the gates, they sat down to eat the supper that had been cooked for the duke's men. They were mighty noisy and merry over it.

When they had finished eating, but the horns of wine were still going round, and the knights were playing the gabbing game, and roaring with laughter at the brags, and especially at Fulcun's that went beyond all, Goulafre the steward came to Hernaut's elbow and says he had just remembered that a peddler came in that very afternoon and he might have news that would be useful to know. Anyway it was always well to ask a peddler what news anywhere.

Hernaut says, "Aye, bring him."

Goulafre brought him, a sandy-haired, red-faced fellow with a bad squint. Hernaut had him to stand beside his chair, and began to question him. The talk and the laughter went on all round the table.

Hernaut asked first, "Can you tell me news of the duke?" No—the peddler could not. "Of Lord Rogier of Montgommeri?" No—the peddler hadn't heard tell anything of him neither. "Where are you from last?" asked Hernaut.

"Fervacques," says the peddler, and Hernaut knew that in all the noise Fulcun had heard that name, and turned.

Hernaut said, "That's no use to me," and waved the fellow to go. But Fulcun leaned across Guion Geroy.

"What news at Fervacques?"

The peddler looked at him and grew flustered before Fulcun's eyes. "Nothing much," he says. "Only there's a lyke-wake there, and I sold them spices for the corpse . . . for to burn about it."

Fulcun waited till his heart beat again and then said, "Whose lyke-wake?"

"It's the man there."

In his mind Fulcun saw again that picture he had seen so often before—four candles, and Mauger lying still in a dark place.

"What man?" he says.

"I've forgot his name. I don't go that way often. Only I heard he was dying and I went to sell my spices. It's the lord there."

"Mauger?" Fulcun said the name in a low voice.

"May be—I dunno. Aye—that is it."

Everyone was quiet now at the table. They looked at Fulcun. He picked up his knife and wiped it on his tranche of bread and stuck it into his belt, his hands were shaking, so he did it very deliberately. Then he stood up.

"Give me leave," he says to Hernaut.

"No, Fulcun. Look here! Wait a minute! You fool—if they catch you—" Hernaut cried after him, but Fulcun was halfway down the hall. He went without another word.

No one said anything about it to Hernaut whatever they may have said among themselves. Next morning, just at dawn, they fired the castle and rode away, leaving it blazing. After they had burned a few villages that belonged to Belesme, they came back to Courville.

Emma asked where Fulcun Geroy was.

Hernaut told her, "Gone off after that woman again. Her husband's dead." He laughed then, but not pleasantly. "I shouldn't wonder if she sent him home again with a flea in his ear. She's tired of him, I think."

"Oh!" cried Emma. "No! She loves him."

"How do you know?"

Emma was flushed and almost in tears between earnestness and shyness.

"She couldn't not," she said confusedly. "She couldn't." She was quite sure that a woman, loved as that woman was loved, "couldn't not," even though it were only Fulcun Geroy who loved, and not Hernaut.

It was twenty-five miles to Fervacques, and the dark just closing with a deep blue sky and a sickle moon sliding down behind the black wall of the trees. There was no use to hurry, for Fervacques gate would not be open till morning. Fulcun let his horse take its own pace; so long as he was going toward Alde tonight he did not need to hurry. The long waiting was suddenly brought to an absolute end.

It was a sweet, soft night now that the wind had dropped. While there was still a glimmer of twilight he could see the primroses in posies and clusters blanched by the dusk, and in one sheltered place where the road dipped to a brook he thought he caught the scent of bluebells, though it was only April. He stopped then, trying to be sure. Something in the darkest parts of his mind needed that it should be the scent of bluebells, because that little thing would, as it were, be an assurance that there was no need to fear. But there *was* no need to fear; tomorrow he would be with Alde.

Though he rode slowly, yet he knew he would get to Fervacques before dawn, so somewhere beyond le Sap he left the road and went up the slope of a hill to a hut whose roof he saw against the sky. It was what he thought it, an empty shepherd's hut. He unfastened the door, turned his horse loose to graze, and went in. There was a bed of bracken there; he lay down on it, and with his arms under his head, and only his helmet laid by, he watched, through the open door, the tall slant of sky, powdered full of stars. He lay there without moving, his eyes on that bright, terrible company of lights, and his mind swung, not with their steady progress, but to and fro restlessly.

Now he would be dreaming of how it should be when Alde and he were together . . . They would go to Caharel perhaps. He saw in his mind a place that might be like Caharel, which he had never seen, and Alde was there; he could see her more clearly than the background of the picture. But first he would take her to Courville, carrying her across Normandy as he had carried her from Falaise. It was easy to imagine that, and easy to imagine how they would come to Courville, perhaps at the evening milking time, and little Emma might be walking with the children along the bank of the river by the big mill, and he would say to her, "This is Alde," while the quiet would be full of the pulsing rush of the water in the turning wheel.

For a moment he was there, at Courville, sitting in the saddle with Alde before him, feeling her fingers on his hand that was about her waist. Then, with a shock and a recoil that was like pain, he knew that, imagine as he might, he was coming to Alde herself—really to Alde; he reached out and gripped the hard shaft of his spear as it lay by him on the ground—it was as real as that. It stunned his mind. It was too great a thing to dream about; it was the truth. He went back, as if for safety, to his imaginings, but for a while they seemed shallow and lifeless.

As he lay, he kept his eyes for the most part on a group of three stars, bright among the rest. They declined and swung slowly across the space of the open door. He thought that when he lost sight of them he would ride on again; but lying here, he was, he told himself, so happy that he would wait a little; there was no hurry now and nothing to fear. Tomorrow, no, today, he would come to Alde.

He got up at last and went out of the hut. The horse came when he called and he mounted. When he got back to the road he looked up. Right before him, high in the sky, unmoving among all the moving stars, stood the small pale pivot of the heavens, the pole star. He was riding straight for it.

Perhaps it was the chill of that hour before dawn, but now, as he rode, he began to discover in his mind thoughts that had lurked there unrecognized. He looked up to find the steadfast star that the swinging wain pointed to, but there was cloud now blotting out all the sky. He muttered in his mind, "She won't be angry. She will be glad I have come so quickly. It is different now he is dead." But he found himself terribly frightened. He whispered aloud, "Alde, don't be cruel . . . my darling!" Then he remembered with a flood of warmth and light in his heart that, being Alde, she could not be cruel. He was only a fool.

The dawn had come, not with deepening blue and sun, but gray, in a weeping shower, when he saw from a hillslope, beside a green-budded hawthorn bush, the village of Fervacques among apple orchards, and the castle at the end of the village—a wooden tower on a mound, a thatched wooden hall, and opposite, a line of outbuildings.

He stopped a moment, staring first at the castle, where she was, then aside, at the hawthorn bush beside him. The whole tree was covered with myriad little globes of green buds, and glassy raindrops hanging from the buds. A lark went up, and his heart with it, choking him with a confidence that was only just not certainty.

He had not thought in the least what he would do. He was quite sure that he would find Alde, and take her hand in his, and that he would ride away with her before him on his horse as he had ridden from Falaise. He had done it once, and no man on earth should prevent him doing it again.

So he rode straight on through the village. It was so early that only women were up in the cottages, and not many of them. One was lighting a fire; he heard the sharp crack of thorns as the flames caught. Another was singing; she stopped when a child cried shrilly; she answered it and then went on with her singing. He came in sight of the gates of the castle, and they stood open.

It was indeed as simple as he had expected. When he had tethered his horse to a ring in the pale just by the gate, he went across the empty yard to a serving woman who was letting down the bucket into the well. He said, "Where does he lie?"

The woman nodded her head to a little low building that stood a little apart; it must be a chapel. Fulcun turned and went toward it; he was quite sure that he would find there, not only Mauger lying between the four great candles, but Alde.

When everyone else had gone away from the wake to get break-fast, Alde would not go. She sat still on the faldstool that they had set for her beside the bier, just by Mauger's right shoulder. She did not look at him—he was covered over with a pall of dark green silk the color of the slime on shadowed pools—nor did she look at the altar, nor up at the candles that burned yellow and pale purple in the daylight. Her heavy eyes rested on the earth floor of the chapel and were too tired to lift.

She was, besides, too tired to think, and now, indeed, there was no need for thinking. She had had time this last two nights and a day; now she had thought, and she knew what it was that she had done.

Here was Mauger—not a man at all, but only a long, still mound under the darkly shining silk. Mauger himself was gone. That common thing had happened that is so blankly, intolerably strange; a man had gone away out of life; he was not; he would not be again.

She moved, turning her head slowly to look at him lying by her, his shoulder not a foot from her arm. She lifted her hand from her lap meaning to touch him, but she caught it back again and clasped it hard on the other upon her knee.

She could have touched him now, when it was too late. She had kindness for him now—it had come to her, pure, pitying, gentle kindness, when he had stirred out of the swoon after that last fit, and raised a gray, dim face, and tried to move his arm under the coverlet. She had put her hand under his head then and had not quailed at the touch of him. And that moment he had died.

So, she thought confusedly, her kindness was in her like the useless milk of a woman whose child is stillborn. But no, the thing was worse, far worse than that, for the woman had loved her child and wanted it, and she had neither loved nor wanted Mauger. And now it was too late.

She raised her head and moistened her dry lips with her tongue. If he could be alive again, she thought, she would give him kindness . . . however much it hurt her, for with a nightmare honesty she knew that if he were alive again, it would be as dreadful as ever to be kind to him. But she would do it so as to escape this worse thing, for now that he was dead, a door had shut in her face.

She heard the latch lift, and someone came into the chapel behind her and then stood still, but she did not turn. She had ruined a man and killed him. She had had time to repent, and she had not repented; in that moment she looked upon the face of irretrievable sin.

The silence drew her from her thoughts more potently than any word. She said, "Who is that?" There was no answer. She turned and saw Fulcun stand inside the door; he stared at her and said nothing; his eyes were shadowed by his helm, and the nasal threw a slanting shadow across his mouth. It was Fulcun. It was sin.

Even now he did not speak, but he took a step toward her. She had thought when she saw him stand there that her body had lost its power to move. But now she sprang up, and before he was halfway across the little chapel the bier was between them, and she looked at him across the dark pall that covered Mauger, and between the tall pale candles.

He stopped short, and said, "Alde," in a strange, startled voice, and nothing more than that, though for a moment she could not answer.

Then she cried at him, "Go away! Go away!"

There was silence again. She did not raise her eyes to his face, but kept them on the place where his shield strap crossed the corner of his gorget that made a little ridge across the leather.

"What do you mean?" he said.

"You must go away," she said. "And you must never come again to me." She was a little troubled as she spoke because she heard herself as if it were someone else. But the words were quite easy to say; she knew that they were the right words too; he must go away; she wanted him to go away quickly.

He said, "Alde . . . why?" She remembered afterward his voice as he said it, but that moment she did not hear it, and his words, like hers, were only words.

"Because it was sin," she told him.

He cried, "But he's dead."

At that she lifted up her eyes and looked at him; there was a glint in them as if of a dreadful laughter at his stupid ignorance. "Aye," she said, "he's dead. So it will always be sin."

She saw his face change and knew that he would speak.

"You know it," she cried. "You know that I'm right," and saw the life wiped again out of his face. She thought, "He must go quickly." She hated him, she thought, for standing there. He was her pain and her sin, and he would not go.

She laid her hands on the dead man, because she must lean on something. She could feel Mauger's hands crossed on his breast under her hands, and his were very cold. "Go away," she said.

Fulcun did not look again at her face. He stayed with his eyes on her hands, spread out upon Mauger's breast, leaning on him. Then he turned away and went to the door. He did not open it at once but stood with his head down, not looking back at her. After a minute he went out.

She sat down again by Mauger. She was very tired. She had driven away her sin. Once a thought leapt at her like a scribble of lightning, "No—it's Fulcun." But she was too tired for it to wake her mind. She was glad that he was gone.

Chapter 17

God hath overthrown me, and hath compassed me with his net. Behold, I cry out of wrong, but I am not heard: I cry aloud, but there is no judgment. He hath fenced up my way that I cannot pass, and he hath set darkness in my paths. He hath stripped me of my glory, and taken the crown from my head. He hath destroyed me on every side, and I am gone: and mine hope hath he removed like a tree.

Job 19:6–10

I

There was a hawthorn bush on the hillside; the raindrops had not dried on it. There was a fox that slipped across the road somewhere and into a wood; its eyes shone as it turned them on Fulcun. There was a place between a pool and a marsh where he pulled up and said to his horse's ears, "This is a very poor jest," and rode on. Then, there was the shepherd's hut on the slope—the hut where he had lain last night. He turned his horse off the road, tied stirrup to bridle as he had done last night, and, just as last night, unlatched the door, went in, and dropped on the heap of bracken. Very soon he fell asleep, and of the hours before remembered afterward only those few trivial things, and one thing more—the knowledge that, like the blackness of a night without stars, hid its own immensity, the knowledge that something was lost—was broken . . .

He wakened suddenly on the bracken bed and began to think, and instead of blackness there was merciless light in his mind. Alde—who had all of him so entirely that he did not belong to himself but only to her—Alde had not even kindness for him. He had thought that their hearts were one heart, but there was nothing at all for him in her—nothing. He meant nothing to her except a thing to be ashamed of, driven off, hated. He saw her again stand leaning with her hands upon Mauger . . . Mauger's wife. He thought, with a pang like death, "She hates me for his sake."

He flung over and lay on his face; the bracken smelled sodden and moldy. He remembered her with horrible sharpness as she had been at Falaise, in the woods of Ecouves, at Montgaudri. She had had something for him then, if you called it love. But what love was it that could change and be cruel? He dared not think. That was not Alde—that wanton, light-loving woman that he saw now in his mind.

He came out of the hut, got on his horse, and went down the hill. On the road he turned north and spurred; he was going again to Fervacques. He would cry to her, "Tell me the truth. Swear to me by your honor, and I'll believe. But I must know."

He rode a few miles, and then he let the horse slacken, and at last pulled up. He dared not go to her again. He turned about and rode for Courville.

Emma was crossing the yard with a piece of scarlet stuff that she had asked from Dame Aldrei, Geroy of Courville's wife, to patch Hernaut's kirtle. She thought, when she heard the horse, that it was Hernaut coming back, and she looked round, scared, and bundled the scarlet cloth under her cloak, because Hernaut had said they must ask for nothing but food and shelter from anyone while they lived on Geroy of Courville's bounty. But you can't, Emma thought with a spurt of unhappy anger, patch a kirtle without any stuff.

She saw that the horseman was Fulcun. He had pulled up, but he sat still in the saddle. Her eyes met his. He moved then and got down. She had not meant to go to him nor to speak, but it seemed that she had to, because they had looked at each other that minute.

She said, standing behind his shoulder, "Sir . . . Cousin . . . Did you find her?"

"Yes."

"You . . . saw her?"

"Yes," says Fulcun, and saw Alde again. He turned on Emma because he must see something else.

"Is she . . . is she well?" Emma grew terrified lest something awful should have happened to her.

"Well?" says Fulcun laboriously. "Yes . . . she is well. But . . . very weary . . . I think . . . with watching."

He met Emma's eyes. He would not let her think, no one should think that Alde was . . . what she was. And they should not know that he was a naked man, that had nothing . . . nothing left.

Emma was red to the edges of her veil. "I thought you might bring her here," she says, stumbling over the words, and then, just because she knew she had said the worst thing, she asked him, "Couldn't you?"

"No," says Fulcun, "I couldn't."

"I'm so sorry," Emma whispered, and he saw her lips shake.

He answered, "It can't be helped," in a light tone that was like a door slammed in her face. She flushed deeper and left him.

He turned away and went into the stable. Emma had meant to be kind. She was kind. That was why he could not endure to listen to her. For Alde was unkind.

That evening Geroy of Courville asked Fulcun where he had been. Geroy had heard it before from Hernaut but he was forgetful. When Fulcun said, "Fervacques," Geroy cried, "Oh—of course . . . and . . . ?"

It was a question, but it got no more answer than Guion had got an hour or two before. He had met Fulcun coming out of the stable carrying a wooden bucket, on his way to fetch water for his horse.

Fulcun did not wait for Guion to speak; he said, "Is supper ready? I'm hungry enough to eat my hood." He grinned at Guion and felt as if he were a skull grinning. Guion said it was ready, and then waited, but Fulcun went past him to the well.

One night, about a week after he got back to Courville, Fulcun wakened. All the folk from Echauffour slept in one room; Hernaut and Emma and little Geva in a bed, and the others on mattresses on the floor. The light had gone out and it was very dark. His body, which was as wide awake as his eyes, sat up, but for a second yet his mind was asleep. He heard the rattle of a swinging shutter and the long, thin whine of a wind about the tower that died to silence.

In that silence he knew at first no more than that a shutter had come open and the wind had blown the lamp out; then at the same instant two thoughts leapt at his mind—Alde under the lamp at Falaise as it streamed, flickered, and went out, and Alde looking at him across Mauger's body—Alde who did not know how to love, did not even know how to pity. Those two were the same Alde; there never had been any other. Not that he thought her wanton now; he could not. But there never had been the woman that he loved. He put his fingers up to his teeth and bit on them, bowing himself over his knees and holding himself very still till the pain of that understanding had, not abated, but grown a little familiar.

At last he got up, very quietly so as to wake no one. He put on his kirtle, then groped about for his sword. When he had it, he went, stepping over Rainald and Guillelm that slept next to him. He let himself out and shut the door behind him, easing the latch down without a sound.

On the hearth of the great hall below there were the embers of yesterday's fire. He stirred the soft ashes, warm to his fingers, and found a brand, black, with red sparks on it and a red glowing core. He blew it up to a flame. When he had made a new fire in the ashes of the dead one, he took from it a piece of the burning wood and laid it to the cords that bound a little packet to the flat top of the cross-pommel of his sword. Many men carried a small packet bound there with a relic of some kindly saint wrapped up in a piece of silk and again in leather.

The cord fell away, burning like a candle wick; Fulcun took off the bundle and laid his sword down. Then for a moment he held his hand out over the fire with the packet in it. He meant to drop it in unopened and let it burn, but he found that he could not.

Crouching down over the faint and wavering flame, with the folk sleeping round about him on the floor of the hall and making a great noise of snoring, he turned his hand over and spread out the bundle on his open palm. First there was the piece of soft leather, then a bit of blue silk, inside that a ragged strip of linen with dark stains splotching it at regular intervals, and in the midst of the roll of linen a tuft of dull golden hair. Those were his relics—the linen that had bound up her foot that night they fled from Falaise, and the tuft of hair that had lain on the boy's grubby palm at Bernay.

For a moment he stared at them while a dumb fury prompted him to throw them into the fire, to turn against the pain and have done with it. Then he knew that he never could have done with it. He could not have done with this love because that would be to live and yet be dead; he shrank from the thought as if he had come upon his own face, dead and corrupting.

He looked again at his open palm. That was her hair; her blood was on the linen. He had meant to hurt these things that were not her, but hers. He could not.

He bowed his head at that, barely knowing what pain it was that had him now. He put his mouth down to them and pressed it there with all the strength of his body, lips closed and teeth clenched in a rage of tenderness. Indeed he could hurt nothing that was hers.

He crouched lower and knelt there a long time. At first this hurt seemed as fruitless as the other. But at last his heart mounted, heavily and slow, on wings that were pain, and the beat of them pain, but yet they raised him to a pitch above either hurt or happiness. Then, for a while released, he cried to God to have pity on her . . . to listen to his pain . . . and somehow . . . with it . . . bless her.

He woke next morning to a vague sense of comfort; then he remembered. When he was dressed and had buckled his sword belt he closed his hand firmly and gently over the pommel, where, wrapped again in their leather and tied with fresh cord from his pouch, were the strip of linen and the tuft of hair. He said to himself, and in his mind to her, "Whether you love me or not, I love you," and he thought then, and for a little while after, that he needed no more than this light to live by. He did not know; and it was well he did not know.

That summer at Courville was very long. Hernaut was a difficult man these days; even Geroy found him hard to get on with. He was proud too; he would not take gifts from Geroy nor let Emma take them for herself or the children. He and all his folk must live of Geroy's bounty, but he'd take nothing for any of them but food and shelter. So Emma spent much time patching and darning, and in spite of it they all grew very shabby. The children must go barefoot to save their shoes; it was summer, and they liked it, but Emma, who was thinner now, and often frowning, cried sometimes at nights quietly, longing that somehow before winter came they might be home again at Echauffour.

One thing Hernaut could do, and did; that was to hunt almost daily. What they brought home was some payment for Geroy's hospitality. Fulcun went along with him; he was glad of it because he could not sit in Courville doing nothing. So they would ride out together most days, with perhaps a couple of the Echauffour men and some dogs.

One evening in June, when they had come back across the river and through the woods to the edge of the open country where the road went by and turned up to Courville on the hillside, Fulcun reined in suddenly.

Hernaut stopped too; the servants were not in sight, for they had killed a couple of buck today, and the men came slowly after, carrying the beasts slung on a fir pole.

Fulcun says, "Listen!" and they sat still, listening.

At first Hernaut could hear nothing in the quiet of the evening except that a silver birch, ghost white, rustled dryly, when all the other trees were still. Then he heard another sound—a dull rattle of wood on wood, the clapping of a leper's bell.

He turned and looked at Fulcun and saw that he was staring up the road toward the north. Hernaut looked too, and now, from behind the mill buildings that lay that way, a man came, walking slowly, stooping, and shaking his bell.

Fulcun says, "It is Raol Geroy," and his horse reared, but he cursed it and brought it round again.

Hernaut laughed. "How do you know? There's many lepers."

Fulcun stared again, then turned his head away with a jerk. He said nothing, but he swung his horse about and broke back into the wood. Hernaut heard him riding as if he rode after a buck. He himself waited a few minutes and then rode slowly along the road toward the leper. If Fulcun was right, Raol would have news.

It was more than an hour after, that Fulcun came again to the place where he and Hernaut had crossed the river once before that evening. He pulled up on the bank and looked over the pale water to the line of trees beyond; there was just light enough still to see them, clear green against clear blue sky as if the whole world was of those two colors only, isolated and intensified just before the dark. His eyes knew that the colors and the lingering light were comfortable and lovely, but now for him there was no life in anything in the world. Or rather, he himself was dead in the living world; but it was death without oblivion. As he rode into the trees again something made him look up; the half moon slipped, a silver flash, through the leaves; he dropped his head again and stared at the horse's neck.

All the way through the woods he was listening for the sound of the clapping bell; if he had heard it he would have fled again. He dared not meet Raol because he was in despair. He had thought that night when he had knelt over the fire with his mouth pressed to the things in his hand that he had not only felt the full pain of loss but had found a sufficient bulwark against it. The long months had taught him otherwise. Now, he knew that the loss of her was like a stone chucked into still water; the stone goes down out of sight, but when it is gone, ring after ring spreads over the water, wider and wider till the pool is full. That was how it was with him; the circumference of those circles of pain that ran out shivering from the one loss had filled the whole world. He could not see beyond their verges; they had swallowed everything.

It did not matter that now he understood rightly why he had lost her—because in her mind he was one with sin, because she thought of him as the enemy of her soul. She had done it, he could tell himself now, for righteousness, but in taking herself from him she had taken from him all the love that had been. For she had never loved him. If she had loved him she would not have dealt with him so—no, not for God's own sake. He loved, and he knew that. But she had never loved him; if she had ever, she could not have changed. Love could not change or die or grow unkind; he knew that too.

He had lived by her love as a man lives by sunlight, and it was no more than a candle burned out to nothing. He had thought it eternal, but it was ended; and with all the power of his soul he was sure of this—that what can come to an end has never been. So for him there was nothing—nothing in all the world.

Yet there was something. There was God.

When that thought came to him he was halfway up the slope to the town, but he wheeled his horse about and sat a long time looking back. The whole sky had deepened to night blue except in the west, where it was suffused with a metallic fiery green; against that deep translucent glow the woods showed black and fiercely distinct. Higher up there were a few, first stars, golden-colored and very large.

Fulcun lifted his head and looked at them. There was something for him still. There was God, who was now his only friend. And always he had his love for her. He looked from end to end of the deepening sky and over the silent woods. Then he dropped his head with a groan. He had learned now, it seemed to him, what love was, and what God was. That should have been enough to fill the world. But for him, in the darkly luminous sky and the brimming gold of the stars, there was nothing but blackness. And when he thought of God, his friend, comfort, and only, sufficient Lover throughout eternity—

He swung the horse about toward Courville and drove it on up the hill. "Oh! No, no, no," he was muttering, as he rode. For he thought, in a vast blank beyond the touch of hope, that unless he had Alde's love, the love of God was as impotent to lighten him as the golden stars. Without her, his soul had rather die than live.

That night when they were all in bed Hernaut called to him across the room.

"You were right," he says, "it was Raol Geroy today. He is come away from Saint-Évroult because now the Bastard has thrust in an abbot of his own, Osbern, the fellow's name is. He's no abbot though, while Robert of Grandmesnil lives."

Fulcun did not answer. In a moment Hernaut spoke again.

"Raol is going back to Marmoutier. But next week we'll ride again into Normandy and burn this fine abbot's granges and spoil his crops. And, by God's Son," cried Hernaut, and laughed angrily, "if I catch this Osbern I'll hang him in his own cloister."

Fulcun thought to himself then that Saint-Évroult, where Raol Malacorona had been a monk, was the last place in the world he would go to. Yet, when Hernaut rode out from Courville next week, Fulcun rode behind him among the rest.

II

Osbern, abbot of Saint-Évroult—if indeed Duke Guillelm could thrust one abbot upon the brothers, having driven out another— sat in the cloister of the abbey on a fine afternoon in late May. The time was between None and Vespers, and all the monks were at work along the cloister walls, except such as were in the infirmary or kitchen or busy in their offices. The sun now was off the north cloister wall, so the light was good for coloring. Abbot Osbern, who besides being abbot, was the best illuminator, copyist, sculptor, and builder in the abbey, was busy over the picturing of the wind-whipped gown of an angel that stooped from a cloud, quick as a swallow, to tell the shepherds there was a child born beyond the winter hills. He smiled as he drew, but with his eyes only, thinking of the rush of dark starlit air and the strong speed of the angel's flight. Then his lips smiled. Was the holy thing pleased to see the hills below, rounded and green, with little brooks among them talking loud in the night? He paused for a moment, holding his pen slanted up lest a drop of ink might fall on the page: he would have liked to be able to picture all heaven and earth, he thought, every living thing, the windy air, the sounds of water, the smell of frosty mornings, the smell of violets, the rocking clamor of bells that was half movement, half sound. But you couldn't do it. No man could. He bent again over the angel.

It was just then that there came a noise of shouting outside. A fellow in a leather hood ran into the cloister from the cellarer's office. It was the abbey porter. He was shouting still, and as he came along the line of monks that had been stooping over their books the length of the cloister walk, one after another jumped up: someone knocked over a desk; many cried out after the man to know what was wrong, and one or two of the novices did not wait for an answer but ran out at once to see for themselves.

Then, while the monks crowded round, the porter told the news. The Geroys were coming. Saint-Évroult village was blazing. Hernaut Geroy had set it alight and now with a strong force was coming to the abbey. And the two abbey serfs that had run through the woods to give warning said that his men were shouting to one another how they would burn Saint-Évroult church and cloister, but Hernaut had beaten one man on the head with the flat of his sword and cried that not one of the monks must be touched, but only the Bastard's simoniac abbot.

The porter told it stammering with haste, and when he finished there was a short lull—then, like ice on a stream that has thinned and breaks quietly at last and scatters, the crowd of monks broke up. Some drew aside and talked, loud and boastfully, of how this abbey was built by the Geroys and the Grandmesnils, and Robert of Grandmesnil its true abbot—none other. Soon they went out by the cellarer's office to the gate to meet the Geroys. Others did not stay to talk, but leaping the low cloister wall so as to cross the garth more quickly, went away to the infirmary gate that opened close on the woods.

A few stayed behind with the abbot. But he had turned to watch those scared and hurried figures that dived under the low arch beyond the chapter house. Even when all were gone he still stared that way. Herman the cellarer plucked him by the sleeve.

"Father," he says, "you must hide."

Abbot Osbern turned his face. He had very bright dark brown eyes that shone and glanced quickly here and there, but now he looked heavily.

"No. I shall not hide."

"But you must."

The abbot looked up. His face had reddened. "In Caux," he says, "my house is a knight's house. I'm not used to hide . . . Besides . . . the holy martyrs did not hide."

Herman says, "They were hunted for by heathens. It is sacrilege for these if they lay hands on you. Think of their souls."

The abbot dropped his eyes. Then he glanced once again at the way those hasty runaways had gone. At last he shrugged his shoulders and turned back to Herman.

"I'll do this," he says, "I'll go into the church. They can find me there if they will. Tell that to Hernaut Geroy." He stared at Herman's puckered square face. "On your obedience," he says.

Herman says, "On my obedience, Father," and bowed his head.

The abbot went up the steps to the east door. Just as he laid his hand on the latch the Geroy's horns sounded outside the gate of the close.

❖

When he went into the church the abbot's only thought was to go to the high altar and kneel before it and let the Geroys lay hands on him there, if they dared. But halfway up the nave he stopped. In the treasury beside the tower were the precious things of Saint Évroult; there was the great staff with its head of crystal, clear as water; there was the shrine where lay Saint Évroult's hand; it was colored all over with enamel work of Limoges, and round about there ran a pattern of vine leaves, wonderfully lively, in silver and silver gilt; and there was the gold chalice too. Was it likely, Abbot Osbern thought, that Hernaut Geroy, exiled and landless and needy, would leave these things behind him? He turned and began to run across the church, his shoes clapping and his keys making a great jingle. He had not been afraid before, but now he was desperately afraid lest they should come in and catch him; it made a man afraid when he began to run—that was his thought and he half smiled at it.

While he bent over the chests, unlocking them and taking out the things, he could feel the sweat run down his back. There was a great deal of shouting now in the cloister; he heard men running about and calling to each other. But they did not come into the church.

He had the treasures out at last, the crystal staff over his shoulder like a shepherd's crook, the chalice in one hand, and the shrine under his arm. He came from the treasury and turned in at the low arch of the tower; as he went through, the top of the staff jarred against the stone—it kept those scratches ever after—and just that moment the west cloister door opened and swung back with a clatter.

Someone shouted, "I don't believe he is gone to Verneuces. If he's hiding here I'll rout him out. Come on, any man who's not afraid!"

Abbot Osbern plunged for the stairs—perhaps—perhaps they had not seen him. Perhaps he had time.

He thought, when he had struggled up the narrow dark steps with his load and laid the treasures on the bell gallery and covered them with some old sacks lying there, that they had certainly not seen him. He stood a second to get his breath, and also to get again the courage this haste had shaken. Then he began to go back down the stairs.

He came to the floor below where the bell ropes ran down from the ceiling to the floor like thin pillars. And then he stopped; a man stood in the doorway; he had his back to the abbot; he had a shield on his shoulder and an iron helm with a bronze rim and cross bands; his sword was out, and he leaned on it with his hands and bent his head forward as though he were listening. As the abbot stopped, he saw the man's head half turn toward him; then he flung a hand out behind him as though he said, "Wait a minute!" and he leaned forward through the door.

"Is that you, Serlo? Try the monks' dortour. I'll seek up here."

Another voice below answered, "Very good."

The man turned.

Abbot Osbern said, "I am the man you want. I am the abbot."

The other glanced at him, but still he seemed to be listening to sounds below. "Be quiet!" he muttered.

The abbot came on. "Let me go down," he says, but the man caught him by the arm then and crammed one hand over his mouth.

"Be quiet!" he whispered. "Unless you'd have them hang you out of hand. They'll harm no one and nothing here but you."

Down below someone shouted. The man loosed Abbot Osbern and turned to the stair, but the abbot caught him by the wrist.

"What are you going to do?" he says.

"Hold the stair if they come up," the other answered him, and Abbot Osbern heard him grind his teeth.

"You're not a Geroy?"

"I am."

Abbot Osbern pulled him back. "No!" he says. "If you're a Geroy I'll not have you shed the blood of your own house for me."

"Let me go!" says the Geroy and tore his hand free.

"What, do you care nothing for your own blood?" cried Osbern. He was honestly shocked.

The Geroy turned his face about. It was a thin dark face and the nasal of the helm made his eyes seem full of shadow, and dull and dead too in the way they looked out. "No," he says, "not now."

Then they were both silent because there was a man on the stairs below. But someone beyond in the church cried out, "Come down. He's not there. Fulcun went up to see."

"That's Hernaut," the Geroy muttered.

The man below ran down again. There was silence.

After a few moments the Geroy turned again to Abbot Osbern. He said, as if there had been no pause, and with a twisted, joyless smile, "It was a monk that told me a man should care for nothing else but God only."

Abbot Osbern answered quick, "Well, he was wrong. The more creatures we love the better. They're all his."

He saw what was like a flicker in the eyes he looked into. It was as if the man had wakened and looked out at him.

"Do you think that?" he muttered so that the abbot only just caught the words, and he brooded a minute, frowning, his chin down on his chest. His eyes came again to Osbern with a kind of eagerness. Then they clouded. He shrugged, as if to say that it might be so, but it was not now to the point.

They could still hear a few distant shouts, but below in the church there was silence. After a little Abbot Osbern spoke suddenly, "I came here to hide the treasures. They're up there." He tipped his head toward the bell loft. "I wasn't hiding from you Geroys."

The Geroy looked at him. He nodded and then saw the monk's face flush.

"There," cried Abbot Osbern. "See my pride! I will have you know—"

The other interrupted him. "I was thinking," he says with a new smile that changed his face, "that you didn't fear to tell me of the treasures."

Abbot Osbern smiled then at him; they found they had a liking for each other that minute.

"Where are all the monks?" the Geroy says after a minute, as a man talking idly to a friend.

"Most of them ran away." Abbot Osbern stared at the ropes. "They'd no call to stay by me. I'm not their choice. And I'm a stranger here. I'm from Caux." He stopped. "But," he says, and hesitated, and then said it quickly, "but Witmund ran away too."

The Geroy murmured, as if he thought he must ask, "Who is Witmund?"

Abbot Osbern told him, "He came with me from Caux." Then he was silent, and at last he said in a very different voice, "Poor lad. He's as gentle as a maid. He makes us music to sing. He could not help it."

The Geroy turned to him. "That isn't enough," he cried in an extraordinarily harsh voice.

"What do you mean?"

The Geroy looked down. The abbot thought he was not going to answer, but he said at last, "It's not enough . . . if any-one is . . . false . . . to go on . . . caring," and then after a minute he muttered through his teeth, "Then—there's—nothing."

The abbot forgot to think of Witmund. He said, keeping his face away from the Geroy—

"There is."

He felt that the other man stiffened; they both stood still. The silence was strained tight so that they could hear each other's breathing and the ticking of a board in the floor under their feet.

But the Geroy did not ask what there was. After a long while he put his sword up and heaved himself off from the wall of the tower. A horn had blown down below in the close.

"There!" he says. "I'll go now. But bolt the door and stay here till you hear us ride out."

He went out to the stairs without any more farewell, but there he turned.

"Your cellarer," he says, "old Herman, he lied stoutly. He swore by God's cross you were gone to Verneuces. You can trust him," he says. "He's not false."

From Saint-Évroult Hernaut Geroy and his men went along to l'Aigle, and there stayed two days with Engenulf. It was there that Herman the cellarer came to him. Herman was as wise an old man as he was bold and eloquent too. He talked with Hernaut in the orchard for an hour, and in the end Hernaut came with him to the gate to bid him farewell and knelt in the road for the monk's blessing.

"And," says Hernaut, "if it's as you say, and this abbot took the abbey in good faith, and without simony, thinking no harm—well, I'll make amends to Saint-Évroult."

He made amends next day; he rode with all his folks to the gate as he had ridden before. But now, when he and his men came through the cloister their feet were bare instead of their swords, and in the church Hernaut laid a very costly mantle of scarlet woven with white and blue upon the high altar, and a moleskin bag with a mark of silver in it. He had plundered the cloak from a manor of Mabille of Belesme, and the silver he had borrowed from Engenulf. The abbot himself blessed them all, and kissed Hernaut, and then the Geroys went away.

But as the abbot lingered, alone in the church, touching with his fingers the curves of a new iron grille that he had wrought and set up across the niche where Saint Évroult's shrine was put for the folk to see at high festivals, he heard the door open and a man come in. It was not a monk; there was the clap of a shield against a mailed shoulder, and iron rang on the wall as the man turned to shut the door. The abbot turned, then waited. The Geroy who had been with him in the tower came over and stood in front of him. He pushed down his sword till the shoe of the scabbard rested on the pavement, and he leaned with both hands on the quillons. He did not lift his eyes to Osbern's face and for a moment he did not speak.

Then he said in a hoarse low voice, "Father, what can I do? I . . . am . . . in hell. And . . . he . . . is not enough."

"Who?"

The Geroy raised his eyes. They were frightened. "God," he says.

Then without waiting for an answer he began to talk, very quick, stumbling over words, with sudden pauses, and sometimes only whispering.

"I can't endure. There is nothing . . . There can be nothing ever—not even in heaven for me. Oh—I know he's kind—and . . . there's . . . no one else. But—" He broke off as if he were breathless.

The abbot said, when he had been silent a moment, "Do you pray to God?"

The Geroy gave something that was like a wild laugh. "Oh, do I not?" he cried, and then, "I used to pray only that he should bless . . . her . . . but now—I must for myself . . . or I'll drown." His voice sank. "But there's no answer. There can be none, unless . . . she should . . ." He left that unfinished.

For a long time they stood together in the empty church. From outside came pleasant summer sounds—a boy calling to his cattle, the confused sweet jargoning of birds, the sound of brother Fulcher whetting his scythe in the garth. Once, when the Geroy moved as if he grew impatient, the abbot threw out his hand quickly. "Wait a minute," he said.

He must think, and he must try to understand without asking questions. He liked this man too well to ask more than he chose to tell. But indeed, he thought that he did understand. He himself had known nights that had no star, and days when the sun itself shone black. He had known the pain that is too absolute to strike out any clear note from a man's heartstrings, but falls with the dull unechoing dunt of a blow on the dumb earth.

He said at last, speaking from his own thoughts,

"I remember . . . then . . . I heard one read this. And when I had waited . . . it came true. Listen, 'My son, if thou come to serve the Lord, prepare thy soul for temptation. Command thy heart and abide patiently, and make not haste in the dark days.'"

The Geroy stared into the abbot's face. "'Make not haste—' I see. But that is not much help."

"It's not all," the abbot told him. "It says then, 'Ye that fear the Lord hope in him, and mercy shall come to you with gladness.'"

"Gladness!" The Geroy laughed, but his voice was different; it was alive with pain and so were his eyes.

The abbot went on, "'Consider the sons of the children of men, and see, for no man hath hoped in the Lord and been confounded. Yea and who hath remained in his fear and is forsaken? Or who hath called on him, and he despised him?'"

The Geroy turned his face away. He said in a whisper, "I must just . . . wait?"

Abbot Osbern says, "'We will fall into the hands of God and not into the hands of men, for as his majesty is, so is his mercy.'"

The Geroy's eyes came to him again, but he said nothing. He turned on his heel and went away.

Abbot Osbern watched him down the nave. He walked with a long stride, stooping a little. The abbot turned to the altar and knelt. He said, "God, help him." He remembered that he did not know the man's name; nor what was his hell; nor would he ever, he supposed. But God did.

Chapter 18

As the trees' sap doth seeke the root below
In winter, in my winter now I goe,
    Where none but thee, th' Eternall root
    Of true Love I may know.

John Donne

I

At the beginning of December, when Hernaut and his folk had been almost two years at Courville, a small company of riders came to the gate. It was a foul day and they were impatient to be in shelter. The foremost of them shouted to the gate watch to know if Hernaut Geroy of Echauffour were here. The gate watch says, "Aye," and let them through. He did not even try to find out what they wanted; he, no more than they, wished to stand in the rain that drove from the banked clouds mixed with stinging hail.

The riders came up to the castle and there asked again for Hernaut Geroy. One of the young men of Geroy of Courville's household, who was hustling across the yard with his head down and his hands under his armpits, stopped just long enough to tell them that they'd find him in the top of the tower yonder, and then ran on. So, leaving two men with the horses under the deep thatched eaves of the outbuildings, the others went up to the tower. On the stairs, one of them, a big man with a face scored with an old sword slash that had twisted his mouth to a strange shape, took out of his pouch a letter with a seal, both white as curd.

Up in the top story of the tower, Hernaut Geroy sat in his shirt and breeches by the brazier, while Emma patched a rent in what had been his feast-tide kirtle and was now his only one. He had caught it on a nail as he sprang up to catch young Rainald, who had got hold of a spear blade and was trying to sharpen it with an old hone.

So now Rainald stood leaning one shoulder on the wall, his face very red and turned away from everyone, kicking at the rushes as hard as he dared. He was sore in person and angry in mind, for the spear blade was an old one, and no use anyway, and the hone one of the carpenters had given him. Emma, who had said nothing while Rainald got his thrashing, but kept her eyes on the linen socks she was making, said nothing now, and was very busy over Hernaut's kirtle, but her face was almost as red and unhappy as Rainald's. Fulcun Geroy, who had watched the whole thing, had set to work again on a boxwood bowl he was carving for a Christmas gift for Petronelle. They and all the rest of the folk sat very silent, while Hernaut brooded, his elbows on his knees and face between his fists, staring into the brazier.

Emma snapped off her thread and stuck the needle into the bosom of her gown, and says, "There, sir." And as she said it someone knocked loudly at the door.

She got up and held out the kirtle to Hernaut. One of the women had moved to the door, but Emma cried, "A minute."

Hernaut turned. "No—let 'em in, let 'em in, whoever it is."

So the woman opened the door and in came the knight with the scarred face and three other men, and found Hernaut Geroy in shirt and breeches by the brazier and Emma still holding out to him the mended kirtle.

"Oh," says Hernaut, "is it you, Raol of Tancarville?" Raol was the duke's chamberlain.

"Hernaut Geroy," says he, "here is a letter and a greeting from Duke Guillelm to bid you come in peace to his Christmas court and be assured of his mercy and friendship."

He held out the letter and Hernaut took it from him. Hernaut said nothing for a moment, and then he laughed.

"What does the Bastard look to get out of this? Will he go against Maine this year?"

Emma cried, "Oh, sir!" to him, and then, though Hernaut bade her be silent, she turned to Raol of Tancarville, "Sir, forget that word . . . I . . . oh, sir, do not . . . do not . . ." She clutched Hernaut's arm, "Let us go home!" and broke into wild desolate crying.

Hernaut tried to loose her hands, then gave it up and tossed Fulcun the letter. "Read it out," he says.

Fulcun cut the silk cord with his knife and read it. There was in it just what the big knight said. Hernaut turned then and thanked him for bringing the letter and bade Fulcun go down with the duke's messenger and find Geroy of Courville's steward and ask for hospitality for him and his folk.

When Fulcun came back everyone was very busy. Hernaut went out to look for Geroy to tell him the news, and Emma and the women and the little boys too grew very merry over the packing up. Not that they had many clothes to pack, Emma says, and laughed, but the gear must all go home, and she caught Rainald and boxed his ears in fun.

Then she stood still and looked at Fulcun, and he saw her face fall.

"But what shall we wear at Christmas court?" she says. "Hernaut has only that brown kirtle with the red pattern. And you—" She looked at him, and her voice trembled into laughter, "Oh, Heron!"

Fulcun smiled at her. It was pleasant to see Emma like this. He says, "Oh, I'll keep my cloak about me."

Emma looked him up and down carefully. "You'll have to." She was serious again. "But what is your cloak like?"

He fetched it and spread it for her to see. She took up a fold in her hand.

"I can see it's a fine cloth, and it must have been a fair color, Fulcun. But look—blue there, and almost green over the shoulder."

He stared at it and forgot her, because looking at the cloak and considering it had reminded him of that hot day at Saint-Céneri when Dame Aelis had pitched it, with the other things, down on the floor beside them. It was Raol Malacorona's cloak. He remembered that Dame Aelis had said then that Raol had not had much luck.

Fulcun says, "It'll do well enough for me; if the duke doesn't like it he can give me a new one." He spoke shortly because his heart was sore remembering Robert eating cherries that day and laughing his great gay laugh. He looked down at the stuff in his hands. There was not much left from that day, except the cloak. He frowned. It was strange and painful to remember that then, he had not seen Alde. Now he had lost her. But the cloak was here still. He bundled it together and threw it down on a bench. He would have liked to trample on it.

The duke kept his Christmas at Lillebonne. They came there on a stormy afternoon with sparse snow on the ground and great banked black clouds in the west rimmed all along their range with a fierce white line of light where the sun lurked. After Caudebec, where they were ferried over the Seine, the road ran between bare woods; the color of bracken was the only warm thing there; the whole world shivered and drew itself close; the ground was hard as iron and rang like iron under the horse's hooves.

At Lillebonne they crowded somehow into one of the smallest of the wooden huts that stood within the pale, and then Hernaut went over to the great hall to wait on the duke.

Emma was so busy for a while seeing to the storing of their gear, and to the lighting of a fire, and to getting food from the steward, that she did not notice the waiting, but when she had time to sit down, then she began to be frightened. What she wanted, and she wanted it so much that she was sure she should not have it, was to go home to Echauffour, and to be as they had been before. She thought of Echauffour, the little brook, the pool that would be gray now with ice and the village lads sliding across it with their arms up and shouting. And the yard, with the box hedge to shelter the beehives that stood each with its doorway to the morning sun; that winter afternoon she heard the bees as they came home through the swimming gold of a summer evening. And the great chamber, and the children's gowns stored away in the red chest under the window. She thought, "Oh, if we could be going tomorrow!" and looked up meaning to say so to Fulcun, but he was staring in front of him with something in his face quite dead and remote . . . it was like the cold world outside. She did not speak.

At last Hernaut came back. He went to the fire and stood by it warming himself and frowning. Emma stared at him, her hands pressed tight together. When Geva came to beg a bit of stuff to wrap a broken stick in for a doll, she chid her sharply and pushed her away.

Hernaut looked up from the fire and across it at Fulcun.

"The duke is angry with you still, Fulcun Geroy," he says. "But I said 'One Geroy, all Geroys. Pardon all or none.'"

Fulcun looked up. "That was good of you, Hernaut." He knew Hernaut had little kindness left for him, but that he was a man that would not leave one of his house in the lurch.

Hernaut only hunched up a shoulder in answer and was silent.

Emma cried out suddenly, "Are we going home?"

At her voice they both turned and looked at her, and then Hernaut laughed, an angry laugh.

"No, my girl," he says.

Her face went slowly white. "Not yet, anyway," says Hernaut. "He'll not trust us yet in Normandy. He says, 'Go away out of my Duchy for a year—'"

Emma cried, "Go? . . . Where?"

"Oh," says Hernaut, "I shall go to Apulia."

She put her hands on her knees and hung her head down as though she were too desperately tired to sit up. He went to her and clapped her shoulder, rough but more kind. "When I come back, then we'll go home, girl," he says, and left her and moved back to the fire.

In a minute he spoke to Fulcun. "You'll come too?"

Fulcun stared at him. "You'd best," says Hernaut. "For you'll have to go out of Normandy as well."

Fulcun said at last, "No."

Hernaut cried out on him, "God's Death! Where will you go then? Back to Courville?"

Fulcun got up and went over to the door. With his finger on the latch, he says, "No. I . . . I'll go to Caharel," but as he said it he was sure that he would not go there. It was not so far as Italy, but yet it was a very long way from Fervacques.

He went out, and as he went he heard Emma begin to cry. He thought as he stood a moment with the bitter wind whipping at his cloak, that it had taken him a long time to learn that the world was a sad place for most folk. But when a man had once learned that it was so, he found sorrow everywhere.

Then he forgot Emma, or rather she became part of the shadow that filled his mind. He went across the yard in the failing light that was yet not quite dusk, and out of the gate and a little way out along the road that ran straight into the dark woods. Some serf women were coming along it bearing home wood for firing; two of them had bundles on their backs, the other dragged a sort of wooden sledge piled with the faggots. All went bowed. Beside them limped a great, gaunt, liver-colored dog; when they came close Fulcun saw that the dog had no toes on his right forefoot—so the beast had been lamed for running the duke's deer.

The women and the dog passed by him and into the pale, but Fulcun stood there still looking out into the growing dark.

Where should he go? Not to Apulia. He was sure of that. To Caharel? He did not want to go there either. Courville? No. Geroy of Courville had been kind, but he had done enough.

He heard a horn blown at the gate behind him and turned. It was the gate watch blowing to give warning that the gate was to be shut. Fulcun went in. But as he went he knew, as if he had known it all along, where he must go. There was one place only for him, and one refuge. It was as though there never had been any other.

When he came back to the little house Hernaut had gone out; only Emma and the women and the little girls were there. Emma was not crying now, but he could see that she had cried a great deal.

"Emma," he says, "it is only for a year."

"Yes." Her voice was not friendly, and she kept her face turned from him.

"Where shall you go?" he asked her.

"To my brother. To Odo."

Fulcun nodded. He remembered Odo the Steward when he came once out of the Cotentin to Echauffour; a big, cheerful, kind man. Perhaps she would be happy there, after a while.

She came to him as he stood by the fire.

"Fulcun, why won't you go with . . . him?"

He looked down at her and knew that she thought he had failed her. She wanted him to go with Hernaut so that Hernaut should be so much the more safe.

He shook his head. He was sorry, and so he must tell her why. He said, "Because . . . it's too far."

She stared at his face and then she understood him. "From her?"

He nodded and she dropped her eyes. When she spoke again it was in a different voice. "Well," she says, "when you are at Caharel, Odo shall bring us to see you someday. The children will miss you, Fulcun." She laid her hand lightly on his arm for a second. "Is Caharel a great fief?"

He told her, "No. Only a little alod. Old Geroy sold the fief." Then he said, "But—I'm not going to Caharel."

"Not?" she cried. "But I thought—"

He says in a low voice, as if he were ashamed, "It's a long way. Right athwart Normandy."

"Then where are you going?"

He was so long in answering that she lifted her eyes and stared at him. He did not look at her, but only into the dying fire. "To Saint-Évroult," he told her at last.

"But . . . ," she says, and hesitated and dropped the tangled thought for another that was simpler. "But . . . that's not out of Normandy."

He gave a sort of smile. "No, I shall be out of the world," and when she cried, "A monk?" he nodded.

Hernaut came in just then, and Fulcun told him. Hernaut said he was sure the duke would not suffer it since Saint-Évroult was in Normandy, but Fulcun said that this new abbot was one of the duke's own men; Guillelm would trust Abbot Osbern to see that a Geroy did not get into mischief. He laughed as he said it, because it was so absurd that Guillelm should be concerned in what he was going to do, now that for him all dukes and counts had ceased to matter, and only one thing was left.

Next day, when they had all knelt before the duke and had kissed his hand, and had received his pardon, Hernaut rode off with five of the Echauffour men. The other two, who were old, would go with Emma, who was to travel in the company of Richart of Avranches to her brother.

Fulcun stood at the gate and watched her go. She had kissed him, and he had kissed the children, and then she had stared at him with her brows puckered up, as if there were something she wanted to say. She had gone away without saying it, but for a long time as she rode behind old Herluin, staring at his dirty white lamb's-wool hood, that looked even dirtier against the snow, she had been puzzling over Fulcun. He had said that Caharel was too far away. But Saint-Évroult, where he would be a monk and out of the world, was not too far. There was something there that did not fit well together, but she could not get it clear in her mind.

There was no questioning in Fulcun's mind at all as he rode out alone from Lillebonne and up the straight road between the dark, snow-spattered woods. He was going to Saint-Évroult so as to be a monk, so as to spend all his life, from this time onward, praying to God for Alde. And, for the rest, waiting upon God to help.

II

It was the eve of Christmas—green Christmas yet, but the wind was blowing cold and the sky was dulling with brownish clouds. Abbot Osbern laid the chisel to the strong upward curve of the capital he was working on—it had on it a leaf like a tight-curled frond of bracken, with all the life of spring in its opening. He gave a few quick strokes with his mallet and stood back and looked at it. Then he turned to the man in the novice's gray gown who stooped over the carpenter's bench.

"Is it said in your countryside, 'Green Christmas, white Candlemas'?" he says.

Fulcun looked up from the coffer lid he was carving.

"No—I've not heard that." Then he gave a little laugh. "There's one thing we say—

Two frosts in November to carry a duck,
And Christmas will be all slush and muck.

The abbot laughed too and turned back to his work.

"Was it so," he says in a minute, "this year?"

Fulcun answered, with a kind of unwillingness in his voice, that he didn't remember, and they said no more. But the abbot, from thinking of November frosts, went on to think of Fulcun Geroy, for just two weeks a novice at Saint-Évroult.

He knew now as much of Fulcun Geroy as anyone in the world, he thought, except that woman. And this Fulcun perhaps was not the Fulcun she had known. No, most certainly he could not be. He was not even the same as the man who had come to Saint-Évroult last summer, as desperate as any hunted beast.

He was cheerful now to talk with. Abbot Osbern had heard him laughing in the garden when the novices took their recreation, and he had heard too the young lads laughing sometimes at things he had said. But now and again, as a minute ago, there would come that lagging note in his voice, and he would be silent. Abbot Osbern knew too much of him not to wonder just what it meant.

He went on working slowly and carefully at the undercutting of the leaf frond, his bright brown eyes intent on it, but his mind still fixed on Fulcun. A queer thing it was that he should have come to Saint-Évroult, of all abbeys in Christendom, where Guillelm of Normandy's abbot had taken the place of his own cousin. And yet that wasn't so queer as the way he had stood in the doorway of the tower room last summer, ready to hold the stair against his kin. And yet again, none of it was queer at all, for that was Fulcun, a man who walked with his eyes on a far distance and simply did not see clear anything that came between.

The abbot smiled in his mind at that. In a fortnight he had indeed learned to know a great deal of Fulcun Geroy. Of course he had learned much of it in Fulcun's confession—but Abbot Osbern smiled now with his lips as he thought, "It's little he knows of me, or cares," and, with a warmth of kindness in his mind, "He'll always be somehow a boy that way, caring only for one thing." Then he frowned. One thing? Yes, but would it always be that woman? Someday would it be God himself instead? For how else, the abbot thought, could the man be ever happy?

He half turned then, without knowing that he did so, and saw Fulcun. He stooped over the coffer lid with one hand resting on it. He had laid down his chisel and mallet and was drawing a circle with the compasses. But as the leg swung he looked up, not at the abbot, but away at the wooden, cobwebbed wall of the workshop.

Abbot Osbern turned back to the stone and worked on fiercely for a minute. Then he stopped. Right or wrong, wise or unwise, he would say what was in his mind.

"Son," he says, and so as not to look at Fulcun he laid the chisel to the stone and flicked at it with the hammer, glancing it along the smooth curve, "have you not thought ever, that perhaps . . . she . . . the woman, sent you from her because she . . . meant right? And only cruelly because it was hard for her, and she forwearied with watching?"

There was a long silence. At last Fulcun says, "Yes. I have thought . . . that. Sometimes." His voice was empty. He laid the compass down and picked up his tools and began again without a pause.

Yet it was he who spoke next. The abbot was hard at work again, the hammer was ringing and the chips flying. He did not catch what Fulcun had said. "What's that?" he asked.

Fulcun gave a sort of laugh. "I said it was a strange thing indeed . . . that which you said to me . . . for a monk to say."

Abbot Osbern knew it. He said, "I'm a poor enough figure of a monk. You know something of how I keep pride by me. And you saw me cuff that lad in the cloister the other day." He saw Fulcun's eyes twinkle and he smiled. "I don't suffer fools . . . not gladly." Then he grew serious. "But this—" he says.

Fulcun broke in on him. "Aye, and you said to me—that day—you said, 'The more things a man loves the better, for they're all his.'" He paused, and his voice dropped. "But when you have loved one thing only, and that . . . above God . . . and cannot leave it . . ."

His eyes were on Osbern's, and there was a deepening shadow in them, as if a fear that had slept was stirring and wakening. He muttered to himself, "I had forgotten that when I came here." But now he had remembered the thing that Raol Malacorona had threatened, and that he himself had always feared.

Osbern stood staring down and frowning, with the cold steel of the chisel laid against his cheek, but before he spoke the bell of the church began to ring. It was time for High Mass. They put their tools down and left the workshop to go to wash. But as the abbot turned from the water trough and Fulcun handed him the towel Osbern spoke, looking down at his hands.

"God must answer you," he says. "I cannot." He gave the towel back and turned away. But he said, without turning to Fulcun, who stooped over the water, "Only . . . don't be afraid. There's nothing there to fear."

It was very cold, that Christmas Eve, getting up just before midnight. As they filed along the row of dortour windows the snow drifted through in soft, loose flakes. One of the novices who stopped and put his head out, whispered that it lay deep, quite so deep on the cloister thatch, and he showed them with his hands though no one could see. After the dark up there, and the night stairs half-lit by a single lantern, the church was ablaze like the hall of a king's palace. Over the high altar every candle in the hanging crown of lights was lit, and the flames flickered and swam till the whole brazen circle seemed to flower and float and dazzle in the gloom. There was a row of candles too on each side of the choir. These were for the novices so that they might follow the office in their books. The monks behind them sat in shadow; they had no need of light, for they had the words by heart. When all were in their places the precentor struck his rod on the front of his stall, and they stood, and the singing began.

For a little, standing or kneeling, Fulcun only listened without thought. The men's voices were like the hollow gloom of the great arches, as somber, strong, and confident as their shadowed curves. The lads' treble fluttered against it like the candle flames, bright, flexible, limpid. And from men's and boys' mouths went up a white steaming cloud of breath, and floated visible in the lit church.

Fulcun forgot again the thing he feared, or rather he was sure that, as the abbot had said, there was nothing to fear. And he had forgotten too all his unending hunger for Alde, his lack, his loneliness, and the irremediable pain of the wound she had dealt him. He remembered now only Alde herself and the kind strength of love. He could wrap love round her like a cloak and so hold her, and God understood and allowed it, because God loved her too.

As the treble voices soared and flickered he knelt in a still happiness. He thought of her, safe in the hold of love, as if she were a little child playing, and God and he looking on at her.

When the long Mass was over they went up again to the dortour. The snow was not falling now; the sky had cleared, and a silver moon, sharp-edged as ice, rode in the profound and empty sky and spilt white slants of light across the floor so that the whole room was not dark but gray with dusk.

Fulcun lay on his side, staring at the moonlight on the floor. A mouse drifted across it, smoothly as a bit of blown gray fluff; the lads had all fallen asleep, it was very quiet. But Fulcun could not sleep. His mind was as wide awake as if it had been plunged into ice water. The musical, fit peace of the church was gone. A darker hour was come upon him. He knew, without at first knowing why, that it was the hour he had dreaded; the hour when he must choose between God and love.

In church he had stood beside God and looked on Alde, safe because God loved her. If now he should turn away and leave her there . . . trust God with her . . . forsake her—it was not to forsake her. It was not he that kept her safe, but God.

And God claimed all his love. God had taken her from him for his sin, and now, because he had loved her too much, God said, "Choose between her and me." Judgment and love had bayed him in on every side. He must choose. This was the hour.

He lay very still. Raol had foretold just this, that God would take away all and then demand his naked soul. It was so now, and yet it was utterly different. There was no fear here, though there was pain, the huge pain of loss. He must lose Alde . . . He could not lose her . . . And then he knew that he could not—could not—lose God.

There was no moment when he made his choice, and he could not have chosen otherwise. He was beaten, and he knew it. Blind, helpless, and empty-handed, one ache of torn love, he turned there where he had always feared to turn. It was less than the smallest lifting of his little finger; as slight as the flicker of a child's eyelids in sleep; and yet, he turned. Soon after, he slept.

Next day, being Christmas Day, there were many and long services in church, joyful but tiring. When dinnertime came everyone was hungry and very cold. But today was a feast, with flesh to eat and wine to drink, and after, almonds and raisins of the sun that Guillelm Geroy, "the Good Norman" as they called him in Italy, dead Guillelm Geroy's son, had sent as a gift to the monks of Saint-Évroult. The monks ate first while the novices served. Fulcun poured the wine; he kept his eyes and his thoughts to that; it was not so difficult because he was sleepy, hungry, and cold, and the frater was warm and steaming after the church. But it had been difficult in church to rule himself, and to keep his mind submitted and obedient to that new, blank emptiness where Alde had been.

After the monks, the novices. It was soon after they had finished there came a knocking at the gate. The porter sent his lad to the abbot to say that here were guests asking hospitality—Guillelm and Robert of Pont Echanfré with a small company. The abbot went out to find Herman the cellarer and welcome them in. On the way Herman told him who they were—Geroys on the spindle side, by Heremburge sister of Robert and Raol Malacorona and the rest, and now, he supposed, come home to Normandy from Apulia.

Abbot Osbern greeted them. Robert was dark-haired and yellow-faced, with square jaw—he looked a quiet man but was a great talker. The elder, Guillelm, was round and cheerful, with fairish sparse hair that curled. When they were dismounted Abbot Osbern bade Herman take them to the frater for dinner—"And," he says, "send Fulcun Geroy to wait on them. They are cousins." On his way back along the cloister the abbot stopped to tell Salomon, the abbey's chronicler, that here were guests that might have news to tell him. Salomon was drowsing over his work, but he woke up at that and collected his tablets and style hastily and went off to the frater. Guests in midwinter were rare.

In the frater, after greeting them all, he sat down at the table in the space between the two knights and their servingmen and waited till they had satisfied their hunger sufficiently to become talkative. But long before he had finished eating, the dark-faced Robert was telling old Salomon how they were on their way to l'Aigle and they would only stop here to eat and then go on. They should have been at l'Aigle last night, but Guillelm's horse cast a shoe close to le Sap and the blacksmith was drunk . . . Guillelm, eating steadily, sat quiet with pleasant, twinkling eyes, and Fulcun Geroy waited on them all.

In the last light of that short afternoon, for the clouds had come down again and the snow was falling dizzily, Abbot Osbern went into the workshop to make a charcoal scrawl, on one of his sheets of linen, of a leaf shape for a capital that had grown and opened in his mind as he sat reading in the cloister with his hands tucked into his sleeves.

It was almost dark here. He rummaged about for the linen and the charcoal, and when he had found them he turned to carry them over to the bench by the window. It was then that he saw Fulcun Geroy standing, leaning with one hand on the bench, the other hanging down by his side. He stood very still, not looking through the window, but into the room; he must have stood there all the time, watching and saying nothing. But now he spoke.

"Father," he says, "I must go from here."

Abbot Osbern could see nothing of his face against the failing light. He came close, and laid down his things on the bench, and stood beside Fulcun, so that he must turn.

Then he asked, "Why?" but he was trying to find out from Fulcun's face.

It was alive; that was certain. The dull look was gone from his eyes; they glanced about, quick and restlessly. He was . . . the abbot groped for the thought and found it, he was like a man set free; and yet not secure. He was alive, but afraid of something. "Why?" says Osbern again.

Fulcun answered him this time. "Because today I heard news of her. They told me—the Pont Echanfré—that Ruald of Saint Pierre—that is—Mauger's brother, who has Fervacques now—he has driven her out. He has refused her dower and driven her out. Robert thought she had gone to the duchess."

The abbot swept a place clear on the bench and hitched himself up on to it. He sat there with his feet hanging and crossed;

he picked up a chisel and balanced it in his hand and rapped with the steel against the wood.

After a little he said, "Will you go to her—again?"

"No," Fulcun told him through shut teeth, and then would not answer the abbot's silence.

At last Osbern said, "If you will tell me, I may understand."

"I want to tell you," Fulcun muttered, and then he swung about and leaned both hands on the bench, looking into Osbern's face.

"I always knew," he said, "that I'd have to choose. I've been afraid—always. Last night, after the Shepherds' Mass, in the dortour, I knew I must do it then."

He paused. Abbot Osbern did not ask what that choice had been. He knew. But he could not guess from Fulcun's face which way the choice had fallen. He waited.

Fulcun stared down at his fingers half buried in the soft saw-dust and curled chips of the bench. "I used to think God wanted of me more than he asked of Abraham. I thought he would want me not even to care that I betrayed . . . my Isaac." He looked up at Osbern, his eyes dark with past dread. "But last night, it was on me. I knew I must choose. I had to. And I had to choose that way." His voice dropped to a whisper. "I had to give her up."

Abbot Osbern did not move or speak. He thought that this was not the end.

"But this morning," says Fulcun, and a quick smile twisted his lips, "there was the ram caught in the bushes."

When he was silent Osbern asked, "What do you mean?"

Fulcun frowned at him. The thing was so abundantly clear, and yet, not to be explained. "I knew," he says, and his voice was impatient, "when they told me that news I *knew* that he'd not have me forsake her." He stopped with a jerk, staring, as if a new thought had struck him, or an old thought come back. "Ever," he says at last. And then, in a low voice, "I am sure, now."

"Sure?" says Osbern.

Fulcun waited before he answered. Then he said, "Yes," and Osbern knew that he was indeed sure. But, as he looked, he saw Fulcun's eyes darken and his mouth grow hard. He was sure of this thing, but there was something yet that he was afraid of. Abbot Osbern dropped his eyes. "I'll give him time," he thought, and he said, "Where will you go?"

"Oh," says Fulcun, speaking hard and impatient, as if he were thinking of something else, "Caharel perhaps." He stood still, and Osbern saw one hand go wandering to the place where his sword hilt should have been and clench there on nothing. Then he cried out, "Father, what can I do? I can't understand. I can't go near her, and she is in trouble. But I can do nothing." He whispered, "I can't understand. I know God loves her, but why does he not keep her safe?"

Osbern laid down the chisel. He reached out and took hold of one of Fulcun's wrists. He had the hard grip of a craftsman and he used his full strength now.

"Fulcun Geroy," he said, "do you think that you love her more than God loves her? If you, who cannot, would do all for her, will he do less, who can?"

He saw the muscles tighten in Fulcun's cheek. For a long time he stood perfectly still; then he said, "No."

He turned his eyes on Osbern, a strange, absorbed stare. He murmured, "No," again, needlessly, as though his thoughts were occupied. Then he said in a great hurry, "May I go soon, at once, tomorrow?"

Abbot Osbern got down from the bench. "You may," he said.

Just before noon next day he and Fulcun stood in the snow at the gate of Saint-Évroult.

When Fulcun was ready to mount they waited a moment, even after Fulcun had got up from his knees and whacked them clear of snow.

The abbot put up his hands and laid them on Fulcun's shoulders.

"Good-bye, Fulcun Geroy," he says. "I'd have been glad to have you stay by me here in Saint-Évroult." Then he kissed him.

Fulcun did not answer, and Abbot Osbern smiled, a little covert smile. That was Fulcun Geroy, always looking into a far distance, so that he didn't see anything that came between. "Get up! Get up!" he says and Fulcun mounted and gathered up the reins.

For a minute he sat there, staring out across the snow; it was scored just here by the perfect half-circle the gate had made in opening, so that the sod showed through, black green; and it was trampled in a broad track the way that Robert and Guillelm had gone down toward l'Aigle. But everywhere else it lay untouched, the very countenance itself of solitude.

Fulcun turned his eyes to Abbot Osbern and for a moment they looked at each other. But Fulcun did not speak. It was the abbot who turned away and went in through the gate, lifting his gown in his hands to keep it out of the snow. He was still thinking of Fulcun Geroy; but as Fulcun touched the horse with his heel and it moved toward the gap in the woods where was the road to Sainte Gauburge, the abbot was not in his mind at all.

The sun, which had come up red in the mist, had climbed now into a clear sky. In the distance the woods were a white mound laced with blue shadows; but when once he was among the trees he moved under an intricate web of shining white. The snow stood ridged along every slender twig, and through the mesh the sunshine came, while beyond the sparkling snow-tangle of the boughs the blue sky shone, pure as a flower; the air was sharp, thin, and delicious as coldest spring water. Sometimes the spear he carried rapped on the bowed branches and scattered over him a spray of snow. He rode on slowly into the deep silence, and his mind was fixed on that thing that he had wanted to say to Abbot Osbern, but had not been able, because it was not come yet within his reach.

At last, in a place where great beeches grew and the woods were open except for their gray and green pillars and the sweeping network of their fine tracery, he pulled up and got off his horse. He propped his spear against one of the trunks and laid his open palm upon the tree and leaned on it; it was cold under his hand; vastly strong; not dead, but of a pulse most slow compared with his own quick blood. And there, in the quiet, alone, he tried to reach that thing that stirred beyond his mind.

A long time ago Robert had said, "I don't believe he'd ever have a man forsake anyone." Yesterday Abbot Osbern had said, "Do you love her more than God loves her?" And today Fulcun himself was certain, though blindly, that God had given her back to him.

He stood there, and those things came through his mind, and after them thought upon thought, like the long groundswell of a far-off, approaching storm; but while his mind lightened and trembled he knew that he waited for something yet to come.

At last he lifted his head slowly, staring at his own fingers moving on the bark of the tree. The thing had come into his mind with the final quiet suddenness of sunrise. He sat down on one of the humped roots of the tree, and hugged his knees and put his forehead down on them.

Here was the end of all his fear. He had dreaded God for the enemy of love, and he was the giver of it. Now, in a still amazement, he knew that of all the whole flood of his own invincible, tender, serviceable love—the love that he had known for the life of his soul and dreaded to lose—God only was the source. Love came, strong-flowing, from that exhaustless fountain, it passed through him, a human conduit, and poured itself out upon Alde—Alde that God loved.

For long he sat there, his face hidden, in the huge silence that was broken only now and again, as the horse moved, by the thin jingle of the snaffle ring, or a whine of leather, and sometimes by the hushed unechoing fall of sun-loosened snow from the boughs upon the deep snow below. His mind, lit clear, and in as pure a quiet as the whole quiet world, brooded; understanding, seeing, and in heartbroken confidence, adoring.

Chapter 19

The Firstë Moevere of the cause above,
When he first made the fairë cheyne of love,
Greet was the effect and heigh was his entente;
Wel wiste he why and what thereof he meant.

Chaucer, "The Knights' Tale"

1

No more snow fell, but a black, bitter frost kept lying all that had fallen, as Fulcun went south out of Normandy, and then westward, making for the Breton border. Day after day he rode under low, steel-gray skies, with a following wind that froze the blood. So it was till he came to Fougères, and there the wind dropped; something changed and softened the air, and that night, when he woke up because of the busy fleas in his bed in the poor hostelry, he heard the gurgle and running of water, and the soft burr of rain on the turf roof; the thaw had come, and the long frost was broken. It was as if, here in the far west, he had come to a place beyond its power, a kindly place where even in winter the spring lurked hiding.

Next day the wind was in his face, a huge wind that shouted and drove heavy slanting showers across the bare green land from which the snow had altogether faded. It was in the afternoon, as his horse went heavily through a miry way, that he met an old man in a sheepskin coat and hood, driving a donkey laden with two bulging sacks of flour. Fulcun pulled up and asked him did he know which way lay Caharel, an alod where a fellow lived called Engeler. The old man tipped his head back— "Engeler the Manceau? Another five miles," he says, "and turn on your right by the Old Stone and up the track. It's nigh the cliff edge toward the sea." When he had gone on a few steps he stopped and called over his shoulder, bidding Fulcun be sure and cross himself and spit over his shoulder when he turned by the stone. He cried out something else too about Engeler, but Fulcun missed that, though a little of it lurked in his mind, so that afterward he wished he had stayed to ask. For anything might have happened to Engeler; no badger skins had come last year, and no deer skins, though that was only to be expected, seeing that Fulcun had been at Courville for the two last summers.

He rode on slowly. His heart had sunk since this morning. It was a long way he had come, and now there was another five miles to put between him and Alde. The Old Stone when he came to it was green and shining all down one side with the rain. There was a rotting mess of dead flowers at the foot among the grass, and some ragged bits of woolen stuff on sticks set in round about. He crossed himself and turned his horse along the track beside it, little used but clear enough. He also spat over his left shoulder. Best to be on the safe side. He was in a strange country now.

The track led up, among white, black-ringed birch trees and sodden, deep copper-colored bracken, to a high open top where there seemed nothing but the roaring wind, and the rain that flung at his face, and more bracken, and more beaten birch trees.

At last, staring out through the rain, he saw before him, against the dark flank of a wood, a low two-storied building. It had a reed-thatched roof, very worn, and in one place the plaster daub that covered the walls was broken away and the withies showed. There was no living thing to be seen anywhere, but as he came on he heard the shrill outcry of a cock inside the building, and then some dogs began to bark. He pulled up close to the door and, taking his foot from the stirrup, kicked on it.

After a moment it opened a little; the long, slavering muzzle of a hunting dog, with the fangs bared, showed in the crack, and above that a woman's face, dirty and smudged, with dull, untidy hair, and eyes of a surprising pure blue.

"Is this Caharel? Is Engelei the Manceau here?" says Fulcun.

It was Engeler's own voice that cried out to know who in the devil's name that was?

"Fulcun Geroy," says Fulcun, and got down and pushed open the crazy door that ground and rattled along the earthen floor, and so went in across the threshold of his home.

He slept that night on a bracken bed rolled in a deer hide, while his cloak and kirtle hung out on a hemp rope by the fire to dry, and his hauberk hung beside it, the scales well smeared with fat. Engeler and the woman slept beyond the fire; the dogs lay near them; at the far end of the room, by the door, in a pen of hurdles, there were a dozen goats; on the hurdles the fowls roosted. Fulcun's horse was tied to a ring in the wall.

It was the cock that wakened Fulcun next morning. He sat up and looked about him. Engeler lay still abed snoring—and might as well, Fulcun thought, for Engeler was a cripple now and would never walk nor go again.

The woman must have gone out, though it was barely light, for the door stood open. Fulcun remembered what Engeler had told him about her last night when she went out to fetch water from the spring. She was a Breton girl; he called her Eve, though it wasn't her name; he'd taken up with her soon after he first came here, when he was after a badger down to the beck below Mont Rouault. And . . . well . . . Engeler grew a little awkward—maids shouldn't look to go so far out of call of their village . . . But she was very angry, says Engeler, and cried a lot too . . . so he left her. And didn't see her again, though he tried, no, not for a year after that, for she'd never let him come near her. And then, Engeler gave a sort of laugh . . . one windy day last Michaelmas year as he stooped to slip the string to the notch of his bow, an elm branch broke and crashed down on him, and there he lay, with no strength to move, for three nights, the third one only just alive and raving for water. And in the dawn after, she came by and heard him; she was gathering sticks. And she'd brought him here, a good two leagues, all the way on her back. And looked after him since. "And that," says Engeler, "when I'm about as much of a man as any dead donkey." He laughed, shamefaced. "Queer cattle, women . . . ," he says, "and well for us." Fulcun only nodded at that, but when Eve brought him a piece of cold bacon and some goat's cheese, as hard as wood chips, he smiled at her, and, though she did not smile back, he felt again that he had come to a kindly, gentle place.

But now, as he sat up on the bracken heap in the dull light and remembered what Engeler had told him, his thoughts went from Engeler's woman and fixed themselves on Alde. She was a woman too, but she had not done as Eve had done. For a second his mind inched away from the fresh pain of that recurrent memory; then, in a new courage, he faced it.

She had not done as Eve. But why? Just because she was Alde that he worshipped, and loved, and now, with his head down on his knees, smiled at in utter tenderness. As he thought of her now he knew that for the first time he was thinking of her as she was herself, not only as his Alde. It was pain but a strange delight too, to think of her so, and it brought her suddenly close to him, and clear, so that he almost cried out at the renewed sharp longing to see her in truth.

But he went on, searching among his memories of her, questioning, trying to know her at last. She had turned to him at Falaise, just as he had turned to her, because she must. She had come with him that night knowing nothing but that she loved and must be with him; she was all his then, and at Montgaudri still all his. At Montgaudri he had begun to fear long before she had. She had not understood what it was that they had done; she was slow to understand, his Alde.

But when she had understood—he shut his teeth hard remembering that last night when she had denied him—now at last he knew why—and the next morning, when his hand had gone out groping for her, and had not found her . . . He knew now why she had dealt so cruelly then; it was because of her loyal simpleness. And she had been cruel to herself too.

But at Bernay? For a moment his mind halted and stumbled into darkness again. Then he understood that too. At Bernay she had sent for him, knowing it was disloyalty; and had hated herself for that, and she had hated him too. Alde that was loyal; she had been disloyal then. But he loved her more for that weakness, he thought, than for all her strength.

At last he came in his remembering to see her face again between the pale, daylight candle flames in the chapel at Fervacques, and to hear the words she spoke then in that hard, toneless voice. But he knew now why she had been pitiless to him. It was because she was pitiless to herself. She had torn her own heart out of her breast; she had murdered her own love; she had no mercy on herself, and therefore she had no mercy on him. But Alde! . . . Oh, Alde! . . .

He flung off the deer hide and scrambled up. With his kirtle pulled on anyhow and his sword in his hand, he went out through the door and across the open hilltop. He had gone a few hundred yards when he stopped short. Before him the ground fell away in a confusion of white rocks, white birch trees with their dark cloud-spray of twigs, and smoldering copper bracken. At the foot of the steep slope there were miles of marshland, dark and patched with pools and black quag. Far away beyond the marsh, a flat, gray, unshining floor that spread wide to the horizon where it met the gray-clouded sky, lay the sea, broken only by the pointed island of St. Michael in Peril and the smaller Tombelaine beyond. The whole space of air was utterly still and quiet. From behind him came the sweet throaty chatter of goat bells; somewhere below in the marsh a curlew cried with a bubbling note as clear and musical as dropping water; and beneath those small sounds, filling the whole silence, he heard the hushed, unceasing murmur of the incoming tide.

He stood there, leaning on his sword and looking out between gray sky and gray sea, and felt the wound Alde had dealt him open again, and ache, and bleed. But now, holding her close in his heart, the real Alde, in her strength, her courage, her pitiful weakness—as if he had only now remembered, after a long forgetfulness, what indeed it was that he loved—he was glad . . . glad of the hurt. Love, mounted in him, triumphant and wounded, touched the extreme height of anguish, and still unsatisfied, proffered itself, in urgent, sharp desire, to be crucified for love. He knew then at last the worth and power of pain. He knew——and bowed his head—how God had bought the world.

When he went back to the house Engeler was lying by the hearth stirring the pot. "She snared a rabbit last night," he says, and sniffed into the steam.

Fulcun looked about him. It was a poor place—worse in the daylight than in the dusk of last night. The earth floor was uneven, broken, and foul. He moved restlessly about the room, picked at the wall where the plaster had flaked off, and rapped at the withies with his knuckles.

Then he said to Engeler, "What is above?"

"Well," says Engeler, "it was a room, but now it's mostly a leak from the roof."

Fulcun said he would go up and see. The ladder had lost several of its rungs, but he swung himself up by his hands and found that it was as Engeler had said. The thatch was so thin that you could see the white daylight through it, and the boards of the floor were rotting away. A pile of old deer hides lay in one corner and they were rotting too. Fulcun kicked open the ramshackle shutters of the window, and threw the whole lot out.

He went back to the ladder opening and sat down on the floor and stayed swinging his legs a moment before he let himself down. There was a lot to be done here; but he'd get it done. This Caharel was his, and besides . . . if someday . . . just because God was so kind . . . and love so mighty . . . *if* she should come . . . someday . . . He caught hold of the edge of the hole with his hands, swung himself down and dropped.

Eve was dipping a wooden bowl into the broth. She brought it out and gave it to him, full and dripping. He did not like the broth running down over his fingers, but all the same, it tasted very good. He thanked her, and her blue eyes came to his, quick and mistrustful. She went away and stood near to Engeler and watched him from there. But Fulcun, drinking up the broth, was thinking not so much of Eve, as that his own mother might have been a woman much like her. And that his mother had known this very place; Caharel; the alod; and the hold that lay beyond. He did not even know what her name had been, for Robert, when Fulcun asked him, could not be sure. But she had gone round about Caharel through the birch woods, and somewhere there Fulcun Geroy of Montgaudri, Fulcun's father, had met her, and somewhere there Fulcun's own life had begun.

⚜

The first thing he did to fettle up the house was to stretch a couple of deer hides across the gap in the thatch and lay peats upon them; the thatching he could not do yet, and did not do till the autumn, when he went down to the marsh and cut reeds and brought them up on his back in a wicker basket Engeler had woven; he did it all afoot because the horse track went too far round about, and Fulcun was impatient always to be done with a thing that was once begun. But long before he thatched the roof he mended the floor of the upper room and carried up bracken for a bed and spread his cloak on it and slept there; Engeler and the woman would not move from the house place below.

In the summer he mended the earth floor of the house place, though Eve almost took a knife to him when he told her that Engeler and she must turn out and sleep, either above, or beyond the house, while he did it; she was never much his friend, nor would she ever willingly count him as the master there. But, when he had rigged up a wattle-and-skin hut for them in the woods, and Engeler had said it would be like old days lying in the open, she went, and Fulcun set to work on the floor. He dug the earth over, and raked it, and watered it with dozens of buck-etfuls of water that he carried from the spring, till it was all of a puddle. Then he left it alone for a fortnight and set to work to build an outside stairway of oak to the upper room, and to cut a doorway through the wall, and close the open trap in the floor. He did not like the opening because when he strawed rushes up there they would blow along and straggle down through the hole; at least, that was the reason he gave to himself, as well as to Engeler; but he knew quite well in his own mind that he did it because once, when they lay awake together at Montgaudri on a windy night, Alde had told him that when she was a little girl she had walked in her sleep.

By the time he had finished the stairway, the floor below was hardening and ready to be beaten smooth with an oak plank that he had cut ready. When it was all done he was prouder of that floor than of anything he had done yet in his life.

It was in the autumn that he rode to Dol with his hauberk lapped up in a goatskin bag. He rode out on the horse that he had had from Hernaut at Echauffour, a great Percheron gelding, with the hauberk strapped to the cantle of the saddle. He came back leading a stocky, rough-coated draft horse, with a bag of seed oats on its back and a bag of rye to balance it, and a plowshare on top of all, and the rest of the price money in his pouch.

So that autumn he worked like a serf, digging, plowing, ditching, and sowing a patch of land below the house for the spring, and when winter came there was work to be done within—plenty of it, and this was what he liked best. It was in the winter that he made two benches for the upper room, with the feet carved in the shape of dogs' feet; and he made a bed frame of birch wood, and stretched hempen rope across and across, and then laid deer skin and bracken on top, and over all his blue cloak, which was the best coverlet he had. Then he set to work on the tie beams, and cut along them a shallow pattern of thin, snake-bodied beasts with claws, and made a raddle of clay, and mixed soot and whites of egg, and colored them black and red. And the last thing he made before the springtime came and he must be out, weeding and sowing, was a chest of oak wood, with a pillar carved out from each of its four corners, and the capitals like, as near as he could remember, to the capitals that Abbot Osbern had been carving last year at Saint-Évroult. But for the lock of the chest he must wait, for he could do no blacksmith's work. He thought he would go some day in summer to the great abbey across the bay—Saint Michael in Peril of the Sea—and find a locksmith in the monks' town there. He wanted the chest to be fine and fair.

And all the time, as he worked, he knew that he was doing it, as he had done everything since those first days at Falaise, because of Alde; and that until she came he was only waiting to be alive . . . if ever she should come.

II

One morning in June, in the second summer that he was at Caharel, Fulcun set out before sunrise to go to market at Saint Michael in Peril. He crossed the sands by the short way, at the last moment possible, when already the flat ripples were coming hissing in over the cold, gray-golden sand and brimming the long pools. The whole world was gray and golden, for the sun, going up beyond Avranches, edged the gray clouds there with cool gold; across the flat sands the Mount itself was a heavy shadow of gray, lit near the top with points of warmer gold where, in the new church, the monks sang their Prime by candlelight.

There were many folk going to market, but most of them went by the higher way that led more safely across the sands, though it was longer. When he came to the gate it was open, and the watch yawning and stretching. Fulcun wasted no time; he went up to the abbey, bought his rye flour from the monk's garnerer, and then, as the sun was well up and warming the east side of the Mount, he led the horse down again to a place between the wall and the shingle where there was a little coarse grass where it could graze. There he hobbled it, put the plump flour sack on the ground, and laying his head on it, fell asleep. He had been up till moonrise last night cutting the hay by the brook, and this morning up again hours before sunrise. So he slept sound.

When he woke the sun was high. He looked out across the bay and saw the empty sands with long shining pools, and the gulls loafing along the edge of the water, or floating and swinging, soft white as flowers, against the blue sky. The tide had fallen low enough for him to get back to Caharel. He scrambled up, loaded the flour, roped it to the pack saddle, and went down at once across the rolling shingle. As he looked back he saw a great number of horses just inside the gate. There must be many guests ridden in today, he thought, for they weren't market horses.

When he was halfway across the sands, he saw a big company of riders coming down from the edge of the marsh toward Pontorson. They were far off now and they would not pass him close, for they were going by the longer way. But when they were abreast of him he could see, among the servants and the men-at-arms, that many of them were women. He wondered a little why all these folk were coming to the Mount. It wasn't any great feast that he could think of. He plodded on, trying to reckon up saints' days in his head, one arm across the horse's withers, his head down, looking nowhere but at the fine-grained sand, clean washed and smooth, or smoothly ribbed with the soft molding of water patterns. He heard the beat of a horse's hooves, distant, and dulled by the sand, but coming toward him. He did not look up to see who came. They reached and passed him, going toward the Mount; from the corner of his eye he had seen a black horse, a man in a leather coat, and a woman in a gold-brown cloak riding behind him; and nothing else but the sand spurts flung up by the hooves. Then he heard the quick regular measure of the hoofbeats change and lengthen and stop. A man shouted. Fulcun turned.

They were riding back toward him. A woman leaned out from the pillion behind the man, staring past him. The woman was Alde.

Fulcun stood quite still. The fingers of his right hand were twisted in the rough, dusty mane of the horse. He could not let go, or move his eyes from her face, or speak.

Alde spoke, but not to him. She said to the servant, "Put me down." When the man did not get out of the saddle she cried again, "Put me down." He obeyed then. He got down, lifted her from the horse's quarters, and set her on her feet. She turned her face again toward Fulcun, staring at him as if she could not look anywhere else. Then she said to the servant—

"Ride on."

"But—"

"Ride on!" She swung round and she lifted her clenched fists and shook them in the man's face. "Ride on!" she cried at him. "Go away. Ride on. Tell Dame Mahalt . . . tell her . . . tell her anything."

She turned her back on him then and faced Fulcun, but she did not move. The servant got up slowly, swung the horse round, and rode away. He stopped once or twice and looked back. Dame Alde and the rough-looking fellow stood as he had left them, a few yards apart. He shrugged his shoulders at last, shook his bridle, and rode on to catch up the others.

Alde looked at Fulcun. He stood leaning against the rough, dull flank of the horse, the fingers of one hand twisted into its shaggy mane. His gown was old and stained and torn, and his bare shoulder showed through the rent, as brown as a serf's at harvesttime. His hair was dusty with flour, and there was a smudge of flour on his cheek.

He dropped his eyes. "What do you want with me?" he said hoarsely. Now that she was here he was most desperately afraid of some new, unimaginable cruelty.

She said in a gasp, "Fulcun," and took one stumbling step. He jerked his head up then, but he did not move toward her. She came on with her hands stretched out till her fingers touched him; they wandered quickly over his gown as if she were making sure he was real. She came closer, and he put his left arm round her then, but he did not take his hand from the horse's mane; he needed something to hold on to.

He said to her, in a voice he could not steady, "You don't . . . hate me then?" and at that her hands came up and clutched his shoulders; she pressed her body against his and leaned her head back, staring into his face. She began to cry, and shake, and say his name over and over.

He loosed his hold on the horse, and pushed off her hood, and began to stroke her forehead and her hair, clumsily because his hand trembled so much. But in a little while she grew quieter and caught his fingers and held them. He waited, looking out over her head across the pale bright sands to the green hills by Pontaubault.

At last she spoke—in a little quavering voice, "How do you come here? Where do you live? I didn't know . . . Fulcun, I saw you . . . I knew you. But we had nearly gone past."

He told her then where he lived. He showed her where Caharel lay, though she did not look up. He went on talking about Caharel with a kind of terrified loquacity, because the chance of seeing her had been so narrow, and because he did not dare to ask her what she would do next.

When he stopped she was silent. She pulled her veil from under her hood and wiped her eyes with it. Then she said in a whisper, "I must come. I am coming with you."

He did not tighten his arm round her, only his fingers closed on the hand he held, as he drew a long breath. He dared not speak or move for a long still minute. Was this thing true?

At last he took his hands away from her and turned and began to uncord the sack from the saddle. When that was done, and he had dumped it on the sand, he turned to her and lifted her up. "Hold to the crossbars," he told her, and put the halter into her hands and then stooped and lugged up the flour sack and shouldered it.

She cried out at that, that she would not ride, but he says, "You must," and took one hand from the sack and for a second laid it on hers. She stooped over it, her head drooping, and felt the tears run warm to her lashes and fall.

He snatched his hand off quickly then to catch a fresh grip of the sack. But she saw him bend his head aside and lay his mouth on his hand a second after, and knew that he had put his lips to a tear that had fallen there. They moved on slowly, he bowed under the weight of the sack, and she looking down at his dark head and stooped shoulders, biting her lips and crying without a sound. She thought that she had known pain before . . . but this . . . but this . . . And she had not tried to find him. But now she must see Caharel . . . and know where it was that he lived . . . and for a few hours be with him again.

Once he looked up with a quick smile, and in his eyes the dancing sparks that she had known. But he saw that she was crying. "Don't," he says, "there's no need now," and he smiled again, but unsteadily.

When he turned his face from her she bit her lips till she tasted blood.

They came to the little slope that led up to the house; Eve was at the door and cried out something, went in and then ran out again and came hurrying to them wringing her hands. She was telling them, long before she reached them, that it was the duke's men, the Normans it was. They had come and they had carried away with them three goats and all the kids, and most of the pullets, and trampled down the rye, look! and broke the fence.

Fulcun let the sack down on the ground.

"Duke?" he says. "What duke?"

Alde said then, "Didn't you know? Duke Guillelm has brought a great host against Count Alain. That is why the duchess came today to St. Michael in Peril."

Fulcun looked up at her. "I didn't think how you came," he said, "only that you had come." Then he put up his hands and lifted her down from the horse. "But it looks," he laughed, "as if you'll get poor fare here," and then to Eve, "What can we have for dinner?"

There was little to have but peas and cakes of rye flour baked on the hearth. Eve made the cakes while Alde sat outside on the stairway and shelled peas. Fulcun sat on the grass and watched her face as she bent over her work; the pods clucked as she broke them, and then she raked the peas out with her thumb so that they hopped and rattled round the curve of the wooden bowl in her lap.

He did not say much, and she hardly anything at all, and what they said was like the talk of children. He made some snares for rabbits as he sat there, "For," he says, "you shall have meat to your dinner tomorrow." She looked at him then as if she were startled, but his eyes were on the osier wand in his hands.

They ate all together in the house place, and Engeler told a long tale of how the duke's men had come, and just what they had said. He made it very funny, and Fulcun, laughing, tried to catch Alde's eyes so that they could laugh together. She did not look up, and it was then that he thought, with a wrench of his heart, that she was not young now, not as she had been, as young as morning. She must have been hurt in these years. He did not hear Engeler's talk for some time after that.

When dinner was finished he stood up. "Come," he said to her, "I want to show you."

He reached down to her and took her hand, and when she got up, he led her out, and up the stairway he had built, to the upper room. He wanted her to see the chest; it hadn't its lock yet, but now he'd get it put on quickly. And the benches; he tilted them for her to see their carved feet. "And Engeler has stitched all those skins together, look, for hangings," he told her. "Eve hasn't a loom, so it's the best we can do." Then he laughed and pointed. "And see my dragon beasts," he says. She looked up at them and then at him; he was eager as a lad about this poor house that was no better than many a serf's house. Her heart moved in her. This was Fulcun who had drawn her to him mightily, as if he were the sun. But now, this was Fulcun. She had never felt this for him before. It was a strange pain and dreadful. When he took her hand again and drew her toward the bed she clung to his fingers; she sat down on it, and he sat down on the floor by her. She put her hands on his hair; but then she thought, "He doesn't understand . . . I can't tell him . . . not yet . . . it's not nearly sunset . . ." and suddenly she was almost angry with him because his poverty hurt her so . . . it made it harder for her, too hard.

He said after a while, what he had said when he lifted her down at the door, "I didn't think how it was you had come. You see, Alde"—he turned his head and looked up at her—"I'm always . . . I have always been waiting for you." His face changed. He muttered, "I know it was not so with you, but I could not help it."

She snatched her hands from his head. "Oh," she cried and pressed them to her breast to keep in the pain and the anger there. "Oh, you don't understand. You don't know how it has been. I have not dared to think of you—I must not think of you."

He twisted round and put his forehead down on her knees. He said, "Forgive me," and for a long time nothing more than that. Then he moved, so that his head rested against her, as he looked out across the room to the small window under the thatch.

"That day," he says, "when I came away from Saint-Évroult . . . it was then I began again to wait for you to come. For I knew then—" He broke off, frowning. "It's hard to remember just how it came through my mind." He went on again after a minute. "I knew then, first of all," he said, "that love was real, so it couldn't be over and done with—never. And . . . you . . . you couldn't escape it . . . So I had you . . . that way . . . for always."

He pushed himself away from her and went on talking, hugging his knees, "And that morning, Alde, or perhaps it was afterward, I was glad again to love you. It didn't hurt as it had done, or if it did, I didn't care. I was glad to love you because you were you, and," his voice dropped, "so dear . . . to love.

"And then, somehow, I knew that there couldn't, in love, be any loss at all, because it's too . . . too strong . . . That was when I began to hope that someday . . . someday you'd come."

She made no sound and held herself very still. She was not listening.

She was staring at him, learning again the look of him, learning the new touch of gray in the short hair at his neck. He went on, speaking very low.

"And it was after I'd thought all these things," he says, "that I understood." His voice quickened. "I understood it was God that all love came from. I knew he couldn't be angry at it. I'd been afraid, all my life, and suddenly, that morning in the woods, I knew that there was nothing to be afraid of."

He turned and stared again into her face, his eyes wide and distant. He did not see her for a moment, for his mind was still full of the glooms and great lights of the eternity it had been moving in. Then he saw her, and his face changed. He cried sharply, "Why . . . why do you look at me like that?"

She must tell him some time; it had better be now. She answered him, her face rigid, her lips hardly moving.

"I must look at you. I must, as much as I can . . . so that I can see you . . . afterward . . . in my heart."

He looked down at his hands, and it surprised him that they were clenched on his knees, and that he could see them shake. He said, and the words hurt his chest as he spoke, "What do you mean, Alde?"

He heard her say, "I must go back soon," but neither of them moved.

At last he spoke, trying to thrust off this nightmare that overwhelmed his mind. He knew now that he had always thought it would happen like this, though he had not dared to do other than hope it would happen very differently. But he must speak, thrust it off, cry out, and wake. It couldn't be true.

He said, "It's different now . . . not wrong . . . now." He spoke with a huge effort, but his voice came in a whisper as if this were indeed a dream.

"We killed him," she said. "So we cannot be together."

He looked at her. He knew now what she was saying—not together . . . that meant dawn to dark with a whole day between, all empty; and the night . . . and another day beyond. He got up, and she stood too. He reached up his hand and caught at the low tie beam where the dragons crawled, and he clutched it with all his strength, standing very still.

She said, "I must go now. I . . . I thought you'd have a man to send back with me . . . But if you will take me back—" She faltered and looked at his face and away.

He let his arm drop. "You can't go now," he told her harshly. "The tide's up."

"The tide?"

"Aye—the Mount's an island in the high tides."

"But—" she said and then was silent.

"You'll have to stay here tonight," he says in the same hard voice.

Her eyes came to his then. There was fear in them. She stepped quickly away from the bed. "I can't . . . ," she cried. "You mustn't."

She had never seen his face as it was then. He looked at her and he smiled. "It was not in my mind," he told her, "till you said it." He laughed. "You needn't be afraid," he says, and turned on his heel and went out.

Down at the foot of the stairway he stopped. There was something that he had to do. He looked about vaguely, saw the snares lying on the grass where he had dropped them, and remembered. He had said she should have meat to her dinner tomorrow; but tomorrow she would not be here.

All the same, the others must eat, and he did not want to go back to her yet. He wanted—he knew, as he picked the sticks up and his hands closed hard on them, that he wanted to hurt her. He knew that he had hurt her when he laughed and told her not to be afraid.

He went off through the wood to the coney warren. He had set nearly all the springes when he suddenly lifted up his head and stared at a crown of yellow ragwort just beyond. He had remembered another time when he had wanted to hurt her; that night on the stairway in Falaise great tower, before Mauger came.

She was Alde still, the same Alde that he had loved and couldn't help loving; but he loved her far more now. And he had hurt her. He dropped the rest of the snares and the cord and went back through the wood, running.

When he came to the upper room she was sitting on a bench, her hands resting on it and her head drooping forward. She looked up, stared at him dumbly, and let her head sink down again. She whispered after a minute, "I thought . . . I thought you would not let me see you again . . . till the morning . . . to punish me . . ."

He did not answer that. He went close to her but he did not touch her. "You're tired," he said. "You'd better sleep."

Her hand came out groping. He took it and took the other too, and lifted her up and led her over to the bed. When she sat down on it he said, "I'm going to fetch a lamp."

He came back with an earthen pot lamp, shielding the pale flame within his hand. She was half sitting, half lying on the bed, her fingers moving about on the old blue cloak, stroking it, feeling it. He put the lamp down on one of the jutting wall beams at the foot of the bed, and as he turned away Alde looked up at him.

"Where will you sleep?" she asked him.

He said, "Alde, you must let me sit by you tonight and watch. I'll sleep tomorrow when you've gone." She stayed very still, not looking at him, and not answering. "You must let me," he said. "I can't waste this night."

She lay down and pulled the cloak about her. He went across the room and fetched one of the benches and set it down by the bed. He had shut the door and the room was dusk, the little light of the lamp showed warm. In a minute his eyes came down to hers.

"You need not mind me," he said, and smiled as if they were children after a quarrel.

She turned away then to the wall, but in a minute she moved again and flung over so that she lay staring up at him.

"Fulcun," she said in a hurry, "please . . . will you let me touch your hand . . . while I sleep?"

He took her hand in his hand and held it gently. "Go to sleep, Alde," he said.

She shut her eyes and felt tears run down from under the lids and into her hair. This . . . this love . . . it was sin.

She woke in the first light of the low sun. She moved, felt the clasp that had kept her hand all night, and lay still again. Then she raised her head. Fulcun sat leaning back against the wall. His head was close to hers, but turned a little away. He was asleep.

She moved cautiously, so as to see him, and then, for minutes her eyes clung to his face, seeing him as he was now. There were lines by his mouth that she did not know; there was a line between his brows that was new too. Even in sleep his face was marked with pain and the endurance of pain.

She looked away at last because she could not bear to look at him anymore. Her eyes fell on the chest he had carved, the chest that he hadn't been able to afford a lock for—Fulcun Geroy of Montgaudri—Fulcun that had been her wonder and desire. Fulcun Geroy that went trudging now to market beside a pack-horse. Fulcun that she had wounded almost to death and today would wound again.

She had loved him before, and yet now she thought that till she knew this pity she had never known love. He was precious; he was pitiful. That was love, a two-edged sword, and her heart was cloven and bleeding. She could not endure the pain while her eyes saw him asleep—pitiful, precious.

She sat up and drew her hand very slowly from his. He did not wake but his hand released hers. He had learned to forgo.

In a minute she was outside and standing on the stairway. She leaned against the wall of the house just beside the door, her fingers clutching at the rough plaster, her head thrown back as if she were choking. She stood so, while her blindfold, simple mind struggled to know if indeed cruelty were right, and pity, sin. Her lips moved, but without any sound. She shut her eyes, and in that darkness her groping, fearful soul laid hold on something. She thought that it was love; then knew that it was God.

She turned sharply at a sound from the room. "Alde!" It was her name only, then silence.

She was in the doorway before Fulcun had taken a step from the bedside. He saw her and stood still except that he turned his face aside.

"I thought—" he said, and stopped. "I was holding your hand," he began again, "and I went to sleep, and then—" He seemed to need to speak, and yet to find it most difficult.

She broke in breathlessly. "I shall never leave you—"

He looked at her now and shook his head.

"You mustn't talk like that," he said, "just because I—"

She cried sharply, "Oh, hush! Oh! You think I don't love you."

He heard the pain in her voice, and he saw her eyes. He sat down slowly and stiffly on the bed and covered his face.

She went to him and knelt down. She did not put her arms about him, or even touch him with her hands. There was no need. She only leaned against his knees and let her head rest against his arm. She said, dragging the words out, "I am not going from you."

"Not—?" he muttered, and then they stayed still, neither moving nor speaking.

It was he who at last stirred, sighed, and touched her cheek.

"Child," he says, "I must cut that hay while the dew is on it."

"I'll come too," she said, and they got up and went down the stair. The drenched grass was gray with dew in the long shadows of the trees, but silver, glass-clear, and golden where the sun touched it. The delicate, gentle, sparkling ecstasy of the unfolding day was everywhere; the world was so still that the long murmur of the tide lay like a shadow across the silence of the air.

He said, "Wait a minute, I'll fetch the scythe," and went into the house. She heard him speaking to Eve. He came out in a minute without the scythe but with a wooden bowl of milk between his hands.

"Drink this first," he says and lifted it. She put her fingers over his and drank. When she had drunk enough he drank too and finished it. "Now," he says, smiling at her, "you've got an old man's mouth as the children say," and he touched her lip with his fingers where the milk whitened it.

He saw her mouth begin to shake and he put his whole hand over it. "No," he says. "No."

Her eyes stared at him for a minute; then she gave a sort of gasp, took his wrist, and pulled it down. She was smiling, though the smile trembled. "Go and fetch your scythe," she said.

When he came back with the scythe over his shoulder, she was barefoot. Her yellow leather shoes stood side by side on the stairway with her stockings in them. She took his hand, and they went on together to the hayfield through the cool heavy dew and the hush of the morning.

Note

The historical part of the foregoing story is founded on the account of the Geroys given by Orderic Vitalis in his *Historia ecclesiastica*.

Any who seek will find them there, but for those who wish to know more of them without seeking, this note is written.

Raol Malacorona died at Marmoutier, probably in 1064.

Hernaut of Echauffour came home to Normandy just about the time the story ends, bringing with him a splendid mantle as a present for the duke, who received him kindly, being in need of knights, and promised to restore his lands. Hernaut retired to Courville, and there died by poison at the hands of Goulafre his steward, who had been bribed for this purpose by Mabille of Belesme. This was her second attempt on Hernaut's life; in the first she had failed, but had inadvertently poisoned her husband's only brother.

After Hernaut's death his wife, Emma, continued to live with her brother in the Cotentin until she became a nun; her daughters also eventually took the veil. The younger son, Rainald, had, just before his father's death, been dedicated to Saint-Évroult. He lived a monk there for many years and Orderic knew him. Guillelm, the elder, went to Apulia, married a Lombard, and prospered.

Robert, Robert of Saint-Céneri's son, also went to Italy as soon as he was grown. He returned to Normandy during the reign of Henri Beauclerc and was restored to Saint-Céneri. He held it for thirty years and continued the family feud with vigor and a fair amount of success against Robert of Belesme, son of Mabille and Rogier of Montgommeri.

Glossary

alod: Lands held without obligation to any suzerain (overlord).

billhook: An implement with a curved blade attached to a handle, used especially for clearing brush and for rough pruning.

borage: An annual herb native to central and eastern Europe, also known as "starflower."

chapman: A peddler.

croft: A fenced or enclosed area of land, usually small and arable.

crupper: A leather strap looped under a horse's tail and attached to a harness or a saddle to keep it from slipping forward.

dunt: A blow.

faldstool: A folding seat.

fettle: To put in proper or sound condition.

gorget: A piece of armor protecting the throat.

hauberk: A long tunic made of chain mail.

homager: A vassal who paid homage to a feudal lord.

jess: A short strap fastened around the leg of a hawk or other bird used in falconry, to which a leash may be fastened.

kirtle: A man's knee-length tunic or coat.

nasal: The nosepiece of a helmet.

pale: A fence enclosing an area.

quillon: A bar, usually of iron, forming the crossguard of a sword or a dagger.

reive: To plunder or to rob.

rime: A white ice that forms when the water droplets in fog freeze to the outer surfaces of objects.

seisin: Having both possession and title of real property.

stook: A small collection of sheaves set up in a field; a shock.

wain: A large open farm wagon.

wattle: A mat of woven sticks and weeds.

whin: A spiny shrub native to Europe and having fragrant yellow flowers and black pods.

Questions for Reflection and Discussion

Use the following questions as guides to deeper individual understanding of the novel or for group discussion.

1. Fulcun's love for Alde has a strongly obsessive quality. In the course of the story, does it become something more than an obsession?

2. Fulcun says he does not dread God's anger but "his love itself, which greedy, bitter, insatiable as any hate, would allow no other object but itself" (317). Is this a fair description of Fulcun's own love for Alde? How does his view of God's love change?

3. The harsh world of eleventh-century Europe is moderated by bonds of loyalty—feudal, familial, marital. Discuss how Prescott's story illustrates the consequences of violating these bonds and the importance of upholding them.

4. One of the key passages in the book is the following exchange between Abbot Osbern and Fulcun. Fulcun says, "It was a monk that told me a man should care for nothing else but God only." Osbern replies, "Well, he was wrong. The more creatures we love the better. They're all his" (370). Do you agree with Osbern? Why or why not?

5. Discuss the four clerical characters: Herfast the priest, the monk Raol, Bishop Ivo, and the abbot Osbern. How do they represent the church? How do they speak of God?

6. Fulcun is tormented by the conviction that his love for Alde is holy but also a sin. Are his feelings for Alde truly love, and does God truly condemn it?

7. Discuss the relationships between husbands and wives in the novel: Geroy and Alianor, Robert and Aelis, Hernaut and Emma. What is the emotional quality of these relationships?

8. At the very end of the story, Alde decides to stay with Fulcun. Did this surprise you? Is this decision consistent with the kind of person we understand Alde to be? If she had left Fulcun, would the meaning of the story change significantly?

9. The novel ends with Fulcun and Alde beginning a life together. How do you imagine this life? Will they be happy?

10. What does the title of the book, *Son of Dust,* mean?

About the Author

Hilda Frances Margaret Prescott was born in Latchford, Cheshire, on February 22, 1896, the daughter of an Anglican clergyman. A brilliant student, she studied modern history at Oxford University and medieval history at Manchester University, receiving master's degrees from both institutions.

Prescott taught in private schools for a time but in 1923 gave up full-time teaching for writing, though she maintained a connection with Oxford University as a tutor in history. Her first novel, *The Unhurrying Chase,* was published in 1925, followed by *The Lost Fight* in 1928 and *Son of Dust* in 1932. Each of these historical novels is set in medieval France and centers on a moral and sexual conflict in the midst of a harsh feudal world. All three novels were praised for their historical depth and their style, "a constant careful beauty which from the first page marks her work as both unusual and distinctive," as the *New Statesman* put it.

Prescott's most acclaimed work was *The Man on a Donkey,* a sprawling historical novel of early Reformation England published in two volumes in 1952. Set mainly in Yorkshire, the novel is a multifaceted historical panorama of the Roman Catholic reaction against the new religious policies of Henry VIII. *Commonweal* lauded the book as "a profoundly moving chronicle, a beautifully executed piece of literature, and a massively impressive work of power, sensitivity and drama." Prescott also received acclaim for *Spanish Tudor: The Life of Bloody Mary,* a biography of Mary Tudor that won her the James Tait Black Memorial Prize.

While many of her historical novels are engrossing epics of romance and adventure, H. F. M. Prescott lived a quiet life for many years in Charlbury, Oxfordshire. A committed member of the Church of England, she had a great fondness for travel and the English countryside. She died in 1972.

LOYOLA & CLASSICS

Catholics	Brian Moore	0-8294-2333-8	$12.95
Cosmas or the Love of God	Pierre de Calan	0-8294-2395-8	$12.95
Dear James	Jon Hassler	0-8294-2430-X	$13.95
The Devil's Advocate	Morris L. West	0-8294-2156-4	$12.95
Do Black Patent Leather Shoes Really Reflect Up?	John R. Powers	0-8294-2143-2	$12.95
The Edge of Sadness	Edwin O'Connor	0-8294-2123-8	$13.95
Five for Sorrow, Ten for Joy	Rumer Godden	978-0-8294-2473-7	$13.95
Helena	Evelyn Waugh	0-8294-2122-X	$12.95
In This House of Brede	Rumer Godden	0-8294-2128-9	$13.95
The Keys of the Kingdom	A. J. Cronin	0-8294-2334-6	$13.95
The Last Catholic in America	John R. Powers	0-8294-2130-0	$12.95
Mr. Blue	Myles Connolly	0-8294-2131-9	$11.95
North of Hope	Jon Hassler	0-8294-2357-5	$13.95
Saint Francis	Nikos Kazantzakis	0-8294-2129-7	$13.95
The Silver Chalice	Thomas Costain	0-8294-2350-8	$13.95
Son of Dust	H. F. M. Prescott	0-8294-2352-4	$13.95
Things As They Are	Paul Horgan	0-8294-2332-X	$12.95
The Unoriginal Sinner and the Ice-Cream God	John R. Powers	978-0-8294-2429-6	$12.95
Vipers' Tangle	François Mauriac	0-8294-2211-0	$12.95

Available at your local bookstore, or visit **www.loyolabooks.org**
or call **800.621.1008** to order.

Readers,

We'd like to hear from you! What other classic Catholic novels would you like to see in the Loyola Classics series? Please e-mail your suggestions and comments to **loyolaclassics@loyolapress.com** or mail them to:

Loyola Classics
Loyola Press
3441 N. Ashland Avenue
Chicago, IL 60657